EYES WIDE OPEN

LARRY BALLARD

EYES WIDE OPEN

To my dear friend Rod

GOD'S FINAL WARNING

Eyes Wide Open: God's Final Warning

Published by Tate Publishing & Enterprises, LLC
127 E. Trade Center Terrace | Mustang, Oklahoma 73064 USA
1.888.361.9473 | www.tatepublishing.com

Tate Publishing is committed to excellence in the publishing industry. The company reflects the philosophy established by the founders, based on Psalm 68:11,
"The Lord gave the word and great was the company of those who published it."

Cover design by Rtor Maghuyop
Interior design by Caypeeline Casas

Published in the United States of America

ISBN: 978-1-63122-811-7
Religion / Christian Life / Social Issues
14.10.16

ACKNOWLEDGMENT

There are two men in my life who have encouraged and inspired me as I wrote this book. They are both men of God, but they are as different as day and night.

The first is my best friend Evangelist, Healer and Prophet Auty Howard of Fire In The Spirit Ministries. To me he is a modern-day Paul. He was on the streets at fifteen taken in by drug dealers and turned into an addict and drug dealer. He spent time in prison and through that experience and a serious illness he had a Damascus experience that changed his life and turned him into one of the most amazing men of God you will ever meet. He is highly anointed and the source of that anointing comes from his incredible humility from the fact that he is thankful that God would so to speak save a retch like him. When I would get discouraged because it seemed that the day would never come to release the message God had given me, he would always give me a scripture of encourage and occasionally a prophetic word when God knew I really needed it. I will forever be thankful for his friendship and support.

The second man is my pastor Sam Conley PhD, Shepherd of The Sanctuary of Hope. Though not a prophet he is prophetic, and the very first time I attended his church a little over a year and a half ago, he singled me out and gave me a prophecy I had waited half my life to hear. He said: "The lord has a message for you. He is going to use you to release a message to the world with power and clarity." Little did he know at the time that I writing *"Eyes Open Gods Final Warning."* Finally a man of God had told me it was time to release my message to the world. In any event that started our relationship and he has both encouraged me as well as introduced me to people in positions to help me get the word out. But most importantly he is very deep in the word, very anointed and an exceptional orator. It is uncanny how many times I would be asking God for guidance on something in the book and then out of nowhere Pastor Sam would deliver a sermon that would give me exactly what I needed.

The most important thing about both of these men is that they have incredible integrity and where ever they go, whoever they come in contact with, they enrich their lives as they have mine. They say when the student is ready the teacher will show up. I guess in my case God knew I needed a lot of help because he sent me two extraordinary men to mentor me and to be my friends. I will be forever grateful.

Thank You Both

CONTENTS

PART 4

Fighting Back: Countermeasures

PART 5

Understanding God's Ultimate Plan

INTRODUCTION

The world is at a tipping point, which has ushered in the planet's sixth mass extinction. This knowledge is the motivating force behind the drive of a group of financial elite who control the world's banking system and are intent on economically collapsing the US, and then every other sovereign government on the planet in order to drive them into a one-world totalitarian government, and once they have secured their power, they intend to commence the systematic genocide of most of us and the enslavement of the rest.

Understanding the motivation of those who would enslave us. The extinction event of which I speak is being brought about by the collision of overpopulation and out-of-control material consumption (greed), colliding with two of the planet's most important finite natural resources—oil and fresh water!

This book will systematically establish these facts in order that you may know the truth, and the truth may empower you to take action to alter the fate of the human race. As an American I am most specifically aware of what is being done to collapse the US, but in most instances if you insert the name of your country where I use the US, as my point of reference, you will be able to see that the same our similar things are being done in every industrialized nation in the world. We are all in the same boat together.

This is doubly true when it comes to the mass extinction event which threatens the world as the result of the collision of overpopulation, and shortages of oil and fresh water. What happens to the planet happens to us all. As I shall prove, a shadow government is intent on establishing a one-world government and then solving the threat of planetary extinction by forcibly reducing global population from its current level of seven billion to one billion, which is the number they believe to represent a sustainable population level. Additionally these events are described by all the world's major religions as the End Time Harvest so God is calling all the people of the world to repent, to come together in brotherly love and to turn away from the false god of materialism and return to the God of creation. We are all fighting for our lives and our souls and we are all in this battle together.

What happens in the twenty-first century will determine if the human race will submit to slavery or pull together to solve the challenges, which threaten all life on planet earth and in the process learn to live in harmony with each other and the planet that sustains us. The information in this book will shock you and challenge everything you think you know about the global political system and its leaders, but if you will open you minds to the possibility that your perceptions of reality have been scripted by a shadow government intent on creating a docile subculture working class, then, you will be able to see the truth and come away with a profound understanding of what is to come!

Selective breeding by elite to create passive, submissive, workers: "Gradually by selective breeding the congenital differences between rulers and ruled will increase until they become almost different species…A revolt of the plebs would become as unthinkable as organized insurrection of sheep against the practice of eating Mutton." (Bertrand Russell. *Keeping The Rabble in Line)*

This quote may sound farfetched, but I assure you it is not. Science has deciphered the genome and as soon as the Financial Elite behind the global shadow government establishes *open dictatorship* there will be nothing to stop them from embarking on Hitler's Eugenics quest to create the perfect human, in this instance a docile slave class. In the book *The Brave New World* Aldous Huxley tells the story of how the Elite plan to genetically alter the human race to create three classes of people: a docile working class, an intelligent but submissive administrative class and of course an genetically superior Elite Class. Thought to be a work of fiction Huxley said in an interview that the book was a **factual account** of the plans of the Financial Elite for the human race.

Our entire perception of reality is carefully orchestrated by a shadow government that controls the media, and educational system, that is demonizing Christianity and systematically destroying the family structures, which together constitute the core of the moral value system which defines our humanity. In order to make absolutely certain they can control us they have taken control of all the necessities of life: food, water and energy and in America today there are more people on Welfare than there are with full time jobs. America is becoming a *Nanny State* just like Europe. A dependent society is a docile society! Wake up before it is too late!

What I am saying probably sounds absurd, but not when you understand that I am not the author of this book. I am just the stenographer. God is the author and revealer of the truth. He cannot lie and his word never returns void. You see, around forty years ago, I had a near-death experience, which I will expound on in chapter 1. Out of that experience came the foreknowledge of what was to befall the world as the result of our greed. Everything that has happened in my life from that point forward has been to prepare me to be God's messenger. My assignment is to assimilate the knowledge, which God has given me and deliver a message to the world "with power and clarity" so that there can be no mistake as to what God wants of us. He is calling his people to open their eyes and recognize their sins, to repent, to turn to him, submit to him, and as he had the Israelites do so many times, stand against our enemies so that having done these things, he can step in and supernaturally deliver us from the hands of our enemies.

What is coming upon the earth is nothing less than the biblical tribulation, but God will not abandon his people. The lessons, which mankind learns through these travails, will forever change the course of The human evolution. We will emerge a kinder, gentler, more loving species that has been tested in the fire of tribulation and emerged ready to commence an evolutionary journey of profound proportion. God is calling his army. Will you be among those that heed his call and inherits his promise? For most of human history, global population has been stable at around one billion. It is only with the advent of the industrial revolution, made possible by oil, that man has been able to tame the planet and bend it to his will. It is oil that has allowed agricultural production to explode and with it, allowed population to correspondingly explode to the point where it threatens the ecological balance of the entire planet. Make no mistake: we are facing a mass extinction event on par with that of the dinosaurs! If we continue to destroy the food chain, we will suffer extinction just as easily as the rest of the plants and animals on the planet! This is the greatest crisis the human race has ever faced!

> "Planet earth is facing a mass extinction that equals or exceeds any in the geologic record. And human activities have brought the planet to the brink of this crisis"(Dr. Peter Raven, director of the Missouri Botanical Garden and adjunct professor at the University of Missouri, St. Louis University and Washington University).

> "By perpetuating the world's sixth mass extinction mankind may compromise our own ability to survive. We need to steer this nation and lead the world toward a sustainable path" (David Wilcove, professor of ecology and evolutionary biology and public affairs at Princeton University).

Global oil production has peaked, and since 2008, it has been falling at a rate of 9 percent per year. Our current agricultural model is utterly dependent on oil—oil to drive our tractors, oil for the ships and trucks, which allows food to be produced anywhere in the world and consumed wherever demand dictates. All pesticides are made from oil, and all fertilizers are made from natural gas, another non-renewing natural resource. For every calorie of food produced, ten calories of hydrocarbon energy are required. So, it is apparent that without oil, our current agricultural system will collapse and that means the population must be reduced in direct proportion to the reduction in food supply. This is an inescapable fact. Also, virtually every product we consume in our industrial world contains oil. If we run out of oil, life on planet earth, as we know it, is impossible.

Now, consider that the US, a nation with only 300 million people, uses 25 percent of the world's oil; and China and India, with a combined population of approximately 2.9 billion people or some 36 percent of the global population, is modernizing at lightning speed, which of course means their oil demands are expanding at pace with their industrialization. The only possible outcome to this situation is that US oil consumption must fall drastically to accommodate the increased demands of China, India, and the rest of the world.

What does this mean to America and the world? Answering that question is the central point of this book, but in a nutshell, it means the US must fall, and it's standard of living must be reduced to that of a third world country. It means that global population must be reduced to what is referred to as sustainable levels, which is a point where utilization and consumption are in balance or in other words resources are renewable or sustainable as opposed to depleting to the point of being exhausted. Make no mistake; human existence is in jeopardy, if we don't take corrective actions!

By the way, a UN document entitled "Agenda 21," which means Agenda for the 21st Century, spells out exactly what the UN intends to do in order to achieve that balance. The key point is that over the balance of this century, they intend to reduce the global population to one billion people, which they believe is the magic number for sustainability. This will be a joint effort of all the major nations of the world lead by the UN in concert with the US, China and Russia. As you will shortly learn we are all one happy socialist/ communist family.

The tragedy is that our scientist and the governments of the world have known about the peak oil overpopulation extinction event for at least the last fifty years. Instead of telling the masses and allowing us to cooperate in reaching a solution, the financial elite—shadow government, which I expose in this book—have decided to cause a crisis of sufficient magnitude that it will allow them to step in and use the crisis they created as an excuse to impose their long sought after one-world totalitarian government. Make no mistake; our government's policies have been intentionally purposed to encourage out of control population growth, over consumption of material goods and natural resources and creation of a catastrophic debt crisis!

What the elite have planned for us peasants, The financial elite has decided that there are simply not enough natural resources to share with us "peasants," so in order for them to live, *most of us must die.* And those of us who are allowed to live must live in poverty, as their slaves, so they can live in luxury. They view us as nothing more than chattel (private property) like a horse, cow, or pig. If we do nothing, this is our fate, but if we will open our eyes to the reality of what is happening, we can forge a solution, which ushers the planet into a new evolutionary cycle where we learn to live at balance with the planet and at peace with one another. In order to avoid the fate the elite have planned for us, America and the rest of the nations of the world will have to stop our cutthroat exploitation of each other and the planet and do something we have hitherto been unable to do, which is to join together to solve the problems which threaten us all.

This book could very possibly save your life and your soul. It is that important! As I explain in my testimony in chapter 1, this book is divinely inspired, and God has been preparing me to bring forth this message for over forty years. He has hidden me in the cleft of the rock till things were sufficiently bad that mankind was prepared to listen!

What you need to know to save America (substitute the name of your country) and your loved ones from what is to come. In this book, you will learn

- *why America must fall* and be reduced to third world status,
- *how our two-party political system has been hijacked* by a shadow government intent on collapsing the US and the entire free market system and imposing a one-world totalitarian government,
- *how and why our leaders have betrayed us*, and why our government is the biggest threat we will ever know. So that you understand their strategy, I have identified their "playbooks" and exposed their tactics for all to see. I have also compiled a list of

key legislation by presidential administration from Wilson to Obama; legislation which has intentionally brought America to the brink of economic collapse,

- *who the traitors are.* I have provided an organization chart of the shadow government, identifying key organizations and individuals, so we may root out the traitors.
- *what your political options are and are not.* I provide a comprehensive political platform entitled "The American Reformation Platform." It details how, if we will stand up and fight to take back our republic, we can regain control of the four centers of power—political, monetary, intellectual, and spiritual. All four are necessary in order for freedom and a republic to flourish! This cannot be achieved through our current political parties. Both parties have sold out. Our only hope lies in a Second American Revolution where we rebuild America from the ground up and reestablish the four centers of power, which have been systematically dismantled. Thomas Jefferson said that "the spirit of resistance to government is so valuable that I wish it to be always kept alive."
- *what to expect between now and the end of Obama's second term.* I guarantee you that your idea of "the fundamental transformation of America" and President Obama's are not the same, and you need to know the truth about what he plans for America.
- *how to prepare for what is coming,* so you can safeguard your loved ones. The government plans to create so much "chaos" that they will have an excuse to declare martial law as the first step to imposing a dictatorship! You need to know how to live day-by-day while at the same time preparing for what is coming. This book provides the reader with the knowledge they need in order to be as self-sufficient as your individual circumstances allow.
- *God's plan as imparted to me.* So that you may have your eyes and ears opened, so that your name and those of your loved ones may be in the "Book of Life" so that no matter what befalls this earth, you will have a better place to go!

Before we go any further, I want to apologize to you. God told me he would give me a message to *deliver to the world with power and clarity.* In order to do that, I cannot dance around the truth, so you are going to get the truth, the whole truth, and nothing but the truth, so help me God. That means I will tell you what is coming in graphic, sometimes shocking, fashion intended to shock you sufficiently to wake you from the slumber your government has inflicted on you with their lies and half truths. It also means that I will be intentionally repeating some material more than once, so I am sure you don't miss the point. In biblical terms, I am a watchman, and that means it is my responsibility to sound the alarm to alert the people to danger, and I take that responsibility very seriously. ***To my foreign readers I pose this question.*** If this book is primarily about the collapse of the US why should you care? Why should you read this book? Because the US is targeted to be the first domino to fall and when it goes all the other dominos (countries of the world) will follow suit. Because if you live in an industrialized nation the same or similar strategies that are being used to collapse the US are being used to collapse your country and the entire free market system. If you understand what is happening to take away US sovereignty you will understand at least in general terms what is being done to take away your sovereignty.

The weapons in the arsenal of the shadow government are the same in every country. They are massive debt brought about by unfunded entitlements and socialist policies, trade deficits caused by slave labor free trade agreements, control of the necessities of life i.e. food, water, energy (oil) and jobs, coupled with control of the monetary system in order to devalue the currency, lower wages and increase the cost of living to the point that we are increasingly at the mercy of corrupt bankers, and government and corporate leaders. From a psychological perspective they control our schools and the media and do everything they can to create division between different religious, social, economic and ethnic groups. In short they attack the four pillars of civilized society ***"political, monetary, intellectual and ecclesial"*** because they know if they can destroy them the fabric of society will be torn asunder and the masses will turn on each other causing chaos and crises which is exactly what they want in order to bring about the birth of their tyrannical New World Order.

So America is the touchstone for the fate of the world. The intent is to collapse the US, and then merge our military with that of NATO creating arguably the most powerful military force on the planet. Additionally approximately one hundred nations depend on the US for food, so if they can get control of the US agriculture production they will be in a position to starve to death millions around the world. Additionally given that the US is the world's reserve currency and that the US has more debt than all the nations of the world combined if they can collapse the US economy it will almost certainly cause a collapse of the global monetary system leading to global chaos and a crisis large enough to usher in the long dreamt of one-world government which is envisioned as being a Super Capitalist Communist Totalitarian Government, the biblical government of the Antichrist.

May God be with you and yours!

PREFACE

Dear Reader:

I wish you were here, so we could talk face-to-face, and I could address your questions and concerns as they arise. Since that's not possible, I will do the next best thing, which is to write in first person where appropriate. Having done a number of presentations and interviews, I am sensitive to where what I have to say will challenge the average person's mindset and loyalties and when I am getting into an area you might not be familiar with, and therefore need background or perspective.

Because the message in this book is so important and because God has told me to write it (bluntly without concern for whether it challenges peoples' sensitivities or perceptions), I will make every effort to tell you why you need to know a particular truth. Without knowing it, people are conditioned from birth to see the world in certain ways. However, when God chooses a watchman, he ordains the circumstances in his life, so he is immune to normal conditioning because it is crucial that he learn to think logically and analytically, not emotionally or out of preconditioning or peer pressure.

I hope that before you have finished this book you will feel like you know me and can come to trust that whatever I say is coming from my heart. God has often chastened me in order to open my eyes to the truth and now, as with the prophets of old, he has sent me to chasten the world so that their eyes may be opened and the truth may set them free!

I hope this book blesses you, and if you end up agreeing with its message please don't be silent. Tell your friends, call them, text then, tweet them, e-mail them, go on Facebook, do whatever you can to help me get the truth out there. God needs workers to spread the truth to an unsuspecting world. Our children's futures are at stake. The fate of the entire planet is at stake. Most importantly, our very souls are at stake. God is knocking. Please answer! Please, for your sake, stand up and be counted among his righteous.

Sincerely,
Larry Ballard

PART 1

The Fall of America: The Enemy Within

DIVINE APPOINTMENT

Mysteries of the ages revealed!

The time is at hand.
Those who will harken to my word,
Their eyes shall be opened
That they shall see,
And their ears that they may hear!

Wonder thee why thou heed my promises
And they be not fulfilled in your life?

By what means
Shall a man inherit the Promised Land
And life eternal?

Thou sinners be not dismayed
For I am a God that loveth thee,
And yet have I provided a way for thee!

Wonder why the way of the sinner seemeth easy,
While the way of the righteous is
Filled with trial and tribulation?
Woe to the wicked generation
That heareth my word and harken not to it!
The spotless lamb have cometh
In righteousness and virtue
His ways to show to a lost generation
Of what have thee learned of his ways?

"All these things and more shall be revealed to you in this book, which I have given to my watchman to reveal to you that you perish not from ignorance!"
This saith the Lord

It was a warm spring day. The sun was shining, a light breeze was blowing, and white billowing clouds floated majestically through the sky. The leaves were budding, flowers blooming, and birds singing as I rode my motorcycle through the Ozark Mountains without a care in the world. Little did I know that my life was about to be permanently transformed. In an instant of time, I would have a divine appointment.

I leaned into a hairpin curve and all the sudden I saw it—road construction, oil, and gravel just before me on the cusp of the curve. My cycle slid on its side while I attempted to regain control but to no avail. In an instant, both the cycle and I were thrown in the air as we left the road and careened over a cliff. I flew headlong into a tree, and the next thing I knew I was laying motionless on the ground, looking up at my cycle perched in the top of a pine tree with its back wheel still spinning as if it had someplace to go. I remembered thinking what a strange sight it was.

Then suddenly, I felt a jolt as though I had been struck by something, and I felt my spirit leaving my body. I was instantaneously wrapped in an envelope of multicolored rays of light, streaking through the universe to some unknown destination. I felt as though I was immersed in a warm solution, which maintained my being at precisely the perfect temperature. But all that was nothing compared to the angelic music, which permeated my being, washing me with a feeling of peace and contentment. In truth, no words can describe what I experienced. It was truly life altering!

Suddenly, before me appeared a brilliant white light! In the midst of the light was the silhouette of a man. I didn't know if it was God, Christ, or an angel, but I had a peace that defied words. At that instant, I knew that the material world, in which I had lived my entire life, which had framed my perceptions and beliefs, was a mere illusion.

Ages of time flashed before me. I could see the rise and fall of civilizations, the errors of man repeated over and over with no discernible understanding as to the cause and effect of their actions!

My mind was flooded with information. There were no words, only a profound knowing. I had been called to a divine appointment.

Before the foundation of time, it had been appointed that man would be sifted and separated and the meek and righteous would take one path and the proud and greedy another. But it was purposed that man's eyes and ears were to be closed till just prior to the time of the judgment. Then, God would call watchmen from the four corners of the earth to open man's eyes and ears, so they could know the truth of all creation and understand the errors of their ways. Those that harkened to God's word would be given the gift of the Holy Spirit and as Jesus before them perform all manner of miracles. However, no such power and authority could be given to the wicked because they would abuse it. Therefore, man must be separated into two groups—the carnal and the spiritual, the wheat and the tares. Thus said the Lord: Only my sheep shall hear my voice.

I heard myself ask, "What does all this have to do with me?" The answer came immediately.

God said that I was one of the watchmen, and I was to be given a gift that would allow me to take the complex, which confounded the mind of man and explain it in simple easy to understand terms. This knowledge would remove the scales from man's eyes so that he might know the secret of good and evil, so he could choose righteousness and salvation or reject God's word and be judged for his sins!

Just as suddenly as my spirit had been snatched from my body, it reentered. I remembered wishing I could have stayed where I was, but at least I knew the magnificence that awaited me when I completed my assignment, and therefore, the events to come held no fear for me.

God told me that in order for me to learn to trust him completely, he would place me in multiple life-threatening situations, any one of which could surely take my life. In each instance, an angel would be there to snatch me from the arms of death. In this way, I would know that at the end of days, when things looked hopeless and the strangle hold of the evil one and his minions seemed absolute and irreversible, his angels would be there to save mankind! Just as an army of angels had been there for Elisha in his hour of need and for me when my life was in danger, they would be there to save his righteous! Not one whose name was written in the book of life would be lost. He reminded me that he is the Alpha and the Omega, the Beginning and the End, and that he is the author and finisher of the Book of Life. The evil that has enslaved the earth for so long was necessary in order to purify mankind and separate the wheat from the tares, the righteous from the wicked.

Lest you think this is just rhetoric, consider what happened to me over the next several years. Within in a matter of weeks, I was in a head-on car accident at seventy miles per hour. I was a passenger, riding in the front seat. When I saw the approaching car coming at us, out of control, I jumped into the backseat. When the car came to a stop, the engine of the car was where I had been sitting. Mark one up for my guardian angels.

At the time, I was working my way through college as an iron worker, building skyscrapers. My next angelic visit came when I was working five stories up, which was no big deal because I was wearing a safety harness—wrong! I leaned back and all the sudden I heard it—*pop, pop, pop* then I fell backward in a perfect swan dive to the ground below. I nearly passed out from fear, but when I regained my senses, I realized I wasn't dead. When I fell back, my foot had caught on something, and I was suspended hanging upside down by one foot. All I could do was remain motionless and pray for someone to rescue me before whatever was holding me gave way, and I plummeted to my death. In what was the longest fifteen minutes of my life, I was rescued. Chalk up two for my guardian angels.

Next, I was off loading steel from a truck on the ground. Couldn't be much safer—wrong! It seems that my spotter, who gives the hand signals to the crane operator some three stories below me in the basement, was girl watching. He gave the up signal without knowing where I was. Hello? I was in the path of ten tons of steel destined for the tenth floor of the high-rise, and I was going along for the ride. I was dangling by one hand several stories up in the air. When the crane operator saw me, his immediate reaction was to stop the crane. The resulting jerk nearly caused me to lose my grip, but somehow I held on. That was three for my guardian angels.

In those days, I did some spelunking (caving) and my buddies thought it would be funny to take my flashlight and leave me in the cave to see if I would panic. I didn't! We were near the mouth of the cave, so I decided I could inch my way along by keeping one hand on the wall of the cave. Not so smart. There was a drop off that I hadn't figured on. I fell and hit my head. You know that prominent vein or artery, whichever it is, in the center of your forehead? Well, I lacerated it. I lost a lot of blood, but I got out of the cave. My friends drove me home. I cleaned up and went to a "doc in the box" to get stitches. He took a suave to clean out the wound and no sooner than he touched the wound, blood started gushing everywhere. If that had happened in the cave, I would have met the Lord a lot sooner than I had expected, but no, I was saved again!

There were several more accidents —divine appointments—but I will tell you about just one more. It was several years later. I was out of college and was on a business trip. I was taking a plane out of the Sue Falls South Dakota. I was sitting near the wing of the plane, and as we took off, I heard a loud pop. I looked down and engine parts were raining down on the runway, and fire was coming out of the right engine. The right engine had exploded on takeoff. The pilot feathered the engine, and the plane immediately pitched several degrees and began circling the airport to jettison its fuel, so we could attempt a landing. Chaos broke out! People were crying, praying, and screaming. By now this was old hat for me. I knew we were going to be okay, because God had promised that nothing would happen to me till I completed my assignment and warned the world of the events to unfold in the future. To this day, I can hardly believe what I did. I got out of my seat, stood up, and shouted at the top of my lungs, "God said not a one of us would be harmed." That show of faith brought my near-death experiences to a halt. I guess I had finally passed the test and showned God that I trusted him no matter what the circumstances.

Since the day of my divine appointment, forty-five years have passed, and God's promise has come to pass just as he said it would. The world is on the brink of destruction and evil abounds. As in the time of Sodom and Gomorra, God's judgment is at hand.

* * *

My time of preparation. So what of all those intervening years? Not a moment of them was wasted because it took all that time for God to equip me for my assignment. While on the spiritual plane, he told me that from time to time, he would send me prophets to show me the road I must travel. He kept his promise!

He told me he would make me a millionaire and then allow me to lose my wealth, so I would know the temptation of riches and would learn to rely on him not money. He kept his promise! Put like that; what I just described sounds very matter-of-fact, but I assure you it was not. Over the course of my life, I had managed to break out of the inner city ghetto where I was raised and had invested in real estate, accumulating eleven rental properties that represented my retirement. I had a net worth of close to three million dollars and was feeling safe and secure.

Before I go any further, I have to make a very important confession. Without realizing it, I had come to trust more in my riches than I did in God. I had looked at all my hard work and believed that it was by my power and my might that I had accumulated those riches. I had failed to see the truth, which was that all my hard work would have been for nothing had God not purposed me to become rich, so I could learn some hard sought lessons.

* * *

My time of testing. Unbeknownst to me, I was about to enter a seven-year period of trial that would forever change me and determine whether or not God could use me. The time of testing was at hand. It was at Wednesday night Bible study, and one of the church members came in, leading a blind lady (a prophet). She said she had come to have the pastor pray a prayer of agreement for her sight to be restored. The pastor laid hands on her and immediately he was hit by the Holy Spirit and fell to the ground. He was shocked because here she had come for prayer and her anointing ended up overpowering him. I think he was flabbergasted by what had just happened. When he got up, he asked her if she would pray for the rest of us and she said yes. It was a small group so she prayed for each of us individually. I don't usually go seeking prophecy because I feel that if God wants me to know something, he will seek me out. When she got to me, she said, "Oh, it's you." Now it was my turn to be freaked out. A blind lady had just singled me out to receive a message from God. That rattled my cage and blew my mind. She definitely had my attention. She went on to tell me that before she came that night God had told her that there would be someone she would meet that He (God) wanted her to taker under her wing. It turned out to be me, and that was what her strange comment was referring to. She said: "God gave me a message for you. I guess if you truly hear from God you don't need to see a person in order to know who they are in God. " She called me "a fence straddler who had gotten rich and self-centered." She said, "God has been calling you, and you have ignored his voice." "You know what I am talking about," she interjected. She was right. I had been feeling that it was time to start writing the first of what God had said would be several books, but I had been procrastinating. "Either you do what God is telling you or he will find someone else as he did with Saul and David," she said. I took the warning seriously, and within a few days, I started my first book, and with her mentorship, I drew closer to God than I had ever been. She chastened me in a way no one ever had. She refined me in the potter's fire so I could serve God. Finally, I was right with God, or so I thought.

But God hadn't even started to test me! The minute I started to write the book, all hell broke loose. My wife was an ex-Catholic, and somewhere in her childhood, something had happened that made her hate God. She had a Jezebel spirit, and she didn't want anything to do with God, so when I started writing a book ordained by God that was the final straw in what had been a shaky marriage.

Not too much later, I got another prophecy from a different prophet. By this time, I had nearly completed my first book, so I thought I was in God's good graces, but to my surprise, I got another warning. The prophet said, "You are going through a divorce and what you decide to do about the financial settlement will determine if God can use you." Unknown to him, I had just consulted an attorney. During the course of our conversation he had asked several questions about my finances and those of my wife. I told him my wife had been a stay at home mom, but her mother was quite wealthy, and that she was not expected to live long and when she passed my wife would inherit several million dollars. He then recommended that it would be in my best interest to delay the divorce till after she passed. He added that once my wife had gotten her inheritance she would have considerably more money than me and it would most likely result in a much smaller divorce settlement. If I took the attorneys advice it appeared that I would be able to get out of the marriage with most of my wealth intact.

I went home to consider what the prophet and the attorney had said. When I have a problem, it is my custom to pray about it and ask God for guidance, and then I usually get the answer just as I awaken, generally around 5:00 a.m. A couple of days later, I got my answer.

God said, "If you take the attorney's advice, you will keep your money, but you will surely lose your calling. If you settle with your wife now, unforeseen circumstances will arise and you will lose most of your money. Additionally, you will be left utterly alone and isolated. But I will use these circumstances to chasten you, so you can finish your assignment." He added that in the end (as with Job), he would restore all that I had lost, but first, I must show him if I worshiped the Living God or if I kneeled down to the false god of materialism.

* * *

The lesson this generation must learn. I chose God, and what he said came to pass. What God knew was that this world has sold out to money and material conveniences, and I could not be used to deliver that message, if I had not already been tested in the fire and come out the other side. Our riches lie with God, not material possessions. The world is divided into the haves and have-nots, and the haves (the financial elite) have no intention of sharing with the have-nots (the rest of us) because they consider us to be their slaves. If this world is ever to have peace and true prosperity, we have to learn to be our brother's keepers, because what happens to the least of us comes full circle and is visited on the rest of us. This is the lesson this generation has yet to learn, if we are to make it into the Promised Land!

How God chastened me so he could use me. Lest I leave you with the impression that the divorce was my wife's fault, I need to make another confession. As an adult, I was trying to escape the poverty of my childhood. Unfortunately, I had no idea how much it would cost me to learn why it is so difficult for a rich man to enter into heaven. He has already gotten his reward here on earth. Unless a man makes stewardship and service to others his number one priority, his riches are a snare!

The vehicle by which God would chasten me was the divorce. It would strip me of my wealth and isolated me. It is amazing how your friends disappear when you are no longer wealthy. I was utterly alone—no wife, no friends, one son who didn't talk to me, and one who was away in the military. I was in a matter of speaking on a sojourn in the desert just as Christ had gone into the desert after being baptized. What a perfect plan to make a man reflect on where he went wrong in life. The wrong choices and priorities he had made and what he wished he had done differently. You see, before we can repent and receive God's grace we first have to realize the errors of our ways. In my case, I came to realize that without knowing it, I had become arrogant, self-centered, selfish, and I had failed to help those less fortunate than me. My money had ruined me.

My life taught me another very important lesson—a lot of pastors teach an oversimplified form of salvation. It is true that when

righteous people who will live according to the Ten Commandments who will love God and their fellow man. Then and only then can the world ever know peace.

Back to my story. Though I would not have said it at the time, my period of isolation and separation made me a better person, more passionate, more compassionate, and tolerant, and most importantly, it made me put my faith in God where it belongs. For me, these lessons were essential, because as a watchman, it is my responsibility to warn God's elect of what their governments are doing to enslave them. But it is even more important to warn the people of where they have gone wrong and without realizing it bowed down to the false idle of materialism rather than worshiping the one and only God, Maker of heaven and earth.

* * *

God enables those he calls. Going back to my initial out-of-body experience, God told me he would cause me to change jobs frequently, working in strategically important industries, so I would understand firsthand how governments and corporations conspire against his children. He kept his promise!

He had me work in health care and for a Canadian company, so I would understand the dangers of socialized medicine. (Canada has had state run medicine for decades.)

He had me work for Monsanto chemical company, so I would learn how the government and Monsanto conspired to control the world's food supply.

He had me work for a nuclear energy company, so I would understand how the government controlled people by controlling their access to energy.

He had me be a real estate investor and broker, so I would understand how the government, international banks, the Federal Reserve and Fannie and Freddie conspired to collapse the housing market and in the process further their goal of limiting ownership of private property.

He had me work for four corporations, which were acquired by corporate raiders, so they could be dismantled, allowing China the opportunity to undermine the US manufacturing base and drive the US into economic ruin!

Around the same time, God allowed me to spend time in China, so I could understand through firsthand exposure exactly how the US Government would aid China to use "free trade agreements" to siphon off the wealth of the US and transform it from the world's wealthiest nation into the world's largest debtor nation. Consider the following quote.

> "We've practiced what I call 'losing trade'—deliberately losing trade—over the last 50 years" (Congressman Duncan Hunter, "Exclusive Interview: Hunter Eyes Presidential Campaign," *Human Events*, Dec.4, 2006).

Getting back to my divine appointment, besides my work experience, God also gave me a love for history, science, philosophy, psychology, and all things spiritual, which are the keys to human understanding and all things political.

Lastly, God gave me the gifts of discernment and word of Knowledge along with visions and revelations, so he could show me how to fit the jigsaw puzzle together, so I could make the complex simple and deliver God's message with power and clarity, so man could have the knowledge to discern good from evil, the spiritual from the carnal and could choose God and his righteousness or the false god of materialism, which the devil purposed to tempt and deceive man!

I should point out that God saw to it that I was not part of the government or any other special interest group. As a watchman, he warned me repeatedly that it was my responsibility to speak the truth without regard for how any person or group might be offended by what I had to say. Once a person knows the truth, he becomes responsible for what he does with that knowledge, but as for me, if I fail to speak the whole truth regardless of the consequences, then I am held accountable!

The truth is that The Second American Revolution is at hand. That is if the American people have the resolve to stand up for the Constitution and for the freedom it guarantees. If not, we will just slip quietly into slavery. It is too late to think we can get out of the mess we have gotten ourselves into, without pain and suffering, but one way or the other, it will come to an end. As I think about what lies ahead for America and the world, I am reminded of the words of warning of Winston Churchill and Patrick Henry, and I ask myself, "Has America become a nation of self-indulgent, cowards who are so concerned for their material comfort that they are willing to give away the future of their children to a tyrannical government intent on making them slaves?" I hope not! I pray not! This same question needs to be posed to all the nations of the world collectively and to us all individually.

> "If you will not fight for the right when you can easily win without bloodshed; if you will not fight when your victory will be sure and not too costly; you may come to the moment when you will have to fight with the odds against you and only a small chance of survival. There may even be a worse case: you may have to fight when there is no hope of victory, because it is better to perish than to live as slaves" (Winston Churchill).

> "Is life so dear, or peace so sweet, as to be purchased at the price of chains and slavery? Forbid it, Almighty God! I know not what course others may take; but as for me, give me liberty, or give me death!" (Patrick Henry).

Thomas Jefferson knew the real truth, "When the people fear their government, there is tyranny: when the government fears the people there is liberty." "The spirit of resistance to government is so valuable that I wish it to be always kept alive...Whenever any form of government becomes destructive of these ends—life, liberty, and the pursuit of happiness—it is the right of the people to alter or abolish it and to institute new government."

President Ronald Reagan echoed Jefferson's sentiments when he said: "In this present crisis, government is not the solution to the problem, government is the problem."

Remember, when it looks hopeless, God will intervene, that is if we repent and turn to him. The fate of our nation and the world is in our hands. This battle will be fought on two fronts—on earth and in heaven—and what is at stake is not only our freedom but even more importantly our very souls. Difficult times call for difficult decisions, but if we stand together united one people under God, we can prevail against any adversary. God rescued the Israelites from seemingly hopeless situations time after time. What we need is courage and faith. I leave you with these words of inspiration from my American hero, John F. Kennedy (JFK).

JFK said, "Each time a person stands up for an ideal, or acts to improve the lot of others, or strikes out against injustice, he or she sends forth a tiny ripple of hope. Crossing each other a million different centers of energy and daring, those ripples build a current that can sweep down the mightiest walls of oppression and resistance." He also said, "Do not pray for easy lives. Pray to be strong men."

Thus says the Lord!

1. *The time of harvest is at hand.* I shall open the eyes of the righteous so they may know the truth and it shall set them free. Know that the truth is a two-edged sword, which cuts to the marrow of he who hears the truth if he departs not from his evil ways!
2. *Be not confused when you see evil take over the earth.* For it is purposed to divide the wheat from the tares and the wicked from the righteous, so that one may inherit life eternal and the other may be judged for his sins!
3. *Only the righteous may inherit the Promised Land.* Because there in shall abound the Holy Spirit who giveth the power to perform miracles which are not to be entrusted to the wicked for they would purpose them for evil not good!

4. *How shall I judge those that come before me?* They shall be judged whether they resisted evil and bowed not before the false god of materialism. Whether they proclaimed my son before man. Whether they walked in righteousness. By what manner of fruit they produced, be it good or evil. By these things shall man be judged!
5. *There shall be no peace upon the earth.* Wherefore shall man be set against man and nation against nation, because ye have lusted after the pleasures, power, perversions and riches of the world, leaning on your own understanding and trusting not in the LORD!
6. *These things does the Lord despise:* ye money lenders, whore mongers, and fornicators. Ye proud and selfish people who care not for them less fortunate than themselves. Chief among that which I despise are liars and those who deceive my people! Surely in the day of judgment shall these be cast down from their high places and be least among men and suffer for thine iniquities!
7. *Woe it be to those shepherds who gardeth not my flock* and allow my teachings to be perverted allowing even mention of God to be stricken from use, by rulers intent on corrupting and enslaving my people and causing them to worship false gods!
8. *Know that the righteous shall I deliver from evil!* Know also that it is only when things appear hopeless that I can intervene, because it is only then that man will surrender to me and repent and cry out, so I may answer his prayers, and he may know that I am the LORD thy God!

This is my testimony, so help me God!

Me: So why did I feel you needed to hear my life story. Not because I am anything special, but precisely because I am not. I wanted you to see just how closely I walk with God and the extent to which he has guided my journey. We can all have that relationship if we will just surrender and learn to put our trust in him and wait upon him. The scriptures say: "Ask, and it shall be given you;

seek, and ye shall find; knock, and t shall be opened unto you:" (Mathew 7:7 KJV) and I can tell you that that is absolutely true, but there is a price to pay for admittance. You must prove yourself righteous by being willing to be tested in the fire. In the time to come we will all be tested and how we stand up to that test will determine what happens to us. All I can say is God will be there for you if you will be there for him and if you will be obedient. The key to the kingdom is selflessness.

UNDERSTANDING THE UN'S SECRET AGENDA

Over time as I researched my books God led me to evidence substantiating everything he had shown me during my Divine Appointment.

God let me see how the globalists lead by the UN were intent on collapsing the US so they could destroy the "free market system" and create a new "highbred capitalist communist dictatorship!

> "The Rockefeller file is not fiction. It is a compact, powerful and frightening presentation of what may be the most important story of our lifetime—the drive of the Rockefellers and their allies to create a One-World government combining super capitalism and communism under the same tent, all under their control...not one has dared reveal the most vital part of the Rockefeller story: that the Rockefellers and their allies have, for at least fifty years, been carefully following a plan to use their economic power to gain political control of first America, and then the rest of the world. Do I mean conspiracy? Yes, I do. I am convinced there is such a plot, international in scope, generations old in planning, and incredibly evil in intent" (Representative Larry McDonald).

On August 31 1983, McDonald was killed aboard Korean Airline flight 007, which "accidentally," accidentally my a——s" strayed over Soviet airspace and was shot down. The media reporting was scant and short-lived, and not a single mention was publicly made about the fact that McDonald had been heading a congressional effort to expose what he called *a dangerous international conspiracy*. The Russians would not have risked starting a war by shooting down a commercial plane, if they had not known ahead of time that there would be no consequences. No. They would have simply flanked the plane with fighter jets and either forced it to land or leave Russian airspace. As you will learn later, Russia, China,

. by the financial elite and they are all one-world government.

, and the truth is revealed—the US must orld Order.

> ıd Order can't happen without US participa- .e the most significant single component. Yes, a New World Order, and it will force the United Sta. change its perceptions" Henry Kissinger [CFR Member], World Affairs Council Press Conference, Regent Beverly Wilshire, April 19, 1994).

Not only will there be a New World Order, but it will be incredibly evil. Listen to what Rockefeller had to say about the Chinese resolution which killed sixty-seven million Chinese.

"Whatever the price of the Chinese revolution, it has obviously succeeded not only in producing more efficient administration, but also in fostering high morale and community of purpose. The social experiment in China under Chairman Mao's leadership is one of the most important and successful in human history." *(*David Rockefeller *New York Times)*

"We know that "the free market is nonsense. We kind of agree with Mao that political power comes largely from the barrel of a gun." *(*Manufacturing Czar, Ron Bloom Obama Administration)

China is the model for the (Anglo-Saxon), Financial Elite's Utopian New World Order. They intend to *destroy the Free Market System* by causing a *global financial meltdown,* collapsing the economy of the US and Europe and the rest of the industrialized world. Then using US and NATO troops they intend to force formation of their long dreamt of *One World Super–Capitalist – Communist – Dictatorship. T*hen following Mao's example they plan mass genocide on a never before dreamt of scale.

Praising a leader that starved to death sixty-seven million of his people should give you an idea of just how ruthless these people are and what they have in store for us as they peruse their agenda of world domination. The intent is to collapse the free market system, and then purge the population just like Mao did.

The UN'S hidden agenda: "Isn't the only hope for the planet that the industrialized civilizations collapse? Isn't it our responsibility to bring that about?" (Maurice Strong, Founder of the UN Environmental Program–Opening Speech, Rio Earth Summit 1992)

Heads Up! This is why the US, Europe and other industrialized nations around the world are being intentionally collapsed under a mountain of debt, and why Obama's Fundamental Transformation is designed to transition the US from a democracy into socialism and eventually into a dictatorship. The UN and our leaders in Washington [Specifically the Office of the President and Key Congressmen] constitute a Shadow Government intent on carrying out the agenda of the UN to *"Collapse The Free Market System."* This means the US must fall! Not only must the US fall, but every industrialized nation in the world. Are you okay with that?

Will you say treason? President Bush pledges the allegiance of the US to the very organization, which is on record, as intending to destroy the US and all the world's industrialized countries. *Will you say treason?*

The American people have been sold out–It is the sacred principles enshrined in the United Nations Charter to which the American people will henceforth pledge their Allegiance."(President George h w Bush Addressing the UN) *US sovereignty is secondary to allegiance to UN.*

Just so we are clear: The UN agenda calls for ending US sovereignty and that of every sovereign nation on the planet, abandoning their Constitutions, collapsing the Free Market System, ending private ownership of property, and oh yes killing six billion of us? Are you okay with that?

The US, China, Russia, and all the major countries of the world are controlled by the shadow government of the financial elite. That is why you hear US and Communist leaders all calling for a one-world government!

We are one happy red family poised to enter the empire of evil. "No one will enter the New World Order unless he or she will make a pledge to worship Lucifer. No one will enter the New Age unless he will take a Luciferian Initiation. "(David Spangler, Director of Planetary Initiative, United Nations)

This is the organization to which our leaders in Washington pledge their allegiance and they dare call themselves Christians. They have taken the *"Mark of the Beast"* and the nations that follow them are destined for God's wrath. I plead with the nations of the world please oppose the UN's communist agenda before it is too late.

* * *

Communism is pure evil.

"Communism is not love. Communism is a hammer which we use to crush the enemy" (Mao Zedong).

"Communism posses a language every people can understand its elements are hunger, envy and death" (Heinrich Hein)

"The idea was that those who direct the overall conspiracy could use the differences in those two so-called ideologies [Marxism/fascism/socialism vs. democracy/capitalism] to enable them [the illuminati] to divide larger and larger portions of the human race into opposing camps so that they could be armed and then brainwashed into fighting and destroying each other" (Myron Fagan, Divide and Conquer).We are all pawns on a global chess board controlled by the Financial Elite and their henchmen in the UN.

"To achieve world government, it is necessary to remove from the minds of men their individualism, loyalty to family traditions, national patriotism, and religious dogmas" (Brock Adams, director, UN Health Organization).

"We are not going to achieve a New World Order without paying for it in blood as well as in words and money" (Arthur Schlesinger Jr., the CFR journal *Foreign Affairs*, August 1975.)

"A world government can intervene militarily in the internal affairs of any nation when it disapproves of their activities" Kofi Annan, UN secretary general.

"In the next century, nations as we know it will be obsolete; all states will recognize a single, global authority. National sovereignty wasn't such a great idea after all" (Strobe Talbot, President Clinton's deputy secretary of state, *Time*, July 20, 1992,

If you think the US government isn't in league with the communist nations, you are woefully mistaken. The mistake comes from thinking of these nations as sovereign nations in opposition to democracy. The rhetoric between them is just that rhetoric, designed to hide the truth. Virtually, all the governments of the world are controlled by a shadow government headed by the international bankers I refer to as the financial elite. If this seems a brash statement, I urge you to finish this book before you make up your mind. They take control by collapsing a country and then bailing them out but at the cost of their sovereignty. The truth is, we are all one happy red communist family and have been for a long time.

* * *

The cast of players in the greatest conspiracy ever perpetrated on any people. They are all in it together—one happy red family.

"He [President Nixon] spoke of the talks as a beginning, saying nothing more about the prospects for future contacts and merely reiterating the belief he brought to China that both nations share an interest in peace and building 'a new world order" (Excerpt from an article in the *New York Times*, February 1972). China and the US are red brothers.

"We believe we are creating the beginning of a new world order coming out of the collapse of the US-Soviet antagonisms" (Brent Scowcroft [August 1990], quoted in the *Washington Post*, May 1991). Russia and the US are red brothers.

"Further global progress is now possible only through a quest for universal consensus in the movement toward a new world order" (Russian Leader Mikhail Gorbachev)

"But it became clear as time went on that in Mr. Bush's mind the New World Order was founded on a convergence of goals and interests between the US and the Soviet Union, so strong and permanent that they would work as a team through the UN Security Council" (Excerpt from A. M. Rosenthal in the *New York Times*, January 1991). Russia and the US are comrades'.

"How to Achieve the New World Order" (Title of book excerpt by Henry Kissinger in *Time* magazine, March 1994).

"How I Learned to Love the New World Order" (Article by Sen. Joseph R. Biden Jr. in the *Wall Street Journal*, April 1992).

"The Final Act of the Uruguay Round, marking the conclusion of the most ambitious trade negotiation of our century, will give birth–in Morocco–to the World Trade Organization, the third pillar of the New World Order, along with the United Nations and the International Monetary Fund" (Part of full-page advertisement by the government of Morocco in the *New York Times* [April 1994]. Title of article by Kenichi Ohmae, political reform leader in Japan in the *Wall Street Journal*, August 1994).

America has been a democracy: A communist order since 1933. That's why the US is referred to as a democracy when it was established as a republic.

US declared bankruptcy: Why is the US is referred to as a democracy and not a republic? Became in 1933 *we declared bankruptcy and became a socialist communist order*. Here is how it came about.

Emergency Banking Act 1933: "...It is an established fact that the *United States Federal Government has been dissolved* by the Emergency Banking Act, March 9, 1933, 48 Stat. 1, Public Law 89-719; declared by President Roosevelt, being bankrupt and insolvent. H.J.R.192; 73rd Congress in session June 5, 1933 ..."

Declaration of bankruptcy: "All United States Offices, Officials, and Departments are now operating within a de facto status in name only under Emergency War Powers. With the Constitutional *Republican* form of Government now dissolved, the receivers of the bankruptcy have adopted a new form of government for the United States. This new form of government is known as a *Democracy,* being an established *Socialist Communist Order* under a new governor for America." (Former Senator James Traficant)

NOTE: *From that time on the FED & IMF [Gangster Bankers] became our de facto government our Shadow Government!* This book will establish the fact that "the President and our elected officials in Washington are irrelevant, nothing more than window dressing for the masses." And this is true of all the governments of all the industrialized nations of the world.

The truth which has been hidden from us since 1933 is that our government has been controlled by a Shadow Government – A Communist Government which has systematically been executing their *"Plan to destroy America from within."* They control our banks, our schools, the media and yes our Presidents and enough Congressmen to assure that their policies are enacted. America is being metamorphosed like a caterpillar, but not into a beautiful butterfly, no we are being turned into the very thing we are supposed to stand against – *"A demonically controlled communist order."* May God help us!

The intent of the one-world government is to create a ruling class modeled after the monarchies of colonial Europe.

Carol Quigley, Georgetown professor, member of Trilateral Commission, and mentor to Bill Clinton wrote that the goals of the financial elite who control central banks around the world are "nothing less than to create a world system of financial control in private hands able to dominate the political system of each country and economy of the world as a whole…controlled in a feudalist fashion by central banks of the world acting in concert by secret agreements arrived at in private meetings and conferences."

President Franklin D. Roosevelt told us essentially the same thing way back in 1933 when he said, "The real rulers in Washington are invisible and exercise power from behind the scenes."

When I questioned the motive for these actions, God showed me two things. First, he said, "Christ was tempted and told that if he would bow down to Satan, he, Satan would give him dominion over the nations of the earth. Christ said no, but the political leaders of the world, being mere men, said yes. As a result evil prevails across all the earth."

Second, he said, "As the end time comes upon the earth, knowledge will increase exponentially" and one of the outcomes of that increase in knowledge will be medical and agricultural breakthroughs that will result in a population explosion so large that the earth cannot support it. Those in power at the time will decide that in the interest of self-preservation they must drastically reduce the population (mass genocide). They will also decide that they must reduce resource consumption because they view the world's natural resources as belonging to them the (financial elite), and they are not to be squandered on the masses. This is what is behind the elites drive to establish a one-world Government, and they are using *debt*, false flag terrorist events, and the hoax of global warming to create crisis after crisis in order to get the people to buy into the lie that their only hope lies in surrendering their freedom to them."

It is as Rob Emanuel said, "You never want to waste a crisis."

"The whole aim of practical politics is to keep the populace alarmed—and hence, clamorous to be led to safety—by menacing it with an endless series of hobgoblins, all of them imaginary" (H. L. Mencken),

Here it is. A clear declaration that they intend to—collapse all the sovereign nations of the world and establish a one-world government dictatorship. It couldn't be much clearer. And as to how they will birth their new government, they will create crisis after crisis till the world is in utter chaos, and if we believe their lies, we will rush into their arms because they will tell us it is the only way to save the planet. (It is a lie. More on this later).

War has been declared. The American public and in fact all the people of the planet have some hard decisions to make. A shadow government has declared their intention to end our national sovereignty and they say our only choice is weather we go along willing or whether they will take over by force.

> "The super national sovereignty of an intellectual elite and world bankers is surely preferable to the National Auto-determination practiced in past centuries"(David Rockefeller, Council Foreign Relations).

> "We are on the verge of a global transformation. All we need is the right major crisis and the nations will accept the New World Order" (Council on Foreign Relations member David Rockefeller, Sept. 23, 1994).

Whether or not we realize it, we are at war. Unlike in WWI and WWII the enemy is not a foreign nation. In this instance, the enemy is a group of subversives from within our own government! The time has come when our own government represents the greatest threat to freedom that this nation and the world have ever known!

They intend to take us over by stealth from within, without us realizing what they are doing till it is too late. But what they don't realize is that God is going to warn us. He always waits till the last minute in order to see what we are going to do, but he always warns his people, and he (God) will always come to our aid, if we surrender to him and cry out for help.

"The New World Order will be built…an end run on national sovereignty, eroding it piece by piece will accomplish much more than the old fashioned frontal assault" (Council on Foreign Relations journal 1974, p558).

The time for action is at hand. If we do nothing, we will be taken over, and the longer we wait to take a stand, the greater the cost in human suffering. Either we become slaves or we fight and endure hardship. There are no other choices. I would add that the United States is the only nation standing in the way of the one-world government. As the US goes, so goes the rest of the planet. God said, "To him that much is given much is expected." Will we simply submit to slavery or will we be that shining nation on the hill that stands between tyranny and oppression? Will we be God's chosen people or will we be minions of the one-world government and their soon-to-emerge leader, the antichrist?

> "If a nation values anything more than freedom, then it will lose its freedom; and the irony of it is that if it is comfort and security that it values, it will lose that too" (Charley Reese, *Orlando Sentinel*)

> "I believe that if the people of this nation fully understood what Congress has done to them over the last forty-nine years, they would move on Washington; they would not wait for an election...It adds up to a preconceived plan to destroy the economic and social independence of the United States!" (Senator George W. Malone [Nevada], speaking before Congress in 1957).

A warning from God: "Freedom, comfort, and security will be taken away from those who allow *man-made chaos* to drive them into the arms of the one-world government because it will be headed by the antichrist, and he will cause them that submit to him to take his mark and swear allegiance to him. In pursuit of material comforts and safety, man will be tricked into giving up his place in the Promised Land. The time is quickly approaching when men will have to choose freedom or slavery. The harvest is at hand, and with it, there will be a revolt in heaven and here on earth. Make sure you are on the winning side. The devil and his minions who head the one-world government will lose."

THE SECRET YOUR GOVERNMENT DOESN'T WANT YOU TO KNOW

The secret that will set you free is that "your government is lying to you regarding virtually everything."

> "The enormous gap between what US leaders do in the world and what Americans think their leaders are doing is one of the greatest propaganda accomplishments of dominant political mythology" (Michael Parent, author and historian).

By the time you finish this book, you will know the truth, and it will set you free. For perhaps the first time in your life you will have the facts at your disposal to make informed decisions regarding your future, that of your family and that of the entire world. The human species is coming upon the most critical time in human evolution. We are at a crossroads. One road brings mankind together. The other divides us. One road leads to putting our greed behind us so that we can learn to live together in harmony with each other and the planet, which nurtures and sustains us. That road leads to freedom and spiritual evolution. The other road perpetuates the greed of the few (the financial elite who control the governments of the world) leading to enslavement and impoverishment of the many (you and I) so that the few may live in luxury. That road leads to death of the many (you and I) in order that the few may live (our corrupt power mongering, narcissist, evil overloads who would play God with our lives).

God doesn't want us to be slaves, but the financial elite do. God gave us dominion over all living things. He wants us to learn to be good stewards and to learn to live together in peace and harmony. The financial elite do everything they can to divide us and pit us against each other.

The truth is the financial elite have an agenda to collapse the US and every sovereign nation in the world and force them into a one-world totalitarian government. To realize their agenda, they lie to us about literally everything and perpetrate every crime known to man. For example:

- *They tell us we are being attacked by terrorist.* It is a lie designed to get us to willing give up the freedoms guaranteed us by the constitution. By the time you finish this book, you will understand that as Ted Gunderson says, literally every supposed terrorist attack in US history has been carried out by the CIA. Ted Gunderson, former FBI chief of LA, Dallas, and Memphis Operations goes beyond suggestions of coincidence and comes right out and accuses the CIA of being behind virtually every major terrorist act in recent years. Gunderson says, "Look what the CIA has done to this country. What they have done to us is unbelievable. Look at the terrorist acts that have occurred. The CIA is behind most if not all of them. We have Pan Am 103, we had the USS *Cole*, we had Oklahoma City, we had the World Trade Center in 1993. Unfortunately, for them (the CIA), there were only six people killed in the 1993 WTC bombing, not enough to pass the legislation so what happened is two years later April 19th 1996 Down comes the Oklahoma City Federal Building. One year later the antiterrorist legislation that takes away many of our Constitutional and Civil Liberties is passed."

The truth of what Gunderson said is detailed in the chapters entitled "Compelling Evidence 9/11 Was A False Flag Attack" and "Wars for Profit and Control." In these chapters, I will prove beyond a reasonable doubt that 9/11 was about oil and laying the groundwork for martial law and imposition of a dictatorship in the US, but for now, I leave you to contemplate the words of three of the world's most infamous leaders.

It is easy to get a nation to go to war: "Naturally the common people don't want war: Neither in Russia, nor in England, nor for that matter in Germany. That is understood. But, after all, it is the leaders of the country who determine the policy and it is always a simple matter to drag the people along, whether it is a democracy, or a fascist dictatorship, or a parliament, or a communist dictatorship. *Voice or no voice, the people can always be brought to the bidding of the leaders.* That is easy. All you have to do is ***"Tell them they are being attacked"***, and denounce the peacemakers for lack of patriotism and exposing the country to danger". (Hermann Goering – Hitler's 2nd in Command)

9/11 was a lie perpetrated on the America people in order to get us to go to war: A war not for honor, a war not for homeland security, but a war intended to secure a foothold in the oil rich Middle East, a war intended to topple regimes which were unfriendly to the US, a war intended to strip away our liberties and lay the groundwork for eventual dictatorship to be imposed in the US, and finally a war intended to financially collapse the US! The truth which this book will establish is that Osama Bin Laden was in league with factions of the US government, particularly his friend and business partner George W Bush who was representing the interest of his handlers in the Shadow Government. America was betrayed from within.

"The Size of the lie is a definite factor in causing it to be believed, for the mass of a nation are in the depths of their hearts more easily deceived than they are consciously and intentionally bad. The primitive simplicity of their minds renders them a more easy prey to a big lie than to a small one… for they themselves often tell little lies, but would be ashamed to tell big lies." (Adolf Hitler's Mein Kamp 1925)

9/11 certainly was a big lie! Hitler used the burning of the German Parliament as an excuse for war and as a means to impose a dictatorship, and our leaders in Washington used 9/11 to do the same thing to the US. Additionally as you will learn a little later 9/11 also laid the groundwork for the 2008 Financial Collapse. So 9/11 gave the US the Patriot Act modeled after Hitler's Enabling Act and the Stimulus with its massive dept and hidden agenda. In both instances the goal was to impose a dictatorship!

George W. Bush

The US Patriot Act laid the groundwork for open dictatorship: Yep @ 3:45 a.m. I pulled the bipartisan version of The Patriot Act & replaced it with one designed to take away your liberties! And the sheep in Congress passed it without even reading it! Yep: I laid the groundwork for Dictatorship!!! Not a quote, a fact! *The interests behind the Bush administration, such as the CFR, the Trilateral Commission–founded by Brzezinski for David Rockefeller–and the Bilderberg Group have prepared for and are now moving to implement open world dictatorship....*" (Dr. Johannes Koeppl Former official of the German Ministry for Defense and advisor to NATO.

I know these quotes don't in and of themselves prove anything, but I have the proof and when you get to the referenced chapters, you will to. This is just an appetizer, a little something for you to think about.

- *They tell us that to be fair, they have to redistribute the wealth.* By taking from Peter, the most productive member of society (the supposed rich guy) and giving to Paul, the least productive member of society. (Those on entitlements; the means by which they make us dependent and docile and in the process drive us into unmanageable debt, their weapon of choice.) That is another lie. Paul, the supposed rich guy, doesn't have squat compared to the vast fortunes of the financial elite. The elite constitute less than 1 percent of the world's population, but they control approximately 95 percent of the world's wealth, so if we are going to redistribute the wealth, they are the ones we should be taking from, and as outlined in the "American Reformation Platform" in the chapter entitled "Political Counteroffensive" I tell you how to do exactly that. No group of self-serving tyrants should be allowed to hold the world hostage the way they do. They control the money supply, credit, and interest rates and through these vehicles, they regularly cause boom bust cycles in the economy (i.e., the Great Depression and the 2008 housing bubble) designed to take the hard-earned money of we, the sheep. So, you see, they have an ongoing policy of wealth redistribution where they take from the many (you and I) to enrich and empower the few, themselves. It is time we demanded a more equitable distribution of wealth, and I will show you how we do that.

The truth is that it is as Thomas Jefferson said, "The democracy will cease to exist when you take away from those who are willing to work and give to those who will not."

"There are two ways to conquer and enslave a nation. One is by the sword. The other is by debt" (President John Adams).

And that is exactly what they want; they want to enslave us. Their agenda calls for nothing short of worldwide dictatorship. Consider this: "It was a carefully contrived occurrence. International bankers sought to bring about a condition of despair, so that they might emerge the rulers of us all" (Congressman Louis McFadden, chairman of the United States House Committee on Banking and Currency.) This is an excerpt from a speech, in which he introduced House Resolution #158 Articles of Impeachment for the secretary of the treasury and the board of governors of the Federal Reserve, charging that they had intentionally caused the Great Depression of 1929. Shortly after delivering his speech, he was poisoned while attending a state function. They are doing it to us again, and I will explain exactly how, in the chapters entitled ("Congress Is Irrelevant and Our Presidents Are Puppets," "The Shadow Government Exposed," and "Our Two-Party Political System Is an Illusion")

Then, there was the lie about Kennedy's assassination.

John F. Kennedy

"There's a plot in this country to enslave every man, woman and child. Before I leave this high and noble office, I intend to expose this plot." (President John F. Kennedy) [seven days before his assassination]

I tell you these men are serious about keeping their money and power. In the chapter entitled "Mind Control Has Turned Us into Mindless Sheep," I expose the assassinations of several high-ranking political leaders, including JFK, who tried to tell us the truth and paid with their lives.

- *They tell us global warming is caused by man-made carbon emissions*, and that in order to reduce carbon emissions, they have to pass job killing Environmental Protection Agency (EPA) regulations and place a carbon tax on virtually every product manufactured in the US. It is another lie. The truth is that the carbon taxes are intended to impoverish and utterly destroy the middle class. The truth is the carbon tax is to force us to reduce consumption of resources they consider to be theirs. The truth is their regulations are intended to collapse the free market system, and in the process, drive the US into unmanageable debt in order to force us into the one-world government.

Every once in a while, there is a politician in Washington that occasionally tells us the truth and in my lifetime, the two that I found most likely to be forthcoming were Kennedy and Reagan. "Approximately 80 percent of our air pollution stems from hydrocarbon released by vegetation, so let's not go overboard in setting and enforcing tough emission standards from manmade sources" (President Ronald Reagan). Gee, that certainly isn't what we hear coming out of the Bush and Obama administrations.

Consider this: Without getting into a lot of scientific mumbo jumbo, it is pretty easy to figure out that if global warming was caused by human activity, here on earth, that earth would be affected, but other planets in the solar system wouldn't be. Make sense? Well, guess what that is not the case. The real culprit is a period of increased solar flares affecting the entire solar system. Pretty simple, right?

"We've got to ride the global warming issue, even if the theory of global warming is wrong" (Timothy Wirth, former US senator [D-Colorado]. Remember the Climategate scandal? Their theory wasn't wrong. It was an out and out lie. Go Figure

> "A global climate treaty must be implemented even if there is no scientific evidence to back the greenhouse effect" (Richard Benedict, State Dept. employee, working on assignment from the Conservation Foundation).

Translation: We are prepared to lie through our teeth in order to force "cap and trade" otherwise known as "cap and tax" on the American people in order to collapse the free market system. And lie they did, till along came the Climategate scandal, which exposed the conspiracy to tax us based on bogus, trumped up scientific data. The endgame was to destroy the free market system by making US manufactured goods noncompetitive in the global market.

Consider this: "We know that the free market is nonsense. We kind of agree with Mao that political power comes from the barrel of a gun" (Manufacturing czar, Ron Bloom).

Translation: Use any means necessary to achieve your goal. Gee, that is a good lead in to my next quote. "The technetronic era involves the gradual appearance of a more controlled society dominated by an elite unrestricted by traditional values" (*Between Two Ages: America's Role in the Technetronic Era* by Zbigniew Brzezinski, US national security advisor).

Translation: It is not only okay to lie, but none of the rules of civilized society apply, gangster rules apply. In the chapter entitled " Congress Is Irrelevant and Our Presidents Are Puppets," I outline how and why the US has practiced intentionally losing trade policies for the last fifty years and how that fact relates to cap and trade initiatives. I also disclose a pattern of betrayal, spanning the administrations from Wilson to Obama. I detail key pieces of legislation that were perpetrated on the American people, all of which were designed to intentionally weaken the US economy, circumvent the constitution, and take away our freedom, all leading to the intentional collapse of the US and the imposition of martial law and open dictatorship.

Gee, when I took Ethics 101, I don't remember hearing the kind of stuff that comes out of the mouth of our illustrious leaders in Washington. I guess they took the class on winning at any cost. Here goes. "The illegal we do immediately. The unconstitutional takes a little longer" (Henry Kissinger). "The Constitution is just a goddamn piece of paper" (George W. Bush Nov. 2005, Capital Hill Blues), and last but not least, "You can fool some of the people all the time, and those are the ones you want to concentrate on" (President George W. Bush). Gee, this kind of honesty makes the cockles of my heart all warm and fussy. Just kidding. It sickens me to think these kinds of men are running our country. They give credence to the saying "power corrupts, and absolute power corrupts absolutely." So, now you know why I say.

Your government is lying to you regarding virtually everything.

- *They tell us that the Green Movement is about saving the planet*—it is not. It is about how it relates to the collision of overpopulation and peak oil, which is the most important topic in this chapter and the book, because it is the root cause of the planets sixth mass extinction and understanding the truth of this matter is crucial to our survival. If we don't see the truth about the Green Movement, they will use it to enslave us.

"Protecting the environment is a *ruse*. The goal is the political and economic subjugation of most men by the few under the guise of preserving nature" (J. H. Robbin).

"America has become little more than an energy protection force doing anything to gain access to expensive fuel without regard to the lives of others or the earth itself" (Political Analyst Kevin Philip). Oil is what our government considers its strategic interest, and it is to protect those interests that it sends our boys off to die in foreign wars. By the time you finish this book, you will understand the truth of what I just said.

- *They lie to us about their planned genocide of the many to benefit the few.* The truth is that the planet is experiencing a sixth mass extinction caused by overpopulation, colliding with peak oil and a shortage of clean water, but from the government's perspective, overpopulation is not the primary issue. The primary issue is conserving their valuable nonrenewable oil supply. Given their perspective, there is no need to inform the public of the problem because they have no intention of working with us to voluntarily reduce the population. They see it as being much easier and expedient to lie to us while they make preparations to impose martial law, lock us down, and begin our systematic extermination.

Psychologist Barbara Marx Hubbard, member and futurist/strategist of Task Force Delta, a United States Army think tank, said, "One-fourth of humanity must be eliminated from the social body. We are in charge of God's selection process for planet earth. He selects; we destroy. We are the riders of the pale horse, death."

While receiving an award at Texas University, Dr. Erick Pianka (biologist) said, "The worldwide aids pandemic was *no good; it's too slow.*" Makes you wonder if AIDS was cooked up in a laboratory by Barbara Hubbard's group or one like it. "The riders of the pale horse, death."

Professor Maurice King said, "Global Sustainability requires the deliberate quest of poverty… reduced resource consumption… and set levels of mortality control." He is right about having to reduce population, but the question is how do we go about it? As to the rest of it, he is wrong, and you will shortly understand why he is wrong.

"In the event that I am reincarnated, I would like to return as a deadly virus in order to contribute something to solve overpopulation" (Prince Philip, reported by Deutsche Press Agentur [DPA] August 1988).

That doesn't work for me! How about you? You okay with that?

After all, we are expendable, and they will keep as many of us around as they need, but as to the rest of us, we are in their way. If they get rid of us, their oil conservation problem is solved. "Military men are just dumb stupid animals to be used as pawns in foreign policy" (Henry Kissinger, former national security advisor, secretary of state [Nixon and Ford administrations], and recipient of the Nobel Peace Prize). This attitude applies to us all. What we have to come to grips with is that to the elite, we are all just dumb animals that exist at their convenience, or not. Their solution is to solve the resource shortage problem and the overpopulation problem by simply killing most of us. For my part I don't like that idea. How about you?

RENEWABLE ENERGY—THE MIRACLE THAT COULD SAVE THE PLANET

There is a better solution than killing us —one where we get to participate in population reduction and we get access to absolutely revolutionary technologies capable of changing life as we know it. The technologies of which I speak are as revolutionary as the internal combustion engine, the harnessing of electricity, and the computer were when they were invented. As a matter of fact, they dwarf those technologies in terms of their ability to change life on planet earth and improve living conditions for people, anywhere and everywhere on the planet. That is the good news. Now, the bad news. Our government knows about all these technologies and has absolutely no intention of implementing any of them that is till they have purged the planet of the virus they call "we, the people" and have imposed a total dictatorship.

* * *

The big picture: understanding the government's lies. The government is pushing their global warming hoax as a control mechanism while hiding the truth from us. The truth is that unless we solve the overpopulation problem and the clean water and oil depletion issues a mass extension event of biblical proportion will be unleashed and once it reaches critical mass there will be no stopping it. In any event we need to recognize that global warming is not the only factor threatening the planet, and it certainly is not caused by human activity. That is a lie straight out of the pit of hell! Global warming is caused by a cyclical event related to a period of maximum sun spot activity, and there is nothing we can do about it.

But there are other serious problems, which are caused by man, and we better take responsibility for them or else we won't have to worry about the government killing us because Mother Nature will do it for them. But in that event we can have solace in the fact that the government will perish along with us. Seriously, we need to consider the effects of

- deforestation as thousands of acres of timber land in the tropics are intentionally burnt in order to clear the land for cattle ranching and many thousands more are logged. Remember trees produce oxygen, which is essential to life.
- destruction of the food chain in rivers, lakes, and the oceans due to agricultural and industrial pollution, over fishing, inappropriate recreational use, and as we now know, the dangers of oil spills. Remember most of the oxygen in the world is produced by planktons and algae in the oceans; kill the oceans, and it is game over.
- loss of habitat due to encroachment by man, and overexploitation of resources due to over population. No man and for that matter no species is an island unto themselves. We are highly interdependent. That is just the way God created the world. We humans live in a very delicate balance with Mother Nature. If we destroy the habitat for other species, it will cause a ripple effect that will come home to roust.
- depletion and contamination of aquifers caused by rising ocean levels and excess human usage. The net effect of this is to take millions of acres of agricultural land out of production leading to famine.
- the threat to the food supply posed by genetic tampering. Four companies control 80 percent of our food supply in the form of genetically designed seeds with a terminator gene, which keeps their seeds from being able to be used as seed stock for planting. Sounds like a perfect way to starve the masses to death. Also, the variety of plant species has been drastically reduced by Monsanto and their like, so what do we do if their seed stock becomes susceptible to some disease like happened in the potato blight in Ireland? I guess we starve. It is dangerous to play God.

- decertification caused by human activity. A study conducted at the United Nations University by over two hundred experts from twenty-five countries suggests that "climate change is making desertification the greatest environmental challenge of our times. If action is not taken, the report warns that some fifty million people could be displaced within the next ten years. Ultimately, this is even more serious than oil. We can live without oil. But we can't live without water.

According to Mark Lynas author of *High Tide*, "We're talking about 30% of the world's surface becoming virtually uninhabitable in terms of agricultural production in the span of a few decades… these are parts of the world where hundreds of millions of people will no longer be able to feed themselves."

- serious fresh water shortages in various parts of the world (e.g., California and the Southwest US, India, Bangladesh, and others. There are literally water wars, breaking out all over the world as areas without water are demanding it from areas with it, and the situation is just going to get worse as glaciers melt, aquifers are depleted, rivers and oceans are polluted. There are just too many people consuming too much water. It is that simple.

If we hope to avoid extinction, all of these issues need to be addressed, but the most serious problem we are facing is "overpopulation" because it is the root cause of all the other problems. The government isn't that concerned about these issues, because their solution is very simple. Just slaughter the sheep (you and I). As the Chinese military strategist Sun Tuz would say, "We are on death ground, and we are fighting for our lives." Are we going to stand by and do nothing till they come to take us to the death camps like in Hitler's Germany? The only way we get a voice in this life-threatening event is if we stand up and take the power from the government and to do that, we will have to stand united as one people, which can only happen if the public becomes aware of the gravity of the situation. Please help me get the word out and rally the people. Please help me take these issues viral on the internet!

If we can solve the *overpopulation issue*, there are revolutionary cheap, clean, renewable energy technologies, which can substantially address the other issues, but the problem is that our government will never voluntarily allow us access to cheap, clean, renewable energy. But for now, let's focus on learning about the technology, and then we will take a look at their implications for solving the greatest crisis the human race has ever faced. Sooner or later, we are going to have to stand up and take the power from the oppressors or suffer the ultimate consequences, but for now, let's just explore our technological options, but first some more quotes for your enlightenment.

> "Giving society cheap, abundant energy…would be the equivalent of giving an addict a machine gun" (Paul Ehrlich, Stanford University).

> "The Environmentalist's dream is an egalitarian society based on: rejection of economic growth, a smaller population, eating lower on the food chain, consuming a lot less, and sharing a much lower level of resources mush more equally" (Aaron Wildavsky).

Energy solutions you may not know about:

- Garbage Recycling: Brian Appel, chairman and CEO of CWT, has developed the technology to turn any organic material (that is anything containing carbon, which is everything on the planet except silicon) into oil, gas, and charcoal. There are twelve billion tons of solid wastes produced each year in the US alone. Appel said, "We can conservatively convert all the agricultural waste in the US, which is six billion tons into over four billion barrels of light oil a year. That is the same number we import."

Note: This technology is real. Appel has plants in operation, which were built for commercial clients, but no money has been forthcoming from the government to capitalize on this amazing technology.

Imagine, we could simultaneously get rid of our garbage dumps and the ecological hazards they pose while developing a renewable/sustainable above ground oil supply, yet the government mandates the use of ethanol as an additive in gasoline, which requires millions of acres of land be taken out of agricultural production for food when people are starving to death around the world. Go figure. Ethanol is impractical and just another form of control.

- Solar Energy: It has been estimated that solar energy has the potential of one day being able to provide 100 percent of our energy needs. That day may not be far away. The Israelis have recently developed a solar cell, which is 1,500 times more efficient than anything previously developed. Gee, to me this seems like a much better investment than Obama's failed investment in the Solyndra solar panel company.
- Compressed Air Engine: Yet another revolutionary technology comes from France where inventor and head of Motor Development International (MDI), Guy Negra, has designed a car that runs on compressed air. Negra is a former Formula 1 race car designer. Since the car runs on compressed air, the only emission is clean air. It can be filled at a service station in about three minutes or plugged into an electrical outlet and filled by an onboard compressor in about four hours at a cost of about two dollars. The top speed is 110 kilometers (68.35 miles per hour) and driving distance is 200 kilometers (124.28 miles). There are also plans for a hybrid that can drive from LA to NY on a single tank of gas. Several licenses have been let to produce the cars, but you guessed it—not here in the US.
- Hydrogen on Demand: Several inventors have patents and working prototypes for cars, which convert water to hydrogen on demand, yet our government and auto makers tell us we have to buy hydrogen at a gas station. Gee, that would conveniently replace oil revenues with hydrogen revenues and keep us dependent on the oil companies and the government. How convenient.
- Stan Meyer's Hydrogen Car: According to Ralf Robinson of Action 6 News, Meyer's invention utilizes a hydrogen fuel cell

that produces hydrogen on demand so unlike the approach of the auto makers, there is no hydrogen fuel tank. The car runs on fresh or salt water. Meyer says, "He was offered a billion dollars for his invention by oil producing companies, but he turned them down." Leonard Holihan, from the Advanced Research Institute of Great Britain, says, "We recently took a delegation to evaluate Stan's work, and we came away saying this was one of the most important inventions of the century."

Meyers died, reportedly the victim of poison. Sounds like a scene from the *Godfather* where the godfather says, "I will make him an offer he can't refuse." Well, Meyers refused the oil producers, and he is dead. Go figure another coincidence. Oh by the way, NASA was also evaluating his technology.

- Denny Cline's Hydrogen Car: He originally stumbled on his invention when looking for an alternative to volatile acetylene in the welding industry. His invention actually produces a flame as hot as the sun.

Inventor Denny Cline of Hydrogen Technologies has patented his revolutionary electrolysis process which converts tap water(H_2O) into HHO, producing a gas that combines the atomic power of hydrogen with the stability of water. As the gas burns, the by-product is water. According to Fox News 26, "The inventor is already in negotiations with one US auto maker and talks are in process with the US government to develop a Hummer that can burn both water and gas. His prototype has passed all performance safety inspections and members of congress recently invited Denny Cline to Washington to demonstrate his invention."

Government cover up! This should have been headline news; instead, Detroit is going ahead with their designs for cars that force us to buy hydrogen at a gas station. The pattern is the government gets involved and then nothing; a big black hole. Go figure.

- John Kanzius's Salt Water Generator: Channel 3 News, Mike O'Mara (Erie, Pennsylvania): While looking for a cure for cancer, Inventor John Kanzius has stumbled on a way to burn salt water as a fuel. He uses radio waves to break the salt water into its chemical components of oxygen and hydrogen and burns it as a fuel. At the AVP Company in Akron top engineers who checked out his invention were amazed. Engineer John White says, "We saw the temperature go up to 1, 500 degrees centigrade. That's incredible."

- John Cristie's Zero-Point Magnetic Energy: Inventor John Cristie has invented an electric motor that is based on the attraction and repulsion force of the positive and negative poles of magnets. The motor is expected to sell for approximately $5, 000 and is capable of supplying the entire electrical requirements of a home, allowing homeowners to get completely off the utility grid. The government will never allow this because it would threaten GE's smart grid and the government's ability to control our electrical utilization. Cristie says his invention "could also be used in cars and could replace the internal combustion engine." Once started with a battery, the motor will run till the magnets are depleted (approximately three hundred years). This technology is called zero-point energy and represents what physicists have long theorized was the most efficient energy source in the universe. Steve Brassington, an independent electrical engineer, has evaluated the invention and says, "It's revolutionary. These guys have thought outside the box." Cristie says, "I think there is an opportunity here to share an invention with the world that goes beyond anything we have ever contemplated before" (Chris Alan, reporter, Sky News, Australia). *Note*: There are at least two others that I know of that have patens for zero-point energy devices.
- Shelved Patents: On a slightly different subject, there are other revolutionary scientific breakthroughs that are also being kept from us, particularly in the field of medicine. Pharmaceutical companies are not in the business of preventing or curing illness. They are in the extremely profitable business of treating chronic illness. They want you sick and dependent on them.

In the chapter entitled "Political Counteroffensive", I discuss how—if we will stand up for our rights—we can get access to shelved patents. Patents were intended to incentivize financial investment in technology. They were never intended to hold the public hostage to greedy, bankers, corporations, and politicians.

The two quintessential natural resources are water and oil, but in the final analysis, water is more important than oil. A technologically advanced society is impossible without oil because virtually everything we consume contains oil. Without oil, our productive output reverts back to horse and buggy days, but life goes on. Without water, there is no life of any kind. But the good news is that we have the capability at our disposal to solve both of these crucially important issues. But I should note that that doesn't mean the overpopulation crisis is any less serious. It is the root cause of the global extinction threat. Read on.

The good news is that the technologies you just read about can solve the oil and water crisis. This still leaves us with the overpopulation issue but that can be solved too if we will face up to it. As you just read, we have current technology, which can convert our garbage into a renewable oil supply. There wouldn't be enough to operate a billion plus gasoline-powered cars, but read on.

More good news: We have technology available to give us—cars run by compressed air, cars run by hydrogen produced on demand with no need to fill up at a fueling station like our government tells us, and cars run by zero-point energy derived from the repulsion of the positive and negatives poles of a permanent magnet.

Still more good news: The Hydrogen and zero-point technology I am referring to are used to power generators, which can be used not only to power electric cars, but they can also power home generators, thus ending our dependency for oil to power our automobiles and freeing us from dependency on the electric grid as electricity would be available on demand at the point of consumption.

Once started by a battery, the permanent magnet, which powers the Zero point generators has a life expectancy of approximately three hundred years.

Still more good news: Electrolysis, which is the conventional way of converting water into hydrogen, using heat, requires more energy to fracture the water, releasing the hydrogen than is generated by the release of the hydrogen, so it is obviously an impractical energy solution But the solutions I have described use either radio waves or electronic resonance frequencies, which actually create several more times energy than what is required to fracture water, so not only is it a clean renewable energy source, but it has a net positive energy output.

Still more good news: The Radio frequency and electronic resonance technologies can use either fresh or salt water to fracture the hydrogen. As I said a short while ago, we are facing a life-threatening fresh water shortage, but three-fourths of the planet is covered by salt water, so we have a virtually inexhaustible supply of fuel to operate our automobiles and produce electricity for our homes. The internal combustion engine and its dependency on oil can be eliminated and replaced by cheap, clean, renewable energy solutions.

Still more good news: Both of the hydrogen technologies I have described have yet another amazing gift to give humanity. They burn at temperatures as hot as the sun. So imagine a cheap, clean virtually unlimited supply of salt water that releases hydrogen, which burns at the temperature of the sun. What could we do with that? Get ready! Here it comes! We could build salt water desalination plants all over the world. We could then build water pipelines like our current oil pipelines and that water could be supplied anywhere in the world it was needed. It gets even better!

Still more good news: There is another event, which is playing a major role in the planets sixth mass extinction. That is decertification. The Bible predicted that the Israelites would return to their homeland and turn the desert into a garden, and they did. And with the technologies I just described, we could pipe fresh water to the deserts of the world and turn them into desert oases. The government would scoff at virtually everything I have said in this chapter, but I say they are liars, and they are guilty of treason and genocide.

The government and corporations deny us access to cheap, clean, renewable energy solutions in order to control and enslave us, and we must put a stop to it if we ever hope to be free!

Comments: If the initiatives outlined above were implemented, and cheap clean energy technologies were made available to the world, it would literally break the control of the financial elite and result in an era of prosperity greater than anything ever imagined. For the first time in human history, cheap clean energy would be available on demand at the point of consumption without the need for any kind of energy grid. We would literally have a second garden of Eden. The financial elite would no longer be able to ration resources, and an era of global cooperation and peace could be ushered in. Again, I say we have more power than we think. Please stand up and join the fight. Please spread the word.

Note: This sharing of resources and technology is exactly what "The American System of Economics" was about, and if we are ever to have peace on planet earth, we will have to embrace its dream of "elevating while equalizing the condition of man throughout the world" (Henry C. Carey, economics adviser to Abraham Lincoln).

What do you say? Are you a dumb sheep to be lead to the slaughter or are you part of the tribe of Judah, the Lion of Courage, who will stand with God and defeat his enemies?

MIND CONTROL HAS TURNED US INTO MINDLESS SHEEP

Chaos and Deceit Are Upon the Earth!

Governments are falling
Economies are failing
Wars are raging
The people are divided

Resources are depleting
The climate is changing
The seas are rising
The oceans are dying
The rivers are poisoned
Drought is spreading
Famine is looming

Yet truth is not to be found
Most of all, the government is lying

Crisis, crisis everywhere
Chaos is upon the earth
Where shall we turn?
Deceit is everywhere
The power brokers are jockeying
The New World Order is birthing
Chaos and slavery are visited upon the earth!

Chicken Little cried, "The sky is falling, the sky is falling! The world is ending! Run for your lives." Sometimes, fairy tales come true, and when they do, they can be frightening!

I think most of us would agree that as we enter the twenty-first century, the world is a scary place. From an ecological perspective, we have climate change, melting glaciers, and shifting weather patterns, causing floods, droughts, and food shortages. The entire ecological system of the planet seems to be unstable and dangerously unpredictable. Then there are concerns over availability and cost of the very essentials of life—food, water, and energy. As if that wasn't enough we have extremely volatile economic and political conditions, with the global debt crisis, terrorism, and the powder keg in the Middle East, threatening WWIII.

The year 2012 was predicted as the time in which the world would reach a crucial tipping point! Everyone from the ancient Egyptians to the Hopi and Aztec Indians, to sears such as Nostradamus and Edger Casey, to the Bible, Torah, and Koran have focused in on 2012 as the beginning of what the Bible calls the Tribulation!

Reader's perspective: People often say to me, "I know things are a mess, but there is nothing I can do about it. I may as well just go about my life and leave things to those in power."

Me: I hear this all the time, but it is the worst possible thing we could do! As Chicken Little would say, "The fox is in the hen house. The fox is in the hen house. Run for your lives!" I hope that as you read this book, you will come to believe me when I tell you a shadow government has taken over the US government and virtually, every sovereign nation in the world. Their intention is to establish a New World Order, a one-world government, a totalitarian-communist government. There will be no middle class, only the elite, and we their slaves.

We have been brainwashed into believing we are powerless. We are not.

In order to establish their New World Order, they need to keep the general public scared, distracted, passive, and convinced we are powerless to stop them, which is a lie! To this end, we are all the victims of mind control that render us blind to the truth of what is being done to enslave us.

This book is probably the most intense book you will ever read, but God specifically told me it had to shock people in order to wake up a blind and complacent society who has been controlled from cradle to grave without them even realizing it. Before we can even think about changing anything, we first have to see the truth, which can set us free, if we have the courage to act on it. Because, virtually everything, which comes out of our government and media, is either an out and out lie—a half truth, distortion, or perversion; it is going to take some strong medicine to get the poison out of your system, so you can see the truth. The general population has been brainwashed. There is no way of getting around that.

Now in the short time I have with you, I am going to try my best to give you the antidote, which is the truth and nothing but the truth delivered in and in your face, fashion and repetitively reinforced till it finally breaks down the protective barriers your mind has constructed in order to give your current perception of reality validity. If this world is to have any hope of escaping slavery, we must see the truth, embrace it, and act on it.

When a drug addict gets clean, he has withdrawal symptoms, the DTs. This is going to have a similar effect on you, but I promise you in the end, you will be better off for having undergone the cure.

The medicine (the truth) may taste bad, but it can set the captives free. Thus said the LORD.

The most serious threat to our freedom is the government sworn to protect us, not terrorist or some foreign government, but our own government! The enemy is attacking us from within using lies, deceit, deception, and divisiveness!

So what we shouldn't do is trust our political leaders! I refer here mostly to those in Washington—in Congress and the White House. We should remember politicians are creatures of opportunity. Most of them are bald face liars who tell us what they think it will take to get elected or whatever the opinion polls tell them the flavor of the day is. Then once in office, they do whatever is necessary to accumulate power and wealth.

Reader's perspective: You had me going there for a second, but now I get it. You are one of those whack job conspiracy nuts. I have heard that crap before, and I don't have time to listen to this garbage.

Me: I wish you were right, and I was just some nut case. But when there is proof, then a conspiracy theory becomes "An Act of Treason." Unfortunately, that is the case. If you will open your mind to the possibility that I could be telling you the truth, I will show you conclusively that our government represents the greatest threat this country has ever faced. The threat is more dangerous than what we faced in WWI or WWII because in those conflicts, we knew who the enemy was, and we were united against what we perceived as a threat to our very lives.

This enemy is even more dangerous, because he is like a cancer that has infected our body and has to be surgically removed. But luckily, I know the cure for this cancer. It is the truth. The light of truth shined on our enemy, will reveal him and allow us to expunge him.

The Government wants to keep the masses distracted and scared; says professor Chumsky "The bewildered herds are a problem. We've got to prevent their rage and trampling. We've got to *distract them.* They should be watching the Super Bowl or sitcoms or violent movies or something… and you've got to *keep them pretty scared* because unless they're scared properly and frightened of all kinds of devils that are going to destroy them from outside or inside or somewhere, they may start to think, which is very dangerous because they're not competent to think, and therefore *it's important to distract and marginalize them.*" (Professor Norm Chomsky From his book: Keeping the Rabble In Line)

This truth explains why our government controls Hollywood and why the CIA not foreign terrorists are responsible for most if not all of the terrorist attacks against America. A fact I will establish in subsequent chapters. The government is intent on distracting us, and scaring us with crisis after crisis so as Chomsky says they can control us and marginalize us.

Like Rob Emanuel said, "You never want to waste a crisis."

9/11 and the patriot act: set the stage for open dictatorship!

Yep, at 3:45 a.m., I (referring to George W. Bush) pulled the bipartisan version of the patriot act and replaced it with one intended to. "Make slaves of you all"—I am proud to say that thanks to my bold actions, the imposition of the one-world government is one step closer! Praise my master Satan! (Not a quote but a fact.)

Bush used the panic of 9/11 to circumvent Congress and impose on the American population a version of the Patriot Act, specifically designed to strip away our freedoms and lay the groundwork for imposition of a legally imposed dictatorship under the guise of some future crisis! *He is a traitor, pure and simple!*

Even worse, we have been brainwashed and lulled into a mind-numbing stupor that renders us passive and docile. It is time for a shot of adrenalin, in the form of the truth to wake us up and alert us to the clear and present danger that confronts us.

Mind control is real. "It is now possible to control and regiment the masses according to our will without them knowing it" (Edward Bernays, father of public relations and modern propaganda).

"Those who manipulate the unseen mechanism of society constitute an invisible government which is the true ruling power of our country…In almost every act of our lives whether in the sphere of politics or business in our social conduct or our ethical thinking, we are dominated by the relatively small number of persons who understand the mental processes and social patterns of the masses. It is they who pull the wires that control the public mind" (Edward Bernays).

What Bernays was referring to is the fact that the financial elite, who controls the shadow government and pulls the strings of our puppet leaders, own the media outlets of the world, and they control the educational system as well, so they therefore control public awareness. The following sums up the situation quite nicely.

The media is controlled by the CFR and TC: *"CIA owns everyone of significance in the media."* (Colby William former CIA director)

Media Is Controlled by CFR & TC

KEY NEWS ANCHORS:	
Dan Rather: CBS–CFR & TC	Barbara Walters: ABC–CFR
Irvin R. Levine: ABC- CFR	Marvin Kalb: NBC–CFR
John Petty: NBC – CFR & TC	John Chancellor:–NBC CFR
Diane Sawyer: ABC–CFR	Tom Brokaw: NBC – CFR
And Many More	

Misinformation in the U.S. today is more efficient than it was in Nazi Germany, because here we have the pretence that we are getting all the information we want. That misconception prevents people from even looking for the truth." (Mark Crispin Miller)

Reader's perspective: Wait a minute! How is it possible to control a free press?

Me: The answer is quite simple. The media outlets have been systematically purchased by the financial elite who control what we the sheeple can and cannot be told.

Control of the media started with the newspapers in the late nineteenth century. The Rothschilds bought the nation's twenty-five largest papers in order to control public opinion! Now, the elite owns virtually all of Hollywood and the entire media industry. For good measure, with the government's help, they have infiltrated our public schools, thereby determining what the next generation perceives as reality, a reality based on brainwashing and propaganda, a reality that makes our children docile, compliant, and oblivious to their mind control and slavery.

Reader's perspective: What did the elite have to hide that required them to control the media outlets?

Me: They had to hide their plans to end the national sovereignty of the US in order to realize their dream of establishing a one-world government. Consider the following quote:

> We are grateful to the Washington Post, the New York Times, Time Magazine and other great publications whose directors have attended our meetings and respected their promises of discretion for almost forty years. It would have

> been impossible for us to develop our plan for the world if we had been subjected to the lights of publicity during those years. But, the world is more sophisticated and prepared to march toward a world government. The supranational sovereignty of an intellectual elite and world bankers is surely preferable to the national autodetermination practiced in past centuries."
>
> —David Rockefeller, speaking at the June, 1991 Bilderberger meeting in Baden, Germany (a meeting also attended by then Governor Bill Clinton and Dan Quayle

In other words, Rockefeller is saying, *"It is better to be ruled by a dictatorial ruling class than to have a republic based on a constitution, which guarantees our freedoms." I think not!* What do you think?

Every once in a while, someone sees through the veil of illusion and subterfuge and challenges the lies. In such cases, the puppeteers employ the following strategy.

1. They try to dig up or fabricate dirt on the whistle-blower.
2. If that doesn't work, they threaten the person.
3. If that doesn't work, they threaten those close to them.
4. If that doesn't work, they resort to violence and the person has an unfortunate accident.

Abraham Lincoln William McKinley Louis McFadden Larry McDonald John Kennedy

All These Men Opposed The Financial Elite And Were Assassinated?

Their actions either threatened to expose the elite or break their grip on the issuance of money, or in Kennedy's case both! *And for that they had to die!* The story of all these men later.

President Woodrow Wilson knew how dangerous it was to oppose the shadow government. "Some of the biggest men in the United States, in the field of commerce and manufacture, are afraid of something. They know that there is a power somewhere so organized, so subtle, so watchful, so interlocked, so complete, so pervasive, that they had better not speak above their breath when they speak in condemnation of it." (The story behind each of these assassinations later.)

The truth about the National Security Agency (NSA) Data Center. Thanks to whistle-blower Edward Snowden, Americans now knows about the NSA's Utah data center. After hiding its existence and the scope of its invasive reach into our personal lives, the government now tells us it is for our protection—"To protect us from terrorist." They say they would never do anything nefarious with the data. The truth is, this is right out of Hitler's playbook. There are reports that the government stores our data in what is called "main core," and it contains a list of eight million or more Americans, going all the way back to 1980s, people the government has identified not as terrorist, but as protesters. This is a political dissident list, not an enemy threat list. This is a list of those the government intends to put in detention centers when it inevitably imposes martial law. This is quite possibly a list of those who will be the first to die as the government embarks on their plan to reduce population to its target levels. All those who might oppose them must be done away with, leaving a docile manageable collective of sheep! That, my friends, is the truth about the invasive collection of data by the NSA.

Revelation 13:16–18 is at hand! How Frightening is that? (Revelation 13:16-18 KJV) "And he causeth all. Both small and great, rich and poor, free and bond, to receive a mark in their right hand, or in their forehead:

17 And that no man might buy or sell, save he that had the mark, or the name of the beast, or the number of the name.

18 Here is wisdom. Let him that hath understanding count the number of the beast: for it is the number of a man; and his number is Six hundred three score and six.

This, my friends, is what the world of the future will be like if we don't stop the mad men who, as Kennedy said, want to "enslave every man, woman, and child."

If you think your government wouldn't use electronic surveillance to control you, think again. What secret weapon did Obama used to win the 2012 Election, and why should you care?

He used electronic data analysis in order to determine your fears and frustrations, and he then bombarded you with targeted TV ads and e-mails, designed to magically target those emotions. That, my friend, is mind control; and it is a tool, which can be used quiet effectively to "enslave us all". Whether used by Obama or some future leader, it spells dictatorship; 1984 is here! Big Brother is watching you!

Still not afraid of your government? Then, consider this—without cash or a global ID, you will not be able to:

- drive a car
- ride a plane or train
- enter a federal building
- open a bank account
- hold a job

Sounds like the mark of the beast to me. What do you think?
What your government has planned for you.

> "The technetronic era involves the gradual appearance of a more controlled society. Such a society would be dominated by an elite, unrestrained by traditional values. Soon it will be possible to assert almost continuous surveillance over every citizen and maintain up-to-date complete files containing even the most personal information about the citizen. These files will be subject to instantaneous retrieval by the authorities" (Zbigniew Brzezinski, *Between Two Ages: America's Role in the Technetronic Era*, 1970). Big brother is here.

> "The most powerful clique in these (CFR) groups have one objective in common they want to bring about the surren-

> der of the sovereignty and the national independence of the U.S. They want to end national boundaries and racial and ethnic loyalties supposedly to increase business and ensure world peace. What they strive for would inevitably lead to dictatorship and loss of freedoms by the people. The CFR was founded for "the purpose of promoting disarmament and submergence of U.S. sovereignty and national independence into an all powerful one world government." (Harpers Magazine July 1958)

> "The New World Order under the UN will reduce everything to one common denominator. The system will be made up of a single currency, single centrally financed government, single tax system, single language, single political system, single world court of justice, single state religion...Each person will have a registered number, without which he will not be allowed to buy or sell; and there will be one universal world church. Anyone who refuses to take part in the universal system will have no right to exist" (Assessment of the New World by Dr. Kurk E. Koch).

Will your greed be the end of you? You may be surprised to know that we, humans, are no smarter than a monkey. Trappers use greed to capture monkeys. In similar fashion, the shadow government has used our greed to enslave us.

Here is how it works: They catch monkeys by putting food in a jar tethered to a stick. The monkey reaches in to get the food, but there is a problem. The opening is not large enough to allow him to get his hand out unless he opens his hand and lets go of the food, but he is too greedy to do so, so he is captured and caged.

Our government (controlled by the shadow government) gives the people handouts in order to buy their votes, but that is not all there is to our human trap. The schools receive federal funding, The Veterans Administration receives federal funding, our churches are given tax exempt status, and in every instance, the string that tethers us and ensnares us is that in order to receive federal funding these institutions, which should be our first line of defense in the fight for liberty, must agree to not engage in political affairs. Put another way—in exchange for handouts from the government, they willingly agree to be muzzled, silenced, neutered, and neutralized as a force in the fight against our slavery. Wait, there is more! Virtually, every American is complicit in their slavery. You see, the financial elite controls the banking and credit system, and by virtue of our dependence on them, they control us. It is as they say, a dog will not bite the hand that feeds it. It is time to wake up! Our greed and addiction to our creature comforts, and material possessions comes at the price of our freedom, our security, and ultimately, our lives. Time to wake up before it is too late. Now, you know why the Bible tells us that money is the root of all evil.

Now, you know the truth. We are controlled cradle to grave. Our greed is used to forge the chains that bind us. So, the question is, "Are you going to go willingly into servitude and slavery or are you going to let go of the handouts and creature comforts and stand for liberty?

The truth can set you free, but only if you are willing to stand up to the government and take responsibility for your life, and only if you will let go of you greed and materialism and surrender to God the source of true wealth!

I ask again, Are you smarter than a monkey or will you let your greed enslave you?

I am sorry to be so blunt, but God told me, "The only hope humanity has is to be told the truth, so that their eyes and ears may be opened and each man would have to decide if he chooses God of Mannon [material possessions], if he would be free or enslaved, if he would be judged righteous, or if his greed would deny him the kingdom of heaven."

CONGRESS IS IRRELEVANT AND OUR PRESIDENTS ARE PUPPETS

Our government is the greatest threat to our liberty there ever has been or ever will be! The public has been brainwashed, and it is time to cut the strings of the puppets and take back our country. Larry Ballard

The Shadow Government Reveled!

The enemy lives amongst us
He is rich, powerful, and cunning
He is charismatic, charming, and ruthless

He comes at us from above and below
He uses the rich and the poor as pawns
He divides us and pits us against one another

He uses propaganda and brainwashing to deceive us
He is patient and strategic, attacking, and withdrawing
He wants the hearts and minds of our
children to enslave them

He is cunning, deceptive, and a liar full of guile and deceit
He creates crisis after crisis to keep us in a state of fear
He controls us by making us dependent on him for the
necessities of life
He intends to use *chaos* to make us surrender to his tyranny

In his *arrogance*, he sees himself as superior
to us in every way
He believes it is his destiny and his right to rule over us
He tells us what we want to hear and does something else

He gives us what we want, and then takes it away
He comes to kill, steal, destroy, and enslave us
He is the shadow government of the financial elite!

Reader's perspective: So you want me to believe that there is some grand conspiracy to collapse the US and drive us into a one-world government headed by a group of bankers, corporate leaders and our own government?

Me: What would you say if I could show that our Presidents are selected by moneyed interest that back their campaigns, in exchange for, favors and that virtually, all of our presidents since Wilson have, knowingly or unknowingly, backed legislation that has contributed to the economic and moral collapse of the US? **Note:** look to Europe, it has been morphed from sovereign nations into a socialist conglomerate where all the member nations have lost their constitutions and sovereignty. That is the world of the future. Well not quite. To truly see the world of the future you have to look to China where dissenters are put in work camps and their organs are harvested, for sale to the highest bidder. Now combine the horror of communism with capitalism and you have the prototype for the world of tomorrow – A Super Communist Capitalist Totalitarian Dictatorship.

Reader's perspective: Well, if you could prove that, within a reasonable doubt, it would go a long way toward convincing me that you are not a conspiracy nut.

Me: No problem. In this chapter, I will show you why I say our presidents are little more than puppets. Then, in the next two chapters, I will go you one better. I will prove that our two-party political system is an illusion, that Congress is irrelevant, and our courts and the media have been hijacked!

Reader's perspective: Sounds like a tall order, but let's see what you have.

* * *

Thesis assumptions

Let's start with the presidents, and as matter of fact, let's develop a complete organization chart of the shadow government. Hold on to your hat or better yet the seat of your pants. This is going to be another choke. Feel free to scream, yell, and cuss, if you feel the need. Personally, it makes me nauseous.

Let me give a little background on the material you are about to read. I started with the thesis that the US is being intentionally driven into economic collapse in order to birth the one-world government we have been discussing, and that this would not be possible unless officials in the highest ranks of the government were part and parcel to the plot (i.e., our legislature and the president).

From there, it was a simple matter to research the records of the various administrations and see if there was a common thread that ran from administration to administration.

Specifically, could I find key legislation that rather than making America stronger economically, made it weaker? You see, I knew that the US emerged WWII with its manufacturing intact and such an advantage over the rest of the world that I simply couldn't believe that any nation could ever catch up with us much less pass us up. It was just impossible, that is unless it was intentional.

I also ask myself: Was there legislation that systematically stripped away our sovereignty and gave it to some other country or governance body? Was there legislation that consistently undermined the Constitution? Was there legislation that threatened our civil rights and made us subject to imposition of martial law and a dictatorship? Was their legislation that consistently caused the American public to be pitted against one another in order to create the biblical house divided that Christ said could not stand?

Government leaders guilty of treason. My research showed that the answer to all these questions was a resounding yes! This conspiracy theory, as so many like to despairingly call it, was now nothing short of "*treason*!" It was a plot to destroy the US from within without firing a single shot. Brilliant though incredibly evil!

Reader's perspective: If you could link all these events together and tie them to our legislators and the executive office, well, I would have to agree with you. I would be forced to say our government is being intentionally collapsed from within and our own government represents the greatest threat to our freedom this nation has ever faced. I would have to add. If you're right, every American needs to know the truth, and we need to stand up and join together to stop it. If we don't, the America we love will disappear to be replaced by a dictatorship. So prove it!

Me: Gladly, but first, I want to add that we are not the only country that is being collapsed from within under a mountain of debt and socialist policies.

The origins of the global conspiracy. Though it is beyond the preview of this book, there is also evidence that this same strategy is being used to collapse Europe by driving it into unmanageable debt through the socialist policies which have led to the recent riots in Greece and elsewhere. And resource rich third world countries all over the world have succumbed to a simpler version of the same strategy. The World Bank, IMF, and USAID would loan money to third world countries ostensibly to develop crucially important infrastructure, and then companies, such as Halliburton would be hired to build the projects, and there would always be problems, and in the final analysis, the country would default; and their oil, timber, and other natural resources would be forfeit as collateral on the defaulted loans. The strategy is infinitely simpler than in the instance of a powerful nation like the US, or Europe but the bottom line is the same. Collapse the country through the creation of unmanageable debt, and take their natural resources. That is for example, why it is now legal for international corporations and countries to own US infrastructure where previously it was illegal. By the way, there is an excellent book on this very topic called *Confessions of an Economic Hit Man* by John Perkins.

In the preface of the book Perkins says, "Economic hit men (EHMs) are highly paid professionals who cheat countries around the globe out of trillions of dollars. They funnel money from the World Bank, U.S. Agency for International Development, and other foreign "aid" organizations into the coffers of huge corporations and the pockets of a few wealthy families who control the planet's natural resources. Their tools include fraudulent financial reports, rigged elections, payoffs, extortion, sex, and murder. They play a game as old as empire, but one that has taken on new and terrifying dimensions during this time of globalization. I should know I am an EHM."

What goes around comes around. This is the strategy that US leaders in conjunction with the financial elite have used for decades to collapse third world countries in order to steal their natural resources and enslave them. Now, it is time for those policies to come home to roost and for the US to be the recipient of the very tactics it has used so successfully to dominate and enslave others. God's judgment is about to be poured out on the US.

Since the takeover of the US centers on world dominance by a group of international bankers, I want to digress a little longer and give you some background that will give you valuable insight as to how they have systematically seized control of the world's banking system and with it, control of the economic systems of sovereign countries all over the world.

The roots of the (privately owned) global banking system, including the World Bank and all the central banks!

History records that after over one hundred years of fighting between England and France, England's treasury was broke. The king of England come to the enormously wealthy Rothschild's and asks for financial help. Rothschild responded: Of course, my king, but I do have one request. Henceforth, I will control the banking system of England. (Not a quote.) And thus was born the world's first central bank and from it, the nest of vipers, which spawned the global banking system that controls the planet's monetary system and spawned this infamous quote.

"I care not what puppet is placed upon the throne of England to rule the Empire on which the sun never sets. The man who controls Britain's money supply controls the British Empire, and I control the British money supply" (Amshell Rothschild).

This is the same Rothschild family that now has a net worth estimated at $500 trillion (half the total wealth of the world). They and a small group of financial elite have seized control of all the central banks of the world and control the entire world's money supply. It is as Henry Kissinger said, "Who controls money controls the world."

It is worth mentioning that our founding fathers came to America to escape the oppression in England. They knew all too well the dangers of banking institutions. Jefferson's warning (found below) is haunting because Americans are indeed waking up homeless in the land their fathers conquered. If we had only heeded his warning.

"Banking institutions are more dangerous than standing armies…I believe that if the American people ever allow private banks [the Fed] to control issuance of currency…The banks and corporations that will grow up around them will deprive the people of their property until their children wake up homeless on the continent their fathers conquered," (Thomas Jefferson, third US president). A *warning from the past.*

Our forefathers knew full well the dangers of relinquishing control of the monetary system to money manipulators. Jefferson's fears have been realized. Millions of hardworking Americans have lost their homes, and America is facing an insurmountable debt crisis, which was intentionally brought on us in order to as Kennedy said, "Enslave us all."

Presidential legacy: A story of betrayal!

Vladimir Lenin Barack Obama
We Are All Socialist Now

Understanding Obama's Fundamental Transformation Of America! "We can't expect the American people to jump from capitalism to communism, but we can assist their elected leaders in giving them small doses of socialism until they wake up one day to find that they have communism" (Valdimir Lenin. Russian Communist Revolutionary)

Obama's *"Redistribution of Wealth"* is exactly what Lenin was referring to in the above quote!

America: Wake up before it is too late. As of 2014 there are more people on Welfare than there are people with full-time jobs. If that doesn't spell the demise of America I don't know what does. Our leaders in Washington have intentionally buried America under a mountain of debt and it is time to put a stop to it. Stand up and be counted!

"The democracy will cease to exist when you take away from those who are willing to work and give to those who will not" (Thomas Jefferson). Obama's redistribution of wealth is exactly what Jefferson was referring to.

"Remember that a government big enough to give you everything you want is big enough to take away everything you have" (Senator Barry Goldwater).

Isn't this the very definition of redistribution of wealth? The weapon that has been most effective in destroying America has been too bury us under a mountain of debt and to turn our own greed/materialism against us by intentionally creating strife between the supposed haves and have-nots. What better way to destroy a nation from within than through debt and division!

These Men Sold Out God & Country For Power & Wealth!
Top row: Wilson Coolidge Roosevelt Nixon Ford
Bottom Row: Carter Bush Clinton Bush Obama

I will prove that: all these men are traitors and puppets of the financial elite. They are committed to creating such *"Chaos"* that we will surrender our freedom and submit to their One-World Super Communist Capitalist Dictatorship! These men and all like them have to go, and the people of the world need to reclaim their governments and set down and learn to live in peace, before we destroy ourselves and the planet! Liars All! Liars, liars, pants on fire!!!!

Proof that these men are puppets of the financial elite! What follows are a series of hypothetical conversations, which help place actual events in context so you can view them from the perspective of the people in Washington, making the decisions, which have shaped our nation.

* * *

Wilson and Rockefeller

Wilson Speaking: *I pledge to the American people there will be no central bank installed during my administration. You have my word on that. I lied.*

Rockefeller's response: They believed you, and you got elected. Now we can get to work on getting the central bank installed. Wilson: But I promised! Rockefeller: Never mind, the public has short memories. You wanted the power. Now you have it, but you have to do this one little thing for the bankers who put us into office. Is that too much to ask? Wilson: No, I guess not.

Wilson: I did what they wanted, but I can honestly say I regret it. When I turned over the money supply to the financial elite, I didn't realize just how ruthless they were. It is like Rothschild said, "Let me issue and control a nation's money, and I care not who writes the laws" (Amshell Rothschild).

May God forgive me? I didn't realize what I was doing when I lied to the American people and circumvented Congress and got the Federal Reserve Bill passed.

I knew the public didn't want a central bank, so I lied to them and convinced them that it would make their money safer and stop all the bank runs we had experienced in the past. I lead them to believe that the bank would be owned by the federal government when in fact it is owned by the financial elite. I didn't tell them that the treasury would no longer be responsible for printing our currency, but instead every dollar printed would enrich the financial elite because we would in fact be borrowing the money from the financial elite (who create it out of thin air) and we would be obligated to pay them interest on the fiat money. When it came time to vote on the bill, I knew I had real opposition, so I called the vote over the Christmas holidays when I knew a lot of legislators would be home with their families. It worked.

I also lied to the American people when I rammed the federal income tax down their throats. I didn't tell them that a federal income tax was unconstitutional and that the Sixteenth Amendment contrary to the claims of the financial elite did not make it legal.

I neglected to tell them that the federal income tax would be used exclusively to pay interest to the Fed for printing our currency. I led them to believe that the tax would be nominal, but that was impossible, if you realize that every dollar printed incurs a debt and an ever increasing amount of money is required to pay the constantly increasing interest and principle payments.

I, Woodrow Wilson, sold out the American people for a political office. May God have mercy on my soul! I neglected to tell the people that the end result of establishing the Federal Reserve Bank could only be the debasing of their currency to the point that at some point the debt burden would be so great that it simply could not be paid and the entire house of cards would collapse, taking with it the wealth and private property of the entire nation.

In Woodrow Wilson, the financial elite found a president who was willing to be bought. It was 1913, and Wilson betrayed the American people when he did as his banker friends wanted and instituted a central bank under the innocent sounding name the "Federal Reserve." Wilson later expressed regret at having been the person who imposed the corrupt Federal Reserve Bank on the American people and said:

> "Our great industrial nation is now controlled by its system of credit. We are no longer a government by free opinion, no longer a government by conviction and the vote of the majority but a government by the opinion and duress of a small group of dominant men. Our great industrial nation is controlled by its system of credit. Our system of credit is privately centered. The growth of the nation, therefore, and all our activities are in the hands of a few men. Who, necessarily by very reason of their own limitations, chill and check and destroy genuine economic freedom. We have become one of the worst ruled, one of the most completely controlled and dominated governments in the civilized world."

Wilson was a Judas goat and a traitor. No other conclusion can be reached!

This event marked the beginning of the fall of the US. A Judas goat by the name of Woodrow Wilson had sold America's hard fought independence for forty pieces of silver, because he wanted the most powerful office in the land!

After doing my research, I firmly believe that today in America, it is literally impossible for any presidential candidate to be elected president unless he has the backing of the financial elite, has been vented by them, and has agreed that in exchange for their support, he will further their agenda of world dominance. I believe what you are about to read in the ensuing pages pretty much proves this statement to be true.

* * *

Colliedge and the Fed

Now that I am out of office, I can confess. I helped the financial elite orchestrate the Great Depression! Here is how we did it. The money supply was expanded. Stocks were sold with 10 percent down, and when we were ready to collapse the market and sheer the sheep all that had to be done was for the financial elite to dry up the money supply, call in the margin loans, and as easy as taking candy from a baby the wealth of the public was transferred to those who never lifted a finger to earn it.

What the American public doesn't realize is that once the financial elite had control of the issuance of the currency, they could orchestrate boom-bust cycles at will. During the boom cycle, wealth is accumulated only to be fleeced when they trigger the bust. Here is how it works: During the boom cycle, the Fed keeps interest rates low and increases the money supply. The cheap money stimulates the economy, and then when it is time for the sheering, all they have to do is constrict the money supply and raise interest rates and poof the economy crashes and the financial elite pick up the hard earned assets of the American public for pennies on the dollar. It works every time.

If one understands this simple truth, the lies of the financial elite and their pyramid scheme no longer works on you. I hope that by knowing the truth, the American people will put a stop to the sheering that I helped institute. May God have mercy on my soul.

Calvin Coolidge aided the elite to bring about the 1929 Depression. Coolidge facilitated the 1929 stock market crash and Great Depression by

- ✓ expanding the money supply 62 percent from 1923–1929,
- ✓ fueling stock MKT speculation with stocks purchased with 10 percent down,
- ✓ expanding the power of the Fed when the 1929 crash saw 1,600 non-Fed banks closed.

Essentially, what caused the 1929 stock market crash was the combination of easy money and speculative investing engineered by the financial elite, who when they were ready to intentionally trigger the collapse, simply dried up the money supply triggering margin calls that collapsed the stock market. Congressman Louis McFadden realized what they had done, and subsequently in 1933, McFadden, the chairman of the United States House Committee on Banking and Currency made a twenty-five-minute speech before the House of Representatives in which he introduced "House Resolution No. 158, Articles of Impeachment" for the secretary of treasury, two assistant secretaries of the treasury, the board of governors of the Federal Reserve, and the officers and directors of the twelve regional banks.

McFadden said of the crash and depression, "It was a carefully contrived occurrence. International bankers sought to bring about a condition of despair, so that they might emerge the rulers of us all."

By the way, they are doing it again except this time, it will be much worse because it is intended to usher in the dictatorial one-world government! Will you say treason?

Call me crazy, but this seems eerily similar to the 2008 real estate collapse and our current recession/depression. The only difference is that this time it was zero down on houses (for the first time in the history of the world) and a 300 percent increase in the money supply. I guess that is why I am a writer. I have a good imagination. Oh, by the way, shortly after levying his charges against the Fed, McFadden was "accidentally poisoned" at a state function. It sure seems like anybody who comes out against the financial elite is accident prone. I sure am glad I have my guardian angels.

The great depression brought unimaginable suffering to millions and the financial elite are doing it again, but this time, it will be much worse!

The government doesn't want the public to know how bad the jobless situation already is, and it is going to get much worse. Recently in Southern California homeless people were rounded up and given the choice of jail or FEMA Camps. (Source Alex Jones Prison Planet) This is how it started in Nazi Germany. First they rounded up the marginalized, then came yellow stars to identify the Jews, then came detention camps and death camps.

Roosevelt's *new deal* relied heavily on borrowing from the Fed, who made a fortune from the interest. Borrowing/printing money didn't work then, and for the same reasons, neither has Obama's stimulus. WWII ended the depression, not FDR's *new deal* spending. You simply cannot borrow/spend your way out of debt.

The plight of the American people during the Depression! By 1932, the Depression was in its fourth year, and no matter what the government did, it didn't seem to work. Over ten million people, approximately 20 percent of the population, were unemployed and locked in the grips of depression, despair, gloom, and the inevitable loss of self-esteem, which besets a person when they have no hope, when their nightly companion is fear of starvation.

No matter where you turned, it was bleak. There was not only an army of unemployed there was also an army on underemployed, as nationwide the combined effects of unemployment and involuntary part-time employment left 50 percent of the American work force unutilized for a decade.

I found this quote by Frank Walker, president of the National Emergency Council (1934) to be especially heart rendering. "I saw old friends of mine—men I had gone to school with—digging ditches and laying sewer pipe. They were wearing their regular business suits as they worked because they couldn't afford overalls and rubber boots. If I ever thought 'there but for the grace of God go I,' it was right then."

I don't include these quotes to depress you, but to wake you up, to encourage you to get your financial house in order. To stockpile food, and do whatever you can to be as self-sufficient as possible, because the time of plenty is coming to an end, and with it, the government handouts.

The house of cards is toppling and the winds of despair are being unleashed. You see, the government is about to collapse the economic system again just like they did in 1929. But this time it will be worse much, much worse!

The 1929 collapse was triggered by a 62 percent increase in the money supply coupled with stocks being sold on 10 percent margins. This time, we have more than a 300 percent increase in the money supply coupled with massive dept. (The US owes more than all the nations of the world combined.) To top it all off, plans are in motion to no longer use the dollar as the "world's reserve currency." As the world's reserve currency, other nations are forced to buy US dollars and debt whether they like it or not, because they can't make international commodity purchases denominated in anything but US dollars. That is about to end, and when it does, the dollar will have a devastating collapse. The question isn't *if*; the question is *when?* I guarantee you it will be soon. Be prepared! The financial elite are about to cause the Second Great Depression and our government leaders are their puppets.

> "The one aim of these financiers is world control by the creation of inextinguishable debts" (Henry Ford, industrialist). Can you see that Obama's reckless spending; his redistribution of wealth as he calls it, is nothing less than a strategy to bury the country under a mountain of debt that is designed to destroy us?

> "History records that the money changers have used every form of abuse, intrigue, deceit, and violent means possible to maintain their control over governments by controlling money and its issuance" (James Madison, fourth president of the United States [1809–1817]

> "Who controls money controls the world" (Henry Kissinger).

> "Remember that a government big enough to give you everything you want is also big enough to take away everything you have" (Senator Barry Goldwater)

* * *

Franklin Roosevelt and Joseph Stalin

Roosevelt: Joe, I am glad you dug up your copy of the Constitution, I couldn't find ours. The press has a lot of nerve, calling me a socialist just because I ignored the constitution and took the US off the gold standard. They don't understand. It was the only way I could implement my "New Deal." Being on the gold standard was just to constraining. I needed to print money and lots of it to realize my dreams. A man is allowed to have dreams without being called names, isn't he? After all, I am the president. I should be able to do what I want.

Comrade: You keep up the good work, and we will talk again soon.

FDR was the president during the Great Depression. Immediately upon entering office, Roosevelt declared a banking holiday. All the banks were closed and all the safety deposit boxes were rifled and the gold confiscated. All Americans were to turn their gold in upon pain of a $10,000 fine and/or ten years in prison. As soon as the government got their hands on the gold, it increased in value 65 percent. How convenient for the government, and how unfortunate for the public.

Shortly after the crash, Roosevelt took the country off the gold standard, which opened the flood gates for the unconstrained printing of money. This was crucially important because Roosevelt's cornerstone program, "the new deal," which was heralded as the way to economic recovery, had to be financed through heavy borrowing and who do you suppose the government borrowed the money from? (The Fed of course).

So, the Fed caused the depression, and then they turned around and loaned the American public money at interest, driving up the national debt. *Will you say treason?*

Roosevelt's "New Deal" and Obama's "Stimulus" were both intended to drive us into unmanageable debt!

Hold on. That can't be. I'll be darn. Guess what, the 1929 and 2008 crashes are instant replays. The only difference is the names have changed. In 1929, the bailout was called the New Deal, and this time, it is called the *stimulus*. By the way, it didn't work last time, so why would we think it will work this time? The truth is, it is not supposed to work quite to the contrary, it is supposed to drive us into unmanageable debt and bring about the Second Great Depression, forcing us into the waiting arms of the one-world government. Point game!

In the book, *FDR: My Exploited Father-in-Law*, Curtis Dall said of the Depression, "It was the calculated 'shearing' of the public by the World-Money powers, triggered by the planned sudden shortage of call money in the New York Market." Will you say treason?

Passage of the Federal Reserve act was an act of treason? Oh, one more thing! Guess what, the "Central Banking Bill" called the "Federal Reserve Act," which created the Federal Reserve, was written by bankers, not legislators, and then it was snuck through Congress over the Christmas break when most congressmen were at home with their families. The bill was pushed through Congress by their front man, Senator Nelson Aldrich, who shortly after married into the Rockefeller family. Even worse, it was illegally passed without the required constitutional amendment! Go figure. Those financial elite sure know how to get things done.

Oh, another repeat of history—amazing, simply amazing! The Federal Reserve Act, the stimulus and Obamacare were all written by special interest groups, not legislators. Then passage was rammed through. In regards to the stimulus, threats were made that if the bill wasn't passed, we could see martial law.

Congress was threatened, "Pass the stimulus or markets will collapse and there will be martial law in America!" (Rep. Brad Sherman).

And Nancy Pelosi (one of my "favorite" people) said, "If you want to know what is in the health-care bill you will have to pass it."

Like I said, this stuff makes me nauseous.

* * *

Richard Nixon and Gordon Liddy

Nixon speaking to reporters: Break-in? What break-in? I don't know anything about a break-in. Where was this alleged break-in? Where? At the Watergate Campaign Headquarters of my opponent. No, I don't know anything about it.

Nixon speaking to staff: Get me Gordon on the phone: Gordon, I am being asked about the Watergate break-in. Do they have anything on me? Mr. President, I don't know what they have on you, but we got caught red-handed. My recommendation is to deny, deny, deny!

Nixon speaking with reporters: I had nothing to do with the break-in. What? Are you calling me a liar? Listen, just because you media types have stuck me with the nickname Tricky Dicky doesn't mean I am a liar.

What is that you say? You have tapes of phone conversations, proving otherwise, and you are going to impeach me? You people don't understand this is Washington. This kind of stuff happens all the time. Once you get this kind of power, it is intoxicating, and you will do anything to hold on to it.

You people are going to ruin everything. The crowning moment of my presidency was when I opened trade with China, but my work isn't done. There are still free trade agreements to negotiate, and now thanks to you, someone else will get the glory. That was supposed to be my job. I could have gone down in history as a great president, and now, you have ruined everything!

Clouded by the Watergate scandal, Nixon's most insidious, destructive action went virtually unnoticed by history. In order to allow the financial elite to drive America into financial ruin, we had to be driven into unmanageable debt, and that could not be done as long as we were bound by the Brentwood Accords, which established the US dollar as the world's reserve currency and obligated the US to convert the currency of any nation into gold upon demand. This was what is referred to as the gold standard, and it assured that the governments of the world would balance their budgets and not print currency that could not be backed by gold reserves. So on August 15, 1971, President Nixon took the US off the gold standard, so that the financial elite could flood the world with fiat currency (worthless currency) and in the process destroy America and lay the groundwork for a global financial meltdown!

"I have directed the secretary of the treasury to take the action necessary to protect the dollar against the speculators. (Bunk: The goal was to be able to print fiat money). I have directed Secretary Conley to temporally suspend the convertibility of the dollar into gold, or other reserve assets, except in amounts and conditions determined to be in the best interest of monetary stability and in the best interest of the United States" (President Richard Nixon).

The suspension was permanent, not temporary, and it marked the death of the dollar. All that remains is for the funeral which will be soon, very soon! Will you say treason and the hijacking of the monetary system?

* * *

Ford and Rockefeller

Rockefeller speaking to Ford: What are we supposed to do with this mess Nixon dropped into our laps? He was supposed to negotiate the Free Trade Agreements with China. I have a serious problem. As the founder of the Trilateral Commission, my reputation is on the line. We have to get those agreements passed, and the public and Congress sees me as one of the financial elite, so it would have been a darn sight easier, if Nixon had done this.

Ford responding: let's go back to the playbooks and see what our predecessors have done when faced with similar circumstances. Remember, the Federal Reserve Act wasn't popular and yet Wilson got it passed. Rockefeller responding: Yes, but treaties are more complicated and they require a two-third majority of legislates present. That is a lot of people to bamboozle. Ford: Let me think on it.

Ford continues: It came to me last night. Let's change the treaty requirements so we can circumvent Congress! Trade negotiations could be controlled by the president instead of Congress, and when we do finally have to go to Congress for a vote, all we will require is a *simple majority* of those present. And if we still have a problem getting the required number of votes, we can do what Wilson did [to get the Federal Reserve Act passed, so he could hijack the nation's money supply]. We could wait till a holiday when our opposition will be home with their families. Rockefeller to Ford. Brilliant. Just brilliant.

Rockefeller continues: I can't wait. The sooner we get started, the sooner we can get about the business of gutting America's manufacturing base and bleeding the country dry. My buddies in the Trilateral Commission are going to be jumping with joy.

* * *

The rest is history. They got their treaty agreements passed, but that alone wasn't enough. The treaties had to be specifically targeted at collapsing the US economy. I could explain what they did but maybe a couple of quotes would better serve the purpose, because they come from a couple of highly reputable sources.

According to Auggie Tantillo, executive director at the American Manufacturing Trade Action Coalition (AMTAC), "Of 138 major manufacturing nations, the US is the only nation that does not take advantage of a value-added tax [VAT] in order to protect its manufacturing base and maintain a favorable balance of trade." Will you say treason?

"Today, other countries around the world employ what they call a value-added tax, in which foreign governments refund to their corporations that are exporting goods to the United States, the full amount of their value-added taxes that, that particular company pays in marketing a product...When American products hit their shores, they charge a value-added tax in the same amount. So they enact a double hit against American exporters. One is that they subsidize their own imports going out, and the second is that they tax us going in. [Tariff] The United States doesn't do this" [(Congressman Duncan Hunter, "Exclusive Interview: Hunter Eyes Presidential Campaign," *Human Events*, Dec.4, 2006).] *Will you say treason?*

The US practices: Intentionally losing trade policies! In other words, other countries reward exporters with the VAT and protect their trade balance by imposing a tariff to prevent free trade goods from China from flooding their markets and destroying their balance of trade and gutting their manufacturing sector. The US does neither of these things, so it is little wonder that our manufacturing base has been gutted our trade balance is upside down and we are the world's largest debtor nation? *Can you say treason*?

But wait the worst is still to come. If a US manufacture chooses to keep his manufacturing here in the States, he gets none of these tax breaks, and in addition, he is burdened with EPA regulations designed to drive up the cost of his products and make them even less competitive in the world market. If that same manufacturer moves his manufacturing abroad, he gets the tax breaks, he gets cheap labor, and no EPA regulations. Is it any wonder that in 1977, after over two hundred years of existence, the US had a total national debt of only $660 billion, less than the stimulus, and as of 2014, our national debt is $17 trillion and climbing? The table below tells the story of the US national debt and the deliberate destruction of the US, our manufacturing base, the source of our wealth was intentionally gutted! *Will you say treason?*

The Strategy For Collapsing The US?
Intentionally Create Unmanageable Debt:
Through Intentionally Losing Trade Policies!

"We practiced what I call 'Losing Trade'—deliberately losing trade—over the last 50 years..." (Congressman Duncan Hunter [R-CA] In an interview with Human Events Dec 4, 2006)

National Debt By President				
President	**Start Date**	**National Debt**	**End Date**	**Debt**
Carter	12/31/77	660B	12/31/81	997B
Reagan	12/31/81	1.029T	12/31/88	2,684T
Bush	12/31/89	2.953T	12/31/92	4.117T
Clinton	12/31/93	4.536T	12/31/00	5.662T
Bush	12/31/01	5.943T	12/31/08	10.700T
Obama	12/31/09	12.311T	6/01/11	17.000T...

The cause of the US debt crisis. The trade imbalance isn't the sole cause of the US debt, but it is far and away the core issue. It will be the iceberg that, like with the Titanic, sinks the ship of State. Other factors are interest payments to the Fed, unfunded entitlements, the cost associated with illegal immigration and the fact that we have not had a balance budget since 1971 when Nixon took us off the gold standard, and now Obama is keeping the printing presses running 24/7. To top things off, the US will soon cease to be the world's reserve currency and when that happens, our ability to print money 24/7 will be suspended, and the US will have the greatest financial collapse the world has ever seen.

Fast track agreements were used to engineer the New World Order. For example, pushing through GATT Tokyo Round, US-Israel free trade agreement, Canada-US free trade agreement, NAFTA, GATT Trade Agreement, and the really important one was GATT Uruguay Round, which created the World Trade Organization (WTO) that opened the flood gates to worldwide free trade and was particularly damaging to the United States' balance of trade. *Who controls trade controls the wealth of the world and who controls the money controls the world! Will you say treason?*

The fox is in the hen house, and we wonder why our economy is in the tank, and we are in danger of becoming a third world country!

Had it not been for intentionally losing free trade agreements and the intentional gutting of America's manufacturing sector, the national debt would be a pittance of what it is. *Will you say treason?*

* * *

Carter and Brezinski

Carter speaking to the American people: You can trust me. I am a good old boy peanut farmer and a born again Christian.

Brezinski to Carter: My palls and I at the Trilateral Commission put you into office. You owe us. You have to turn on that charm of yours and convince the American people that trade with China will be a good thing for the country. Never mind if it guts the manufacturing sector and bleeds the nation's wealth out like a hog at slaughter! All that really matters is what my buddies at the Trilateral Commission want. This is going to be a tough assignment, but I know you can do it. We will create whatever crisis you need, in order to stall the economy, to give China time to gear up. Just keep smiling, and tell them they can trust you.

Carter: Okay, I can do that. You can count on me,

* * *

Most people I talk to describe Carter as somewhat of a buffoon. I don't see him that way at all. The way I look at these men is they are given an agenda by their puppet masters. The closer we get to their endgame, the more accelerated their agenda becomes. Carter just got dealt a tough hand and the only way it could be played was by looking the fool.

Reader's perspective: So in your opinion, what was Carter's assignment?

Me: For now, we can call it my opinion, but as you will shortly see, history bares out what I say. Carter's agenda was to stall the US economy while China geared up their manufacturing for their assault on the American manufacturing base. Additionally, key US corporations had to be disassembled because they stood in the way of the elite's agenda. This was handled by corporate raiders who purchased perfectly sound companies and then broke then up and sold them off piece by piece so they were no longer large enough to be a threat to the takeover by China, of the US domination of global manufacturing.

Just like Wilson was put into office by banking interest and became their pawn, Carter was put in office by the Trilateral Commission and was their pawn. Carter was the first president groomed for the presidency by the Trilateral Commission. The following quotes will give you an idea of just how ruthless the Trilateral Commission and Council on Foreign Relations really are.

"The Trilateral Commission is intended to be the vehicle for multinational consolidation of the commercial and banking interest by seizing control of the political government of the United States. They rule the future" (Felix Frankfurter, justice of the Supreme Court). *Will you say treason?*

"The Council on Foreign Relations is the American branch of a society, which originated in England… [and]… believes national boundaries should be obliterated and one-world rule established" (Dr. Carroll Quigley, CFR member, college mentor of President Clinton, author of *Tragedy and Hope*). *Will you say treason?*

"The Trilateral Commission doesn't run the world; the Council on Foreign Relations does that!" (Winston Lord, assistant secretary of state, the US State Department). *Will you say shadow government?*

Reader's perspective: That is very interesting, but what does that have to do with Carter's agenda?

Me: I needed to establish the agenda of Carter's puppet masters, so his actions could be seen not as blundering mistakes but as part of a very sinister plan to drive the US into unmanageable debt and force its economic collapse. I am going to be connecting a lot of dots, so we can see the big picture that evades us when we are in the moment, but fortunately, that is the advantage that history provides. Please give me your undivided attention. Here we go:

Three years prior to the 1976 election, Carter was introduced to David Rockefeller, chairman emeritus of the CFR, and Zbigniew Brzezinski, CFR member and founding member TC, who openly acknowledged that he had helped groom Carter for the presidency. Incidentally, his VP Walter Mondale was a member of the TC as well. Once in office, *Carter appointed twenty-six TC members to key positions in his administration.* I will list a few of the more important ones starting with Zbigniew Brzezinski, national security advisor—a position he held under five US presidents; Michael Blumenthal, secretary treasury; Fred Bergsten, undersecretary of the treasury; Cyrus Vance, secretary of state; James Schlesinger, secretary of energy; Harold Brown, secretary of defense; Andrew Young, ambassador to the UN; Elliot Richardson, delegate to Law of the Sea; and most importantly, Labor Leader Leonard Woodcook was appointed chief envoy to China, etc.

This constituted nothing short of a takeover of the White House by the Trilateral Commission. The chessboard was set. The game was on. The time had come to "seize control of the political government of the United States." *Will you say shadow government?*

As I proceed, I need to remind you of the government's propensity to use crisis to their advantage. Without having access to highly classified documents that will never see the light of day, we have no way of knowing if a given crisis was just a coincidence or if it was perpetrated. I will say this however: *It sure seems to me that every time the elite want to drive us in a particular direction, there is an all too convenient crisis.* In this instance, I am referring to the oil embargo that occurred early in Carter's presidency.

The (oh so convenient) oil embargo provided the Fed the excuse it needed in order to be able to tamper with the economy. We experienced a period referred to as stagflation, which is an economic term referring to a period of inflation occurring simultaneous to a period of stagnant business activity.

How coincidental; the US enters into unfavorable free trade agreements with China, and then suddenly, the US experiences the perfect financial crisis where it encounters both inflation and stagnant business activity at the same time. The oil crisis aside there was one other requirement to create this perfect economic storm and that was high interest rates. Never mind, the Fed was there to accommodate the agenda of the Financial Elite. According to *Time* magazine March 24, 1980, President Carter announced a crisis in which both inflation and interest rates exceeded 18 percent. The economy came to a screeching halt. China had time to gear up their manufacturing for a full-fledged frontal assault on the very lifeblood of the US economy, our manufacturing might, which was the very foundation of our wealth.

Finally, the financial elite were positioned to collapse the US, which they saw as essential to the formation of the New World Order.

"The New World Order cannot happen without US participation, as we are the most significant single component. Yes, there will be a New World Order, and it will force the United States to change its perceptions" (Henry Kissinger, World Affairs Council Press Conference, Regent Beverly Wilshire Hotel, April 19, 1994).

This calls for the ending of US sovereignty! *Will you say treason?*

From Carter on the office of president of the United States has been controlled by the shadow government. As you shall see in the next chapter, you simply cannot hold a key position in Washington unless you belong to the Trilateral Commission or Council on Foreign Relations, both of which are on record as being dedicated to the demise of the US.

Do you have enough evidence yet? If not keep reading, if you dare. I have more much more. You might say I have so much evidence that it is damming!

Reagan's legacy: I don't have much of anything bad to say about Regan. He, Eisenhower, and Kennedy were the only presidents in my lifetime I had any respect for. By the time Reagan came into office, the Chinese had geared up their manufacturing, and key US corporations had been neutered. So, not wanting to push us into open revolt, the financial elite decided to allow us to have a breather from the economic vice the Fed had us in. With that said, all it took to cause an economic recovery was for Reagan to "end price controls on domestic oil and for the Feds to lower interest rates," and poof, like magic, instant economic recovery! Go figure!

* * *

George H. W. Bush and Fed Chairman Alan Greenspan

George H. W. Bush: "Read my lips. No new taxes. No new taxes."

Greenspan to Bush: Mr. President, a call from Mr. Greenspan. Put it through. George, it is time to raise the taxes. There is not enough revenue in the treasury to pay us our interest payments for printing the nation's fiat currency.

Bush: But I promised there would be no new taxes!

Greenspan: Don't make me threaten you. You know very well that the Fed runs the country. Are you forgetting what happened to Kennedy when he tried to buck us?

He went before Congress and referred to the Federal Reserve as an "establishment that virtually controls the monetary system that is subject to no one, that no congressional committee can oversee, and that not only issues the currency but loans it to the government at interest."

He even went so far as to try to shut us down, and he got his brains accidentally blown out. We wouldn't want a similar accident to happen to you, would we?

Bush: No, I will make the tax increase happen. You can count on me.

Greenspan: Good, I am glad to hear that. Oh, one last thing. Don't forget you also swore your allegiance to the UN.

Bush: I know, and I will bring the power of the presidency to bear in order to accomplish their agenda of implementing the one-world government. I will see to it that we keep the public in a constant state of fear with crisis after crisis till they submit to the UN and the one-world government. You have my word.

Greenspan: Good. I knew we could count on you.

* * *

"It is the sacred principles enshrined in the United Nations Charter to which the American people will henceforth pledge their allegiance" (President George Bush, addressing the UN).

The UN is dedicated to ending US sovereignty so that makes bush a traitor! Will you say treason?

"Out of these troubled times, our objective a New World Order can emerge. Today, that New World Order is struggling to be born, a world quite different from the one we have known" (President George Bush Sr., addressing the general assembly of the United States, Feb. 1, 1992.

Never fail to take advantage of a crisis! Will you say treason?

I don't know about any of you, but I am an American, and in my opinion, the UN is one of the most evil organizations ever spawned, and it will never get my allegiance, but the quotes above speak volumes for where the allegiances of our presidents reside.

And in one voice, the multitude cried traitor! So exactly what legacy did Bush Sr. leave us, and did it make America stronger or weaker? He continued in the tradition of his predecessors to undermine the US balance of trade. In 1990, he signed the Immigration Act, which increased immigration by 40 percent and negatively impacted unemployment. Though actually signed under Clinton, Bush spearheaded the North American Free Trade Agreement (NAFTA) between the US, Mexico, and Canada. According to John J. Sweeney of the Boston Globe, "The trade deficit with Canada and Mexico ballooned to twelve times its pre-NAFTA size, reaching $111 billion in 2004." Will you say treason?

It was suppose be good for the economy. I guess they lied. And according to Henry Kissinger when campaigning for the passage of NAFTA, "NAFTA is a major stepping stone to the New World Order." Will you say treason?

Like I have said previously, the financial elite is dedicated to collapsing the US in order to birth their New World Order, and our politicians in Washington are in league with them. This is especially true for our presidents.

* * *

Bill and Hillary Clinton

Bill speaking to the press: I did not have sex with that woman! Those charges are ridiculous.

Hillary speaking to the press: My husband is the president. Show him the respect he deserves. And another thing; regarding the Whitewater scandal, Bill and I did nothing wrong. Those charges are ridiculous as well. You people are just out to slander us.

Bill: That's right, Hillary and I did nothing wrong.

Bill speaking to the press: What is that you say? Another person scheduled to testify against Hillary and me has been found dead. Hillary, how many does that make now? No answer. Bill replies: No, we didn't have anything to do with it. Those accidents are just coincidences. I repeat, Hillary and I did nothing wrong.

Bill speaking to the press: What is that you say? My what? My semen has been found on Monica's dress? *Oops*!

Hillary to Bill: You B——-d you lied to me. Lying to the American people is one thing, but lying to me is another thing entirely. You B——-d!

* * *

I commend Clinton for his policies regarding deficit reductions, which certainly contributed to his popularity, but nonetheless, the agenda of the financial elite was advanced during his administration. And he and Nixon certainly tarnished the office of the president.

Anyway, back to politics. He signed the NAFTA agreement spearheaded by his predecessor, and though started prior to his term, he also signed the repeal of the Glass-Steagall Act, which had prohibited commercial banks from being owned by full service brokerage firms (securities companies). Repeal of the act allowed merger of banks, securities firms, and insurance companies and set the stage for the predatory lending practices, which lead to the 2008 collapse of the housing market. Had Glass-Steagall remained in effect the predatory lenders would not have been able to combine conventional home mortgages with high-risk zero down no-doc loans and adjustable rate mortgages (ARMS) to create the collateralized debt obligations (CDOs), which were bundled together, given fraudulent AAA ratings and sold to unsuspecting investors all over the world.

The housing collapse was no accident; it was a collaborative effort involving Clinton, Bush Jr., and then Senator Obama along with Fannie, Freddie, and the Fed. They conspired to intentionally cause the housing collapse in order to further the financial elite's agenda to collapse the US and limit private ownership of property.

The millions of us who lost our homes (yes, I lost everything I had), our jobs, our life savings deserve to know that what happened to us was done intentionally. And we deserve to know who was behind it and how they did it.

Agenda 21: The 2008 Housing Bubble is part and parcels of the UN's Agenda 21, and their plans to limit ownership of private property. It was part of the largest land grab in the history of the world. Remember, under a communist government, virtually everything is owned by the state. I tell you these things in the hope that by knowing what has been done to us and what lies ahead we will stand up and resist, and their heinous plans can be thwarted. I should note that though the 2008 housing collapse was primarily a US phenomenon. It was intended to affect the entire world and it did. Rating companies gave the caustic collateralized debt obligations bogus AAA ratings and the banker gangsters sold these fraudulent securities to investors all over the world. The target of this crime was the entire free market system. Remember the UN is on record as saying that it is their responsibility to see to it that the Free Market system falls. In any event, here is what they did to hardworking Americans here at home and unsuspecting investors around the world.

It is as President Thomas Jefferson said, "If the American people allow private banks to control the issuance of the currency, first by inflation and then by devaluation, the banks and corporations that will grow up around them will deprive the people of all their property until their children will wake up homeless on the continent their fathers conquered."

Wake up! Our property is being taken before our very eyes! Will you say treason?

Obama **Clinton** **Bush Jr.**

We Are Proud To Say That Our Actions Caused The 2008 Financial Collapse, And Very Nearly Collapsed The Entire Free Market System!

Don't let the smiles fool you. These men are traitors. Read on and decide for yourself.

The attorney generals and governors of all fifty states tried to put a stop to the *predatory lending practices* which caused the 2008 financial meltdown, but we told them to *"butt Out"* because it was a federal issue. Thanks to us the end is near!

How We Collapsed The Housing Market:

- I Senator Obama: Sued Citi Bank on behalf of ACORN for racial discrimination forcing them to lower their lending standards. I am revered as a hero. If the people understood what I really did they would know that I am a traitor not a hero.
- I President Clinton: Repealed "*The Glass Steagall Act*" thus allowing the merger of banks, security companies, and insurance companies creating banks which *"Were Too Big To Fail."* My actions also led to the creation of the Collateralized Debt Obligations [CDO's] which precipitated the collapse of the housing market. Any it great?
- I President Bush Junior: Opposed all fifty Governors & States Attorneys in efforts to pass Anti-predatory Lending Laws. I guess I showed them!
- On Behalf Of The Financial Elite We Fannie & Freddie: Scooped up foreclosed homes by the millions furthering the goal of the UN to end private ownership of property which is one of the tenants of communism and the soon to come New World Order. Ant it great!
- We The FED, The Real Rulers of the U.S.: Recently announced we are going to start buying $40 B per month in mortgage backed assets setting the stage for a 2nd housing collapse! Ain't great that the masses are so stupid!

Yep You Have Us To Thank For The 2008 Financial Collapse!

The bottom line is that Obama, Clinton, and Bush conspired to collapse the residential housing market. Then (privately owned)

Fannie and Freddie, who were bailed out with taxpayer money, turned around and scooped up the mortgages of millions of unsuspecting Americans, leaving them homeless. Meanwhile, millions of investors around the world who bought the fraudulently rated (CDOs) lost their investments. Lastly, the Fed has joined the party and is also buying mortgages. I tell you anyone who would do these things would do anything. *They are pure evil.*

Well, how am I doing? Am I proving my thesis that "Congress Is Irrelevant and Our Presidents Have Become Puppets of the Financial Elite?" Instead of upholding the Constitution and our national sovereignty, they conspire to create crisis after crisis, so they can drive us into the one-world government. The reality we face is that:

The government sworn to protect us: Is the biggest threat this nation has ever encountered?

Reader's perspective: I have to admit you have presented some pretty convincing evidence. But at the same time it all seems hopeless. How can we ever stand up to such a powerful evil group of men?

Me: Time and time again, the Israelites were up against much larger, more powerful enemies and at the last minute God stepped in and saved them. The first step to our victory is for us to understand what is being done to us. Then we have to remember they want to take us over by stealth. Once the truth comes out, the entire game changes. There are three chapters dedicated to our counteroffensive. Please be patient, and once we have fully disclosed their plan, we will be ready to talk about how we take the country and the planet back. Remember, God's people win, but God doesn't promise it will be easy. Matter of fact, I can guarantee you it won't be easy. But it's a darn site better than the alternative!

"It is difficult for common good to prevail against the intense concentration of those who have special interest, especially if the discussions are made behind closed doors" (President Jimmy Carter).

* * *

Bush Jr. and Cheney

Bush speaking to Chaney: Dick, isn't it great? Here we are in the White House and along comes 9/11 and the housing bubble—two of the biggest crises this country has ever seen. And both of them are on our watch. Just think of how much we can get done. We can use these crises to scare the crap out of the public and force them to agree to things they would never otherwise agree to!

Chaney speaking to Bush: Yep, George, we can use these events to strip the people's liberties out from under them while all the while they think we are protecting them. It will be like taking candy from a baby.

Bush speaking to Chaney: Yep, Dick. Normally the g——n Constitution would get in the way of our plans to lay the groundwork for martial law and the takeover of the country by our pals at the Trilateral Commission. But we can force our agenda on the public in the name of "homeland security." Ain't it great?

Chaney speaking to Bush: Just think of it George. It is the same thing our role model Adolf Hitler did to implement the Third Reich. He had the German parliament set on fire, found a patsy, passed the Enabling Act, which we modeled the Patriot Act after, and in the name of homeland security, he attacked his neighboring countries and dismantled the German constitution and in no time declared himself dictator for life. Just look at the possibilities.

Bush responding to Chaney: Yah, Dick. The public makes too much of the Constitution. It is outdated and its "just a goddamn piece of paper!" George Bush, the White House blues; besides, it stands in the way of creation of the New World Order. Bush speaking to Chaney: And Dick, it is like our old pal Henry Kissinger said, "The illegal we do immediately. The unconstitutional takes a little longer" (Henry Kissinger, secretary of state and CFR member).

Chaney speaking To Bush: Just think of the opportunity we have. We can get away with doing all kinds of unconstitutional things, and if anyone complains, we can call them unpatriotic and say what we are doing is for homeland security.

Bush Speaking to Chaney: That gives me an idea. Do you remember what one of our other role models said? Chaney responds: Who are you referring to? Bush continues: Herman Goering, Hitler's right hand man. He said, "Why of course the people don't want war. That is understood. But after all, it is the leaders of the country who determine the policy, and it is always a simple matter to drag the people along, whether it is a democracy, or a fascist dictatorship or a parliament or a communist dictatorship…voice or no voice, the people can always be brought to the bidding of the leaders. That is easy. All you have to do is to tell them they are being attacked, and denounce the pacifists for lack of patriotism and exposing the country to danger. It works every time." Bush continues: We can use 9/11 as an excuse to invade the Middle East and get a strategic foothold there as well as get control of the oil. The sheep will never figure it out. And there is even a bonus. The war will make a fortune for our friends at the Fed, and it will drive the national debt to the stratosphere. Excellent, let's do it.

Bush continues: I just had another idea, while the people are distracted and cowering from fear over terrorism and crying over the state of the economy, we can sneak in another big win.

We can have a secret meeting with the leaders of Mexico and Canada and conspire to merge the US with Canada and Mexico. Even better, we can appoint a panel of bureaucrats to write regulations to integrate the three counties while at the same time undermining the US constitution and even the Supreme Court. Our buddies at the Trilateral Commission will be ecstatic. It is after all exactly what they did with the European Union and look how that turned out.

Chaney responds: What if the public should get wind of what we are doing? Bush retorts: No problem. I have the perfect cover story. We call the meeting "The Security and Prosperity Partnership" (SPP) Doesn't that have a warm and fuzzy ring to it? People are so dumb!

Secret meeting to plan merger of U.S, Mexico and Canada to lay plans to end US Sovereignty:

Baylor Hosts President Bush, Mexican President Fox and Canadian Prime Minister Martin For Historic Meeting March 23,2005 (By Lori Scott Fogieman)

Baylor University welcomes President George W. Bush, Mexican President Vincente Fox and Canadian Prime Minister Paul Martin on March 23 for meetings the leaders said provided a framework for the next generation of trilateral relations between the North American Countries.

The truth is the Security and Prosperity Partnership was a cover for talks to establish an American Union, modeled after the European Union. Like what started out in Europe as just trade agreements and ended up costing the nations of Europe their constitutions and their sovereignty. And that is exactly what it is intended to do here in the US as well.

The (SPP) is establishing tribunals: which are destroying U.S. Sovereignty & taking precedence over the Constitution, U.S. Law & The Supreme Court! Bureaucrats Are Writing Regulations Governing: Transportation–Law Enforcement – Agriculture – Banking – Manufacturing–Construction–Education – Immigration & Military.

These appointed *(Unelected)* bureaucrats are completely circumventing all three Branches of the U.S. Government and are secretly morphing the U.S. into a servile member state of the New World Order. All in all there are ten such trading blocs being formed by The Shadow Government of The New World Order. They are intended to replace all the Nation States of the world which are to be eliminated in order to make way for the New World Order! In my opinion the ten trading blocs being established represent the ten-headed beast referred to in the Book of Revelation.

All I can say is, if this isn't treason I don't know what is!

Let's take a look at the facts. Bush Jr. presided over the largest increase in national debt of any president in US history (that is till Obama) with the debt skyrocketing from $5.493 trillion to $10.700

trillion. Not a bad accomplishment, if you want to collapse a nation under a mountain of debt.

Following 9/11, Bush initiated what he called "the war on terror," which has us fighting wars in both Afghanistan and Iraq, but what I never could understand was that if he was so concerned about terrorist attacks, how could he leave our border with Mexico wide open and support legalization of illegal immigrants. Maybe, just maybe the war was really about oil and a strategic foothold in the Middle East.

Bush also signed a tough new bankruptcy law, which was coincidently written by Maryland Bank National Bank commonly referred to as MBNA the nation's second largest credit card company, which was coincidently Bush's largest campaign contributor. I don't suppose this could possibly be considered *influence peddling or maybe even treason?*

Most Americans know that Bush signed the Patriot Act, which significantly infringed on our civil liberties (one of those things we would not have done minus a crisis), but what most do not know is that hours before the bill was to be voted on, Bush pulled the Congressional Bipartisan Bill and replaced it with a bill written by the White House. It contained provisions, which had previously been rejected by Congress. This was just another underhanded power ploy which in this instance was designed to set the stage to make it easier for Obama to impose a police state. *Will you say dictatorship?*

At 3:45 a.m. I pulled the Bipartisan version of the Patriot Act and replaced it with one designed to take away your liberties and there isn't a thing you can do about it. [Fact, not quote] Will You Say Treason?

Bush also signed EO#12803 expressly allowing privatization of US infrastructure by private international investors. By the way, prior to this, it had been illegal for foreign investors to own US infrastructure, built and maintained by US citizens. This is an indication that our debt holders do not want worthless US dollars, preferring instead hard assets.

Bush signed the Medicare Drug Benefit Program that, according to Jan Crawford Greenburg, resulted in "the greatest expansion in America's welfare state in forty years."The bill cost approximately $7 trillion dollars. David Walker, controller general of the US, called the bill "the most fiscally irresponsible piece of legislation since the 1960s."

Bush's efforts to support the agenda of the financial elite were if nothing stellar, not to mention reprehensible and criminal. In reality, the 2008 housing collapse would probably never have happened, if 9/11 hadn't crippled the stock market giving the Fed the perfect excuse to use the crisis to lower the interest to historic lows. The combination of easy money and the actions of Obama, Clinton, and Bush them came together to create the perfect financial storm. Don't think for a second it was accidental. It was planned, and it was diabolical. *It was treason—pure and simple.*

Obama and Biden

Obama to Biden: Do you think the American people have figured it out yet? Biden: Figured what out? Obama You know! Biden: Know what! Obama: That I am a liar and the front man for the financial elite, the one whose job it is to lead them like dumb sheep to the sheering table.

Biden Replies: The halo does seem to be slipping a bit. You know what they say. You can fool some of the people all the time, but you can't fool all the people all the time. But I think you can buy enough votes to get reelected.

Obama replies: What do you think we should do? Do we need to make them more hollow promises? Biden responds: No. That strategy is wearing a little thin. Obama: How about blaming the republicans? Biden: No. That one is getting old too. I think your best bet is to keep up the entitlements, the divisive rhetoric and false statistics that make it look like your stimulus is working. And keep up the misinformation campaign so you keep them so confused they don't know what to think or who to believe. Confusion is our friend. And if we have to we can throw in another crisis, a big one, big enough to scare the shit out of them.

Obama replies: Boy, I hope they don't figure out that the stimulus is just a retread of "Roosevelt's New Deal" and that it is impossible to spend your way out of a financial crisis. It didn't work in 1929, and it won't work now. It is simply impossible. And if they figure that out, they might figure out that I am forcing the registration of gold, so I can confiscate it like Roosevelt did in 1933.

Biden replies: I think you are okay. As long as you keep giving them handouts, their greed will keep them blind to the truth, and you will get reelected, and then you can do whatever you want.

Obama replies: I sure hope you are right. It would make my job a lot harder, if they figured out that everything I am doing, all my rhetoric, is to mask the fact that it is my job to collapse the US and drive the idiots into the one-world government and utter servitude. It would be a really serious threat to our power, if they figured out that the real problem is the trade imbalance, the reckless spending and the government regulations intended to make America noncompetitive in the global marketplace. If they figured that out, they might actually figure out that their government is the biggest threat to their liberty they have ever faced or ever will face. And if that happens, well then, there is no telling what they might do!

Barack, you give them too much credit.

Obama replies: It would be an utter catastrophe if they ever woke up and figured out that regardless of which party they vote for, the financial elite will be pulling the strings because the president is just a figure head. I can't believe how easy it has been so far to lead the idiots to slaughter but if they ever were to wise up. Well, they might just revolt, and there are a lot more of them than there are of us, and they have those darn guns. I sure hope they don't figure out that the "small arms treaty" with the UN is designed to circumvent Congress and finally take away those d—n guns. First, we force them to register the guns, and then we send in our palls at the UN to disarm them. We finally got the law changed, so it is legal to deploy foreign troop on US soils, so when the time comes, we can control them and herd them wherever we want. I just hope they don't wise up before we get our plans in place. The urban deployment vehicles I ordered haven't been delivered yet, and we need then to quell the riots when they finally wake up to the truth.

Obama continues: Joe, I just thought of something else that could go wrong.

Biden responds: What is that, Barack?

Obama replies: What if they became more afraid of us than the crises we have been inflicting on them?

Biden responds: No, Barack they are not that smart. They believe in the demons we have created to control them.

Obama retorts: Hear me out.

Joe replies: Okay.

Obama expounds: What if they were to see that all the executive orders I have been passing behind the scenes were intended to force them to be utterly dependent on the government, so when we were ready, we could pull the plug on them, literally starve them to death, and incarcerate them like our pal Mao did in China. That kind of fear can cause even a mouse to fight back!

They could even figure out that my "million-man army" is what Hitler did when he created the Brownshirts and SS in Germany and used them to strike fear in the hearts of the German people. Our founding fathers were expressly opposed to standing armies.

Biden responds: Barack you give them too much credit. We have been very successful in distracting them, confusing them, dividing them, and dummying them down. They are as harmless as a kitten.

Obama in frenzy responds: I just hope the kitten isn't a lion. When they grow up, they have big teeth.

Biden flippantly says: Don't worry; be happy. We have the idiots, eating out of the palm of our hands. They are so busy fighting each other that they don't have time, or for that matter, the balls to fight us! I tell you they are sheep, not lions.

Obama agitated: Joe I tell you some of them are even getting wise to my redistribution of wealth rhetoric. They realize that it is intended to destroy the upper and middle classes, leaving only two classes—us, the ruling class; and them, our slaves. Some of them have even gone so far as to figure out that the only group with enough money to restore the economy of the US, or for that matter, the world is the financial elite, and they are not about to share.

I heard the other day that they know that the Rothschild's alone control one half of the world's total wealth, and if you add in the rest of the elite, only 5 percent of the entire world's money supply is left to be shared among seven billion people. It would be a big problem, if they figured out that we do need to redistribute the wealth, but not from the upper and middle classes, but from the financial elite. Just think of what the world would be like if all that wealth was used to help people instead of to enslave them. We would lose control!

I also heard rumblings about passing a national usury laws and revamping mortgages so they don't start over every time they refinance or buy a new home. That would nearly put an end to our money laundering scheme. Some of them are even waking up to how we use energy and war to control and enslave them. I tell you if the word gets out, they will even demand control over their own currency, then our entire money printing pyramid scheme would go up like a puff of smoke, and they might actually revolt against us no matter what the cost, because they would realize that it is better to die a free man than to live as a slave. I tell you they are waking up. We have to do something fast.

Barack, calm down. Like I have been saying, you give them way too much credit.

Obama in a panic: I have one other concern. Biden replies: What is it this time? Obama looking distraught: My popularity is slipping. I don't think they see me as the anointed one any longer. Some of them even see through the mask and realize that I am pure evil the sun of perdition.

Oh, I just had the worst thought imaginable. What if they figured out that it is like our pal Stalin said, "It doesn't matter who votes, it only matters who counts the votes"? They could put two and two together and realize that I used the census to reconfigure the congressional districts to favor the democrats. That my opposition to voter identification is to ensure I can stuff the ballot boxes with fraudulent ballots. That the reason I am making it hard for military personnel to submit absentee votes is I know that the military is overwhelmingly republican. And I can't even imagine what they would do, if they realized that their votes are going to be counted by a server in Spain by a company owned by my pal George Soros.

Barack, you have to stop being so negative. We have them right where we want them.

No Joe: Obama visibly shaken: I have this gut feeling that they are waking up. Hear me out. Remember that interview where I was asked about my faith, and I responded my "Muslim faith," and the interviewer had to correct me and say you mean your Christian faith. That was a big screw up. You know I do a lot better when I have my teleprompter. It is just so hard keeping up with all those lies. And sometimes I get confused and let things slip that they are not supposed to hear. Like the time I told Putin I could be a lot more flexible after the election. Damn it; they might figure out that the one-world government we are pushing is actually a super capitalist communist dictatorship, and actually, Putin and I are both working to bring the US down. The only difference is that one is on the inside and the other is on the outside.

If they figure that out they might take it a step further and realize that the US, China, and Russia are all controlled by the financial elite, then they might figure out why I gave China a Brazilian oil well and Russia one-half of the Prudhoe Bay Alaska oil field (one of the largest oil finds in the world). We are all brothers, all communist, all controlled by The Elite. And at the same time they might figure out that my ban on drilling in the gulf and my veto of the keystone pipeline was to cripple the US and make it dependent on unreliable foreign oil sources so we could be sure of high oil prices and could trigger an oil crisis, if and when we need to.

And Joe, I think my past is catching up with me as well. Some of them have actually figured out that my real father is not a goat herder from Kenai, but Frank Marshall, a communist organizer, and it was he that got me into community organizing, introduced me to my radical friends, and got me into Harvard. The resemblance between me and my real father is just too strong to ignore, especially when you realize I look absolutely nothing like my politically contrived father from Kenai.

Bear with me a minute. Before we go on with the conversation I need to tell you about Obama's real father.

Please Google President Obama and Frank Marshall Davis and look at side by side pictures of them. You will see what appears to be a remarkable family resemblance. Then if you Google Barack Obama Senior you will see there is absolutely no resemblance. The documentary Dreams of My Real Father develops a strong case for the fact that Communist Organizer Frank Marshall Davis and not Kenyan Goat Herder Barack Obama Senior is Obama's real father. The documentary contends that Marshall mentored Obama and fostered a hidden Communist agenda. It further documents that Obama's Mother Ann Dunham married a second time, this time to Lolo Soetoro, a Muslim from Indonesia. It was during this time that Obama attended a State run school in Indonesia and recited the Muslim Call to Prayer, making him by Muslin law forever a Muslim and *prescribing the American people as infidels to be defeated at any costs.* Sorry I had to send you to the web to get the pictures, but I couldn't find any photos that were not copyrighted.

Back to our conversation:

Obama continues: Then the unthinkable. What if they figured out that I am not only a Communist but also a Muslim, and that I hate the US and everything it stands for. No telling what they might do.

Biden responds: Barack, you are paranoid. You are out of your mind!

Wait, Obama interrupts: Joe, if they figured out that I attended Muslim school and regularly recited the "Muslim call to prayer"? It would be a no-brainer to realize that I am a Muslim. If they figured that out, all they would have to do is realize that *as a Muslim, it is my responsibility to lie to infidels in order to subdue them*, and poof, they would know that everything I have done and will do is to bring them down because I hate them. Then, there is no telling what they might do.

And you have to admit it is a bit hard to believe that when you pastor regularly preaches hatred against the whites and against America and says things, such as "goddamn" America." It is hard to deny adherence to his teachings when people realize I have been going to his church for over twenty years.

Obama ranting: What really scares me is the UN was stupid enough to put our endgame in writing in that dam Agenda 21 document. It spells out that our endgame is to reduce the world population from seven billion to one billion to drastically reduce resource consumption, control access to education, jobs, housing—literally everything. They might even figure out that my affordable health plan is a Trojan horse for population control and mass genocide.

Damn it. If things get far enough out of control, they might even catch on to our brainwashing strategies and how over time we intend to genetically alter them to the point that they are literally like dumb sheep, too dumb and too docile to ever fight back.

I tell you, if they figure out the truth, nothing will keep them from rising up because they will realize it is better to fight and die than to live as slaves.

Biden trying to calm Obama down: Get control of yourself. Our handlers don't want to hear that kind of childish quibbling! Remember what Warburg told Congress on behalf of the Rothschilds? "We shall have world government whether or not you like it. The only question is whether World Government will be by conquest or consent" (James P. Warburg, representing Rothschild banking concern, while speaking before the United States Senate, Feb. 17, 1950).

Obama getting agitated responds: That kind of rhetoric is all well and good, but at the end of the day, there are seven billion of them and only a few thousand of us, and the biggest fear of all is what would we do if they repented to their God, and he came to their rescue? I have read their Bible, and their God has unlimited power. That is why I have been doing everything I could to nuttier Christianity. If their God comes against us, I tell you, we are screwed.

Barack, *shut up*! Listen to yourself. We know who we serve, and he has enthroned us in the seat of power. Now is the time. We have to enslave the world in his name and kill his saints. That is what we pledged to do and we better do it.

Obama responds: I am just saying what if they wake up? That's all.

Obama regaining his composure: You are right. The dumb idiots reelected me. It is game on. Balls to the wall. We will bury them in their own ignorance!

* * *

Self-indictment by Obama! "If the people cannot trust their government to do the job for which it exists—to protect them and to promote their common welfare—all else is lost" (Barack Obama).

Obama has unwittingly indicted himself, his administration, and the entire federal government with the words out of his mouth. Without realizing it, he has told us it is time to take our country back!

Reader's perspective: Okay, uncle. You have convinced me that our presidents have sold out and that Congress is irrelevant. Even if we have some honest congressmen, there are so many ways to circumvent Congress that it has become irrelevant. What you have shown me reminds me of the Jimmy Steward movie *Mr. Smith Goes to Washington*. The only difference is the corruption portrayed in the movie is nothing compared to the picture you have painted. You also said you would put names and faces to the shadow government, which you haven't as yet done.

Me: Well, I guess we better do that then.

THE SHADOW GOVERNMENT EXPOSED

Best Laws Money Can Buy

Politicians in Washington serve themselves and special interest groups and not "We The People:" "The liberties of the people will never be secure when the transactions of their rulers can be counseled from them." *(*Patrick Henry)

How is it our congressmen & senators can write a bill that they know full well will cause a given company's stock to sore & then behind the scenes invest in that company making vast fortunes? *They are an elected elite above the laws they pass!* As Time Magazine put it they give us **"The Best Laws Money Can Buy."**

Unlike you & I they are *"Exempt From Insider Trading Laws."* which they passed! Will you say enough is enough?

America is a two-party dictatorship!

Global Governance and the Plan to End National Sovereignty!

They come in peace
With outstretched arms
Making promises most grand

To care for us
To heal the land
To keep the peace

Their power is great
Their reach is vast
Extending all across the land
Across the sea
And around the globe
Their words are sweet
But they don't ring true
Their hearts are black
And a trap they have planned
To enslave all in the land
And overthrow all the nations

They are the shadow government
The United Nations
The financial elite

By any name they are
The spoon of the devil

As I recall, I promised you an org chart of the shadow government and to show you just how deeply the Trilateral Commission (TC) and Council Foreign Relations (CFR) has penetrated the government. So let's get to it.

Abbreviations of Global Governance Organizations used in graphic below:

EXECUTIVE BRANCH OF THE SHADOW GOVERNMENT: Responsible for strategic planning includes the following groups and organizations: Bilderberg Group (BG) North Atlantic Treaty Organization (NATO) United States Agency for International Development (USAID) World Trade Organization (WTO) World Health Organization (WHO) World Bank (WB) International Monetary Fund (IMF) United Nations (UN)

IMPLEMENTATION BRANCH OF THE SHADOW GOVERNEMNT: Responsible for executing the plans of the Executive Branch includes the following groups and organizations: Council Foreign Relations (CFR) Trilateral Commission (TC) Federal Reserve Bank (Fed) TV, newspapers, magazines, etc. (Media) Politically Connected Corporations (CORP) Government Agencies (GOVT) Community Organization Groups i.e., ACORN and SEIU etc =. (COMM. ORG) Politically connected unions, such as SEIU (UNIONS) Educational system, particularly left-leaning Ivy League Universities (Academia)

The Organization Chart Of
The Shadow Government

The global governance organizations: I refer to the Bilderberg Group (BG) as the super secret strategic planning/executive branch of the shadow government, while the Tilateral Commission (TC) and the Council on Foreign Relations (CFR) can be thought of as the feet on the ground, which carries out the day-to-day initiatives of the organization. Meetings for all three entities are conducted under what is referred to as "Chatham House Rules," which specifies that nothing discussed in the meeting is to be repeated or quoted outside the meeting or in the press. *Will you say secrecy and*

treason? All three entities are in one way or another committed to ending national sovereignty and establishing the one-world government. The Bilderberg Group is comprised of the wealthiest and most powerful power brokers in the world (approximately 125 people). North American Treaty Organization (NATO) is the military enforcement organization, which forces compliance with United Nations (UN) directives. The International Monetary Fund (IMF), World Bank (WB), and United States Agency For International Development (USAID) are all banking organizations, which in concert with Central Banks, such as the Fed, control the world's monetary system on behalf of the financial elite. Their job is to drive us into unmanageable debt. The World Trade Organization (WTO) is the free trade organization whose job it is to collapse the free market system by driving major industrialized nations, particularly the US, into unmanageable debt by creating trade imbalances. The World Health Organization (WHO) is responsible for establishing global health accords favoring major corporations and designed to kill those in third world countries through malnutrition and starvation.

***The implementation organizations*:** Are the feet on the ground, which carries out the directives of the various global governance bodies, particularity the Bilderberg Group, which is responsible for strategic planning? The TC and CFR are high level organizations, working to implement the directives of the Bilderberg Group from within the government, military, media, academia, unions, community organization groups, and key corporations, which carry out strategically significant roles for the government (i.e., Halliburton, Monsanto, GE, etc.)

Reader's perspective: My God, how can we ever hope to stand up against such powerful organizations?

Me: How did David stand against Goliath? How did Gideon defeat an army may times larger? How did Alexander the Great conquer one-half the known world while fighting thousands of miles from home and when consistently outnumbered? Easily—

that's how it is. Easily—in one instance, it is divine intervention, which will be ours if we will only drop to our knees and repent and ask for God's help. Having lived the life I have lived and seen the things I have seen, I believe emphatically in God and his power. In the second instance, the answer is by knowing your enemy and by having a superior strategy. As God told me to tell you, "the truth will set you free." You are learning about your enemy, and by the time you finish this book, you will know exactly what his vulnerabilities are and how we can defeat him. I promise, but one step at a time. You are not ready to tackle that yet, but you will be. Remember, we win. Not without a fight, but we do nonetheless win.

I promised I would give you the names and positions of those who would enslave us and the charts below will do just that, but first a little further elaboration is in order. It is impossible to identify every single person, nor is it necessary. According to Representative Ron Paul, there are about twenty-five thousand people worldwide who are dedicated to birthing this New World Order. What I am going to give you, in the charts that follow, are the names and titles of key individuals in our government who also belong to the (TC) and or (CFR), the very organizations on record as being dedicated to the collapse of the US. These traitors are in the seat of government and they are dedicated to destroying everything this nation stands for.

Before we get to the Organization Charts of TC and CFR members in our government I want to remind you that there can be no question that these organizations are emphatically dedicated to the destruction of the US. It is impossible for a person to serve the US Constitution and the CFR and TC at the same time because one is dedicated to the destruction of the other. There can be no question that the men I identify are traitors to everything this nation stands for. With this in mind please read and contemplate the quotes below so you have fresh in your mind the objectives of these traitorous organizations. May God save America and the American way of life?

The *US must fall in order to birth The New World Order:* "We shall have world government whether or not you like it. The only question is whether World Government will be by conquest or consent" (James P. Warburg Representing Rothschild Banking Concern While speaking before the United States Senate Feb. 17th 1950)

"The New World Order will be built… an end run on national sovereignty, eroding it piece by piece will accomplish much more than the old fashioned frontal assault" (Council on Foreign Relations Journal 1974, P558)

The US is a two party dictatorship controlled from the top down and the bottom up: "Council on Foreign Relations is the establishment. Not only does it have influence and power in key decision-making positions at the highest levels of government to apply ***pressure from above***, but it also uses individuals and groups to bring **pressure from below**, to justify the high level decisions for converting the U.S. from a Sovereign Constitutional Republic into a servile member state of a one-world dictatorship."(Former Congressman John Rarick 1971)

Obama

Obama was groomed and put into office by the elite in order to destroy America from within. While at ACORN, as a Community Organizer, Obama controlled us from the "***bottom up***" and now as President he controls us from the "***top down***". I say again: America is a Two Party Dictatorship! ***Congress Is Irrelevant!*** America is controlled by a Shadow Government intent on our destruction and the Office of the President has been hijacked!

Down with the US and up with the New World Order:

> "The most powerful clique in these [CFR] groups have one objective in common: they want to bring about the surrender of the sovereignty and the national independence of the US....What they strive for would inevitably lead to dictatorship..." (Harpers, July 1958)
>
> "The Trilateral Commission doesn't run the world; the Council on Foreign Relations does that!" (Winston Lord, assistant secretary of state, the US State Department).
>
> "Our government will soon become what it is already a long way toward becoming, an elective dictatorship" (Senator J. William Fulbright).
>
> "I believe that if the people of this nation fully understood what Congress has done to them over the last forty-nine years, they would move on Washington; they would not wait for an election...It adds up to a preconceived plan to destroy the economic and social independence of the United States!" (Senator George W. Malone [Nevada], speaking before Congress in 1957).
>
> "The New World Order can't happen without US Participation, as we are the most significant single component. Yes, there will be a New World Order, and it will force the United States to change its perceptions" (Henry Kissinger [CFR] World Affairs Council Press Conference, Regent Beverly Wilshire, April 19 1994).

As I said earlier, it is literally impossible to hold a key position in Washington without belonging to either the TC or CFR. This also goes for the courts, military, and the media. The charts below show just how deeply the TC and CFR have penetrated the inner workings of our government and institutions. ***Their presence renders our two-party political system irrelevant*** as they drive all the decisions of any importance. Our presidents are just puppets of the shadow government run by the CFR and Trilateral Commission,

The shadow government: CRF and TC members in Congress

Name	Position	Title
Z. Brzezinski	Security Advisor to five presidents Founding Member	CFR TC
Colin Powell	Chairman Joint Chiefs of Staff	CFR
George H. Bush	US President	CFR
William Clinton	US President	CFR
Jimmy Carter	US President	CFR TC
Walter Mondale	US VP	TC
John McCain	Senator Presidential Candidate	CFR
Albert Gore. Jr.	US VP	CFR
Hillary Clinton	Secretary of State, Obama Administration	TC
Condoleezza Rice	Secretary of State, Bush Administration.	CFR
John Kerry	Senator and Chairman, Foreign Relations Committee	CFR
James Woolsey	Director, CIA	CFR
Robert Gates	Secretary of Defense and Former Director, CIA	CFR

Henry Cisneros	Secretary, Housing and Urban Development	CFR
Dick Chaney	Vice President	CFR

Congress is irrelevant! Every decision made by our elected officials in Washington is influenced by people dedicated to destroying the national sovereignty of the United States and making slaves of us all!

The financial elite run the country! Senator Barry Goldwater warned in the 1960s that "both houses of congress are irrelevant. America's domestic policy is now being run by [the Chairman of the Federal Reserve (Fed)], and America's foreign policy is now being run by the International Monetary Fund."

The US political system is controlled by the FED and IMF. Our presidents are nothing but puppets. Alan Greenspan said when appearing on (PBS the Lehrer Report) when asked: "What is the proper relationship between the Chairman of The Federal Reserve and the President of the United States?"

"Well first of all the Federal Reserve is an independent agency and that means basically that, uh, there is no other agency of government which can overrule actions that we take. In so long as that is in place… what that relationships is, uh, don't frankly matter."

The Shadow Government: World Bank Presidents

Name	Position	Term in Office
Robert McNamara	President	(1968–1981)
A.W. Clauson	President	(1981–1986)
Barbara Conable	President	(1986–1991)
Lewis Preston	President	(1991–19950
James Wolfenson	President	(1995–2005)
Paul Wolfowits	President	(2005–2007)
Robert Zeellick	President	(2007–Present)

Big Problem: World Bank presidents are appointed by the president of the United States! So if the president is sold out so are all the people he appoints!

Since 1968, all but one of the presidents of the World Bank have been members of the Trilateral Commission.

The Shadow Government:
CFR and TC Members in the Treasury Department

Name	Position	CFR/TC
Henry Paulson	US Treasury Secretary	CFR
Robert R. Glauber	Undersecretary, Finance	CFR
David C. Mulford	Undersecretary, Intn'l Affairs	CFR
Robert M. Bestani	Dept. Asst. Secretary, Intn'l Monetary Affairs	CFR
J. French Hill	Dept. Asst. Secretary, Corp Finance	CFR
John M. Niehuss	Dept. Asst. Secretary, Intn'l Monetary Affairs	CFR
Roger Altman	Deputy Secretary	CFR

> "The money power preys upon the nation in times of peace and conspires against it in times of adversity. It is more despotic than monarchy, more insolent than autocracy, more selfish than bureaucracy" (President Abraham Lincoln).

> "History records that the money changers have used every form of abuse, intrigue, deceit, and violent means possible to maintain their control over governments by controlling money and its issuance" (James Madison, fourth president of the United States [1809–1817]).

Congressman Louis McFadden said of the 1929 crash and depression: "It was a carefully contrived occurrence. International bankers sought to bring about a condition of despair, so that they might emerge the rulers of us all."

Mc Fadden was poisoned at a State function. So, the money changers run the country!

The Shadow Government:
CFR and TC Members in the Judiciary

Name	Title	CFR
Sandra Day O'Connor	Assoc. Justice, US Supreme Court	CFR
Steve G. Breyer	Chief Judge, US Court of Appeals, First Circuit, Court Boston	CFR
Ruth B. Ginsburg	US Court of Appeals, WA, DC Circuit	CFR
Laurence H. Silberman	US Court of Appeals, WA, DC Circuit	CFR

"All the rights secured to the citizens under the Constitution are nothing and a mere bubble, except guaranteed to them by an independent and virtuous judiciary" (Andrew Jackson).

Remember, our presidents appoint our Supreme Court Justices, so if the office of the president has been hijacked, then by default, so has the Supreme Court!

The purpose of The Council On Foreign Relations and Trilateral Commission is to collapse the US: "The Trilateral Commission (TC): is intended to be the vehicle for multinational consolidation of the commercial and banking interest *by seizing control of the political government of the United States*...They rule the future." (Felix Frankfurter, Justice of the Supreme Court)

The Shadow Government: CFR Members in the Department Of Defense

All the individuals listed below are members of the CFR

Name and Title

Les Aspin, Secretary of Defense
Charles M. Herzfeld, Director, Defense Research and Engineering
Frank G. Wisnerll, Undersecretary Policy
Andrew Marshall, Director, Net Assessment
Henry S. Rowen, Asst. Secretary, International Security Affairs
Michael Stone, Secretary of the Army
Judy Ann Miller, Dept. Asst. Secretary, Nuclear Forces and Arms Control
Donald B. Rice, Secretary of the Air Force
Bruce Weinrod, Dept. Asst. Secretary, Europe and NATO
Franklin C. Miller, Dept. Asst. Secretary, Nuclear Forces and Arms Control
Adm. Seymour Weiss, Chairman, Defense Policy
US Arms Control and Disarmament Agency
Thomas Graham General Council
Richard Burt, Negotiator on Strategic Defense Arms
William Schneier, Chairman, General Advisory Council
David Smith Negotiator, Defense and Space

Dwight Eisenhower said in an address to the nation (January 17, 1961), "We must guard against the acquisition of unwarranted influence...by the military-industrial complex. The potential exists for the disastrous rise of misplaced power." Beware of false flag events!

In order to birth the New World Order the US must fall. Are you going to go quietly into slavery or are you going to fight back?

Henry Kissinger

The US must fall in order to birth the New World Order: Henry Kissinger Former Secretary of State "The New World Order can't happen without U.S. participation, as we are the most significant single component. Yes, there will be a New World Order, and *it will force the United States to change it's perceptions.*" (Henry Kissinger: [CFR] World Affairs Council Press Conference, Regent Beverly Wilshire, April 19th 1994) If this isn't treason then what is?

> "In the long history of the world only a few generations have been granted the role of defending freedom in its hour of maximum danger. I do not shrink from this responsibility, I welcome it" (President John F. Kennedy).

> "We, the people, are the rightful masters of both Congress and the courts, not to overthrow the Constitution but to overthrow the men who pervert the Constitution" (President Abraham Lincoln).

> "Those who make peaceful revolution impossible will make violent revolution inevitable" (President John F. Kennedy).

> Ronald Reagan was speaking of our foreign enemies when he said, "Above all, we must realize that no arsenal, or no weapon in the arsenals of the world, is so formidable as the will and moral courage of free men and women, It is a weapon adversaries in today's world do not have."

Are you prepared to stand up for your freedom and that of your loved ones?

OUR TWO-PARTY POLITICAL SYSTEM IS AN ILLUSION

Understanding the shadow government's "chess game of global primacy." If the financial elite are to realize their dream of establishing a "one-world dictatorship," they must collapse the US and take over our government and military.

The plot to take over America and then the rest of the world has been generations in the making, so over time, lots of credible people in positions to know have tried to expose them, but unfortunately, given their control of the media their warnings have not gotten widespread exposure. They nonetheless exist. In other instances, the arrogance of these conspirators has lead to then saying things that expose their agenda. So thankfully, there is plenty of evidence to share.

Here goes. Our leaders in Washington may not themselves be the financial elite, but for the most part they, are owned by the power brokers and special interest groups who make it lucrative to see things from their perspective. They have become a "ruling class," who see themselves as being privileged and superior to those they were elected to serve. They, for the most part, have betrayed our trust, and it is time they were exposed for what they really are. They regularly conspire to do everything they can to dismantle the Constitution and take away our right to bear arms.

Our Founding Fathers never intended for us to have carrier politicians because they knew that to do so would invite the kind of corruption and elitism which we see in Washington and other governments around the world. It was intended that there be term limits and when the terms were up people would return to their former positions in the private sector. Even more importantly lobbyists were illegal because our Founding Fathers knew that they would insure that the interest of the people would not be served. The apple barrel is rotten and the apples need to be thrown out so we can get a fresh start.

Reader's perspective: Before you go any further, I have a complaint to make. You have used some of these quotes several times, and I am getting tired of your badgering by constantly asking, "Will you say treason? Will you say shadow government? Will you say dictatorship? Will you say genocide?"

Me: Well, are you ready to stand up and say those things? Are you ready to take responsibility for your life and your actions? Are you ready to tell the government they can take their handouts and stick them where the sun doesn't shine? Are you ready to demand the truth? Are you ready to take a stand for liberty and the pursuit of happiness? Some of you are ready to stand up and be counted. To you, I apologize for frustrating you. To the rest of you I say it is my job to stay in your face till you see the truth and come to grips with it. I am honestly sorry, but this is what God told me to do.

To those of you whose eyes are open, again, I apologize, but to the rest of you I say the best way to drive home a point is with repetition and emotion! After this chapter, I will stop asking, "Will you say treason? Will you say shadow government? Will you say dictatorship? Will you say genocide?" I will simply present the facts without the annoying commentaries; well, may be a few where I can't help myself. I want you to know that what I do I do out of love. God has put it on my heart to tell the truth so that those who will see and hear may be saved from the worst of what is to come. May God bless you and yours. Now back to the badgering! Sorry! It is my job.

Our right to bear arms. Congress knows this is a political hot potato that is too controversial to touch, if they ever want to get reelected. That is why Obama and Hillary have circumvented Congress and the American people and are negotiating away our rights under the "UN small arms treaty," which would force us to register our guns, and from there it is just a matter of time till under a UN resolution, circumventing the US Constitution, our guns are taken away, and we are left defenseless. Will you say treason?

"Our task of creating a socialist America can only succeed when those who would resist us have been totally disarmed" (Sara Brady, Chairman, Handgun Control to Sen. Howard Metzenbaum, the National Educator, January 1994, page 3). Will you say treason?

It is as Noah Webster said, "Before a standing army can rule, the people must be disarmed."

"We, the people, are the rightful masters of both Congress and the courts, not to overthrow the Constitution but to overthrow the men who pervert the Constitution" (President Abraham Lincoln).

"The Constitution is just a goddamn piece of paper" (George W. Bush, Nov. 2005, Capital Hill Blue). *Will you say treason?*

This is from a man who swore an oath to protect the Constitution. No, my friends, these men are not intent on protecting the Constitution. They are intent on dismantling it, so as Obama says, "They can fundamentally transform America," and what they want to do is transform it into is a dictatorship.

Reader's perspective: Wait a minute. Not all politicians are corrupt! And what do you mean when you call them a "ruling class?"

Me: Of course you are right, but that doesn't make what I said wrong. In a second, I will show you why I say they are a ruling class, but more than that, the system is corrupt and it renders those who are honest ineffectual, so the system has to be changed. We are past the point of doing that within the confines of the Republican and Democratic Parties because they have been rendered irrelevant! It is as President Jimmie Carter said, "It is difficult for common good to prevail against the intense concentration of those who have special interests, especially if the discussions are made behind closed doors."

Why I call congress a ruling class. They serve their interest, not those of the public. If they served our interest, they would be subject to the same rules and laws as we are, but they aren't!

For example, they are not subject to the laws they pass (e.g., Social Security and Obamacare). They can pass bills that they know will cause a particular company's stock to skyrocket and then turn around and invest in that company and make a fortune (i.e., GE and the regulation making it mandatory to buy their new mercury-filled environmentally hazardous light bulbs). That is called insider trading, and if one of use makes investments based on privileged information, "We go to jail, directly to jail. Do not pass go. Do not collect $200." Like I said, they are a privileged ruling class; a class above the law. Will you say treason?

They vote on their own salary increases. Who among us wouldn't like to have that privilege?

Contrary to the intent of our Founding Fathers, they have no term limits. They can reconfigure congressional districts, not in order to better represent their constituents, but to create a voting block favorable to their party so they can stack the deck in favor of reelection. Will you say treason?

They pass landmark legislation without even reading it (i.e., the Stimulus Act, the Patriot Act and Obamacare. How is that representing our interest? Maybe they don't have to read the bills because they are written by special interest groups they owe allegiance to (e.g., the Stimulus and Cap and Trade; both of which were written by the Apollo Group, which is a coalition of unions, such as SEIU and social justice groups, such as ACORN, both of which Obama has close ties to, and both of which have left leanings). Will you say treason?

Then way back in 1913, the banking interest took over the treasury's right to mint money and gave it to the privately owned Fed who now prints our currency and charges us interest for printing fiat money backed by nothing but hot air. Will you say treason?

"Let me issue and control a nation's money, and I care not who writes the laws" (Amshell Rothschild).

The US is run by the Fed and IMF: Congress and the president are just puppets. If we can believe the following quotes, and I do, the Fed tells the president, what to do and they not Congress or the president run the country, and they do so for their interest, not that of the public.

Alan Greenspan was asked when appearing on PBS the *Lehrer Report*, "What is the proper relationship between the chairman of the Federal Reserve and the president of the United States?" He answered, "Well, first of all, the Federal Reserve is an independent agency, and that means basically that, uh, there is no other agency of government, which can overrule actions that we take. In so long as that is in place…

what that relationships is, uh, doesn't frankly matter." Will you say treason? Will you say our presidents are puppets of the Fed?

"Our great industrial nation is now controlled by its system of credit. We are no longer a government by free opinion, no longer a government by conviction and the vote of the majority, but a government by the opinion and duress of a small group of dominant men...Our great industrial nation is controlled by its system of credit. Our system of credit is privately centered. The growth of the nation, therefore, and all our activities are in the hands of a few men, who necessarily, by very reason of their own limitations, chill and check and destroy genuine economic freedom. We have become one of the worst ruled, one of the most completely controlled and dominated governments in the civilized world" (President Woodrow Wilson). Will you say treason?

Senator Barry Goldwater warned in the 1960s that "both houses of Congress are irrelevant. America's domestic policy is now being run by [the chairman of the Fed], and America's foreign policy is now being run by the International Monetary Fund." Will you say treason?

In other words, the Fed, acting on behalf of the financial elite, tells the president and Congress what to do, and they do it.

Why John F Kennedy had to die: Appearing before Congress, President John F. Kennedy referred to the FED as: "This establishment that virtually controls the monetary system; That is subject to no one; That no Congressional Committee can oversee; and that not only issues the currency, but loans it to the Government at interest."

JFK was so outraged at this usurping of power by The Financial Elite that he signed Executive order #11110 to dismantle the Fed. To accomplish this: he issued US Silver Certificates to replace the dollar. He was also taking action to limit the power of the CIA and he refused the demands of the Military Industrial Complex to commit more troupes to Vietnam. For these reasons he had to die!

Johnson Reversed All Kennedy's Positions!

Had JFK lived, the Fed and the financial elite would be history! We would be living in a safer world! Our children would have a future. The world would be at peace. If his dream is to live on, the Fed must go, and at the same time, we must withdraw from the United Nations (UN), World Trade Organization (WTO), and all global governance bodies. I know that sounds impossible, but Jackson got rid of the first central bank, and JFK nearly succeeded in getting rid of the second (the Fed)! I know this sounds crazy and impossible, but the time is coming when we will have to stand against the financial elite or be utterly destroyed. Before you finish this book, I will show you how we can end the financial elite's strangle hold on money and credit and regain our freedom. Put your trust in God. There is a way. He showed me.

The Federal Reserve Bank not the president or Congress is in charge of the United States government! The Fed must go, if we are to ever be free!

If Congress or the president served our interest (no matter how inept they are) occasionally something they did would benefit us and our failing economy, but it doesn't! All they do is spend money we don't have.

"There are two ways to conquer and enslave a nation. One is by the sword. The other is by debt" (John Adams, second US president). *A warning from the past!*

When Obama came into office, the national debt was $10.7 trillion, and now, it is $17 trillion and climbing. When we fall off the cliff, and we will, it is going to be a long fall. Since the housing crash, Americans have lost 40 percent of their wealth, but that is nothing compared to what is coming when the dollar crashes.

Reader's perspective: I do see that the system has flaws, but it can't possibly be as bad as you make it out. After all, our Founding Fathers built checks and balances in the three branches of government, so if some mysterious shadow government wanted to take over they would have to take over all three branches.

Me: Precisely, and that is exactly what they have done. Read on, and all will become clear.

Presidential overreach renders Congress irrelevant! For example, Candidate Obama pledged that under his administration, there would be no:

1. Signing statements. Obama promised no signing statements, *"saying they were illegal,"* but the very first-bill signed by Obama had a signing statement attached. I realize that some of you may not know what a signing statement is, so I will explain. After weeks or months of debates and compromise, a minor miracle occurs. Both houses of Congress reach agreement, a vote is held, and a bill is passed. The bill them goes to the president to be signed; at which point, the president can attach a signing statement that can invalidate any portion of the bill. So, in the final analysis, the president trumps the Congress, and he effectively nullifies the bill the Congress passed. Remember, Obama is the President that threatened that if Congress wouldn't enact his policies, he would govern by decree. *Will you say dictatorship?* That brings us to the second presidential overreach.
2. Executive orders. For example, Obama recently circumvented Congress when he announced he would stop enforcing certain parts of the American Immigration Law. The tool he used was an executive order. Oh by the way, that particular decision is most likely unconstitutional. But the strategy in Washington is to do whatever the president wants, and then fight it in the courts, if it comes to that. As the following quotes show this flagrant disregard for the "Balance Of Power," imbedded in the

Constitution is shared by republicans and democrats alike. *Will you say dictatorship?*

"The illegal we do immediately. The unconstitutional takes a little longer" (Henry Kissinger, secretary of state and CFR member). *Will you say treason?*

"The Constitution is just a goddamn piece of paper" (George W. Bush, Nov. 2005, Capital Hill Blue) *Will you say treason?*

Did you ever watch those infomercials on TV where they say, "Wait a minute. There is more. We are going to double your order." Well, I have two more examples of executive over reach for your reading pleasure.

3. Regulatory czars. Appointed, not elected bureaucrats empowered to enact legislation with "No congressional oversight." For example, after Climategate, the public got the drift that our government was lying to us when they said global warming was caused by human activity, so cap and trade died an agonizing death. But never fear, the regulatory czars to the rescue. They would just go through the EPA and enact regulations, effectively giving us cap and trade by fiat. The net result was to pass job-killing regulations. And we wonder why there is no economic recovery. Hint: The government doesn't want a recovery, because they want to collapse the US economy so they can get their one-world government. *Will you say treason?*
4. Fast track treaty agreements. Simply put, "fast track treaty agreements" require fewer votes to pass than normal treaties, so they can be used to ramrod through agreements that might not otherwise get ratified by Congress. There goes another of our safeguards. Where you see this tactic most prominently used is in passing "intentionally losing free trade agreements," which are responsible for gutting the US manufacturing base by intentionally sending those jobs over to China. And we wonder why China owns the US? We gave it to them. That's why. *Will you say treason?*

According to Auggie Tantillo, executive director at the American Manufacturing Trade Action Coalition (AMTAC), "Of 138 major manufacturing nations, the US is the only nation that does not take advantage of a value added tax (VAT) in order to protect its manufacturing base and maintain a favorable balance of trade." In other words, the US trade balance and manufacturing base are being intentionally sabotaged. *Will you say treason?*

Don't just brush past this. This is huge! This is probably the biggest single cause of the economic demise of the US economy, and it was intentionally perpetrated on an unsuspecting American Public. In 1977, just prior to the opening of trade with China, the US—after over two hundred years of existence—had a national debt of only $600 billion. That was less than the Stimulus. Then, we opened trade with China, and as of 2014, our national debt has jumped to $17 trillion. Oh by the way, that value added tax you just read about, if a manufacturer were to manufacture his goods overseas, he is eligible for the tax break, but if that same manufacturer chooses to be a loyal American and keep his manufacturing in the US, he gets no tax break. So much for American patriotism! Is it any wonder the US economy is now based on the service industry and our manufacturing base is eroded away to next to nothing? We are feeding on the bottom of the economic food chain? *Will you say treason?*

I bet you thought we were done with why Congress is irrelevant. Sorry! There is one more branch of government, the judicial, and then I saved the best for last. That is how global governance bodies (e.g., the UN and others) circumvent not only Congress, but the US Constitution as well. And they don't just do it to the US. They undermine the sovereignty of every nation in the world, because their goal is to destroy all sovereign nations so they can institute their totalitarian super capitalist communist one-world government and as Kennedy said become the rulers of us all. They are pure evil. What I want my readers to understand is that how the US goes the rest of the world goes. If the US falls and the forces of evil get control of US agricultural production there are no less than one hundred countries that could be starved to death just the way Mao starved to death 67 million of his people. And then if they get control of the US military and combine it with NATO they will have control of the most advanced military force on the planet and it will be as the bible says: *Who can stand against the Antichrist?*

These guys have been really busy figuring out how to topple the US. I promise I will get through this as fast as I can, but this is absolutely crucial foundation material. You see, if we hope to launch a counteroffensive to put America back on track, then it is essential that we first understand what has been done to destroy our economy. In that knowledge lays the key to our economic restoration. When we have all the facts, we can launch a counteroffensive, and we can say, "Enough is enough!"

The judicial system is compromised! "All the rights secured to the citizens under the Constitution are nothing and a mere bubble, except guaranteed to them by an independent and virtuous Judiciary" (Andrew Jackson).

1. The president appoints the Supreme Court justices. Bottom line is that if the office of the president is compromised, as it is, then he can stack the Supreme Court with judges who will vote in line with his policies. *Will you say dictatorship?*

Reader's perspective: Wait just a gosh darn minute! Where do you get off saying the office of the president is compromised? There may have been a specific president that has done some questionable things, but to say the entire lots of them have sold out, that is just ridiculous. Maybe you need to go back and read the last chapter again!

Me: I thought this one would raise a few eyebrows. Ridicules, you say. Not if I can prove it, and prove it I can, but first, let's get the rest of our foundation laid.

2. International treaties can override the US Constitution and Supreme Court. This is an atomic bomb with unbelievable implications! Let me give you a few examples of just how crucial this issue is to the survival of America as a sovereign nation.

As I am writing this, Obama and Hillary are circumventing the congress and going to the UN to negotiate, "the small arms treaty," which could force us to register our guns with the UN. Then thanks to an executive order signed by Bush, it is now legal to deploy foreign troops on US soil. So at some point it is conceivable that UN troops might be deployed on US soil and take away our guns.

"Today, America would be outraged, if UN troops entered Los Angeles to restore order. Tomorrow they will be grateful. When presented with this scenario, individual rights will be willingly relinquished for the guarantee of their well-being granted to then by the world government" (Henry Kissinger).

There you have it. All we need is the right crisis (maybe a false flag event), and we can have UN troops on US soil, ready, willing, and able to take away our rights. Oh by the way, did you know that Russian troops have been conducting urban crowd control exercises on US soil, something that till recently was illegal and still should be. *Will you say treason. Will you say dictatorship?* Because that is what is coming. All they need is an excuse to declare martial law (the right crisis) and that will be the end of the US Republic! Now contrast this next quote to the one above and see what you think: "If a nation values anything more than freedom, then it will lose its freedom, and the irony of it is that if it is comfort and security that it values, it will lose that too" (Charley Reese, *Orlando Sentinel*). So I ask again, are we smarter than a monkey? Are we going to hold on to the government handouts at the cost of our liberty, or are we going to have the courage to bight the hand that feeds us, the hand that would enslave us?

Then, there is the World Health Organization and the "Codex treaty," which if implemented would make it illegal to buy therapeutic levels of vitamins and minerals. It would put us at the mercy of the pharmacy companies and it would kill billions.

According To WHO and AFO's own projections, "Implementation of 2009 vitamin and mineral guidelines will result in a minimum of one billion deaths by starvation and two billion deaths from preventable diseases associated with malnutrition! *Will you say genocide!*

So how could they even contemplate such legislation? Oh, I remember now. They want to reduce the world's population to one billion. After this, only four billion to go. I wonder how many of those will be Americans, possibly our sons, daughters, parents, or grandparents.

This is our government's and the UN's plan for our future. It is the plan to commit mass genocide on a never before imagined level, take away our freedom and regreen America and make upwards of 75 percent land off limits for human settlement. It is Agenda 21. The plan for the twenty-first century.

Agenda 21 The UN's Plan For Sustainable Development
Called Agenda 21; Agenda For The 21st Century

- An end to national sovereignty
- Abandonment of the Constitution
- Presumption of guilt till proven innocent *"No inalienable rights."*
- Abolition of private property
- Educational system focused on the environment as the central organizing principle of society
- Restructuring of the family unit with education focused on allegiance to the state
- Limitations on mobility with up to 75 percent of land being off limits
- State control of access to higher education and carrier opportunities
- Limitations on private ownership of property with state owned residences along rail corridors
- Reduce population to sustainable levels of one billion or less

In order to accomplish their objective, our property will be confiscated and we will be herded into designated areas connected only by Monorail. We will live in state owned apartments as the state will own everything. Is this the future you want for your children? If not then you need to stand up and take back America before it is too late. Most of these initiatives are already in place in Communist China, the nation the New World Order is modeling their Utopian Dictatorship after!

THIS CAN ONLY BE REFERRED TO AS SLAVERY & GENOCIDE!

Will you say slavery and genocide? Who among you will stand up for liberty?

Guess what? I have been to China, and most of what Agenda 21 calls for are in place there already. I guess I would certainly agree with Obama. This does indeed represent a "fundamental transformation." Just not the kind I would like. Oh by the way, did you know that in China, you can buy organs from political prisoners? Just tell them what you want, and they will harvest it from dead or living, but not so willing prisoners. Now, who wants to live in China? Who wants to live under a dictatorship? Who is willing to stand stand up and say enough is enough, give us back our government?

Horrific new evidence of Chinese organ harvesting revealed by: (Jan JekieieK Eopch Times Staff on assignment in Warsaw.) "The incredible thing is that the doctor would ... go down the names on a sheet of paper looking for blood types and tissue types and so on, and he (the patient) would point at names on the list..."

"A military surgeon had eight Chinese citizens killed to supply a single foreign patient with a new Kidney, said former Canadian Secretary of State for Asia – Pacific David Kilgour on November 14. Kilgour spoke to a special guest at the Asian Human Rights Week forum in Warsaw, on day two of a five day program".

THIS IS COMING TO AMERICA UNDER THE NEW WORLD ORDER

Back to Agenda 21. It took ten thousand generations for the world to reach two billion people, and thanks to modern medicine, it has jumped to seven billion in one generation. The globalists know that if we keep up this growth rate in another generation, the earth will be uninhabitable. Additionally, they see the world's resources as belonging to them, and there are just not enough resources to share with us peasants. Rather than tell us the truth and allow us to be part of the solution, they have simply decided we are expendable. These are real problems, and they do need to be addressed, just not by a group of narcissist who engender mass genocide as the solution. If you still doubt what I am telling you, munch on these quotes, and see if you feel better.

The UN intends to kill most of us and enslave the survivors! "Isn't the only hope for the planet that the industrialized civilization collapses? Isn't it our responsibility to bring that about?" (Maurice Strong, founder of the UN Environmental Program, Opening Speech, Rio Earth Summit 1992).

"It is the sacred principles enshrined in the United Nations Charter to which the American people will henceforth pledge their allegiance" (President George Bush, addressing the UN). Wait a minute. Bush swore allegiance to an organization intent on collapsing the Free Market System!

Psychologist Barbara Marx Hubbard, member and futurist/strategist of Task Force Delta, a United States Army think tank, said, "One-fourth of humanity must be eliminated from the social body. We are in charge of God's selection process for planet earth. He selects; we destroy. We are the riders of the pale horse, death."

If the New World Order is birthed it will mean billions will die. As they execute their plan to reduce global population from seven billion to one billion, which is what they consider to be a sustainable population level. In other words: We must die so they may live in luxury in their version of UTOPIA! Wake up! If you still don't believe our government is dedicated to depopulation: Then consider the following quote.

"Dr. Henry Kissinger proposed in his memorandum to the NSC that "depopulation should be the highest priority of US foreign policy towards the Third World." Henry Kissinger Was Secretary Of State Under Richard Nixon. Make no mistake. Mass genocide will come to America as soon as the New World Order is in power.

Mark my words Obama Care will eventually be used as a means of population control and genocide of the elderly and infirmed!

What about us? How can they starve us to death? Well for one thing, Obama recently signed an executive order, allowing the government to enter your home and take your food. That would be a good start, and then there is that genetically altered food that does not germinate leaving the human race at the mercy of a few corporations, and of course, the government.

The Plan To Starve Us To Death!

Monsanto Patent

God didn't give Monsanto Chemical the right to patent life. Our corrupt politicians in Washington did. Thanks to them approximately 80 percent of our food supply has been genetically altered with a terminator gene which renders the seeds sterile. What better way to control the population than to control our access to the necessities of life, in this instance food?

Now don't you feel better? You have to excuse my somewhat morbid, flippant sense of humor. It is the only way I can deal with this crap. It is just too much to contemplate without a little sarcasm. At any rate, we have two more ways in which the judicial system is compromised. Then, you can ask some questions, and we can move on to another topic.

3. Supreme Court rulings disregarded.
4. Lower courts told Supreme Court rulings are inadmissible. The Supreme Court, the highest court in the land, is deemed inadmissible at the direction of—you guessed it—the federal government. My example for both of these is implementation of the "illegal Federal Income Tax."

- In 1895, the Supreme Court ruled (in eight cases) that a direct tax on Income or wages was illegal.
- Also ruled sixteenth amendment granted no new taxing authority (Brushaber vs Union Pacific R.R. Co., 204 US1, the Supreme Court).

In the insuring years, several people were brought up on income tax evasion charges and all of them were found not guilty. Why you ask? Because they cited the obvious fact that according to the Supreme Court the federal income was illegal. The federal government couldn't tolerate this challenge to their Gestapo rule, so all the sudden, the situation took a 180-degree turn about, and virtually, everyone charged with income tax evasion was found guilty. *What changed?* The lower courts were directed by the federal government that they were to no longer allow the eight Supreme Court decisions to be used as a defense! On that day, our judiciary system died and was laid to rest, taps were played, and a eulogy read. It was a solemn occasion. *Will you say treason? Will you say dictatorship?*

"All the rights secured to the citizens under the Constitution are nothing, and a mere bubble, except guaranteed to them by an independent and virtuous Judiciary" (Andrew Jackson).

Reader's perspective: This is more than a little overwhelming. Okay, Uncle! You have convinced me that our government is our worst enemy! What you say goes a long way toward explaining our current financial situation. If our manufacturing is gutted, that is kind of like taking the engine out of our car, so to use an analogy, it would be kind of hard to jumpstart the economy and get people back to work without an engine. And if our currency is devalued that would be like putting gas in your car that had water in it. It wouldn't run.

Let me see, if I understand what you have said so far. These mysterious overlords you refer to have supposedly made us passive by first, making us dependent on the government for entitlements and the necessities of life (e.g., food, water, and energy) and second, by intentionally creating division, so we would be unable to mount any form of cohesive resistance. So as long as we remain ignorant to what they are doing, submissive, dependent, and divided, they win by default. I hate to say it, but it sounds pretty hopeless.

You also contend that our executive, legislative, and judicial branches of government have been rendered irrelevant and our government is actually controlled by the Federal Reserve and IMF, which are in turn controlled by the World Bank and UN, which are at the head of this mysterious shadow government.

Let's see. Have I left anything out? Oh yes. You also say global governance bodies, such as the UN, intend to end national sovereignty of governments around the world and create crisis and chaos in order to drive us into a one-world high bred capitalist communist government that would be a ruthless dictatorship. Oh yes, the US must fall so they can use our global presence along with that of NATO to force compliance with their policies. And the endgame is to reduce world population to one billion, drastically reduce resource utilization, lower our standard of living, and literally enslave us. Boy! This reads like a science fiction novel, except I have to say it does make a lot of things make sense.

Me: You pretty much summed it up. I know this is a lot to grasp, but it is what the Bible predicts, and if we follow the headlines, we can see it coming together before our eyes. My role in all this is to open people's eyes so we can hopefully wake up and fight back rather than just standing ideally by while our freedom and that of our children is snatched out from under our very eyes.

You said this all seemed pretty hopeless. As a watchman, I can assure you God would not have sent me to warn the world, if it was too late to do anything. Let me ask you a question. If you were a football coach and you had the other team's playbook; do you think that would give you an edge? That is of course a rhetorical question. Of course it would. Well right now, our adversary is pretty cocky because they see it as being the fourth quarter, and we are so far behind they think we can never catch up. But if all the sudden we got the opposition's playbook and knew in advance exactly what they were going to do, it could make all the difference between defeat and victory. Wouldn't you agree?

I make you this promise. Before you finish this book, you will have the enemy's playbook and the playing field will be leveled!

The reason it took God forty years to get me ready for my assignment was I had to have an extremely broad background in order to be able to see the big picture and formulate a strategy. Remember, I had a lot of help, such as direct revelation from God, pertinent work experience, knowledge of history, politics, science, psychology, religion, and military strategy. I guarantee you God equipped me to equip you. We can win, if we will just open our eyes and fight back.

PART 2

The Next Four Years: What Lies Ahead?

A TRAITOR IN OUR MIDST

The fools will never know what hit them. Praise Allah!

A traitor in our midst! In President Obama, we have a President who is dedicated to the destruction of the US through his associations and actions he has shown himself to be a communist, a racist, and a Muslim, masquerading as an open-minded transparent leader.

Obama is the enemy of America and Christianity, and he is dedicated to our destruction! He lied to us about all the things below and many more.

- No warrantless wire tapping
- No Lobbyist in his administration
- No bill would be signed till posted on internet for five days so public could review it
- No Signing Statements (they are unconstitutional)
- Said NAFTA was a mistake (handlers called statement just campaign rhetoric)
- Would immediately withdraw troops from Iraq
- Would not renew Patriot Act
- Would hold the bankers accountable

Our presidents tells us what we want to hear and do what they are told.

Big Brother Is Watching You!

[NSA] Data Center Has Your Data! What Do They Want With It?

Could our government be compiling a list of dissidents so they can do like Hitler did and whisk us off in the middle of the night never to be seen again?

Obama's associates and their agendas

- Saul Alinski, author of *Rules for Radicals*. He exposes creating "agitation and racial tension" intended to "divide the country" and using "community organizing" to register voters who are encouraged to vote for "entitlements" designed to "collapse the economic system by burying it under a mountain of entitlements." I would say they have been very successful, wouldn't you?

  In Obama, we have a president who taught (Rules for Radicals) for four years while a "community organizer at ACORN." It is a philosophy of division and subversion of everything America stands for. Even more frightening the following quote proves that Obama knew that "Rules for Radicals" was demonically inspired: "Lest we forget an over the shoulder acknowledgement of the very first radical…The first radical known to man who rebelled against the establishment and did it so effectively that he at least won his own kingdom "Lucifer" (Saul Alinsky, *Rules for Radicals—from the foreword of the book*).

- Bill Ayres, founder of the Weather Underground (which was responsible for bombing the Pentagon in 1972), mentor to Obama and the author of his books.
- Reverend Jeremiah Wright (known for his racist anti-American black liberation rhetoric), Obama's pastor and spiritual leader.
- Frank Marshall Davis, communist organizer, mentor to Obama and postulated to be Obama's real father.

Why Obama's Birth Certificate Was Withheld?

There is compelling evidence that Obama's goat herder father from Kenai is not his real father. Evidence indicates that his real father is Frank Marshall Davis, a card carrying Communist Organizer, but that could never be allowed to get out because it would be politically damaging. I urge you to get the documentary ***"Dreams From My Real Father."*** It builds a compelling case that Obama's birth father is Communist Organizer Frank Marshall Davis who mentored Obama and is responsible for his Socialist/ Communist leanings. The documentary shows side by side photos of Obama, Frank Marshall Davis and Obama's politically correct goat herding Kenyan father. The resemblance between Obama and Marshall is striking and there is absolutely no resemblance to Obama's politically correct father. Photos also on Google images

The documentary further explains that Obama's Mother later remarried a Muslim and moved to Indonesia where Obama attended Muslim school and recited the *"Muslim Call To Prayer"* making him forever a Muslim. This biographical information goes a long way toward explaining why Obama said "America is not a Christian Nation" and why his every action is to destroy Christianity and impose Socialism and Sharia Law.

Once a Muslim always a Muslim! Obama attended Muslim school in Indonesia and "recited the Muslim call to prayer," which by Muslim law makes him a Muslim and makes the American people infidels and his enemies. Also, Muslims are allowed to lie to the infidels in order to further their cause. This accounts for all of Obama's broken promises/lies!

It is time we wake up to the fact that we have a traitor in the White House. President Obama's affiliations and his actions show him to be a communist, a Muslim, a racist, a purveyor of demonic rhetoric, and a man dedicated to the destruction of America. He is the student of a pastor who said, "Goddamn America," and his actions indicate that he shares that opinion. His economic policies are designed to drive us into unmanageable debt, leading to chaos and social disobedience, which he intends to use as an excuse to take away our guns, "our last defense against a corrupt government." His policies invite economic collapse and are additionally an invitation for our enemies to attack an economically weak, militarily weak, racially divided America!

The fundamental transformation of America: What does it mean? Obama promises to "fundamentally transform America," but he never explained what that statement meant. He left it to a disgruntled and disillusioned American population to interpret it as a message of hope as he constantly repeated the mantra of "change you can believe in."

Four years later, he has once again been elected despite the fact that his promise of "a transparent government" proved to be a lie. And despite the fact that he promised to cut the deficit in half but instead it went from $2.1 trillion to $5 trillion (more than double Bush's second term). And despite the fact that it is increasingly apparent that his vision of "fundamental transformation" is not designed to unite the nation and create economic stability, but instead to divide it, creating unmanageable debt eventually resulting in economic collapse and erupting into racial tension and chaos so severe as to cause the American public to surrender their freedom to a government, which intentionally brought these hardships upon us.

As evidenced by his reelection, even today, despite overwhelming evidence to the contrary, the majority of Americans seem to still cleave to this charismatic figure and believe that in him America's future is in good hands.

The Obama deception. Our votes have been bought by a big government that promises to take care of us from cradle to grave. Our government-run schools teach our children "political correctness," which is code for an agenda of tolerance, which undermines the godly virtues upon which our nation was founded. Our news, media, and entertainment industry have become propaganda machines, infusing our society with a communist agenda cloaked in the guise of "fairness." For example, Obama wants to make it a crime, punishable by imprisonment, to speak out against the Muslim religion yet under Sharia law, women have virtually no rights. Go figure! He appointed a Muslim head of homeland security at a time when we are supposedly facing the threat of terrorism sponsored by Muslim countries. How is that even imaginable? Oh, by the way Obama recently ordered some 2, 700 urban deployment vehicles to be deployed in the US. It looks like he is preparing for civil disobedience, no doubt, brought about by an economic crisis precipitated by the government.

Our communist leaning government in Washington is intentionally undermining our values in an attempt to transform America. It is as Lenin said, "We can't expect the American people to jump from capitalism to communism, but we can assist their elected leaders in giving them small doses of socialism until they wake up one day to find that they have communism."

With the help of our leaders in Washington, this is exactly what is happening to America. We are being transformed from within, ever so slowly, without most of us even realizing it. My fellow Americans, this is what Obama meant by "fundamental transformation." It is not a message of hope, but an agenda designed to enslave us!

"Our founding fathers understood that if you could destroy *Christianity and morality*, you could destroy *the family*, and if you could destroy the family, you could *destroy the nation*" (Larry Ballard).

"Our constitution was only for a moral and religious people. It is wholly inadequate to government of any other" (John Adams, second president of the United States).

The evils of socialism.

> "Socialism destroys all the things that made America great! It destroys our work ethic, our self-reliance, our sense of community, our patriotism, and our family values. It must above all else destroy Christianity because it is the basis of the value system upon which our family values and our Constitution are based. Communism is evil and demonic, and in its wake are death, destruction, and misery!" (Larry Ballard).

Obama's Socialist entitlement and immigration agenda are designed to create division, and as Christ said, "A house divided cannot stand." Our government does everything they can to create a "consumer society where materialism becomes our God, and the state becomes our provider." The idea is that a dog will not bite the hand that feeds it. That is how they see us—as dogs with no more rights than a dog and as sheep, sheep that are as Lynen said, "Useful idiots." It is time to wake up and fight back.

The minute anyone makes statements the likes of which I am making, he is branded as a "conspiracy theorist, a nut case, a whack job." That might be true, if it were not for the fact that those intent on transforming America have left us a clear and concise agenda, outlining exactly how and why they plan on destroying America.

A history lesson: Unfortunately, the vast majority of Americans have not learned the lessons of history. Entitlements lead to big government that leads to socialism that invariably leads to communism. There has never in history been an instance in which a socialist or communist government, once entrenched in power, did not turn on the very people who put them into power and killed them and enslaved them by the millions. Stalin, Hitler, and Mao all promised "power to the people," but in the end, millions of their supporters were put in concentration camps, executed and starved to death. It can't be any other way because communism is dedicated to eradicating the middle class and creating a two-tier society comprised of the elite ruling class and the serfs, peasants or poor. Regardless of what you call them, the masses are reduced to poverty, and their liberty, their freedom, and very often, their lives are taken from them.

Wake up! This is what Obama's fundamental transformation actually forebodes for America!

Call For 'Planetary Regime' To Usher In One World Government!

John Holdren – Obama's Science Czar Advocates:

- A "Planetary Regime" to control the global economy and dictate by force the number of children allowed to be born.
- We need to surrender "National Sovereignty" to an armed international police force.
- Mass sterilization of humans through drugs as long as it doesn't harm livestock.
- Single mothers should have their babies taken away by the government or they could be forced to have abortions.
- As of 1977 we are facing a global overpopulation catastrophe that must be resolved al all costs.

Once the one-world government is established you can expect: UN troops to occupy the U.S., impose martial law, imprison dissidents and kill anyone they deem to be nonproductive! That is the truth about Obama's Fundamental Transformation of America! Open your eyes before it is too late!

Ponder the following quotes and ask yourself if you want to live under socialism or communism.

> "Communism has been responsible for the mass murder of more people in times of peace than all the wars of history" (Jim Simpson, researcher/writer, former White House staff economist).
>
> "The goal of socialism is communism" (Vladimir Lenin, founder, Soviet Union).
>
> "My objective in life is to destroy capitalism" (Karl Marx, Father of Communism).
>
> "When you are asking, 'What is the legacy of Marxism (Communism)?' It is the greatest killing machine in all of human history" (Dr. David Noebel, founder/president, Summit Ministries).

So, if communism is so evil and is responsible for such atrocities, how is it possible that they get people to buy into it? Perhaps the following quotes will shed some light on this perplexing and puzzling question.

> "Communism succeeds because most people who support communist causes are not communists. The useful idiots, as Lenin called them, give communism an air of legitimacy it would never have, if it was identified with communist and communism" (Whittaker Chambers).
>
> "If I could control Hollywood, I could control the world" (Joseph Stalin, Russian leader and mass murderer). *Will you say brainwashing?*
>
> "Give me four years to teach children, and the seed I have sown will never be uprooted" (Vladimir Lenin, founder, Soviet Union). *Will you say brainwashing?*
>
> "The organized minority will beat the disorganized majority every time" (Vladimir Lenin, founder, Soviet Union).

Isn't that what is happening in America today? We are increasingly controlled by a vocal minority with an agenda to destroy the American way of life! This is the cost of our passivity!

Wake up and smell the roses! The very fabric of America's greatness has been destroyed! "America is like a healthy body, and its resistance is—its patriotism, its morality, and its spiritual life. If we can undermine these three areas, America will collapse from within" (Joseph Stalin, Russian leader and mass murderer). *Will you say brainwashing?*

Time to take a stand. So what is the final outcome of a communist takeover, and are we going to allow this fate to befall our children and our children's children? Are we going to wake up to the truth and stand up for liberty and the American heritage, which so many generations of Americans have died to preserve?

Why people don't fight back? Increasingly, Americans are waking up to the fact that our own government poses the greatest threat our nation has ever faced, but still, people do not stand up and fight back. Why? There are many reasons. For many people, they don't want to bite the hand that feeds them. But of all the reasons, I think the primary reason people don't fight back is they truly don't understand what the government has done to them, how they have done it, and in their ignorance, they believe they are powerless!

We are anything but powerless. But in order to exercise our power, we must have three things. First, we must be informed. Second, we must have a plan and the willingness to stand resolute against our common enemy. If we do these things, it will be like David and Goliath. David (the people) will slay Goliath (the government). Third, the final thing we need is God's help, and in order to get that, we will have to turn away from our materialism and turn to God and once again become a moral society. If we do these things, our victory is assured.

In the pages of this book, I will provide you with the requisite knowledge and a detailed plan for how to take back America from our corrupt politicians. But in the final analysis, we will have to have the courage to fight the good fight because only then will God come to our aid and will our victory be assured. The way I see it the real danger is in not taking a stand. If we don't take a stand, our children will live under tyranny and oppression. I don't know about you, but I couldn't live with myself, if I allowed that to happen. How about you? *Do you have the courage to take a stand? Are you with me in the fight for liberty?*

"Socialism destroys law, morality, prosperity, productivity, education, incentive, and finally, life itself. It creates conditions for dictators to come to power" (Karl Marx, Father of Communism).

* * *

Could Obama be the antichrist? You decide. How the Bible says we will know the antichrist? Thus Saith The Lord: "The Tribulation Is At Hand And The Antichrist Walks The Earth!"

How The Bible Says We Will Know The Antichrist?

- He shall come at the time when knowledge shall be increased [now].
- He shall come in peace [be elected receive Nobel Peace Prize]
- He will think to change the times and laws [fundamental transformation]
- He shall magnify himself above all [the anointed one]
- He shall exalt himself and do as he pleases [anointed one. rule by executive order]
- He shall obtain the kingdom by flatteries [movie star status]
- He shall speak blasphemy against God. [mocked Christianity & Sermon On The Mount]
- He shall make war with the saints [Muslim pretending to be a Christian]
- He shall do according to his will [executive orders, circumvent Congress]

- He shall cause all to take his mark [health care is a Trojan Horse for RFID chip]
- He shall not regard the desires of women [he will support Sharia Law]
- Trouble from East & North [laying groundwork for WWIII]
- He shall break his promise & become strong with a small nation [not a friend of Israel]
- He shall put his palace on the holy mountain [to be determined]
- We shall cry out because of the King we chose [our President]
- In the end he shall fall and none shall come to his aid [the antichrist looses]

Above are sixteen things the Bible says will identify the antichrist. I challenge you to come up with even one other human being on the planet to which all these things apply. I know I couldn't, and I am pretty well politically conversant. Heck, I challenge you to come up with one person to which even one half of these things apply. Bet you can't!

The Demonically Controlled UN Will Be:
The Launching Platform Of The Antichrist!

"No one will enter the New World Order unless he or she will make a pledge to worship Lucifer. No one will enter the New Age unless he will take a Luciferian Initiation."(David Spangler, Director of Planetary Initiative of the UN)

"It is the sacred principles enshrined in the United Nations Charter which the American people will henceforth pledge their Allegiance." – (President George H W Bush Addressing the UN.) Remember The UN is dedicated to collapsing The Free Market System, which indirectly means it is dedicated to collapsing the US. To pledge allegiance to the UN is nothing short of treason.

Obama Taught Rules For Radicals While At ACORN. It is a book dedicated to Lucifer and intended to bury America under a mountain of debt. "Lest we forget an over the shoulder acknowledgement of the very first radical… The first radical known to man who rebelled against the establishment and did it so effectively that he at least won his own kingdom." Lucifer. (Saul Alinsky, Rules for Radicals) [from the foreword]

The UN'S Agenda 21 details plans to exterminate 6 billion people and enslave the world. The UN is the enemy of all humanity. Obama is the only US President to Chair the UN and if he ever leaves the office of President of The U.S. I believe he has eyes on the UN; a position from which his reach can truly be global.

OBAMA'S FUNDAMENTAL TRANSFORMATION OF AMERICA

The framers of the Constitution got it wrong! But my executive orders will straighten things out.

The US is the hope of the world! There are forces at work dedicated to seeing the US fall in order to birth the New World Order.

The US stands as the only real obstacle to implementation of a world wide capitalist/communist dictatorship. Our enemies know a united America is invincible, so it must be divided and destroyed from within. President Obama is dedicated to that end!

"America must be fundamentally transformed!"

There is a saying that goes, "My enemy's enemy is my friend." When it comes to the plan to collapse America, truer words were never spoken. We see an uneasy coalition comprised of the Anglo-Saxon financial elite (the banks, which are touted as too big to fail), radical Islam, and communist governments around the world, namely Russia and China. Their objective is to destroy America from within, and if necessary (when we are sufficiently weakened), occupy us by force. An economically weak nation is by its very definition militarily weak.

The strategy for conquering America from within. The communist agenda: their goals and accomplishments! I have alluded to some of these things thus far, but now, it is time to connect all the dots, so you can see that in fact there is an agenda designed to collapse America from within. Our politicians in Washington are not inept! They are our enemies! They represent more of a threat to our nation and our way of life than any army we have ever faced! Think of what follows as a "report card," grading the effectiveness of our government's agenda to "fundamentally transform America into a communist state!" (By any unit of measure, they have a 4.0 grade point!)

If our government can achieve the following goals America is assured of collapsing from within.

1. *Goal*: Attack and destroy Christianity because it is the basis of our morality and family values and the cornerstone of our liberty and our Constitution. (Grade A+)

   Destructive activities:

   - ✓ Our communist leaning government has eliminated prayer in schools on grounds it violates "separation of church and state." This is a perversion of the Constitution.
   - ✓ They have used "social justice rhetoric" to promote the philosophy that there is no absolute right and wrong (as taught by Christianity) and those that believe there is are labeled intolerant.
   - ✓ They are endeavoring to neuter Christianity by merging it with Islam to create Chrislam. As mentioned above, our president is even attempting to pass a law, which would imprison those who say anything against Islam while at the same time doing everything he can to remove reference to God from our public institutions.

Outcome: "Christianity is on the endangered species list and persecution is on the horizon!" (Larry Ballard).

2. *Goal*: Promote immorality because a free society is only possible if the people are moral and stand for the common good. (Grade A+)

Destructive activities:

- ✓ The federal government has "banned obscenity laws" on grounds they violate freedom of speech, yet they promote pornography regardless of its negative impact on society.
- ✓ Washington "promoted hate crime legislation," which made it a crime to even say anything against the homosexual movement.

Outcome: "Freedom and free enterprise are simply fruits on the tree of morality [and our morality is being systematically stripped away]" (Unknown).

3. *Goal*: Destroy the nucleus family because it is the basis of every civilized society known to man. (Grade A+)

   Destructive activities:

   - ✓ The financial elite (Rockefellers) financed the "feminist movement" in order to make women dissatisfied with their role as mothers and caregivers. As a result, the majority of women now work outside the home, the divorce rate is over 50 percent, and 40 percent of children are born out of wedlock.
   - ✓ The government welfare program pays for and incentives having multiple illegitimate children.

Outcome: "The nucleus family is having cardiac arrest!" (Larry Ballard).

4. *Goal*: Control and subvert the educational system in order to make our children willing tools of the state. (Grade A+)

   Destructive activities:

   - ✓ Because the majority of mothers are in the workplace their children are subject to a "nanny state" where a hostile government and subversive school system dumb down our children in order to make them wards of the state, teach them homosexuality, and same sex marriage is a normal and acceptable lifestyle; use "social justice rhetoric" to create divisiveness, foster socialism, and undermine the role of the family.

- ✓ They have gotten control of the teachers' unions and subverted the school curriculum in order to support globalism, socialism, and communism and to achieve their anti-American, anti-God, anti-family, anti-free enterprise agenda!
- ✓ "He alone, who owns the youth, gains the future" (Adolf Hitler).
- ✓ The goal is to create a generation of sheep who are too dumb and docile to challenge the government and therefore willingly accept servitude in exchange for being taken care of.
- ✓ Thanks to a curriculum which turns out students which do not have the requisite skills for the high tech jobs of the twenty-first century America is increasingly forced to hire foreigners who do have the necessary skills.
- ✓ The government has taken over the college curriculum and student loan program in order to make sure our students graduate with massive debt and are then unable to get jobs, making them wards of the state who can be controlled because they are dependent on the government!

Outcome: "America has become a 'nanny state' where a hostile government controls the minds and financial futures of our children!" (Larry Ballard).

5. *Goal*: Infiltrate our institutions from the top-down and from the bottom-up in order to transform America from within. (Grade A+)

   Destructive activities:

   - ✓ Top-down control: The buying of the first US president! The strategy of buying political power by buying the president began with the 1896 election when William

Jennings Bryan was campaigning on a strong antitrust platform. The three wealthiest and most powerful men in the US (John D. Rockefeller of Standard Oil, Andrew Carnegie of Carnegie Steel, and Banking Tycoon J.P. Morgan) saw their empires being threatened and decided to put aside their rivalries in order to protect their interest by buying the office of the President of the United States of America. They put their money and enormous power behind, industrialist sympathizer, William McKinley and got him elected over Bryan. That was what I call "Patient Zero" (the first president to be bought) in the scheme to control the US government by controlling those elected to the highest offices in the land. I am referring to the "inception of the shadow government," which today pulls the strings of our elected officials and is the real power on Capitol Hill (*The Men Who Built America*, the History Channel).

✓ Bottom-up control: collapse America under a mountain of debt! Through organizations, such as ACORN, SEIU, the TIDES Foundation, etc., the "Left" orchestrates the "organized minority" to create the agenda that supports the top down decisions coming from Washington, even though those decisions are in opposition to the "unorganized majority." While serving as a community organizer at ACORN, Mr. Obama drove the bottom-up decisions of the minority (by teaching *Rules for Radicals*), and now as president, he implements those same policies from the top down. The entire political system is controlled through this process.

Outcome: "The entire US federal government, including Congress, the office of the President and the Supreme Court (appointed by the president) have been taken over by the communist leaning left and are irrelevant! Our only political hope lies at the local and state level, which is where we must wage the war to save America! There and in our homes and our churches!" (Larry Ballard).

Note: In the pages of this book, you will find a complete political agenda designed to restore the Free market system and return America to the Christian values upon which our Founding Fathers based our Constitution!

6. *Goal*: Destroy national patriotism, and replace it with allegiance to the planet (code word for one-world government). (Grade A+)

   "To achieve world government, it is necessary to remove from the minds of men their individualism, loyalty to family traditions, national patriotism, and religious dogmas" (Brock Adams, director UN Health Organization).

   Destructive activities:

   - ✓ During his first campaign, then candidate Obama made an "apology tour," and when he was elected, his wife, Michelle, said, "For the first time in my life I am proud of America."
   - ✓ During his first term, President Obama refrained from saluting during the Pledge of Allegiance and openly denounced the American flag as a symbol of oppression.
   - ✓ "It is the sacred principles enshrined in the United Nations Charter to which the American people will henceforth pledge their allegiance" (President George Bush, addressing the UN).

Outcome: "Our national patriotism is being systematically destroyed and replaced with loyalty to the UN and their one-world communist agenda!" (Larry Ballard).

7. *Goal*: Divide the nation by creating racial and economic tension, leading to open "class warfare" eventually culmination in "chaos and rioting" (Grade A+).

   Destructive activities:

   - ✓ How do you transform a nation from within? One way is to change the demographics through immigration. America is now a bilingual nation with millions of illegal aliens of

Mexican descent. Obama and Bush before him has chosen to ignore federal immigration laws because: "The Security and Prosperity Partnership" initiated under Bush Junior is intended to merge Mexico, Canada and the United States and average out the economic standards of the three countries with the US being the looser. America is to follow Europe and become the "Amerounion" with a common constitution (a Communist Constitution) and merged economies.

- ✓ Obama has made it possible for refugees from Palestine and Syria, two Muslim countries who hate America, to immigrate to America. So thanks to Obama we are as they say *"sleeping with the enemy"* an enemy that might one day wakeup and commit who knows what atrocities against us!
- ✓ Europe has been inundated by Islamic immigrants and is increasingly facing a growing Islamic minority calling for Sharia Law. Obama is a Muslim, and America is next.
- ✓ Obama and those in Washington are intentionally creating economic, racial, and religious tension in order to divide the nation and keep us fighting amongst ourselves instead of fighting "our real enemy, our government."

Outcome: "A united America is invincible, but a divided America is easy prey for our enemies." It is as Christ said, "A house divided cannot stand" (Larry Ballard).

8. *Goal*: Use the press and media to brainwash us so we can't distinguish fact from fiction, truth from lies! (Grade A+)

   Destructive activities:

   - ✓ The financial elite own most of the media outlets and control what is and is not reported. "Whoever controls the media controls the mind" (Jim Moris).
   - ✓ "Misinformation in the US today is more efficient than it was in Nazi Germany, because here we have the pretense that we are getting all the information we want. That misconception prevents people from even looking for the truth" (Mark Crispin Miller).

Outcome: "America was founded to get out from under the tyranny of an intellectual and financial elite and they have imposed their tyranny again!" Larry Ballard

9. *Goal*: Hijack the monetary system and create unmanageable debt as a means to collapse the US and all of the Free market system! (Grade A+)

   Destructive activities:

   - ✓ How the financial elite hijacked the banking system and with it, the government itself!

     This is what I call "patient zero" for creation of the network of Central Banks, which today allow the financial elite to control the global banking system with ruthless disregard. Our story starts at the battle of Waterloo. Amshell Rothschild had spies overlooking the battlefield, with orders to dispatch carrier pigeons with news of the battle as soon the victor was known. We all know that the English defeated the French, but Rothschild spread a rumor that the French had won. He then used the panic that ensued to amass a vast fortune in ill-gotten gains. Then, some years later, a bankrupt king of England came to the Rothschilds for a bail out. The condition for the loan was that the Rothschilds takeover the banking system of England, leading to formation of the world's first central bank and this famous quote: "Let me issue and control a nation's money, and I care not who writes the laws" (Amshell Rothschild).

     Today in America, the financial elite control the nation's money and they care not who writes the laws. The global banking system has been taken over by the financial elite, and they, not our elected officials, run the country.

     "The dirty little secret is that both houses of congress are irrelevant. US's domestic policy is now being run by Alan Greenspan and the Federal Reserve. US's foreign policy is now being run by the International Monetary Fund" (Robert Reich, member, President Clinton's cabinet, Jan. 7, *Today*).

I don't know about you, but to me, this fits my definition of a dictatorship, which is exactly what the quotes below say the shadow government is, "A group of unelected power mad men acting behind closed doors, in secrecy, making decisions to subvert the national sovereignty of America."

- ✓ The goal of our left-leaning government headed by (former community organizer) Obama is to drive America into unmanageable debt by expanding voting roles, expanding welfare rolls, increasing the tax burden on the middle class, in order to economically collapse America!
- ✓ They have infiltrated the environmental movement and supported the false doctrine of "global warming" in order to use it as an excuse to write regulations designed to destroy America's ability to compete in the global market place.
- ✓ America is the only major industrialized nation to have "no tariff or value added tax" to protect our economy from the ravages caused from the uncontrolled influx of "free trade slave labor goods from China."

Outcome: "America has a national debt of $17 trillion. It borrows 46 cents of every dollar it spends. Our credit rating has been downgraded, and the US dollar is in the process of ceasing to be the world's reserve currency! Economic collapse is the only possible outcome of such events" (Larry Ballard).

10. *Goal*: Use crisis and fear to get us to give up our liberty in the guise of providing security. (Grade A+)

    Destructive activities:

    - ✓ Obama's chief of staff, Rahm Emanuel, said, "You never want to fail to take advantage of a crisis." Whether our recent crises were providential or perpetrated by our government there is no question that our government has used crisis to systematically strip away America's liberties.

- ✓ "At 3:45 a.m., President George W. Bush pulled the version of 'The Patriot Act' drafted by Congress and replaced it with a much more damaging version (which undermined our liberty) written exclusively by the White House. Our Congress then passed it without ever reading it." How much more irrelevant could Congress get?
- ✓ Our government uses crisis to create chaos as a justification for government intervention to solve the chaos the government itself caused!
- ✓ The war on terror and the wars in Afghanistan and Iraq have substantially added to our national debt yet President Obama has cleared the way for Palestinian refugees (potential Islamic extremist terrorist) to immigrate to the US and our southern borders remain wide open to incursion from our enemies.

Outcome: Hitler started WWII in the name of "Homeland Security" and under the same guise, he declared himself "Furor for Life" (dictator)! Our government is using the same playbook with the same goal—to establish a dictatorship! (Larry Ballard).

11. *Goal*: Weaken our military in order to eventually make us vulnerable to invasion of the US mainland, if deemed necessary. (Grade A+)

    Destructive activities:

    - ✓ During his first presidential run, then candidate Obama said he would "disarm America to a level acceptable to our Muslim brothers."
    - ✓ During his second campaign, Obama told Russia's Putin, "I can be more flexible after I am reelected."
    - ✓ Obama is cutting our military budget, which makes us vulnerable to our enemies, yet he continues on a path to raise taxes on the middle class without implementing cuts to entitlement programs. The only outcome to such policies is financial collapse.

Outcome: "A financially weak America is a militarily weak America. History demonstrates that a financially weak, divided nation is always subject to attack and occupation by its enemies" (Larry Ballard).

12. *Goal*: get control of all private property because under communism, the state owns everything, and the people are completely dependent on the state.

    Destructive activities:

    - ✓ As discussed earlier the government intentionally caused the 2008 housing collapse. The government in concert with the Fed, Fannie and Freddie allowed real estate to be sold to bad credit risks with nothing down, and then allowed perfectly good conventional mortgages to be bundled with caustic subprime loans floated on the derivatives market creating collateralized debt obligations knowing perfectly well it would collapse the residential housing market forcing millions of Americans to lose their homes to foreclosure. Privately owned Fannie and Freddie along with the Fed now own the mortgages on millions of American homes in what was the largest land grab in history.
    - ✓ Since the CDO'S were sold around the world the 2008 "financial crisis and housing bubble" was designed to bring *"the entire free market system"* to the brink of collapse and to further the elites goal of "abolition of private property."
    - ✓ "Isn't the only hope for the planet that the industrialized civilization collapse? Isn't it our responsibility to bring that about?" (Maurice Strong, founder of the UN Environmental Program, opening speech, Rio Earth Summit 1992).

- ✓ Now the Fed has announced that it is buying $40 billion per month in mortgages. It will then, once again, use the derivatives market to cause a second housing collapse and cause millions more Americans to lose their homes.

Outcome: "The American dream of home ownership is an illusion. The strategies discussed above are intended to eventually give the government control of all mortgages in America. Additionally, no American owns his home because if they are unable to pay their property taxes the government will take the property. As the government pursues its tax and spend policies even working Americans will be backed into a financial corner where they will be forced to choose between paying their mortgages and taxes or putting food on the table for their families. We are all tenants of a tyrannical government intent on eliminating the middle class and creating a two-class system comprised of the *elite* and the *poor*" (Larry Ballard).

13. *Goal*: Get control of all natural resources (the necessities of life) as the ultimate control mechanism. (Grade A+)

Destructive activities:

- ✓ The government now controls all water (the essence of life).
- ✓ Four companies control 80 percent of all food production with non-germinating genetically altered seeds and the government can take farmers land. (What better way to starve the population into submission just like Mao starved sixty-seven million of his people to death.)
- ✓ The smart grid when complete will allow energy to be controlled and metered out. Fossil fuels are intentionally kept in short supply, and we are denied access to available sources of cheap, clean renewable energy. (An industrialized nation ceases to function without energy. Our government knows that and uses energy as a weapon.)

- ✓ Thanks to Obamacare, our access to medical treatment is controlled by a government, which wants to drastically reduce the population. (What a perfect recipe for genocide!)

Outcome: "Can you say slavery? Can you say genocide? Will you stand up and fight back before it is too late?" (Larry Ballard).

14. *Goal*: The endgame is to establish a totalitarian one-world government, seize control of all private property and natural resources and cull the population from its current level of seven billion to one billion. (Grade A+)

Destructive activities:

- ✓ The United Nation's Agenda 21, which stands for agenda for the twenty-first century), outlines this exact strategy.
- ✓ The justification for such an agenda is that it took ten thousand generations for the human population to reach one billion, and now, with the advent of modern agriculture and medicine in the span of one generation, the population has exploded to seven billion. The contention is that this population explosion has caused what they refer to as "the planets sixth mass extension," and in the span of the next generation, they project the population to explode to approximately twenty-eight billion, which they say is absolutely unsustainable. Given this, they say that the population must be culled to one billion, and the only way that can be done is through implementation of a worldwide totalitarian communist government, willing to take the drastic measures necessary to save the planet. In other words, they will save the planet for the ruling class by killing off the masses that Lenin called the "useful idiots."

Outcome: "If we don't wake up and take a stand for liberty, we will most assuredly become sheep to the slaughter!" (Larry Ballard).

The future of America and the world are in your hands! Combined the initiatives listed above are intended to accomplish the "fundamental transformation of America" from a sovereign republic based on constitutional law into a servile member of a one-world dictatorship! The question is, "Are we going to allow that to happen to the nation our brothers, sisters, mothers, and fathers fought and died for?"

Are you willing to stand up for liberty and the pursuit of happiness?

THE AGENDA FOR OBAMA'S SECOND TERM

America is at a tipping point. The goal of the financial elite to collapse America and usher in a one-world government is near completion. Their puppets in Washington have passed all the laws necessary to legally declare martial law and impose a dictatorship, but they would rather collapse us economically than have to fight us in the streets of America though they are prepared to do that if necessary, otherwise why would Obama order 2, 700 tanks for riot control? This knowledge and the fourteen agenda items discussed in the previous chapter give us the ability to look into the future and predict with relative accuracy what we can expect in the next four years. Read the following quotes and reflect on them. They expose the future the financial elite plan for America. The question is how they will achieve their endgame?

"We shall have world government whether or not you like it. The only question is whether world government will be by conquest or consent" (James P. Warburg, representing the Rothschild Banking Concern while speaking before the United States Senate, Feb. 1, 1950).

"The New World Order will be built, an end run on national sovereignty, eroding it piece by piece will accomplish more than the old fashioned frontal assault" (Council on Foreign Relations journal 1975, p558).

Understanding the government's endgame. America must fall to birth the new world order!

The financial elite want to collapse the United States of America because an economically and militarily strong, Christian America stands in the way of the imposition of their long dreamed of demonically inspired one-world government, a government headed by what they describe as "a supernatural sovereignty (demonic sovereignty) of intellectual elite and world bankers" (self-important, power mongering money lenders committed to ending national sovereignty and imposing a totalitarian dictatorship). This is the agenda Obama is committed to birthing. He is their closer. To him comes the assignment to make America so indebted and its people so dependent on the government that they will willingly relinquish their freedom in exchange for the promise of peace, security, and food on the table.

The key phrase in the above paragraph is "willingly relinquish their freedom." It holds the key to understanding what the next four years forebodes. The financial elite don't want to push too far too fast because they are afraid that if they do, we just might rise up and foil their plans of world dominance. They would rather bury us in debt and then offer to step in and fix the very problems they created. I refer to it as a death of a thousand cuts where we bleed to death without even realizing it.

The final demise of America! During Obama's second term, we can expect the following agenda.

1. Agenda: An assault on our second amendment rights to bear arms because it is as George Washington said, "Firearms are second only in importance to the Constitution because they are the people's liberty teeth." Before the government imposes martial law and begins their genocide, they want to make sure we are disarmed and defenseless.

   Their initiatives:

   - Use the UN small arms treaty to circumvent Congress and our Second Amendment Rights to bear arms.
   - Take advantage of the unfortunate incidents of mass murder involving assault weapons, and blame the problem on guns, instead of the real issue, which is the moral decay of America brought about by violent video games, the government's attack on Christianity and family values, Hollywood's propensity for violence and moral depravity

and the divisive social justice and political correctness agendas espoused by the government and educational system.

I am formerly from Chicago, which has one of the toughest gun laws in the nation and also one of the highest murder rates. The problem isn't guns. It is our stressful, immoral society and the isolation created by the breakdown of morality and the nucleus family and the preference for electronic interface instead of human interaction. Dysfunctional, lonely, antisocial, depressed, angry people kill people. Guns are only the tool.

- Limit availability of ammunition through price increases or lack of availability.
- Eventual imposition of martial law and a dictatorship. The government has already passed all the necessary laws to legally impose martial law and incarcerate US citizens with no legal recourse and to deploy UN troops on US soil in order to put down civil disobedience, should it arise, but their preference is to take us over without firing a shot.

Countermeasures/Public response:

- A well-armed civilian population is essential to counter Obama's efforts to impose a million man domestic army that is reminiscent of Hitler's brownshirts, which terrorized the German population. Obama's million man domestic army is in effect a standing army, which our founding fathers warned us against.
- Get nonregistered guns and ammunition while you still can.

2. Agenda: Promote Racism And Religious Intolerance: So we are too busy fighting amongst ourselves and to divided to unite against our common enemy, our own government.

Their initiatives:

- The government will continue to use illegal immigration as a means to divide us.

- Look for Muslim President Obama to allow millions of Muslims into the country: just like has happened in several European countries. Then expect them to form a vocal minority (supported by Obama and the Left) and expect for them to push for imposition of Sharia Law under the guise of religious freedom whereas all the while, Christianity is stripped from our schools, our judicial system, our legislative system, and society at large. The intention is to make Obama's statement that "America is not a Christian nation" a reality! In order to collapse America, Christian morality must be obliterated from the public conscience! Obama's intention is to eventually impose Sharia Law and nullify the US Constitution!
- Washington will use the fairness doctrine to make it literally illegal to speak out against such policies.
- The government will continue to create social strife between what they call the rich millionaires and the middle class and the poor by pushing tax increases on the millionaires, despite the fact that their tax plan is estimated to generate only enough revenue to run the country for approximately one week. Conversely, their plan will severely limit the incentive for those entrepreneur millionaires to invest in job creation, which will hamper economic recovery and result in increased unemployment all of which is intended to make the majority of Americans dependent on the government as a control mechanism.

Countermeasures/Public response:

- We must recognize that Obama's redistribution of wealth is nothing but a plan to eliminate the middle class and create a two-class system. The real wealth is not in the hands of the so-called rich millionaires, the supposed upper class, which Obama is targeting. They are only convenient scapegoats. Taxing then is simply a diversionary tactic to take our attention off of the fact that they intend to tax the middle class out of existence. The truth is that 95 percent of

the world's wealth is controlled by 1 percent of the population—"the financial elite billionaires and trillionaires." If America and the world are to solve its financial woes, we must stop redistributing the money from "the supposed rich millionaires" and redistribute it from the financial elite billionaires and trillionaires who control the world's banking system, to the other 99 percent of us who labor under their oppression. In a subsequent chapter, I outline a detailed plan to do exactly that. As long as the financial elite control the world's money supply and credit, we are nothing more than their slaves, and intentionally created debt is their weapon of choice with which to control and enslave us.
- If we can come to see Obama's redistribution of wealth ploy for what it is—a plan to divide, impoverish and enslave us—then we can end much of the divisiveness, which his administration is using to keep us from uniting against "our real enemy our own government." It is time to take a stand!

3. Agenda: Access to health care will be rationed. Medical care will be focused primarily on those deemed to be most productive (forty years of age or less). Because in the soon to be instituted one-world government, we will all exist to serve the state, and when we can no longer serve that function, we no longer have any value. Obamacare will be one of the tools used to "purge society of those deemed to be nonproductive." *Can you say genocide!*

Their initiatives:

- Expect as many as 40–50 percent of medical professionals to leave the medical field.
- *Why*? Because once fully implemented, doctors will be utterly controlled by the government. Their salaries will be controlled, and there will be handheld devices in doctors' offices. When they diagnose your condition, they will be required to electronically submit a medical diagnosis code to a government office who will in turn tell the doctor the approved course of treatment. That treatment will often be

based on cost rather than efficacy. If the doctor fails to follow the government's designated treatment, he can be fined $100,000 for the first offense and actually go to jail for the subsequent offences. Would you work under such a totalitarian system?

- Obamacare is rationed medicine and legalized genocide. It is expected that Obamacare will add approximately thirty million people to the health-care system, and if at the same time upward of 50 percent of the doctors leave the medical field, how could it result in anything but rationed care? Additionally, treatment will be determined by what the government calls "comparative effectiveness," which is another way of saying *rationing*. The cost of care will be divided by the number of years the patient will benefit (their age) in order to determine if they can be treated. This is nothing short of genocide for the elderly who are deemed to be of no value to the state.
- Obamacare will not provide coverage for all Americans as promised. To the contrary, Obamacare will cause severe financial hardship for millions of American families. The big box retailers, such as Wal-Mart and the fast-food chains, such as McDonalds, will limit employment to twenty-nine hours per week in order to avoid having to provide workers health care coverage. The net effect will be that a large segment of Americans will not only, not get healthcare coverage but they will be forced to try to live on part time low paying jobs.

Countermeasures/Public Response:

- States are fighting implementation of Obamacare. Join the fight!
- Assume responsibility for your families medical treatment by stockpiling medical supplies and learning about alternative medical options.
- Be prepared to pay for medical treatment yourself and to go outside the country for treatment if necessary.

4. Agenda: America will become a nanny state, and the last vestiges of our two-party system will become irrelevant, as the majority of Americans become dependent on the government, because the government believes our dependency will assure our nonresistance to the takeover of America. Currently approximately 40 to 45 percent of Americans receive benefits from the government. As the dollar is devalued, as inflation increases, as taxes increase, and as unemployment skyrockets we can expect upwards of 75 percent of all Americans to receive payments of some sort from the government (e.g., unemployment, Social Security, government pension or paycheck, Medicare, Medicaid, welfare, food stamps, etc.) At that point, we will be at the mercy of big government. The Left will have taken over the last vestiges of our two-party system. By virtue of their entitlements, they will control the election process effectively neutralizing the last remaining vestiges of the two-party system!

Their initiatives:

- Expect a number of hidden taxes to be imposed on the middle class to the point that it will eventually back the middle class into a corner where even fully employed families will have to choose between paying taxes or feeding their families. In other words, we are witnessing the demise of the middle class and imposition of a permanent lower class, existing at or near the poverty level. We have already seen imposition of a new payroll tax and Obamacare has been determined to be a tax. Additionally, the EPA is being used to pass onerous regulations, which will continue to systematically make it impossible for the US to compete in the global market. The cost of these onerous regulations will be passed on to American consumers in the form of hidden carbon taxes and higher purchase prices as well as unemployment!
- Estate/inheritance taxes are to skyrocket with their current exemption levels going from $5.1 million to $1 mil-

lion with rates over $1 million being as high as 55 percent. This is nothing short of the immoral confiscation of assets as homes and businesses will have to be sold to pay these obscene taxes. By the way, one of the planks of communism is to end private property and the transference of wealth from one generation to the next is one way to achieve that goal.

- Energy and food prices will soar due in part to inflation and in part to price fixing. Food and gasoline are weapons, which are very effective in controlling the population and the government will not refrain from manipulating both cost and availability as a control mechanism. Once Syria and Saudi Arabia are toppled expect gas to sky rock, going to $6 or more per gallon.
- College students will graduate from school with massive student loans and will not be able to find jobs, so the government will be in a position to control them by virtue of their dependency on the government!
- Taxes will be increased but spending and entitlements will not be cut because the financial elite learned from the recent demonstrations and riots in the Middle East, and Greece as well as the union agitation in Wisconsin that if they take away entitlement too soon, it can lead to violence in the streets. In the instance of an armed America, it could thwart their plans for a voluntary relinquishing of our rights to a government we have become dependent on for literally everything.
- There will be no attempt to balance the budget because our current debt is so great that it is impossible. We borrow 46 cents of every dollar we spend. The 2013 US budget is $3.8 trillion but we only collect $2.5 trillion, leaving a shortfall of approximately $1.3 trillion. Coincidentally, that is almost exactly the amount required to operate the federal government, so even if we shut down the government, we still couldn't balance the budget. The government won't cut

entitlements because they know it would cause social disobedience, which could threaten their plans to take us over from within by consent rather than by force. So you can see that by design, our national debt will continue to climb till it implodes in on us. As of 2014, our national debt is $17 trillion, and by 2022, it is projected to be $22 trillion, which is unsustainable.

Note: For the first time in US history, the US has lost its AAA rating. We can expect that once they have forced us into the one-world government that not only will entitlements be drastically cut but millions will be incarcerated, executed, and starved to death in order to achieve the goals of the UN's Agenda 21. Remember the government and their co-conspirator banks and corporations control access to all the necessities of life. They will control our access to food, water, energy, health care, and literally all of the necessities of life, either by legislative measures, by pricing us out of markets or by artificially controlling availability.

Countermeasures/Public response:

- Our only political hope lies at the local and state level, and in the pages of this book, I provide a detailed plan for how we use the very strategies, which have been used against us to restore our Constitutional liberties.
- Be as self sufficient as possible! In subsequent chapter, I provide recommendations for how to limit your dependency on the government. It will require a shift in mindset back to the rugged individualism and self-sufficiency of our Founding Fathers.

5. Agenda: Collapse the dollar because it will cause such chaos that we can be expected to willingly relinquish national sovereignty in exchange for financial stability and false security.

Death of the dollar: The truth about fiat money and the US dollar. In 1971, President Nixon took the US off the gold standard, making the "dollar fiat currency" backed by nothing!

- History shows that FIAT money (money back by nothing) has a 100 percent failure rate, ending most frequently in hyperinflation which utterly destroys the value of the currency!
- The US has run a budget deficit every year since 1971, when we went off the gold standard.
- As of 2014, the national debt is $17 trillion.
- The US owes more money than all the rest of the nations of the world combined.
- One hundred ninety-two nations have meet to make plans to go off the US dollar as the world's reserve currency, which will result in

    - ✓ the US becoming a third world economy
    - ✓ repeal of the US's license to print "counterfeit fiat money"
    - ✓ currently, we borrow 46 cents of every dollar we spend. Our credit will be abruptly ended, resulting in the wholesale demise of government entitlements and social chaos on an unparalleled level. That is why Russian troops are conducting crowd control exercises on US soil.
    - ✓ consumer spending, which is 70 percent of GDP will come to a screeching halt, resulting in unemployment levels of 50 percent or more
- Over night, all paper assets will be worthless. That means your stocks, your bonds, your 401K, your pension, your life insurance, all your paper assets will become worthless, and since the value of your home is tied to paper through the credit market, your home will be worth substantially less as well. With no jobs and their wealth destroyed, virtually, all those with mortgages will lose their homes. The current

stock market and real estate resurgence will be short lived! We are at the end of the fiat currency road. Those who are caught in paper assets will lose everything they have. When the end comes, there will be no warning. The world as we know it will change virtually over night and it will never be the same again. Knowing this and acting on it could save your life.

This will not be a typical recession. It will be an order of magnitude worse than the Great Depression! America will be forever transformed, and it will take decades to recover, but it will never reclaim its status as the world's leading economy. Both rich and poor will be starving in America!

Are you ready to face the reality of an economically destitute America?

Their initiatives:

- Unbridled spending will kill the dollar. It will cease to be the world's reserve currency: This means nations around the world will no longer be required to buy dollars in order to transact international commodity transactions. The outcome will be that Obama's unbridled spending will bring about hyperinflation and the demise of the dollar!
- Why would the nations of the world want to abandon the US dollar as the world's reserve currency? The answer is quite simple. The US has more debt than all the other nations of the world combined. That means that our unbridled printing of dollars is devaluing the US dollar, but it also negatively affects their economy, making us a monetary pariah.

  Note: Because of the size of the US debt bubble when the dollar finally collapses—and it will—what is happening in Europe and in countries, such as Italy, Greece, France, and Ireland, will be nothing compared to what will happen in America. America will experience hyperinflation on the order of magnitude of what happened in the Weimar

Republic of Germany following WWI. Our currency will be destroyed along with all paper assets (e.g., your insurance policies, your IRAs, your 401Ks, your mutual funds and annuities, your bonds, all paper assets destroyed. History can and does repeat itself when circumstances repeat themselves. Those under the age of fifty can expect to never see their pensions and that goes for Social Security as well.

- Is there evidence that the dollar will cease to be the world's reserve currency? *Absolutely!*

  a. The BRICKS coalition comprised of Brazil, Russia, India, China, and South Africa have agreed to trade amongst themselves using the Chinese currency not the US dollar. They comprise 18 percent of global GDP, 43 percent of the world's population, and 53 percent of the world's wealth.
  b. February 2012: China (the world's second largest economy) and Japan (the world's third largest economy) agreed to buy and sell with each other using other than US currency.
  c. April 27, 2012: China signed an agreement to buy crude oil from Iran with payment to be in gold.
  d. March 2012: India signed an agreement to buy crude oil from Iran with payment to be in gold.
  e. Saudi Arabia, the largest supplier of oil to the US, agreed to build a refinery in China and sell China crude oil using their currency.
  f. Germany, Africa, and the Bank of Africa all agreed to trade using the Chinese currency.

- Debt limit will be suspended, making way for unbridled spending, leading to hyperinflation and the utter demise of the dollar. Source interview with Pastor Lindsey Williams on *Alex Jones*.

Note: This always happens when a currency goes into its death spiral!

Countermeasures/Public response:

More detailed solutions are offered elsewhere in this book, but for now, suffice it to say:

- Hedge your risk by diversifying your investments in order to protect you from abrupt market changes that do not give you time to react.
- Consider getting out of paper assets in favor of tangible assets, such as gold, silver, food, medical supplies, farmland, barter items, etc. India and China are buying oil with gold. The financial elite are also buying gold and silver. Draw your own conclusions.
- If you have appreciable paper assets, find a financial advisor who is aware of the impending tipping point of the world financial system and can advise you from that perspective rather than from the perspective of the Wall Street bandits.

6. Agenda: Expect there to be a second housing collapse. The intent will be for the banks to own all mortgaged property. That is one of the agenda items of both the UN's Agenda 21 and the Communist Manifesto. More on this later.

Their initiatives:

- Reduce our purchasing power to literally nothing. The combination of tax increases, unemployment, underemployment, devaluation of the dollar, and inflation will force people into a situation where even working families will fall behind on their mortgages and millions more Americans will lose their homes to foreclosure as they are forced to either put food on the table or pay their mortgage.
- End private ownership of real estate by buying all mortgages and then forcing mass defaults, leaving the banks owning literally all real estate in the country (e.g., residential real estate, commercial real estate, businesses secured by real estate and pastors, even your churches). Here is how they will do it. On Sept. 13, 2012, Fed Chairman Bernanke

announced that for an indefinite period of time it will be purchasing $40 billion per month in mortgage backed assets. Why would they do that?

- Historically, 80 to 90 percent of US treasury notes (used to pay our national debt) are purchased by investors. Because the nations of the world are systematically going off the US dollar as the world's reserve currency they are shunning the purchase of US T-Bills, resulting in a situation where 80 to 90 percent of the T-Bills are now being bought back by the Fed in a classic money kiting scheme. This cannot go on indefinitely because it would cause the US government to default on our national debt and the dollar would have an immediate collapse. The financial elite want the dollar to die a slow death over the next couple of years making sure that in the process we are driven into such desperation that we will agree to accept their new currency and their one-world government in exchange for the false promise of peace and security.

Countermeasures/Public response:

- If at all possible, pay your home off, so you have a roof over your head.

  Note: You also have to make provision to pay your property taxes or the government will take your paid for property in a tax sale.
- Spend your money now while it still has purchasing value. Use it to buy tangibles (e.g., food, barter items, and other necessity items), which you will need to survive when the financial system collapses. This may free up the money to pay your mortgage and or property taxes so you don't lose your home.
- Consider buying some gold and or silver because it will be a medium of exchange when the dollar becomes worthless.

  Note: If you do buy gold or silver, I do not recommend putting it in a safety deposit box because in 1933, the government declared a bank holiday and riffled all the safety deposit boxes and confiscated the gold. Look for it to happen again!

Silver historically trades at eighteen to one to gold, and currently, that ratio is in favor of purchasing silver over gold. Also, if you purchase US minted gold or silver coins, you have a good chance of using them as legal tender when the dollar will no longer be accepted.

7. Agenda: Simultaneously collapse all of the world's currencies creating global debt crisis of such magnitude that the people of the world will gladly give up their liberty and national sovereignty and accept rule by the New World Order in exchange for their promise to issue a new world currency (backed by gold and silver and probably oil) and the promise of the UN to restore social order.

Their initiatives:

- Collapse the quadrillion dollar "derivatives market" as the means to collapse all the world currencies simultaneously thus creating total global chaos.
- How? The largest banks in the country, owned by the Fed and World Bank, will take the $40 billion (the Fed created out of thin air) to buy mortgage backed securities (your mortgage) and use the leverage of the fractional banking system to invest that money in the (highly speculative derivatives market), and then take their enormous profits and use then to buy US T-Bills so they can be sure that the interest on the national debt is paid till such time that they choose to collapse the currency market which they will most likely do by increasing interest rates which automatically increases the debt service on the national debt.

Countermeasures/Public response:

- Obviously, before this happens, you want to be out of paper because it will instantaneously be worthless.

Note: One of the strategies often used to hedge against devaluation of a given currency is to invest in other currencies. Though that might insulate you against a failing dollar, in the short run, when the elite collapse the derivatives market, *all currencies will collapse*, so in the long run, you should be out of all paper assets including foreign currencies.

It is also worth mentioning that countries can make their products more competitive in global markets by manipulating the exchange rate. That is why we have a world reserve currency—to stabilize the currency market and limit speculation. With the US ceasing to be the world's reserve currency and with the formation of various trade agreements, we can expect currency/trade wars, which will cause volatility in the currency markets.

- When the currencies of the world fall, all trucks will cease to move products, and services will likewise be suspended till such time that a new currency is instituted, so you better have enough food and other necessities on hand to last you at least six months.

8. Agenda: Expect World War III as the direct result of the power vacuum caused by a militarily weak US because the uneasy alliances between the Anglo-Saxon financial elite, communist super powers, chiefly Russia and China and the Islamic nations, will collapse once they have destroyed their common enemy, the US, and they will turn on one another, and all hell will break loose.

Their initiatives:

- Once the US has been collapsed we can expect the various factions to turn on one another resulting in WWIII.
- The Anglo-Saxon financial elite (Monarchs of Europe) came to dominate the banking system as the result of their control of trade during the colonial era. They believe they are in control of the world's financial system and will be successful in ushering in a super capitalist/communist one-world government. They have used China as a tool to once

again institute the "colonial free trade slavery system" in order to control world trade, and in particular, to collapse the American economy.

Note: Now, China sees themselves as a world power in their own right, and they may not be able to be controlled.

- Don't discount Russia as a threat. They have been somewhat left out in the cold as they have not enjoyed the financial benefits, which China has. The Bible tells us to "beware of the sleeping bear," which is Russia. With an ambitious Putin in power and with America militarily and economically weakened and with Muslim Obama, saying, "After the election, I could be flexible," Putin may decide that the time is right for Russia to move on the Middle East oil fields as a way to leverage his power.
- The Muslims hate the Christians, and in particular, America and Rome because the Catholic church was responsible for the crusades (a holy war, which lasted two hundred years and utterly destroyed the Islamic empire). Now, America has attempted to control the Middle East oil reserves for more than sixty years and that along with our support of Israel have made us their mortal enemies.
- The wild card in all this is Obama who was put into the presidency by the financial elite, but has betrayed them in favor of his Muslim Heritage. He is therefore in a position to make sure that America's military strength is curtailed, creating the power vacuum, which will invite WWIII. The question is what will the financial elite do to a US President who betrayed them? Kennedy passed Executive Order 11110, ordering the disbandment of the Federal Reserve controlled by the financial elite, and he was assassinated. Will they likewise attempt to assassinate Obama,? No man knows exactly what will happen, but one thing is for sure, a power vacuum is emerging, which will invite old enemies to try to grab power and settle old scores, and if we believe we are in the end times and if we believe in the Bible, then it seems likely that the situation is right for WWIII.

- Expect Syria and Saudi Arabia to be toppled. Thanks to Obama, the US stood on the sidelines while one nation after another came under control of the Muslim brotherhood, and it is just a matter of time till the entire region is under their control.

  Note: Saudi Arabia is the US's largest oil supplier, and Obama has done everything he could to make the US dependent of Middle East Muslim oil supplies, so when Saudi Arabia falls, expect gas prices to go through the roof, causing severe economic ramifications to an already weak US economy. That is exactly what Muslim Obama wants.
- Don't expect the US to invade Iran. I am not a US diplomat, so what I am about to say is based on my analysis rather than insider information. When the US told Iran they were placing sanction on the sale of Iranian oil, what happened? India and China did not support the US. Instead, they told Iran they would not only buy their oil, but they would pay them in gold. Additionally, despite anything Obama may say to the contrary, I believe he intends to leave Israel out in the cold. In my opinion, the net result will therefore be a nuclear Iran and a very volatile situation in the Middle East, which is again exactly what Muslim Obama wants. Most recently we signed a deal with Iran to give them money and to allow them to continue to enrich uranium, just not to weapons level. Bunk! They will have the bomb and when they get the chance they will use it against both Israel and the US. Think about this! They certainly won't have a nuclear arsenal like Russia, but they could bring down the US with just a couple of bombs set off in the atmosphere which would fry all electronics, which means no transportation, no communication absolutely nothing would work. The US would be in the stone age in the flash of a bomb. What a perfect scenarios for a land invasion say by China or Russia and America is wiped off the global chessboard.

* * *

Open your eyes or suffer the consequences! If you hope to survive what is coming, you will have to stop being in denial with your head in the sand like an ostrich and see our government leaders for the traitors they are. You will likewise have to stop listening to the media propaganda. You will have to get informed and take the necessary steps to get prepared. Your survival will require a "complete change of mindset." The global financial system is on the brink of collapse, and when it happens, all paper assets will be worthless. If you know what to do, you cannot only survive, but when the dust settles, you might be wealthier than you were before the crash, but if you are not prepared, you will probably lose all your material assets, and you may starve to death. I am not trying to be melodramatic or an alarmist. I am simply trying to get you to face the facts, frightening though they are. In the pages of this book is the information you need to know. God has prepared me for the last forty years so that when this time comes, I could help those with eyes to see and ears to hear. Are you one of those people?

High treason! Our political leaders, controlled by the shadow government call for subversive measures, to convert the US from a sovereign constitutional republic, into a servile member of a one-world dictatorship!

How could this be considered anything but *treason*? Is Obama the next furor?

A warning from God To America—Wrong way, go back!

- If you think America can't fall, you are wrong! Like all the great empires of the past, America will fall, and when it does, chaos and tyranny will follow. That time is fast approaching, and will overcome us, if we don't wake up and change our ways and fight back against the forces of evil!
- If you think your wealth can protect you, you are wrong! It can and will be taken from you in the blinking of an eye!
- If you think the Book Of Revelation is fiction, you are wrong! God cannot lie. All of its horrors are very real, and they will befall a wicked world consumed by materialism!

- If you think you are powerless, you are wrong! God has imparted to me, and I have put in the pages of this book all you need to know to allow you to put on the full armor of God and be victorious over the forces of evil that would as President Kennedy said, "Enslave Us all!"

Will you stand up and be counted? Will you fight for freedom and "The American Way of Life", or will you willing submit to the forces of evil? Will you take the "Mark of The Beast" & surrender your soul, or "Will You Persevere To The End And Inherit The Promised Land?" Will you let your children be sold into slavery? ***It Is Time To Choose:***

Fight For Freedom Or Surrender & Be Enslaved

The "false god of materialism" is about to be sacrificed on the "altar of greed." Those who continue to worship him will become the "tares," which are burnt in the eternal fire. Those who turn their backs on our "material world" will become the "wheat," which God will lovingly preserve and whose name he will put in the "Book of Life." Our greatest hope for the future lies in returning to the godly principles, which made America the greatest nation the world has ever known! Please join me on this journey of discovery and enlightenment by allowing God to open your eyes to the deception which has been wrought on an unsuspecting world. I promise you we can change the world for the better, and in the process, we will find the meaning of true happiness!

That, my friends, is change you can believe in!

PREPARING FOR MARTIAL LAW

Police State: America's New Way Of Life!

US military deployed against US citizens and freedom of speech threatened: Repeal of Posse Comitatus allows deployment of US military to police US citizens on US soil & HR 1955 *"Violent Radicalization & Homegrown Terrorist Prevention Act"*:if passed *will* ***classify dissenters as terrorist!***

What we are talking about here is ***"Imposition of a Standing Army."*** Couple that with the government's efforts to disarm us and keep us from exercising our Constitutional right of freedom of speech and the outcome can only be open dictatorship. Wake up before it is too late!

"A standing army is the greatest mischief that can possibly happen." (James Madison Founding Father)

Then all we need is the right crisis and we are ripe for imposition of martial law and open dictatorship and here it is. *Executive Order 51:* ***Grants the President authority to declare an undefined national***

emergency & impose martial law without the approval of Congress! Grants President the power to assume; all national essential functions for continuity of government including directing all federal, state, local & tribal governments as well as private sector organizations! Executive Order 11921: states that: "...when a state of emergency is declared by the President, *Congress cannot review the action for six months.*"By then the US will be a dictatorship.

Camp FEMA: Dissidents Welcome!

Ask yourself why our government is building internment camps if not to incarcerate dissenters and those deemed to be nonproductive? "KBR has been awarded a contract announced by the Department of Homeland Security's [ICE] component. The indefinite delivery/ indefinite quantity contingency contract is to support ICE facilities and has a maximum total value of $385 million over a five year term. The project provides for establishing temporary detention and processing capabilities in the event of an emergency influx of immigrants into the United States or to support the rapid development of new programs." [Alex Jones] **Bunk! They are concentration camps pure and simple.** Wake up! We have never needed these kinds of facilities before, so why do we need them now? What do you think? What other explanation could there be?

Uncle Sam wants you dead! Internment camps, starvation and death await! Your government is afraid of you and what it is afraid of must either die or be incarcerated, after all, "Power comes from the barrel of a gun," or so the Obama administration says! The government is building internment camps for activist, dissidents, the intellectuals, the poor, the elderly, and the unemployed, those on welfare, anyone who is either too old or too sick to work, doesn't possess the desired skills, or might take a stand against them. Those on the endangered species list also include the Christians. They are a particularly big threat because they might actually fight back. And we mustn't forget the *veterans*! The government is so afraid of them that they have labeled them "terrorists." And last but not least, we don't want to forget the gun owners. They are the biggest threat of all! The internment camps are not for refugees.

In addition to the FEMA camps there are storage sites for millions of FEMA coffins: What are they for? They are for your mothers, fathers, sisters and brothers, for any of us who will not submit to the government. The US is on the brink of financial collapse and the day of government hand outs is about to come to an abrupt end. When that day comes, and it will, **anyone who cannot produce more than he consumes will be eliminated pure and simple.** Additionally anyone who the government suspects might stand up against them will also be incarcerated or killed. That is Communism and that is what is coming to America and the rest of the world! Consider the following quote.

"A part of eugenic politics would finally land us in an extensive use of the lethal chamber. **A great many people would have to be put out of existence** simply because it wastes other people's time to look after them." (George Bernard Shaw, Lecture to the Eugenics Education Society, Reported in The Daily Express, March 4, 1910.) California recently started rounding up homeless and giving then a choice prison or FEMA Camps. (Source Prison Planet Alex Jones) Who will be next?

It takes a lot of coffins to get rid of six billion people which is ultimately what the New World Order's utopian extermination plan call for. Alex Jones host of "Infowars" and former Minnesota Governor Jesse Ventura host of the TV Show "Conspiracy Theories" filmed not only the coffin storage sites, but also the long rumored FEMA detention centers. Google it for yourself. If you do Google it pay attention to the barbwire fencing around the compounds. The barb wire faces in, not out as you would expect. *"These are not harmless resettlement facilities. They are prison camps."*

As if that wasn't enough there have been numerous documented sittings of truck and train convoys on U.S. soil loaded with UN assault vehicles. From a military perspective you always stockpile equipment prior to any military engagement. They hope to take over the US through **"Consent",** but just in case some of us prove to have a backbone they need a military solution as well. That is where the UN comes in. The UN, The organization who wrote "Agenda 21" the document dedicated to ending the ownership of private property and exterminating the majority of us!

So armed with these insights what is the likely takeover scenario of the New World Order? I believe the endgame will materialize something like this. With the US and the entire Free Market System teetering on the brink of economic collapse the government will create an event [financial or otherwise] resulting in economic chaos. It could be something as simple as the Fed raising the interest rates or it could be another 9/11 etc. The intent will be to create an economic collapse which will create chaos causing riots to break out all across America. This will give the government the excuse to declare martial law and they will bring in UN/NATO troops to quell the riots and ***"they will remain as an army of occupation!"***

Meanwhile the President will have six months in which to consolidate the occupation and lock us down so that the Dictatorship of the New World Order can be birthed. The United States will cease to be a sovereign nation. We will be absorbed into the nations of the NATO alliance most ostensibly the EU, our military will be merged with that of NATO and we will be ruled by the UN which is the seat of power from which the Antichrist will rule. **America will be a nation no more.** We will be taken into bondage just as the Israelites before us.

Then in the throes of a *"global monetary collapse"* the world will descend into chaos and the financial elite who caused the crisis in the first place will step in and offer economic assistance if the world will consent to their authority. Any nation who refuses their generous offer will, as they said in the movie the "God Father," be given an offer they can't refuse. Comply or suffer the wrath of our economic and military might.

You have just read the perfect plan for birthing the New World Order a Super Capitalist/Communist one-world dictatorship.

This is the last call for freedom! Stand up now and take America back or live in slavery! There you have it! The endgame has been spelled out for you. You now know why the government wants to collapse the US and you have a pretty good idea as to how they are going about executing their plan. The balance of this chapter will elaborate in more detail on some of the key components of their strategy, particularly Agenda 21 and HAARP which were alluded to without detailed explanations. By the time you finish this chapter you will know the facts concerning the government's plan to collapse America and enslave us.

Make no mistake they intent is to:

- Have an army of occupation in America
- Implant RFID chips in order to utterly control us
- Systematically incarcerate and kill those of us they deem dangerous or unable to produce more than we consume like for example the homeless in California.

By the time you finish this book all your questions will be answered. Your eyes will be opened to the truth. The only questions that will remain will be:

- Will you consent to your slavery and that of your children? or
- Will you stand up and fight for liberty and freedom and Godly principles?

- Will you surrender to God and renounce the False God of Materialism?
- Will you hold on to the illusion that the human race can continue to proliferate and consume natural resources at the expense of the very planet that sustains us?

Agenda 21: The UN's plan to commit genocide by reducing the global population from seven billion to one billion. Agenda 21 calls for severe restrictions on resource consumption (collapse of the free market system), an end to national sovereignty (the demise of the US and every sovereign nation in the world), abandonment of the US and other Constitutions, presumption of guilt till proven innocent (no inalienable rights), abolition of private property, education focused first and foremost on environment, restructure of the family unit, education to create allegiance to the state, limitations on mobility with upwards of 75 percent of the land off limits, limitation on education and carrier opportunities with state control of access to higher education and employment opportunities, lack of privacy with state owned residential units along rail corridors. This is the Brave New World of the future, the future not just of America, but of the entire world.

Will you say slavery? Will you say treason? Will you say genocide? Will you say no? By the way, most of these things are already in effect in China, the country our leaders seem to admire so much, where if you have enough money, you can buy organs harvested from live political prisoners. This and more is coming to America and the rest of the world!

Reader's perspective: Wait just a minute. From what you have said, so far these people you call "the financial elite" pretty much run the world as it is, so why would they want or need to impose such a diabolical scheme?

Me: You have no drought heard the saying "Power corrupts and absolute power corrupts absolutely." Well, it applies here. According to documentary film producer Aaron Russo and personal friend of Nick Rockefeller, the endgame is to put Radio-frequency identification chips (RFID) in every person on the planet. This of course is the "mark of the beast" referred to in the Bible. It would track our location, and without, it we couldn't buy, sell, travel, get medical care, or literally anything. Excerpt from interview of Russo on *Alex Jones Show*: At one point, Russo asks Rockefeller, "What's the point of all this? You have all the money in the world, all the power you need. What's the point? What's the end goal?" Rockefeller responded, "The end goal is to get everybody chipped (referring to RFID chips) to control the whole society to have the banks and the elite people and some government controlling the whole world." *Will you say absolute slavery? Will you say no?*

Now, let's go to a quote from David Rockefeller for some more of their endgame strategy. " "Some even believe we are part of a secret cabal working against the best interest of the United States, characterizing my family and me as 'internationalist' and conspiring with others around the world to build a more integrated global political and economic structure – one world, if you will. If that's their charge, I stand guilty and I am proud of it" (David Rockefeller, *Memoirs*).

Me: Oh boy, I get chills from this quote. It sounds all noble and humanitarian; that is till you read the next two quotes. Then you realize that in order for Rockefeller to achieve "his more integrated society," billions of us useful idiots as Mao called the peasants of China must die!

Listen to what Noble-sounding David Rockefeller had to say about the tyrant Mao. "Whatever the cost of the Chinese Revolution, it has obviously succeeded not only in producing more efficient administration, but also in fostering high morale and community of purpose. The social experiment in China under Chairman Mao's leadership is one of the most important and successful in history" (David Rockefeller, *New York Times*).

Mao: Yes, I do deserve to be praised for my bold action. I killed over sixty million of my own people in order to realize my dream of reforming China. (A fact, not a quote). Now, Rockefeller and his motley crew of financial elite want to kill six billion of us to realize their dream of a "more integrated global political and economic structure." *Diabolical*, that is all I can say!

Will you stand up and fight or will you allow your children to either be killed or live a life of servitude?

Me: Gee, I wonder what the Obama administration thinks of Mao. Oh yes, I know. There is an interesting quote from manufacturing czar, Ron Bloom, "We know that the free market is nonsense. We kind of agree with Mao that political power comes largely from the barrel of a gun."

Reader's perspective: I know that there are power crazy narcissistic people in this world, like Hitler, Mao, Lenin, Stalin, and Napoleon, but none of them even came close to reeking the kind of carnage you are talking about. This whole Agenda 21 thing seems like science fiction. Is there more to it than just an insane quest for power?

Me: Matter of fact, there is more to it than just a quest for power. First of all, this is the biblical tribulation of which God says. There never has or never will be a time such as this upon the earth. So from a biblical perspective, this is the time of the harvest, "the time of testing" when the righteous (the wheat), shall be separated from the sinners (the tares). God also tells us that many shall be called but few will be chosen and the road to salvation is narrow but the road to perdition is broad. We all have to be tested to see who is righteous and who is not, who will prevail to the end and who will not, who will serve God and who will serve the devil and the false god of materialism. To this end, evil must be loosed upon the earth to test us all.

Reader's perspective: Okay, I hear you. That spiritual stuff is all well and good, but is there a logical reason that can help me understand and accept that the kind of evil you are referring to really exist and the elite really do plan on killing six billion of us and enslave the rest of us?

Me: Actually, there is a very real and plausible explanation, and like everything in the world, it has its origins in the Bible. The Bible tells us that just prior to the tribulation, knowledge shall increase greatly. So, I guess you are wondering what that has to do with the plan to kill six billion of us. The answer is everything, absolutely everything!

Here is your answer: It took ten thousand generations for the world's population to reach two billion, and now, thanks to modern medicine and agriculture (knowledge), in the span of one generation, it has exploded to seven billion, and by the next generation, it is expected to be upward of thirty billion. The bottom line is the planet can't handle the population explosion and "overpopulation is the direct cause of what scientist are calling the planet's sixth mass extension." The financial elite are acting out of self-preservation. So that they can live we must die! It is that simple. So they can have more, we must have less. It is a story as old as empire, as old as time, as old as greed, as old as *Lucifer*! From their vantage point high above us, the financial elite look down on us peasants and decree that there simply are not enough marbles to go around (natural resources). so most of us must die and the rest must live in poverty as their indentures slaves. Is that logical enough for you? Simply put the herd must be culled and reduced to a manageable level.

The UN knows everything I have just told you. That is why they wrote Agenda 21, which stands for agenda for the twenty-first century. And rather than tell us the truth and try to solve the problem together, they have chosen to take actions in their own hands and just "*cull the herd*!" (Kill six billion of us useful idiots!)

After all, when viewed from their "elitist's point of view, we are just chattel" (personal property like cattle, goats, etc.). We are nothing more than "collateral damage" in their march toward their utopian one-world government where the few of us who are allowed to live will exist to serve our masters, our overlords, who long ago sold their souls for power, and as they say, "Power corrupts and absolute power corrupts absolutely."

If you still doubt that the elite would kill billions of us, consider these heartwarming quotes.

Henry Kissinger, who was secretary of state under Richard Nixon, said, "Depopulation Should be the highest priority of foreign policy toward the third world." Psychologist Barbara Marx Hubbard, member and futurist/strategist of Task Force Delta, a United States Army think tank said, "One-fourth of humanity must be eliminated from the social body. We are in charge of God's selection process for planet earth. He selects, we destroy. We are the riders of the pale horse, death."

"In the event that I am reincarnated, I would like to return as a deadly virus. In order to contribute something to solve overpopulation" (Prince Philip, reported by Deutsche Presse-Agentur [DPA], August 1988).

John Holdren – Obama's Science Czar Advocates: A planetary regime' to usher in one-world government!

- A "Planetary Regime" to control the global economy and dictate by force the number of children allowed to be born.
- We need to surrender "National Sovereignty" to an armed international police force.
- Mass sterilization of humans through drugs as long as it doesn't harm livestock.

- Single mothers should have their babies taken away by the government or they could be forced to have abortions.
- As of 1977 we are facing a global overpopulation catastrophe that must be resolved at all costs.

I am glad he Obama and Holdren are on our side! Har, Har! If you doubt what I say, it is all in his 1977 book *Ecoscience*.

You know this reminds me of Hitler's "eugenics program" intended to create the master race. We all know how that turned out. Wait, this reminds me of something else too. I got it. The book *Brave New World* by Aldous Huxley. Hollywood turned it into a movie, starring Leonard Nimoy of Star Trek fame. Interestingly, when interviewed about the book that was assumed to just be so much science fiction fantasy, Huxley indicated it was based on the Utopian plan of what I call the financial elite. When viewed as nonfiction, it is scarier than any horror movie ever made. The premise is that there has been a cultural revolution and the world is now controlled by a consortium of banks and corporations, (The New World Order) and all babies are (test tube babies) genetically altered to produce a dim-witted worker class, an intelligent, but docile administrative class and of course a genetically superior ruling class. The family is obsolete as all children are raised by the state for the benefit of the state, kind of like how we raise cattle. The prime directives are to consume and to indulge yourself in any form of pleasure you desire. This is the world your children and grandchildren will inherit, if this generation doesn't stand up and take control from these power crazy mad men!

In a sick and perverted sense of humor, the elite take pleasure in telling us in advance what they intend to do to us before they do it. Then, they sit back and laugh at how stupid we are that we couldn't see what was right before our eyes.

They create crisis after crisis in order to get us to accept things we would not otherwise accept. Oh, speaking of foreknowledge, I have another of those oh-so-convenient coincidences coupled with their propensity to tell us what they intend to do before they do it. It has to do with Hurricane Katrina and the fact that two weeks before Katrina hit New Orleans with such devastation, Hollywood released a movie entitled *Oil Storm*. It just so happens that the movie depicted a hurricane hitting, of all places, New Orleans and affecting oil platforms and pipelines. Go Figure.

Reader's perspective: What does a natural disaster and a Hollywood movie have to do with our government, imposing martial law?

Me: More than you would think. We have already established that our government has put in place all the necessary legislation to allow them to legally declare martial law with the potential of imposition of a dictatorship, but they need an excuse. They need a disaster that can't be blamed on them. They need a natural disaster, which makes then look like good guys coming to our rescue rather than an occupation force. They need an excuse that would allow them to bring in NATO troops instead of or in addition to US troops. US troops are not knowingly going to participate in a coup against the American people, but NATO troops report to the UN who just happens to be the very organization dedicated to collapsing the US and imposing a one-world government. The UN just happens to be the organization committed to reducing the global population to one billion by any means necessary. NATO is therefore crucial to any plans to impose martial law and morph the US into a dictatorship.

Reader's perspective: I still don't get the connection. Where are you going with this?

Me: What if the government caused Hurricane Katrina as a training exercise and to lay the foundation for an oil shortage at some point in the future? An industrialized society simply cannot function without oil. Thanks to Katrina and the BP oil spill, Obama stopped all oil exploration in the gulf. Though not related to Katrina, he also vetoed the Keystone Pipeline and prevented oil exploration on federal land out west. So thanks to Obama, we are dangerously dependent on foreign oil from Middle East countries that hate us. The perfect scenario or an all too convenient crisis at some time in the future.

Reader's perspective: Do you have any idea how crazy that sounds? First of all, hurricanes are natural disasters so there is no way the government or anyone in Hollywood could have known beforehand that Katrina was going to hit New Orleans. Do you even know how crazy that sounds?

Me: Don't be so sure. You are about to take a trip through the twilight zone where science fiction becomes reality. It turns out that the US government has a weapon called HAARP, which is capable of causing hurricanes among other things. So you see, Hurricane Katrina could well have been a man-made disaster, not a natural disaster!

HAARP Facility In Alaska Used To Weaponize Weather

HAARP is possibly the most dangerous weapon ever known, because it simulates natural disasters and as such has total deniability! You pick a natural disaster and whatever it is our government can cause it: Hurricanes **[Done]** Droughts **[Done]** Floods, **[Done]** Earthquakes, **[Done]** Volcanic Eruptions **[Done].**

HAARP stands for High Frequency Active Aural Research Project. It utilizes an array of microwave antenna to achieve a variety of functions. Essentially, what it does is super heat the upper atmosphere, causing a bubble of super heated energy that can be projected at a desired target, at a desired frequency, to achieve a desired objective. It can affect weather patterns, creating hurricanes, floods, and droughts on demand. It can also cause earthquakes, tidal waves, and volcanic eruptions. HAARP is the perfect weapon because it can be used to create crisis after crisis with perfect deniability, because it cannot be proven that events such as hurricanes, floods, droughts, and earthquakes were anything other than natural events. It is the perfect weapon to use to create chaos and create a situation where martial law can be imposed without reprisals from the public, because they see the troops as coming to their aid rather than locking them down.

Reader's perspective: If you expect me to buy into this flight of fantasy of yours, you are going to have to prove to me that our government actually has the capabilities you are claiming.

Me: My pleasure, but you know that when you are dealing with top secret government facilities, finding a smoking gun is pretty difficult. Wait. I think I have something that might convince you. Consider this:

Government admits HAARP is a weapon! It can cause hurricanes, earthquakes, volcanic eruptions and climate change! At a (DOD News Brief April 27, 1977) Secretary of Defense William Cohen (Clinton Administration) @ the University of Georgia sited the *existence of: weapons systems utilizing Electro Magnetic Energy* for targeting earthquakes, volcanic eruptions and climatic alterations.

Cohen sites 1977 Treaty: US ratified treaty agreeing not to use environmental manipulation as a ***weapon of war*** to create earthquakes, tidal waves, and volcanic eruptions or to disturb the weather across national borders. The treaty doesn't say anything about using HAARP within the US.

Me: How is that for proof? To me, it as good as a confession. So what do you say to that? It kind of makes me wonder about all the droughts, floods, tornados, and hurricanes we have had recently, which have increased in both frequency and intensity. They have cost the nation billions if not, trillions. When you are trying to economically collapse a nation as great as the US, you have to come at them from every conceivable angle, entitlements, trade deficits, and yes, man-made disasters disguised as natural disasters.

I want to go back to my comment about the BP oil spill in the gulf. It is just chocked full of those oh-so-convenient coincidences. What I am about to tell you is from a TV series entitled *Conspiracy Theories* hosted by former wrestler and Minnesota governor, Jessie Ventura. I am going from memory here so I don't remember the names of all the companies involved, but the facts are accurate. His expose exposed the fact that the oil platform was leased and just days before the explosion, that destroyed the platform, the company sold their stock short and made a fortune. *Coincidence?* Then it turns out that Halliburton, one of the governments, go to companies, had a remote robot doing maintenance on the well head just prior to the explosion. *Coincidence?* I don't suppose it could have been used to plant explosives., or not. Even more interestingly, it turns out that weeks prior to the explosion and oil spill, BP purchased an oil clean up company, the very company that got the contract to do the clean up. *Coincidence?* Isn't it amazing that whenever the government is involved in one of these crises, there are a statistically improbable number of coincidences, all favorable to the government's agenda to create crisis and chaos in order to systematically, ever so slowly drive the American people into financial collapse culminating in slavery?

Reader's perspective: Wait. Let's go back to HAARP. Do you honestly believe our government would use such a weapon against us?

Me: Absolutely, I do. If you believe, as I do, that our presidents are puppets of the financial elite, and they have sworn their allegiance to the UN in deference to the US Constitution, then it is entirely believable. More on this in a second, but first I want to say one more thing about HAARP. I am not a prophet, so I want to be careful how I say this. This book is absolutely inspired by God, but he gives me unctions, dreams, and visions that serve to guide me rather than to show me specific events, but for several weeks now, I have had the strongest feeling that the government is going to use HAARP to trigger an earthquake of biblical proportion in the US, probably the New Madrid fault in the Midwest.

Reader's perspective: You are crazy. That would destroy our cities, our infrastructure, or bridges, roads, etc and if the quake was large enough over a large enough area, it would bring the US to its knees.

Me: Precisely. That is exactly what the elite want. They want to reduce the US to the level of a third world country and drastically reduce our resource consumption. They don't care what happens to us. All they care about is that we stand in their way and we are using too many of their natural resource. I hope I am wrong, but I generally hear God pretty well.

As I close this chapter, less you have any doubts as to the fact that the UN is our enemy and our leaders in Washington have sold out to them, I want to leave you with a compilation of quotes for your reading pleasure.

"It is the sacred principles enshrined in the United Nations Charter to which the American people will henceforth pledge their allegiance" (President George Bush, addressing the UN). And here I thought the president swore allegiance to the Constitution of the United States. I guess that is a passé concept.

"The United Nations will spearhead our efforts to manage the new conflicts (that afflict our world)...Yes, the principles of the United Nations Charter are worth our lives, our fortunes, and our sacred honor" (General Colin Powell). Says who? Not me, and I bet not you! The herd must be culled!

"The super national sovereignty of an intellectual elite and world bankers is surely preferable to the national auto-determination practiced in past centuries" (David Rockefeller, Council Foreign Relations). Didn't I tell you the bankers rule the world! We are just their chattel.

"The Technetronic era involves the gradual appearance of a more controlled society that would be dominated by an elite unrestricted by traditional values" (*Between Two Ages: Americas Role In the Technetronic Era*). Ouch! I guess that means they can do whatever they want to us. After all we are just chattel. Will you say dictatorship!

"National States as a fundamental unit of man's organized life has ceased to be the principal creative force. International banks and multinational corporations are acting and planning in terms that are far in advance of the Nation States" (*Between Two Ages*, Zbigniew Brzezinski, CFR member, founding member TC, secretary of state to Carter Administration, and security adviser to five presidents. Darn it. There goes the United States. We are just outdated! Too bad nobody told us! Oh, check out the TV series *Continuum*. It just so happens to depict this very scenario. Coincidence or sadistic humor?

"We know that the free market is nonsense. We kind of agree with Mao that political power comes largely from the barrel of a gun" (Manufacturing Czar Ron Bloom). Gee, if they had only told me I could have moved to China a long time ago! Oh, if they get guns, I want one too. It is only fair.

"Isn't the only hope for the planet that the industrialized civilization collapse? Isn't it our responsibility to bring that about?" (Maurice Strong, founder of the UN Environmental Program, opening speech, Rio Earth Summit 1992). And you believed the president's economic recovery plan. Too bad you didn't realize it was a demolition plan not a construction plan!

"Further global progress is now possible only through a quest for universal consensus in the movement toward a New World Order" (Mikhail Gorbachev). We are all brothers. It is just one big happy Red family! We are all comrades!

"The New World Order cannot happen without US participation, as we are the most significant single component. Yes, there will be a New World Order, and it will force the United States to change its perceptions" (Henry Kissinger, World Affairs Council Press Conference, Regent Beverly Wilshire Hotel, April 19, 1994). Aren't you glad to know we are good for something? But there we go again. Another one of those veiled threats. We will be forced to change our perspectives. Say from free men to slaves!

"The Rockefeller file is not fiction. It is a compact, powerful, and frightening presentation of what may be the most important story of our lifetime—the drive of the Rockefellers and their allies to create a one-world government combining super capitalism and communism under the same tent, all under their control, not one has dared reveal the most vital part of the Rockefeller story that the Rockefellers and their allies have, for at least fifty years, been carefully following a plan to use their economic power to gain political control of first America, and then the rest of the world. Do I mean conspiracy? Yes, I do. I am convinced there is such a plot, international in scope, generations old in planning, and incredibly evil in intent" (Congressman Larry P. McDonald, 1976, killed in the Korean Airlines 747 that was shot down by the Soviets).

The Trilateralist Commission is international (and) is intended to be the vehicle for multinational consolidation of the commercial and banking interests by seizing control of the political government of the United States. The Trilateralist Commission represents a skillful, coordinated effort to seize control and consolidate the four centers of power—political, monetary, intellectual, and ecclesiastical. What the Trilateral Commission intends is to create a worldwide economic power superior to the political governments of the nation-states involved. (A dictatorship). As managers and creators of the system, they will rule the future" (Former Senator Barry Goldwater).

Seriously, they need our military because of our global presence, but as for our economy, they want to see it devastated and the US reduced to third world status. We are the hope of the world. If the light of liberty is extinguished in America, it will be extinguished in all lands.

> Will you submit to a satanic government and lose you soul?
>
> *The harvest is at hand and we will be judged based on the decisions we make in the coming days so choose carefully!* I hope this registers with all you out there. This is not just about what is going to happen to America. What happens to the US happens to the world because the US is the only country capable of thwarting the elite's plans. Once they have gotten us out

of the way they will be free to unleash their tyranny on the rest of the world.

The endgame is to end the national sovereignty of virtually every country on the planet and form *"Ten Super Trading Blocs/Kingdoms"* like the European Union and the emerging Amero Union comprised of the US, Mexico and Canada. It is by design that the Federal Government allows millions of illegal Mexicans to enter the US. Like a caterpillar we are being morphed into something else. Likewise it is no accident that Europe is inundated with Muslims who are taking over Europe by virtue of their birth rate and vocal demands for Sharia Law. Europe is being morphed. And we might have our old friend (Henry Kissinger) to thank for the ethnic clensing in Africa. Old Henry said: "Depopulation Should be the highest priority of foreign policy toward the third world." Africa is being morphed. And last but not least the Middle East is being morphed as we see the aftermath of the Arab Spring which was no spontaneous event. The Middle East is to be the fuse that lights the powder keg that will be known as WWIII. That too has its purpose. The world is being morphed and the question is are you going to go along with the takeover of the world by the forces of evil or are you going to stand up and say no?

The CFR has been working to implement their ten Kingdom/Trading Block for decades. As outlined in "Sovereignty and Globalization" by (Richard N. Haass, President, Council on Foreign Relations February 17, 2006 Project Syndicate) here is what the elite envision as the future of the world. No sovereign nations only "Ten Trading Kingdoms" controlled by the UN and their leader the Antichrist.

1. The Amero Union comprised of the USA, CANADA, Mexico.
2. The E.U. – countries of the European Union, Western Europe as a whole
3. Japan
4. Australia, New Zealand, South Africa

5. Eastern Europe, Pakistan, Afghanistan, Russia and the former countries of the Soviet Union
6. Central and South America, Cuba and Caribbean Islands
7. The Middle East and North Africa
8. The rest of Africa, except South Africa
9. South and Southeast Asia, including India
10. China and Mongolia

If you have paid any attention by now you should have realized that my touchstone for forecasting world events is the Bible, so maybe it can shed some light on this proposed global configuration.

1 Thessalonians 5:2-7 (KJV)

2 For yourselves know perfectly that the day of the Lord so cometh as a thief in the night. 3 For when they shall say, **Peace and safety**; then sudden destruction cometh upon them, as travail upon a woman with child; and they shall not escape. 4 But ye, brethren, are not in darkness, that that day should overtake you as a thief. 5 Ye are all the children of light, and the children of the day: we are not of the night, nor of darkness. 6 Therefore let us not sleep, as do others; but let us watch and be sober. 7 For they that sleep sleep in the night; and they that be drunken are drunken in the night.

The key phrase in the above scriptures is "Peace and Safety." This is typically thought of as the Peace Treaty with Israel that is to be broken after three and a half years, but it also has a more global inference. When the elite collapse the global monetary system there will be *"global chaos"* and they will come in offering to restore stability and peace. That olive branch is the forty pieces of silver of Judas. The New World Order will buy our loyalty with the false promise of "Peace and Safety," which will actually be the equivalent of taking Christ to the cross, because once we say yes all hell will break out and the entire world will literally and figuratively be taken to the cross of persecution. We will have turned our back on God and chosen to serve the Devil and we will pay the consequences just like Christ did 2,000 year before. He died to take away our sins, but because we didn't follow his teachings and establish heaven on earth through brotherly love we will now have to go to the cross and learn the hard way the wages of sin.

2 THESSALONIANS 2:3-4 (KJV)

3 Let no man deceive you by any means: for that day shall not come, except there come a **falling away** first, and that man of sin be revealed, the son of perdition; 4 Who opposeth and exalteth himself above all that is called God, or that is worshipped; so that he as God sitteth in the temple of God, showing himself that he is God.

Well we certainly have **fallen away**. Communism is a godless political system so that means Russia and China are by in large Godless nations, and in Europe and America Christianity has been systematically expunged from the public forum, and in America religious leaders have allowed themselves to be muzzled by tax exemptions that preclude them from speaking out from the pulpit. Hollywood has launched an all out attack on family values and replaced them with promiscuity and same sex relations as the norm. "If I could control Hollywood, I could control the world" (Joseph Stalin, Russian leader and mass murderer). Sorry Mr. Stalin the Financial Elite beat you to it.

"The case for government by elites is irrefutable." (William Fulbright US Senator)

Revelation 17:12-13(KJV)

12 And the ten horns **(Nations)** which thou sawest are ten kings, which have received no kingdom as yet; but receive power as kings one hour with the beast. 13 These have one mind, **(World socialism/Communism)** and shall give

their power and strength unto the beast. (Comments in parenthesis)

Gee go figure **2,000 years ago God foresaw ten kings which had received no kingdoms, because they are not kingdoms as we would think of them.** They are ten trading coalitions run by the UN and their leader the Antichrist. I don't say for sure that that person is Obama but the sixteen points I outlined earlier from the bible would certainly suggest that to be the case. If Obama leaves the office of the President of the US and goes to the UN watch out.

The Enemy Is at the Gate!

The hour is late!
The enemy is at the gate!
The enemy is not from without!
The enemy is from within!
The enemy is our own government!

The enemy has lulled us to sleep!
They have transformed us while we slept!
They dismantled us brick by brick!
They sold us bit by bit!

They are enslaving us without a fight!
They have stolen our wealth!
Left us a shadow of our former self!

Wake up! Wake up!
For God's sake, wake up!
The enemy is at the gate!
Wake up before it is too late!

Time to choose! Fight for freedom or surrender and be enslaved!

"When the government fears the people, there is liberty; when the people fear the government there is tyranny" (Thomas Jefferson).

Will you stand up and be counted?

PART 3

War: The Ultimate Control Mechanism

9/11 IN BIBLE SCRIPTURE

The following material is inspired by the bestselling book *The Harbinger*. It builds a convincing case that 9/11 was a warning to America, a warning that our political leaders disregarded and in so doing have brought judgment on America. As I will prove in the next chapter US leaders not only disregarded God's warning but were complicit in the events of 9/11.

The now famous *"Cross At Ground Zero"* which rose from the wreckage of the Twin Towers was God's reminder that his hand was in the events of 9/11!

On 9/11God called America to repentance and we ignored his warning. What awaits America if we continue to turn away from him and refuse to heed his warnings? Like Israel before us America will be taken into captivity?

Does Ground Zero hold special significance to America? You bet it does! The symbol of America's economic power *"The World Trade Center & Wall Street"* became the symbol of its economic downfall!

Is that all there is to the significance of Ground Zero? Not by a long shot! Ground zero was the places of America's Consecration and as such God choose it as *"The place of Americas' judgment!"* Make no mistake God's hand of protection has been removed from America and it will not be restored unless we repent and surrender to him, and unless we turn away from the false god of materialism and decide to become The self-reliant, moral, God fearing nation who inscribed on its currency and monuments ***"In God We Trust."*** If we return to God America may yet be saved, otherwise God's hand of judgment will not be stayed and America like Israel before us will be occupied by its enemies and its people taken into slavery. Hearken to God's final warning!

America's consecration to God. The date is April 30, 1789. George Washington is inaugurated at Federal Hall (in New York City at the site of ground zero; Washington, DC did not exist yet, so NY was America's first capital), and America is officially founded as a fully Constituted Republic under God.

In his inaugural address, President Washington said, "The Propitious smiles of heaven can never be expected on a nation that disregards the eternal rule of order and right, which heaven hath ordained."

Our first president and the first joint session of Congress then walked from Federal Hall to St. Paul's Cathedral (located on the corner of "ground zero," which by the way, was land originally owned by St. Paul's Cathedral) where President Washington gives a speech, in which he said, "It would be peculiarly improper to omit in this first official act my fervent supplication to that Almighty Being who rules over the universe, who presides in the councils of nations, and whose providential aids can supply every human deficit, that his benediction may consecrate to the liberties and happiness of the people of the United States, a government instituted by themselves for the essential purpose."

Can there be any question America was founded and consecrated to serve God, to serve as a shining example to the world, to spread Christianity to the four corners of the world? For that reason, we have been blessed as no other nation in the history of the world. But on the day of 9/11, people all across America were asking how God could allow such a thing to happen. They forgot how before America, Israel had been chosen to be God's people, and to be in covenant with him, how he blessed them and put a hedge of protection around them, but when they broke their covenant, the blessing became a curse. So it must be with America. If we break our covenant, we are warned, and if we do not heed the warning, progressively, worse and worse judgments will befall us till as with Israel, we are *utterly destroyed and taken into captivity.*

America's turning away from God's covenant. We have taken prayer out of our schools. Our pastors are prohibited from speaking out against a corrupt ungodly government! We worship many false idols—idols of sexual immorality, idols of greed and materialism, idols of comfort and security, idols of power and military might, idols of self-importance and self-worth, and we have forgotten the God who bestowed our blessings upon us. We drove God out of our personal and social life, and then we dare to ask, "Where is God in our hour of need?"

I say to America, "Where is our covenant with God? Where are the godly people who founded this nation and upon whom God bestowed so many blessings? Where is our praise and worship for the God who made America the greatest nation the world has ever known?

Repent, America, before it is too late! If we don't restore our covenant with God, this nation is lost, pure and simple! As with Israel before us, we will fall and go into captivity!

We cannot say God didn't warn us. "If my people, which are called by my name, shall humble themselves, and pray, and turn from their wicked ways; then I will forgive their sin, and will heal their land" (2 Chronicles 7:14 KJV).

American leaders ignored God's warning and were defiant. "The bricks are fallen down, but we will build with hewn stones: The Sycamore are cut down but we will change them into cedars" (Isaiah 9:10 KJV).

I can hear a refrain of people saying, "What in the world does this obscure Bible verse have to do with America?" It has everything to do with the warning of the fall of America, and we better head it, if we don't want to be utterly destroyed as Israel before us and taken into captivity as they were.

Israel's first warning was when they were attacked by Assyria (modern day Iraq). They ignored God's warning. They did not reflect on why judgment had befallen them. Instead, their leaders stood in the nation's capital of Samaria and vowed to build with hewn stones instead of bricks and to replace the sycamores with cedars (Isaiah 9:10).

Translation: "They would rebuild stronger than ever." Hewn stones are stronger than clay bricks. The Assyrians had cut down the sycamores native to Israel, but they would plant stronger trees "cedars." The declaration of Isaiah 9:10 was made by the leaders of the nation in defiance of God's warning, so a defiant Israel was taken captive by the Babylonians for seventy years.

Why seventy years of captivity? Because God wanted to guard against the accumulation of material goods and power, so the masses would not be downtrodden by the money lenders. To this end, he instructed the Israelites, saying thus:

> "Speak unto the children of Israel, and say unto then, When you come into the land which I have given you, then shall the land be kept a Sabbath unto the LORD. Six years thou shall you sow thy fields, and six years thou shall prune thy vineyards, and gather in the fruit thereof; But in the seventh year there shall be a Sabbath of rest unto the land, a Sabbath for the LORD: thou shall neither sow thy field nor prune the vineyard" (Leviticus 25:2–4 KJV).

> "At the end of every seven years thou shall make release. And this is the manner of the release: Every creditor that lendeth aught unto his neighbor shall release it; he shall not exact it of his neighbor, or his brother; because it is called the LORD's release" (Deuteronomy 15:1–2 KJV).

So I say again why seventy years of captivity? Because Israel did not keep God's covenant and honor the Sabbath, and seventy years just happens to be the number of Sabbaths Israel ignored, so one year of captivity under Babylon for each Sabbath not observed (no coincidences in God's kingdom).

> "And I will scatter you among the heathen, and will draw out a sword after you: and your land shall be desolate and your cities waste. Then shall the land enjoy her Sabbath, as long as it lieth desolate, and you be in your enemies land; even then shall the land rest, and enjoy her Sabbaths. As long as it lieth desolate it shall rest; because it did not rest in your Sabbaths when ye dwelt upon it" (Leviticus 26: 33–35 KJV).

America has made the same mistake as Israel before us and will suffer the same fate. In America today, we are utterly controlled by banks, which are "too big to fail." A corrupt banking system inflicts predatory lending practices on us, which make us their slaves, slaves without chains, but slaves nonetheless. As with all things, God foresaw the ending before the beginning, and he warned us, but we didn't listen so we have to suffer the consequences. When will we learn?

America's response to God's warning on 9/11: Just as the Israelites before us, we defied God and ignored his warning. We defied God not once but three times!

- September 12, 2001, Senate Majority Leader Tom Daschle said in response to the shocking terrorist attacks the day after, "I know that there is only the smallest measure of inspiration that can be taken from this devastation. But there is a passage in the Bible from Isaiah that I think speaks to us all at times like this: 'The bricks have fallen down but we will rebuild with dressed stone; the fig trees have been felled but we will replace them with cedars.' That is what we will do. We will rebuild and we will recover."

- *Third anniversary of 9/11—September 11, 2004.* From the nation's capital in Washington, DC, John Edwards, the democratic VP candidate said these exact words, "The bricks have fallen, but we will rebuild with dressed stones. The sycamores have been cut down, but we will put cedars in their place."
- *Feb 24, 2009, Obama's inaugural address.* Barack Obama vows to rebuild America in inaugural address (key points of speech). Barack Obama was sworn in as the first black president of the United States with a vow to rebuild America and tell the world, "We are ready to lead once more."

President Obama's utterances on

- *CBS News*: "We will rebuild."
- *CNN*: "We will rebuild."
- *MSNBC*: "We will rebuild."
- *The Guardian*: "We will rebuild."
- *National Public Radio:* "We will rebuild."
- *Timesonline*: "We will rebuild."
- *Fox News*: "We will rebuild."
- *Al Jazeera*: "We will rebuild."
- *Drudge Report*: "We will rebuild."
- *Associated Press*: "We will rebuild."
- *New York Times*: "We will rebuild."

Isaiah 9:10 "We will rebuild."

Obama, the evil one, stands in open defiance of God. He mocks scripture and God, so when he says, "We will rebuild," it is nothing short of a "mockery of God, and it brings down judgment on America."

June 28, 2006, Senator Obama, taking scripture out of context in order to mock God and the Bible, said in a speech, "Which passage of the Bible should guide our public policy? Should we go with Deuteronomy, which suggests stoning your children, if he strays from the faith, or should we just stick with 'The Sermon on the Mount,' a passage that is so radical that it is doubtful that our own Defense Department could survive its application?" (Don't forget Mr. Obama, Deuteronomy gave us the Ten Commandments, which fly in the face of your mockery).

America, you be the judge. Is the Sermon on the Mount something to be mocked?

Mathew 5:1–48 KJV (Selected verses only. Please read it all.)

3 Blessed are the poor in spirit: for theirs is the kingdom of heaven.
5 Blessed are the meek: for they shall inherit the earth.
6 Blessed are they that hunger and thrust after righteousness: for they shall be filled.
7 Blessed are the merciful: for they shall receive mercy.
9 Blessed are the peace makers: for they shall be called the children of God.
16 Let your light so shine before men, that they may see your good works, and glorify your father which are in heaven.
19 Whosoever therefore shall break one of these least commandments. And shall teach men so, he [Obama] shall be called the least in the kingdom of heaven but whosoever shall do and teach them, the same shall be called great in the kingdom of heaven.

Oh, Mr. Obama, what curse have you brought upon yourself and upon the nation that elected you?

Nothing about 9/11 was accidental. "The place of America's consecration became the place to herald our downfall! How much more symbolic could God have been? How much clearer could the warning have been? *Repent, or else.*"

How Isaiah 9:10 relates to Israel and America:

- Just like in Israel, we vowed to rebuild stronger and bigger. (For Israel, it was the rebuilding of the Temple Mount, and for America, it was the building of the One World Trade Center).

"One World Trade Center now rises to 1, 271 feet, surpassing the Empire State Building as New York's tallest building and symbolizing the city and the nation's recovery from the 9/11 terrorist attacks."

The Temple Mount represented Israel's covenant with God, so its destruction was the ultimate sign the covenant was broken. President George Washington dedicated America to God at St. Paul's Cathedral on what was to become ground zero, symbolizing as with Israel that America's covenant was broken, and its hedge of protection had been removed.

- Just like the Israelites, we ignored the first warning. (For Israel, it was the Assyrian invasion; for America, it was 9/11.)

  Following 9/11, the stock market closed for six days, and when it opened, it had the largest one day point drop in history. By 2003, the interest rate was 1 percent, setting the stage for the easy money credit bubble that led to the 2008 economic collapse. Had we repented, 2008 could have been obverted.
- Just like the Israelites, we ignored the second warning. (For Israel, it was the Babylonian captivity; for America, it was the 2008 economic collapse.)
- Just like Israel, we vowed to replace the sycamore with the cedar. The founding of the US Stock Exchange (the symbol of America's economic might) took place under a sycamore tree at Ground Zero. When that sycamore was uprooted on 9/11, it signaled the uprooting of America's economic might. Then, in fulfillment of scripture, we replaced the sycamore with cedar.
- Israel abandoned God's "Sabbath seven-year jubilee forgiveness of debt" and was lead into a seventy-year captivity. America allowed the money lenders to make the American people virtual slaves to the debt they intentionally created, and precisely, seven years following 9/11 came the 2008 economic collapse with coincidentally (no coincidences in God's kingdom) a 7 percent loss of stock value and a 777 point drop. God is warning America.

What does the future hold for America? If America refuses to repent and the seven-year cycle created by God continues, it may well be that September 2015 could see a third judgment on America. I don't know what that judgment will be, but if it follows the same course as with ancient Israel, America may well see itself invaded and taken into captivity. An economically weak America is a militarily weak America, and America has many enemies. We also have a president who has vowed to "disarm America to a point acceptable to his Muslim brothers." Only God knows the future, but I do know this:

> The harvest is at hand. Contemplate this. Heaven is reserved for the righteous. The evil must be cast aside. America is in defiance of God, so how will God judge a nation and its people if they do not stand up in defiance of the evil that pervades and contaminates the land? Our very souls may well depend on the stand we take. Repent, America, and return to God or suffer the consequences!

Either America repents or it is in store for ever worsening judgments till it is utterly destroyed.

Break time: Go get a cup of coffee, take your blood pressure medicine, and get someone to keep you company and to hold your hand. You are going to need it. It is finally time for the *unimaginable truth* that has enslaved us all!

The world as you know it is about to get turned upside down. I do not breach this next subject lightly. Matter of fact, I prayed to God for weeks, asking him if I could just skip this *truth*, because sometimes, the truth can be a bitter pill best not taken because once taken you never see the world the same again. God answered, "That is exactly why you have to tell this truth. It will open my people's eyes and set them free. They will finally know who the real enemy is, and they will have a choice to make—resist the evil and be free, or submit and be slaves, but for the first time in their lives, they will know who the enemy is."

Me: Think about this over break. It is as President Obama said in these prophetic self condemning words, "If the people cannot trust their government to do the job for which it exists—to protect them and to promote their common welfare—all else is lost."

COMPELLING EVIDENCE 9/11 WAS A FALSE FLAG ATTACK

It is finally time to contemplate the unthinkable. Was the US government complicit in the Events of 9/11?

In the instance of this extremely sensitive subject, I am not going to draw a definitive conclusion, though I certainly have my own opinion, which I will share. I will present you with information, which most Americans are unaware of and then let each of you draw your own conclusions.

What I will ask of you is that you put aside you biases and emotional road blocks and look at the data from an analytical, scientific view point the way any good police detective would. Then you decide where the body of evidence lies.

Examine the evidence and decide for yourself. Is the government guilty or innocent of taking some three thousand American lives in order to further their agenda of collapsing the US and establishing a one-world communist dictatorship?

- *What brought down the Twin Towers?* Demolition experts say that to bring down a building by controlled demolition, you first cut all the support beams in the basement at a forty-five-degree angle facing in, so that as the building collapses, it will fall in on itself, making the *V* shape that is the signature of a controlled demolition. I have photos showing that all the columns in the basement were in fact cut on a forty-five-degree angle facing in just as demolition experts describe, but unfortunately because of copyright issues I could not reprint them in the book. But you can Google them and see for yourself. The evidence is out there for those who are willing to find it as I did. Second, in order to initiate the collapse, you "crack it at the top," which is accomplished by simultaneously setting off explosions on all four sides of an upper floor, causing it to collapse, and in the process, bring the rest of the building down in free fall fashion. I have photos depicting this as well. These photos may be a little harder to find, but if you look you can find them on Google Images.
- *Evidence that spells controlled demolition.* Both of the towers and building 7, which collapsed, had tons of ***molten metal in the basements***, but it was conspicuously absent from the buildings, which remained standing. Why? Because scientists say it is impossible for a fire fuelled by jet fuel to melt metal because the temperatures are nowhere near hot enough. That is why prior to 9/11 no steel building had ever collapsed due to fire, and then on 9/11 we are told that three buildings collapsed due to fire. Bull crap! Building 7 had two small fires and no structural damage. In a minute I will tell you why it had to come down, but make no mistake it was brought down. It did not collapse due to two small fires. No way! But thermite used in controlled demolition burns at 4,000 degrees F and produces massive amounts of molten metal in its wake. There are lots of photos of pools of molten metal that can only be explained by a controlled demolition using Thermite. ***"This is your smoking gun!"*** I urge you to Google 9/11 molten metal and see the smoking gun for yourself.

The government's lame pancake theory does not stand up under examination of the facts. I urge you to get on the web and do some research on your own. There are tons of pictures and video footage. ***The only thing that explains the collapse of the towers is controlled demolition.*** Now that you know what to look for, I am sure you will find collaborating photographic evidence. The truth has been staring us in the face, but we couldn't bring ourselves to even contemplate that our own government could kill some three thousand US citizens to further their goal of collapsing the US in order to establish a one-world dictatorship.

Why would the government deny that the buildings were brought down by controlled demolition? How about this as a possible explanation? Because then they would have to explain how "Muslim terrorist" got access to the towers to rig the explosives, which demolition experts say is a time-consuming job, requiring several days. The evidence I am about to present clearly establishes that to plant explosives in the towers required an inside man and the facts point to Mr. Larry Silverstein, Marvin Bush, and the US government. You decide for yourself.

Who had access to Dulles Airport and the Twin Towers? Could 9/11 have been an inside job?

Let's examine the evidence, and you decide.

- *Who had the security contracts at both Dulles and the World Trade Center?* On 9/11, President Bush's younger brother Marvin Bush was a principal in Securacom Strategies, which had security contracts at both Dulles Airport and the World Trade Center. The connection was never investigated despite a suspicious down at the WTC the weekend prior to 9/11. Scott Forbs of Fiduciary Trust reported the incident, but no one would investigate it. He indicated the building's security system was down over the weekend, during which time men were working in the building with no security cameras. Could this have been the cover for wiring the building for demolition?

- *How could the Twin Towers have been rigged for demolition?* Politically connected real estate investor, Larry Silverstein, acquired a ninety-nine-year lease on the WTC just six weeks prior to 9/11, and immediately rewrote the insurance policy to cover acts of terrorism and to provide for rebuilding in the event of demolition. Suspicious! The building had a $1 billion asbestos liability. Additionally, the building was operating at a loss due to occupancy rates below 50 percent. Sounds like a horribly bad real estate deal; that is unless there was foreknowledge of coming events, and the purchase was made in order to secure access to the buildings for the planting of explosives so that on 9/11 the towers and building 7 could be brought down by controlled demolition. By the way, immediately following 9/11, Mr. Silverstein was awarded a $7 billion insurance award. Even though this looks like an obvious case of insurance fraud, this also was never investigated. Why not?
- *Who had opportunity to plant explosives?* Immediately following the signing of the lease, several tenants were moved, leaving several upper floors completely vacant, supposedly for renovation. (Remember, the explosions on the upper floors just seconds before the building came down and remember that demolition experts say you crack a building at the top to bring it down. What a coincidence!) Commencing immediately after the lease was signed, a gray powder was reported to be present throughout the building on Monday mornings. Demolition experts said such dust would be consistent with the drilling, which would be required to plant explosives for a controlled demolition. One thing is for certain, and that is that no band of Middle East terrorist walked into the Twin Towers and rigged it for demolition. They simply couldn't have gotten access, and that is precisely why the government had to deny that there could have been a controlled demolition. It would have pointed to an inside job, which would have put suspicion on them and Mr. Silverstein
- *Government had motive, means, and opportunity no terrorist had!* Since none of these things were ever investigated, it cannot be

proven that they were the cover up for the planting of explosives for a controlled demolition, but it certainly does provide motive—for Mr. Silverstein, a $7 billion insurance award, and as you will see shortly, for the government, an excuse to invade Iraq. Means and opportunity: The access to the buildings and the airport compliments of Mr. Silverstein and the president's brother. You decide what all this means. Oh, and as we will see shortly, the government benefited big time from 9/11. Just one more of many coincidences.

The mystery of the collapse of building 7!

- *Building 7 had only minor damage, so why did it come down?* It was the furthest away from the Twin Towers and sustained only minor damage with only small fires on two floors, yet it collapsed while buildings 3, 4, 5, and 6, which sustained catastrophic damage, all remained standing. How is that possible? Oh by the way, none of those buildings had their basement columns cut at forty-five-degree angles, and they were suspiciously devoid of the tons of molten metal, which was present in the twin towers and building 7. Go figure. Just another coincidence I suppose, or maybe not!
- *The mystery that is building 7:* Building 7, with almost no damage collapses while bldg's [3, 4, 5, & 6] with catastrophic damage remained standing! Why? How is that possible?
- *How could fire fighters have known in advance building 7 was coming down?* I viewed video footage, in which firefighters told onlookers to move back because building 7 was coming down. How is that possible unless they knew the building was being brought down by controlled demolition?
- *Could there have been an ulterior motive for demolishing building 7?* As it turns out, building 7 housed all the records for all the white color crimes in the country, including the Enron energy case. When building 7 was destroyed all those case files were lost. How lucky for all the financial elite banker-gangsters and their friends! Will the coincidences never cease?

- *Prior to 9/11, No steel-framed building had ever collapsed due to fire for the simple fact that it is scientifically impossible:* A carbon based open air fire (which would include the fire caused by the jet fuel from the planes) burns at a maximum temperature of 1, 200 F, and it requires temperatures in excess of 2, 750 F to melt steel, accounting for the governments "pancake theory," much less to produce the pools of molten metal, which were found in both the towers and building 7 and were conspicuously absent in the other buildings. Go Figure! As I said before, thermite used in controlled demolition burns at 4, 000 degrees, and it would certainly account for tons of molten metal, which can't be accounted for any other way. Go Figure!

Experts say no commercial airliner hit the Pentagon!

French Accident Investigator Francois Grangier said: "What is certain when one looks at the photos of the facade that remains are that it is obvious that the plane [the 757] did not go through there." Again there is photographic evidence on Google.

No commercial airliner hit the Pentagon. The hole in the façade was too small to have been a 757. It was more what you would expect from a military plane, such as drone!

Daniel O'Brien Air traffic Controller at Dulles. "The speed, the maneuverability, the way that he turned, we all thought in the radar room, all of us experienced controllers, that that was a military plane." **(*New Pearl Harbor*)**

"We were told that the bodies were able to be identified either by fingerprints or DNA. So what kind of fire can vaporize tempered steel. (The government claimed the jet engines vaporized and yet have human bodies intact?)" (David Griffin, author, *New Pearl Harbor*).

- *There was a conspicuous absence of wreckage,* and FBI agents removed what little wreckage there was from the sight and even more bazaar within hours of the crash huge dump trucks covered the lawn of the Pentagon with gravel and dirt. Can you say cover up literally and figuratively? Again, I urge you to go to the web and find your own evidence. Oh, by the way, the Pentagon has one of the most sophisticated missile batteries in the nation to protect this high value asset. Like at NORAD, planes didn't take off for eighty minutes when ten minutes is the norm; the missiles batteries at the Pentagon didn't fire. How is that possible? It is possible if as air traffic controllers suspicion the aircraft was a military not commercial aircraft (say hypothetically, an unmanned drone). It would have a military transponder, and the missile batteries would therefore not open fire on what would have been considered a friendly a US military plane. And as to the comments from the French accident investigator, saying it was obvious no 757 hit the Pentagon. (The opening in the façade simply was too small, more in keeping with what you would expect from a much smaller plane, say a drone.)

- *Crash site conveniently under construction and reinforced to withstand bomb blast.* It just so happens that, the area where the Pentagon was hit was under construction, so there were minimal personnel present, and most of them were civilian construction workers. Additionally, just coincidentally, it was the only area in the entire vast multi-acre Pentagon Complex that had been reinforced to be bomb proof. Go figure! I am sorry but that is no coincidence. The Pentagon is too valuable to allow it to be destroyed so they made sure the damage would be localized. *Will You say false flag attack? Will you say treason and mass murder?*

The mystery of the crash site of flight 93 in Shanksville, PA!

- *A photo taken by the US geologic survey prior to the plane crash clearly shows the existence of the crater prior to 9/11.* It supports the statement of (Coroner Wally Miller), at the crash site on 9/11, "It looks like somebody took a scrape truck and dug a ten-foot ditch and put trash in it." *(New Pearl Harbor)* Check it out yourself.
- *Conspicuous absence of bodies and wreckage.* When was there ever in the history of aviation a crash of a commercial airliner with no bodies and no wreckage? I will tell you when. *Never.* Yet Miller

said, "There is nothing there…there were no bodies… I have not to this day seen a single drop of blood."(*New Pearl Harbor)*

- *What really happened to Flight 93?* The author of the New Pearl Harbor has an explanation. There were reports that Flight 93 was being shadowed by a military jet. There was also reportedly wreckage found over an eight-mile radius. Experts say this is consistent with a midair explosion, not an impact with the ground where the wreckage would be more confined. You may recall this was the flight where the passengers had taken over the plane from the hijackers. If the military jet shot down Flight 93, that would explain the inconsistencies of the crash site. My conclusion is that it would have been embarrassing for the government to explain why after passengers had taken over the plane, it was shot down, so a fake crash site had to be provided. Draw your own conclusions.

  Note: The flight recorders of all the planes were found and the recordings were released, that is except for the last three minutes of Flight 93's recorder, which was withheld. Go Figure!

Who had motive, means, and opportunity? Was there a cover up? You decide!

Allegations 9/11 Commission was a cover-up:

- *Families of 9/11 victims charge government with cover-up*, and demanded that Executive Director Philip Zelikow resign as commission director 9/11 because he was a White House operative in charge of a cover-up and his job was to make sure that the CIA, FBI, Pentagon, and Justice Department were not investigated and the American public never found out the truth.
- *White House obstructed 9/11 Commission.* Provided only 25 percent of eleven thousand documents requested, and twenty-eight pages of the final report were censored. Why?
- *Government intimidation tactics.* Anyone who questioned the events of 9/11 was labeled a nutcase and called "truthers" mind control 101.

What did Bush and Chaney have to hide?

- *Bush and Chaney were asked to appear separately and testify under oath.* They refused. Why? They appeared together, refused to testify under oath, did not allow the interview to be recorded, and no transcripts were allowed. What did they have to hide? By not testifying under oath, they are protected from impeachment for obstruction of justice, if they lie. Sounds more than suspicious; sounds down right incriminating!
- *FBI and CIA told to "back off Bin Laden family."* Why? FBI leaked order W1191, in which George Bush orders them to back off Osama bin Laden and his family. Some agents refused to follow the orders and were fired.
- *George Bush benefited from arms deals.* Wayne Madsen, former intelligence analyst, says Bush Sr. used his Oval Office Connections to broker arms deals, on behalf of the Carlyle Group, which he benefited from financially.
- *Bush/Carlyle abuse of power. EO 12803:* Allowed privatization of US infrastructure, which had hither to been illegal. Bush's buddies at the Carlyle Group then announced they were forming an eight-man investment team to raise a multi-billion dollar fund to purchase US infrastructure. Another coincidence.
- *US infrastructure for sale to bankers.* Euromoney hosted a conference in New York. The brochure noted that given that it takes $90 billion per year just to maintain US infrastructure that virtually all US infrastructure was up for grabs. Attendees included Lehman Brothers, Goldman Sachs, the Royal Bank Of Scotland, HSBS, J.P. Morgan Assets Management Group, and the Carlyle Group etc—the royalties of the banking industry. I guess Jefferson got it right when he said, "If the American people ever allow private banks to control the issue of their currency, first by inflation, and then by deflation, the banks and corporations that will grow up around them will deprive the people of all property until their children wake up homeless on the continent their Fathers conquered. I believe that banking institutions are more dangerous to our liberties than standing

armies. The issuing power should be taken from the banks and restored to the people, to whom it properly belongs."

- *Dick Chaney benefited from defense contracts.* Former CEO of Halliburton benefited from defense contracts. Chaney received deferred salary package from Halliburton.

Allegations Afghan war Operation Enduring Freedom, Oct.7, 2001, was planed months before, and 9/11 was only a pretext.

- *War plans drafted before 9/11.* Why? *NBC News* reported May 2002, a former national security presidential directive "submitted two days before the 9/11 attacks" had outlined essentially the same war plan that the White House, the CIA, and the Pentagon put into action.

NORAD: Possible stand down scenario.

- *General-in-charge of NORAD Relieved just before 9/11.* Why? Prior to 9/11 the general–in-charge of NORAD was relieved of command and replaced by Vice President Chaney. This was the first time in US history a US general had not been in charge of NORAD. Could it have been to allow Chaney to order a stand down?
- *Was stand-down order given?* NORAD's typical interception time to a suspected hijacking is ten minutes, but on 9/11 it took eighty minutes before fighters were airborne. Was there a stand-down order given? And if so, by whom? Certainly not by Bin Laden?
- *On 9/11, NORAD was conveniently having war games.* Coincidentally, on 7/7 the day of the British Rail Attack, Britain was also having war games. It just so happens that troops were deployed at the very stations that were attacked. Coincidence or was this a cover up for covert operations buy the British Government?

Bush-Bin Ladin-CIA connection:

- *Did President Bush protect Bin Ladin?* He had a long standing relationship with the Bin Ladin family and protected them in the days following 9/11.

- *Al-Qaeda was created by the CIA* in the 1980s to fight the Russians and continued to receive funding even after the Russians withdrew.
- *Bin Laden was CIA asset* (a.k.a. Tim Osman) trained by the CIA during the Russian/Afghan conflict.
- *Covert meeting with Bin Laden and CIA Section chief prior to 9/11.* CIA agent alleged to have meet Bin Laden on July 13. Medical reports substantiated by officials at American Hospital in Dubai that while receiving dialysis at the hospital, Bin Laden meet with CIA Middle East section chief for ten days in July 2001 just prior to 9/11. One has to ask why he was meeting with the CIA just before 9/11?
- *Bush-Bin Laden business connections.* George W. Bush started his first oil company, Arbesto Energy, in 1976 funded by and in partnership with the Bin Laden family. Coincidence?
- *Suspicious oil drilling contract.* (Quid pro quo) Obscure Harken Energy received an off shore drilling contract in the Persian Gulf. When questions arose as to how a tiny cash strapped company could beat out all the major oil companies, it was discovered that Bush Junior was on the board. Go figure!
- *Bin Laden family flown to safety.* Document showing that between Sept. 11 and 15, at a time when all flights were grounded by the Pentagon, that 160 members of the Bin Laden family were flown from the US to Saudi Arabia to safety. Go figure!
- Bush took FBI agents off Bin Laden family trail. Why?

Indications 9/11 was joint effort of US and Taliban/Al-Qaeda

- *Taliban generals released.* Why? *Washington Times*, Dec. 18, 2002, top US generals were told to release Taliban generals. In frustration, some generals went public.
- *Taliban leaders flown to safety.* Why? At the end of the three-week Afghan war, eight thousand Taliban and Al-Qaeda leaders were flown to Pakistan on aboard US C130s (*New Yorker Magazine*, November 29, Michael Moran).

- *Taliban and Al-Qaeda soldiers flown to safety.* Why? In the past week, and a half a dozen or more Pakistani air force cargo planes landed in the Taliban-held city of Kunduz and evacuated to Pakistan hundreds of non-Afgahn soldiers who fought alongside Taliban and even Al-Qaeda against the US ((*New Yorker Magazine*, November 29, by Michael Moran). What is wrong with this picture?

US government refused surrender of Bin Laden.

- *Government didn't want Bin Laden put on trial.* Why? According to *NBC*, on Oct. 14, 2001, seven days into the bombing, the Taliban offered to surrender Osama bin Laden to a third country for trial, if bombing was halted, and they were shown evidence of his involvement in September 11 terrorist attacks. This was their second offer to surrender Osama, and it was also refused by US President Bush who declared, "There's no need to discuss innocence or guilt. We know he did it." Ask yourself why in the world President Bush would refuse to have Osama surrendered for trial? Could it be that there was no evidence? Could it be that Osama was more valuable to Bush alive as the face of terror than he could ever be in a jail? Could it be they were accomplices in crime?

Insider trading/fortunes were made. How did traders know to short stocks affected by 9/11?

- *Insider trading American Airlines.* September 10 saw 4, 516 put options vs. 748 call options. A put option is a bet that the stock value will fall.
- *Insider trading American Airlines:* September 6 and 7 saw 4, 744 put options vs. 396 call option
- *Insider trading Stanley Morgan:* WTC tenant: Average number of put options per week was 27, and for the three days prior to 9/11, they were 2, 157
- *Insider trading Merrill Lynch:* WTC tenant: Just prior to 9/11, 12, 215 put options were placed, which was twelve times normal. It was estimated profits from inside trading was $15 billion.

They always say follow the money, but in this instance, the government didn't think this was important enough to investigate. Why?

US government interest furthered by 9/11.

- *Project for the New American Century (PNAC).* The report written in 2000 outlines three major US military objectives—first, the need for strategically positioned military bases around the world; second, the need to bring about regime change in countries unfriendly to US policy (say Iraq and Afghanistan; third, the desire to increase military spending by upwards of a trillion dollars, most especially for "missile defense," not to defend the US but to provide the US "a prerequisite for maintaining preeminence by keeping other countries from being able to deter the US. Go figure. 9/11 accomplished all the government's objectives. Will the coincidences never cease?
- *9/11: Second Pearl Harbor.* PMAC noted that the government's plans to transform the military would probably be unattainable "absent a catastrophic and catalyzing event like Pearl Harbor." Within a year, the authors of PMAC had their Pearl Harbor and a chance to "turn their imperial fantasies into reality." Will miracles never cease?
- *Pentagon budget increase of $48 billion.* Was in and of itself more than any other country spent on its entire military budget. *Will you say imperialism?*
- *CIA and FBI power grab.* The Patriot Act and other similar legislation have widely increased the purview of the CIA and FBI. And that is why Bush pulled the version passed by Congress and replaced it with his own! *Will you say treason?*
- *Iraq provided strategic foothold in Middle East.* Strategically positioned between the Tigress and Euphrates, Iraq controls critical water supplies. It has access to the Persian Gulf, and from a military standpoint, it is in easy missile range to both Israel and Russia.
- *Regime change and oil as a motive.* The US wanted to control Iraq's oil, and now it does, but there was another reason Iraq had

to fall and Saddam had to be ousted. He was threatening to sell oil denominated in euros and that couldn't be allowed so he had to go, just like Kennedy issued Executive Order 11110 intended to do away with the Fed, and he had to be done away with as well. You don't buck the financial elite and live.

Allegations 9/11 was pretext for regime change!

- *Afghan war planned months before 9/11.* The *BBC News* reported (on September 18, 2001, exactly one week after the September 11 attacks) that Niaz Naik, a former Pakistani foreign secretary, had been told by senior American officials in mid-July that a military action against Afghanistan would proceed by the middle of October at the latest. The message was conveyed during a meeting between senior US, Russian, Iranian, and Pakistani diplomats.

Oil interest furthered by 9/11.

- *Oil, the ultimate motive!* US is the world's largest oil consumer, and it is expected that in approximately ten years, demand will exceed supply. Oil is crucial to the US economy and political power! "America has become little more than an energy protection force doing anything to gain access to expensive fuel without regard to the lives of others or the earth itself" (Political Analyst Kevin Philip). This speaks to the opening of this book where I disclose the fact that the world is facing mass extinction caused by the collision of overpopulation with peak oil. So the endgame is for the US to control as much of the world's oil as possible, impose a one-world-government and then commit mass genocide in order to, over the next several decades, reduce the world's population from seven billion to one billion. Game over! Mission accomplished! Could their possibly be a more powerful motivation? I think not, how about you?
- *Pipeline deal.* US oil companies had long standing ambitions to build a pipeline from the Caspian Sea, and one day, after a US puppet government was installed, their dreams were realized.

- *Foothold in oil rich Middle East.* Sixty percent of the world's oil fields are in the Middle East. Now, we have a foothold in the region.

Interest of arms dealers furthered by 9/11.

- *Cart Blanch to arms dealers:* Cart Blanch to arms dealers: Arms industry has been given virtual "Cart Blanch" with Bush, saying, They would be given whatever it took to win the war.

Accusation: CIA behind virtually every terrorist attack in recent years. CIA chief charges FBI behind most if not all terrorist attacks against US. Ted Gunderson, former FBI chief of LA, Dallas, and Memphis Operations, goes beyond suggestions of coincidence and comes right out and accuses the CIA of being behind virtually every major terrorist act in recent years. Gunderson says, "Look what the CIA has done to this country. What they have done to us is unbelievable. Look at the terrorist acts that have occurred. The CIA is behind most, if not all of them. We have Pan Am 103, we had the USS *Cole*, we had Oklahoma City, we had the World Trade Center in 1993. Unfortunately, for them (the CIA), there were only six people killed in the 1993 WTC bombing, not enough to pass the legislation so what happened is two years later, April 19, 1996, down comes the Oklahoma City Federal Building. One year later, the anti- terrorist legislation that takes away many of our Constitutional and civil liberties is passed."

"If tyranny and oppression come to this land, it will be in the guise of fighting a foreign enemy" (James Madison). Gosh, our Founding Fathers sure were smart.

Aaron Russo's tell-all interview about his friendship with Nick Rockefeller and the elitist agenda. Aaron Russo who died in 2007 was a well-known documentary film maker and political activist. At one point, he ran for governor of Nevada as an independent. During this time, he met and became friends with Nick Rockefeller (Interview by Alex Jones, Infowars).

Russo, speaking to Alex Jones: "9/11 was done by people in our own government, in our own banking system to perpetuate the fear of the American people to subordinate themselves into anything the government wants them to do. That's what it's about, to create an endless war on terror. Look, this whole war on terror is a fraud, a farce. It's very difficult to say that out loud because people are intimidated against saying it; they want to make you into a nut case. But the truth has to come out. That's why I am doing this interview."

At one point, Russo asks Rockefeller, "What's the point of all this? You have all the money in the world, all the power you need. What's the point? What's the end goal?" Rockefeller responded, "The end goal is to get everybody chipped (referring to RFID chips, which hold individual medical and financial data) to control the whole society to have the banks and the elite people and some government controlling the whole world."

MY CONCLUSIONS

After reviewing all the evidence, here is what I concluded. I wonder what you will decide.

I believe 9/11 was planned by the US government in advance of 9/11 to further what it called its vital interest (control of the planet's oil supply). I believe it was a covert attack on US citizens by CIA operatives, working in conjunction with George Bush, Dick Chaney, elements of the US military, the FBI, and foreign nationals (Osama bin Laden/Al-Qaeda) hired by the US government.

Any decent detective always looks for motive means and opportunity. The government had plenty of all three. On the other hand, Bin Laden and his band of terrorist had motive but means and opportunity were limited. They would have been able to get on the planes (if they were helped, say from a security company owned by the president's brother), but from there on out, they would have been powerless to control any of the day's activities. They could not have kept NORAD plans from intercepting the hijacked plans, like the vice president who was in charge of NORAD). They could not have scheduled a military training exercise, which was the governments excuse for not getting the planes off the ground. They could not have gotten access to the WTC to wire it for demolition, like say the president's brother and Mr. Silverstein could have. They could not have impeded the investigation or buried evidence, like say the president and vice president are accused of. Only the US government had the capability to do all these things and so they make a much better suspect than a group of rag tag terrorist with limited access to crucial resources necessary to pull off such a sophisticated attack. This said, you draw your own conclusions. These are only my opinions.

Wait there's more! Before you make you final decision, I have one more piece of information for you to consider. Remember earlier when I mentioned the financial elite have a playbook and that if we could get our hands on it, their actions would become crystal clear, and we would even be able to predict their future plans. Actually, they use several playbooks. In this instance, the one of interest is a book by General Sir Frank Kitson, commander-in-chief, UK Land Forces, who was the innovator of a strategy he called "pseudo gangs," which was a concept trailblazing "fake terrorism." It utilized state sponsored groups to further the government's agenda while blaming the events on the opposition. It is the strategy, which was used in the formation of Al-Qaeda. Go figure yet another coincidence.

Now, you have all the information you need to reach your verdict. Was the US government complicit in the deaths of over three thousand American citizen in the 9/11 attacks? Even though I did not want to broach this topic, God told me it was essential.

Thus said the Lord, "As long as the citizens of any nation can be tricked by its leaders into going to war, there can be no peace, and it is time the lies of the enemy were exposed so mankind can begin a journey toward peace."

WARS FOR PROFIT AND CONTROL

The Grim Reaper Roams the Land!

Rhetoric was flying
Tempers were flaring
Rage was in the air

Nations were posturing
Their leaders were shouting
Insults were flying

Drums were beating
The march was proceeding
Lovers were pleading
Boys were leaving

Hearts would soon be breaking
Hatred was everywhere
And war was in the air

All were infected
None were protected
For lies were everywhere
War not for honor
War not for glory

But war for *greed* was to proceed

The truth about war. "If my sons did not want wars, there would be none" (Gutle Schnaper, wife of Mayer Amschel Rothschild).

This, coming from the wife the man who said, "I care not what puppet is placed upon the throne of England to rule the empire on which the sun never sets. The man who controls Britain's money supply controls the British Empire, and I control the British money supply" (Amschel Rothschild).

"In other words, war is a business, and the currency of war is human lives—yours, mine, and our children's, and it is time we wake up to that fact and stop sacrificing our lives for a pack of lies fed to us, like a narcotic, by a bunch of power crazy men who see us as nothing more than expendable resources in their narcissistic quest for power" (Larry Ballard).

"Military men are just dumb stupid animals to be used as pawns in foreign policy" (Henry Kissinger, former national security advisor, secretary of state in Nixon and Ford administrations, and recipient of the Nobel Peace Prize). To our brave soldiers, I ask, "How does it make you feel to be referred to as a pawn in foreign policy? My, my, Henry, what a pedigree! Your mother must be proud! Now, folks, let me break it down for you. This man who obviously has no regard for our military, for our sons and daughters, who uses them like pawns in a chess game without any regard for the sanctity of their lives, he and men like him send our children off to die in foreign wars to as he said, "Be used as pawns in foreign policy." Then, when the wars are over, he and men like him are given Nobel Peace Prizes when instead they should be put on trial for crimes against humanity. War is a business, and our children are the leverage used by the elite to gain power, money, and natural resources. That is the truth of the matter, pure and simple. Oh. By the way, Kissinger was also instrumental in opening relations with the People's Republic of China, so our manufacturing sector could be gutted, our balance of trade turned upside down, and our nation lead like a blind donkey down the path to unmanageable debt. Yes, Kissinger is a great man, and I am sure God has a special place for him somewhere in the down under.

As you are about to learn from some of the world's most ruthless men, war is never about what the masses think it is about. It is about the world's most powerful men, lying to the masses in order to get them to give up their liberty, their dignity, their humanity, their sanity, their vitality, their wealth, and their lives in order to benefit leaders who consider them to be "resources to be expended in pursuit of something they consider more valuable than our lives." They feed us a pack of lies in order to make us feel it is our moral obligation, our patriotic duty to go to war to defend what they portray as our "duty to God and country." Life is cheap to the power crazed leaders of the world.

Julius Caesar on the folly of war and patriotic fervor: "Beware of the leader who bangs the drums of war in order to whip the citizenry into patriotic fervor, for patriotism is indeed a double-edged sword. It both emboldens the blood, just as it narrows the mind. And when the drums of war have reached a fever pitch and the blood boils with hate and the mind has closed, the leader will have no need in seizing the rights of the citizenry, (who) infused with fear and blinded by patriotism, will offer up all of their rights unto the leader and gladly so. How well I know? For this I have done. And I am Julius Caesar."

Goering, Hitler's second in command, on leading a nation into war: Just tell them they are being attacked. It works every time!

"Naturally, the common people don't want war. Neither in Russia nor in England, nor for that matter in Germany. That is understood. But, after all, *it is the leaders* of the country who determine the policy, and it is always a simple matter to drag the people along, whether it is a democracy, or a fascist dictatorship, or a parliament, or a communist dictatorship. Voice or no voice, the people can always be brought to the bidding of the leaders. That is easy. All you have to do is *tell them they are being attacked*, and denounce the peacemakers for lack of patriotism and exposing the country to danger. *It works the same in any country*" (Goering at the Nuremberg Trials). As you saw in the last chapter, this is in all probability what 9/11 was about—to get us to be willing to go to war over oil interests in the Middle East.

Hitler, the master of propaganda. Tell them a big enough lie, and they will believe it!

"The size of the lie is a definite factor in causing it to be believed, for the mass of a nation are in the depths of their hearts more easily deceived than they are consciously and intentionally bad. The primitive simplicity of their minds renders them a more easy prey to a big lie than to a small one, for they themselves often tell little lies but would be ashamed to tell big lies" (Adolf Hitler's *Mein Kampf*, 1925). After reading volumes of information about 9/11, I firmly believe 9/11 was one of the biggest lies ever perpetrated on humanity, and we swallowed it hook, line, and sinker, and our boys and girls are still paying the cost of our naiveté. Our government is the biggest threat we will ever face.

Like I have said before, the war on terror is about oil. "America has become little more than an energy protection force doing anything to gain access to expensive fuel without regard to the lives of others or the earth itself" (political Analyst Kevin Philip).

That's why we are in Afghanistan and Iraq. America has blood on its hands.

* * *

It is time their hold over us was broken and the invisible chains loosened, so we can go free, free to pursue a world at peace rather than at war!

There is a way. Once we understand that the root cause of war is selfishness, greed, and abuse of power, we can decide to beat our swords into plow shears and create a world where the resources of the world are not hoarded by a few incredibly ruthless men but are shared for the betterment of all.

"If a nation expects to be ignorant and free, in a state of civilization, it expects what never was and never will be" (Thomas Jefferson). The truth will set you free.

God has prepared me for over forty years for this exact moment in time, and he has charged me with the responsibility to "open the eyes of the people of the world," so that we may see the truth and "the truth may set us free."

Peace is impossible as long as we serve the evil rulers of this earth. We have to see them for what they are—evil overlords. We have to surrender to God and repent our sins, and if we do, we can walk into the future promised in the Bible,—a future where man and beast live in harmony.

"The wolf shall dwell with the lamb, and the leopard shall lie down with the kid; and the calf and the young lion and the fatling together: and a little child shall lead them" (Isaiah 11:6 NKJV).

This is a parable describing what the world can be like when we no longer have to serve evil masters intent on destroying us. We can learn to live as the family of man and to trust as a small child.

WHAT IS IMPERIALISM, AND WHY SHOULD WE CARE?

"I define imperialism as the process whereby the dominant investor interests (the financial elite) in one country bring to bear their economic and military power upon another nation or region in order to expropriate its land, labor, natural resources, capital, and markets—in such a manner as to enrich the investor interests. In a word, empires do not just pursue 'power for power's sake.' There are real and enormous material interests at stake, fortunes to be made many times over" (Michael Parenti, author, *Against Empire*, February14, 2010, commondreams.org).

- Our two wars in the Middle East are about oil and a strategic foothold in the region and not about Homeland Security. You protect the homeland by closing the borders. And you certainly do not foster good relations with the Muslims by invading them and killing them.

"Is there any man, is there any woman, let me say any child here that does not know that the seed of war in the modern world is industrial and commercial rivalry?" (Woodrow Wilson).

America is often referred to as "The nation forged on war!" What does that mean, and why should we care?

War good for a few bad for most. "The enormous gap between what US leaders do in the world and what Americans think their leaders are doing is one of the great propaganda accomplishments of the dominate political mythology" (Michael Parenti, author and historian).

- It is time we woke up and realized that America has arguably more blood on it's hands than any nation in the history of the world. If we don't put a stop to it God will stop it for us and the consequences will be grave.

"From 1945 to 2003, the United States attempted to overthrow more than forty foreign governments and to crush more than thirty populist-nationalist movements fighting against intolerable regimes. In the process, the US bombed some twenty-five countries, caused the end of life for several million people, and condemned many millions more to a life of agony and despair" (William Blum, *Rogue State: A Guide to the World's Only Superpower*).

- Is it any wonder nations around the world hate the US?
- So much for all our rhetoric about human rights. Let's face it; the US will support any regime no matter how ruthless and corrupt they are as long as it furthers our interest. So who is the bully of the planet?

So why should we care? "America's permanent war economy has endured since the end of World War II. Since then, the US has been at war, somewhere, every year, in Korea, Nicaragua, Vietnam, the Balkans, Afghanistan—all this to the accompaniment of shorter military forays in Africa, Chile, Grenada, Panama, and increasingly at home against its own people" (Seymour Melman, author of several books from an article "In the Grip of a Permanent War Economy," Counter Punch, March 15, 2003).

- The legal foundation has been established to declare martial law at will.

So why should we care? The US spends more on military expenditures than the combined totals of the worlds next 10 highest military spending nations.

"We are like the British at the end of World War II: Desperately trying to shore up an empire that we never needed and can no longer afford, using methods that often resemble those of failed empires of the past—including the Axis powers of World War II and the former Soviet Union. There is an important lesson for us in the British decision, starting in 1945, to liquidate their empire relatively voluntarily, rather than being forced to do so by defeat in war, as were Japan and Germany or by debilitating colonial conflicts, as were the French and Dutch. We should follow the British example..." (Chalmers Johnson, author of *Blowback*, *The Sorrows of Empire*, and *Nemesis: The Last Days of the American Republic*, in an article titled "Dismantling the Empire, July 30, 2009, Tom Dispatch.com).

- Our military spending is one of the things driving us into economic collapse, and it is not to protect our homeland as they tell us. It is to secure strategic military advantage and to secure the world's resources.

Roosevelt, talking to Churchill at the end of WWII, "I am firmly under the belief that if we are to develop a stable peace, it must entail the development of backward countries, backward peoples."

So why should we care? "According to the 2008 official Pentagon inventory of our military bases around the world, our empire consists of 865 facilities in more than forty countries and overseas." (Chalmers Johnson, "Dismantling the Empire").

- This is why we are crucial to establishing the one-world government. We are the world's only truly global military presence. They want us in concert with NATO in order to be able to control the rest of the world by force, if necessary.

Do we have blood on our hands? Is America an imperialist aggressor? "America has become little more than an energy protection force doing anything to gain access to expensive fuel without regard to the lives of others or the earth itself" (Political Analyst Kevin Philips).

The birth of Iran's Hatred of the US. According to Stephen Kinser, author of *All the Shah's Men: American Coup and The Roots of Middle East Terror*, in 1951, the Iranians rebelled against a British oil company, which was exploiting them. In response, the "democratically elected, popular leader" of Iran Mahammad Massaden, who I might mention was *Time Magazine*'s "Man of the Year," nationalized the Iranian oil resources. England, seeking to reverse this decision sought the help of the US. After careful consideration, it was decided that because of Massaden's popularity that military intervention would not be advisable. Instead, it was decided to conduct a covert CIA led incursion. The grandson of Theodore Roosevelt, CIA operative Kermit Roosevelt was sent in with instructions to destabilize the government. For a scant few million dollars, he bribed people, threatened others, and orchestrated a series of demonstrations and riots that made it appear that Massaden was inept and unpopular. He was deposed and spent the rest of his life under house arrest. He was replaced by pro-American dictator and tyrant Mahammad Reza Shah, known as the Shah of Iran (the king of kings). In subsequent years, this low profile low budget coup would be refined and serve as the model for future US covert operations and imperialist endeavors.

Unfortunately for the US, the Iranian people despised the pro-American Shah, and in 1979, they revolted, led by religious leader Ayatollah Khomeini and overthrew the Shah who fled to the US. Hatred for the US spilled out into the streets of Iran, and in November 1979, an Islamic mob seized the US embassy in Tehran and held fifty-two Americans hostage for 444 days. In April of 1980, President Carter attempted a failed military rescue, and on this note, ended twenty-nine years of US intervention into the affairs of Iran. The hostages were eventually released. The seeds of Middle East terrorism had been sown by the US and British exploitation of the Iranian people and their oil resources.

Unfortunately, most Americans were too busy living their lives of luxury to realize what we had done in Iran and elsewhere in the world. To this day, few Americans understand why so many nations of the world see the US flag as a symbol of hatred and oppression. By the time you finish this chapter, you will understand, and you will have to decide if you want to be complicit in this game of empire, this game of modern slavery, or are you willing to say that it is the right of all people to enjoy the "inalienable rights promised by the Declaration of Independence."

Birth of the economic hit man (EHM). Out of the events of the 1951, Iranian coup evolved a subtler less risky plan for future covert operations. The problem with the Iranian model was that Kermit Roosevelt was a card caring CIA operative. If he had been caught, the US would have no deniability; they would have been caught orchestrating a coup of a popular democratically elected leader of a sovereign nation. The answer to this problem was to enlist the services of a group of men that would come to be known as the economic hit men (EHM) of which John Perkins was one. He recounts his life as a CIA surrogate and explains he never received any money from the CIA, NSA, or any other government agency. He was hired as a consultant by the private sector so that if ever exposed, his activities would appear to be the result of corporate greed rather than government complicity. He recounts that in addition, "the corporations that hired him, although paid by government agencies and their multinational banking counterparts (with taxpayer money), would be insulated from congressional oversight and public scrutiny, shielded by a growing body of legal initiatives, including trademark, international trade, and freedom of information laws."

In the preface to his book, Perkins defines exactly what an EHM is. He says "Economic hit men (EHMs) are highly paid professionals who cheat countries around the globe out of trillions of dollars. They funnel money from the World Bank, U.S. Agency for International Development, and other foreign "aid" organizations into the coffers of huge corporations and the pockets of a few wealthy families who control the planet's natural resources. Their tools include fraudulent financial reports, rigged elections, payoffs, extortion, sex, and murder. They play a game as old as empire, but one that has taken on new and terrifying dimensions during this time of globalization. I should know I am an EHM."

Perkins coined a name for the confluence of the international banks, international corporations and the would be one-world government. He calls them collectively the "corporatocracy," which is just another name for what I call the "the financial elite." He goes on to say that the corporatocracy's use of debt, bribery, and political overthrow is what he defines as "globalization."

In the name of foreign aid America in concert with the World Bank, IMF, the US Agency for International Development (USAID) have for decades engaged in a worldwide scheme to drive resource rich underdeveloped nations into bankruptcy.

- The US uses economic hit men, such as John Perkins to loan billions to third world countries for infrastructure projects and then makes sure they default on their loans and then their natural resources are taken as assets against the default. Guess what? Now they are doing it to the US. That is why it is now possible for foreign investors to buy US infrastructure, and it is why we recently gave oil reserves to both Russia and China. America is for sale to the highest bidder.

We have been duped, and it is time to wake up!

"The whole aim of practical politics is to keep the populace alarmed—and hence, clamorous to be led to safety—by menacing it with an endless series of hobgoblins, all of them imaginary" (H.L. Mencken). Wake up! This is what 9/11 and the war on terror is really about!

Hopefully, you begin to have an appreciation as to why so many nations hate America. Why they burn our flag. Why they feel exploited by both American corporations and the American government. As long as we persist with our current policies of exploitation, we will continue to be a symbol of global hatred. And think long and hard about this. The weaker we get, the more likely the next war will be on American soil. There is always a time of reckoning. It is time we perused peace not war.

A note to all you mothers and fathers out there:

> The military-industrial complex spares no expense in recruiting our children to use then as fodder to serve their interest. For example, they sponsor paint ball tournaments and video game tournaments and then approach our impressionable teens and tell them how good they are at what they do and how Uncle Sam could use their talents. *Use* is the right word. They glorify war; but war, unlike a video game, has no reset button, and the bullets they shoot don't just splatter on your clothing—they kill and main. But the recruiters don't tell them that. If you have teens, I encourage you to try and get them to read this book so they can be armed with the truth.
>
> Sincerely,
> Larry Ballard

PART 4

Fighting Back: Countermeasures

STRATEGIC COUNTEROFFENSIVE

A House Divided Cannot Be Victorious!

Victory lies in knowing yourself and
knowing your enemy even better!
If you are to win, you must know the end
even before the beginning.
Victory comes not necessarily to the mightiest
but to him with foreknowledge.
Foreknowledge comes not to the rash
but to the quiet and contemplative.
Victory is conceived by intellect and
is realized by courage and resolve.
Passivity and lack of resolve are fatal wounds
to be inflicted on your enemy.
He who makes a frontal assault will lose to
stealth and attack from within.

The greatest victories are those
won without bloodshed!
War is a game of intellect more than a
game of power and might.
It is a game of illusion; using secrecy, deception,
misdirection, and diversion.
It is more a game of psychology and strategy
than of force and strength.
In any event, strive to win with minimal
resources and casualties.
He who decides where, when, and under what
conditions to fight has the advantage.

Moral and political context are more important
than military context.
Victory is conceived in leadership, discipline,
loyalty, resolve, and belief in a cause.
Victory is birthed in moral superiority and
knowing that to lose is to die.
The wise leader avoids his enemy's strength and
attacks his weaknesses.
Above all, a people must *stand united* for a house
divided cannot be victorious!

Our strategy to restore America to greatness is comprised of four steps:

Step one. *We first have to know our enemy as well as we know ourselves.* That means we have to have his playbooks and understand his tactics, so we can counteract them.

Step two. *We have to learn how to outthink our enemy* for that we will study the military tactics of the greatest military strategist of all time Sun Tzu as outlined in his book *The Art of War.*

Step three. *We have to have a plan to fix what is broken*: Most revolutions, even if they succeed, erode into some form of dictatorship because when those in power are removed, a vacuum is created, because there is no plan in place to run the government and fix what was wrong with the old system. So, our third step will be a comprehensive political platform designed to restore the republic.

It is not rocket science. It's mostly a simple process of replacing those things, which have been stripped away in order to enslave us. Additionally, it takes into considerations that in a highly technological society some provisions are required, which were not in a more agrarian society, like that which existed when the US was founded.

Step four. *The American people must come together with one accord.* Lastly, in order to keep America from being intentionally collapsed and driven into the one-world government, we must put into place measures to "restore unity, equality, peace, liberty, and morality." Only then can we hope to maintain national sovereignty and take the United States of America into the twenty-first century. Otherwise, we will surely be absorbed into the tyrannical one-world government, and our freedom and quite possibly our lives will be forfeit.

Will you choose freedom or slavery? Well, you stand up and fight to restore what made America the greatest nation the world has ever known.

By the time you finish this book, we, collectively, will have the requisite knowledge to defeat our enemy—the financial elite and the puppets they have installed in the US, and virtually every sovereign nation in the world. I know this sounds a little utopian, but I think you will be pleasantly surprised when you see the entire picture.

Stand up and be heard! The time is now or never.

COUNTEROFFENSIVE MEASURES: TAKING BACK THE REPUBLIC

Step One: Know Your Enemy

At last, it is time to go on the offensive, or nearly so. In order to defeat an enemy, a commander must know his adversary as well as he knows himself. A great leader must literally know his adversary so well that he can become him and anticipate his actions in advance and therefore have his counteroffensive planned and ready to execute even before his enemy launches an offensive. In other words, you must know the end before the beginning or put another way he must possess foreknowledge.

The key to attaining foreknowledge. Get your enemies' playbooks, and use the information in them against him in order to defeat him at his own game! That is precisely what we are going to do. We have discussed some of these books in passing. But in order to make sure we are focused, I am going to give a synopsis of each before we proceed with our strategic planning. I want to assure you that God is the one feeding me the information in this book, and he knows the end before the beginning so we are in good hands.

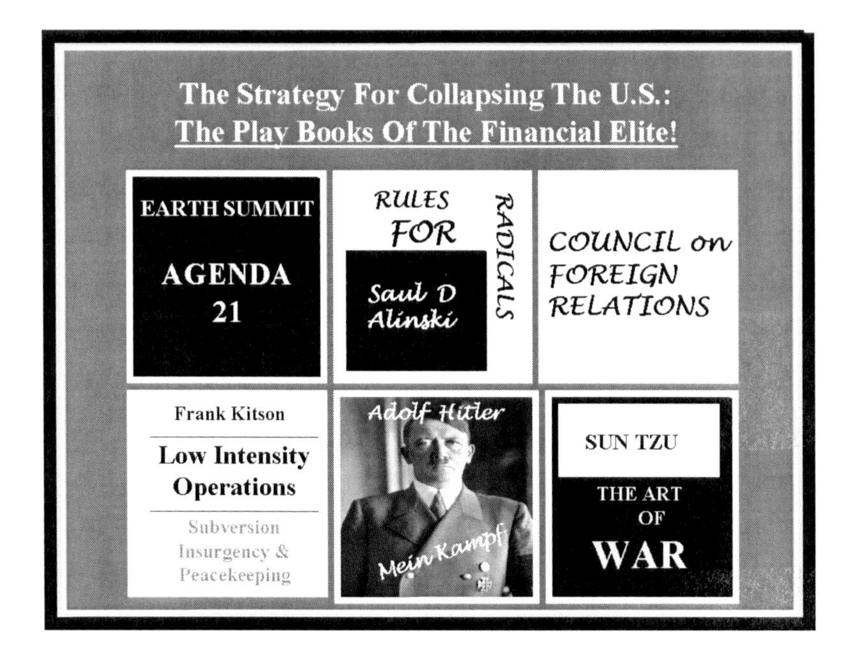

The Strategy For Collapsing The U.S:

The Play Books Of The Financial Elite!

1. *The Council On Foreign Relations HandbooK:* Lays out the plan to collapse the US from within.[Playbook for formation of the Shadow Government]
2. *Rules For Radicals:* (by Saul D. Alinsky)–Lays out the plan to collapse the US under a mountain of unmanageable debt and the strategy for creating divisiveness among "We The People." [Playbook for the financial and moral collapse of the US]
3. *Mein Kampf:* (By Adolf Hitler) – Details Hitler's plan for formation of the 3rd Reich, a plan which our government has followed in detail. [Playbook for 9/11 & military occupation]
4. *Low Intensity Operations: Subversion, Insurgency & Peacekeeping*: (By British General Frank Kitson) – Details a plan used by the British to rule their empire whereby they committed acts of terrorism and blamed them on others just like our CIA in order to scare us into willingly relinquishing our Constitutional

Freedoms. [Playbook for dismantling of the Constitution and our freedoms]

5. *Agenda 21:* The document which came out of the UN's Earth Summit which details their plan to control the earth's resources by collapsing "*The Free Market System*", imposing a global dictatorship and exterminating six billion people. [Playbook for genocide of most of us].
6. *The Art Of War:* (By Sun Tzu)—The military strategy book which describes how to defeat your enemy (The American People) by using our strengths against us through subversion, deception and betrayal. [Playbook for victory at any cost].

Further Synopsis of the Enemies Playbooks:

The Council On Foreigh Relations Handbook: Was written with one goal in mind, and that is to subvert our political leaders in Washington and provide them with a plan for carrying out the *collapse of the US from within*, orchistrated by the very people elected to protect and serve the Republic. It is vitally important that we understand that our political system has been corrupted.The enemy is among us and he is more dangerious than any external force because up till now he has operated under the cloak of secracy. No longer. It is time to expose our corrupt politicians for the traitors they are. They are part of a Shadow Government intent on Collapsing the US by any means necessary. They are enemy # 1. The following quotes will give you a glimpse into their sinister plans. Sorry I repeat so many quotes but they have to be read in context of different situations in order to get the full implication of the elites plan.

"Council on Foreign Relations is 'the establishment.' Not only does it have influence and power in key decision-making positions at the highest levels of government to apply pressure from above, but it also uses individuals and groups to bring pressure from below, to justify the high level decisions for converting the US from a sovereign constitutional republic into a servile member state of a one-world dictatorship" (Former Congressman John Rarick, 1971).

"The New World Order will be built…an end run on national sovereignty, eroding it piece by piece will accomplish much more than the old fashioned frontal assault" (Council on Foreign Relations journal, 1974, p558).

"We shall have world government whether or not you like it. The only question is whether world government will be by conquest or consent" (James P. Warburg, representing Rothschild banking concern while speaking before the United States Senate, Feb. 17, 1950).

So the Council on Foreign Relations is on record as intending to do an end run on national sovereignty and forcing the US into the one-world government by any means possible. And according to former Congressman John Rarick, those at the highest level of our government are complicit in their treasonous plans. That is why in an earlier chapter, I warned you about the shadow government in Washington and listed the names of key government officials who belong to the subversive Council on Foreign Relations and their sister organization, the Trilateral Commission. As far as I am concerned, any individual who belongs to one of these subversive organizations is a traitor to the American people. Unfortunately, that is virtually anyone of importance in Washington. How unfortunate.

Rules For Radicals—taught by Obama while at ACORN. The book endorses collapsing the free market system by burying it under a mountain of debt. So in Obama, we have a president committed to collapsing the economy of the US by burying it under a mountain of debt, debt from unfunded entitlements, debt from intentionally losing trade agreements coupled with crushing regulations, debt from any and all forms of reckless spending, *including war.*

Obama is modeling his "non-recovery" after Roosevelt's "New Deal," which failed miserably. His strategies are intended to fail. They are intended to devalue the dollar and eventually collapse it. He is intent on driving up the national debt with all his borrowing, which will of necessity lead to higher taxes, and in the final analysis, he intends to crush the middle class and implement a highbred capitalist, communist one-world government modeled after China.

Most importantly, I want to stress that he has been the most divisive president in the history of the nation. He absolutely wants to pit different ethnic, religious, and political groups against each other so we are so busy fighting each other that we cannot fight our real enemy, "our own government." Lastly, I urge everyone to look at what is happening in Greece. When the house of cards falls and the economy finally falls, and it will, all the unfunded entitlements will come to an abrupt end. They are only a means to collapse the economy and once that is accomplished the free handouts will go away—*guaranteed*!

Let's take another look at this quote from the Council on Foreign Relations in light of Obama's role as president. I think you will be shocked. "The Council on Foreign Relations is 'the establishment.' Not only does it have influence and power in key decision-making positions at the highest levels of government to apply ***pressure from above***, but it also uses individuals and groups to bring ***pressure from below***, to justify the high level decisions for converting the US from a sovereign constitutional republic into a servile member state of a one-world dictatorship" (Former Congressman John Rarick, 1971).

So while at ACORN, Obama applied pressure from below (community organizing groups), and now as president, he is applying pressure from above (his use of executive orders to force the policies of the Left down our throats). Here is a clear example of the tactics of the Council on Foreign Relations being implemented in order to collapse the US from within from the top-down and the bottom-up just like they threatened to do. Now you know what Obama means by The Fundamental Transformation of America.

Mein Kampf: Many of the strategies being used to collapse the US and in particular to undermine the Constitution and strip us of the liberties it guarantees come directly from *Mein Kampf*. As we discussed, the "Patriot's Act" is a retread of Hitler's "Enabling Act." Hitler established his Brownshirts and SS, which was a standing army that he used to crush all dissenters and eventually declare himself dictator. Now Obama is calling for a million man standing army. 9/11 is a replay of Hitler's burning of the German Parliament. Hitler built concentration camps and so is our government. The only difference is they are hiding their real purpose behind the innocent sounding name of "resettlement camps." Please open your eyes.

"How fortunate for governments that the people they administer don't think" (Adolf Hitler).

"It is not truth that matters but victory" (Adolf Hitler).

"Communism is the death of the soul. It is the organization of total conformity—in short, a tyranny—and it is committed to making tyranny universal" (Adlai E. Stevenson, ambassador to United Nations).

Just like Hitler, our present government in Washington is lying to us and by their own admission trying to end US sovereignty by collapsing us from within in order to drive us into a super capitalist communist one-world tyrannical government. They are our enemy, the enemy from within, the most dangerous enemy we will ever face.

Low intensity operations: Subversion, insurgency, and peacekeeping. As we discussed in the **chapter entitled** "Preparing for Martial Law" this book endorses the use of state sponsored groups to further the government's agenda while blaming the events on the opposition. It is the strategy, which was used in the formation of Al-Qaeda, and in my opinion, to perpetrate 9/11. Was Osama involved in 9/11? You bet he was, but what you may not know is he was a CIA asset recruited and trained by the US in the Afghan/Russian war. Was the US government involved in 9/11? As I discussed in the chapter entitled "Preparing for Martial Law", the events of 9/11 could not have been orchestrated from a cave ½ a world away. Only the US government had the motive, means and opportunity. A quick review: Only our government had motive, means, and opportunity.

1. 9/11 furthered the government's imperialist's plans. In 2000, a report was issued "Project for New American Century" (PNAC). It called for massive military expenditures, which the report said were not likely short of a second Pearl Harbor. Well,

there you go. Just one year later, they got what they asked for and some three thousand American souls were lost. Coincidence?

2. Marvin Bush was a partner in Securacom Security Company, which had the security contract for the Twin Towers. (Opportunity)
3. Access for getting terrorist into Dulles Airport: Securacom had that contract as well. (Opportunity)
4. Ordered a stand-down of US fighters. One month before 9/11, the general-in-charge of NORAD was relieved from duty and replaced by VP Chaney. (Opportunity)
5. Bush and Chaney refused to testify under oath. (Cover-up and avoid impeachment, if they got caught lying under oath.)
6. Illegally removed evidence from the crash sites. FBI removed evidence from Pentagon and the lawn of the Pentagon was covered with gravel and dirt. (Cover-up and control the seine.)
7. Ordered military exercises to take place on 9/11 just like on 7/7 when the British rail stations were attacked. (Cover-up and control the seine.)
8. Relatives of the victims charged Warren Commission of covering up the government's involvement. (Cover-up)
9. Ordering that building 7 be brought down. It had minimal damage compared to buildings 3–6, which remained standing. So why did it collapse in free fall fashion? Could it be because it housed the records for the ENRON scandal and other white color crimes the bankers wanted expunged. (Motive, means, and opportunity)
10. Probable insurance fraud. The Twin Towers were sold to politically connected Larry Silverstein just weeks prior to 9/11. He immediately had the insurance policy rewritten to cover terrorist attacks and in such an event to allow the buildings to be rebuilt. Just six weeks later, that is exactly what happened and he got a $7 billion settlement for a piece of real estate that was in the red and had a $1 billion asbestos removal liability. (Opportunity to install explosives.)
11. Failed to investigate insider trading. Billions were made by selling the companies in the towers short. Don't they always say follow the money? (Motive, means, and opportunity)

Will the coincidences never cease?

The really shocking thing is none of these things were investigated. I guess the Warren Commission just thought they were coincidences, or could it be as the relatives of the victims charged and our government did everything they could to cover up their involvement in 9/11? A government who would kill three thousand of its own citizens would not hesitate to kill six billion. After all, it is just a few more decimal points, and as Kissinger said, we are just pawns.

Stand up! Wake up!

"Demoralize the enemy from within by surprise, terror, sabotage, assassination. This is the war of the future" (Adolf Hitler). Isn't that what 9/11 did and isn't that what terrorism does, and isn't that exactly what low intensity operations calls for and isn't that exactly what the government sponsored Al-Qaeda does? What a coincidence? Is it just me or does something stink around here?

If you combine the philosophy of Hitler's *Mein Kampf* with that of Kitson's *Low Intensity Operations*, we have a pretty good explanation of the "War on Terror" where a government creates a crisis (in this case, a terrorist attack) and blames it on opposition forces. I believe that the facts support the thesis that CIA operative Osama bin Laden was in fact complicit in the events of 9/11, but without internal support from the US government, he would never have been able to pull off such a sophisticated attack. As we discussed, he simply could not have gained access to the Twin Towers or Dulles Airport, he could not have scheduled the all so convenient military exercises, he could not have ordered the suspected stand-down of fighter planes, and he would not have had the boots on the ground to cover up the truth, but our government had both the means and opportunity to do all these things. 9/11 is an example of the combining of the strategies of multiple playbooks in order to achieve a desired goal. In this instance, the economic collapse of the US.

The facts support the statement that no terrorist operating from a cave half a world away could have pulled off 9/11 without support from the US government. It is important that we stop and think hard and long before we allow our government to use another terrorist attack to take away our remaining freedom.

The quote below is from the previous chapter, but I repeat it here because I believe that in this particular context it is particularly revealing as to the events of 9/11 and the two playbooks we have been discussing.

"Naturally the common people don't want war neither in Russia, nor in England, nor for that matter, in Germany. That is understood. But, after all, *it is the leaders* of the country who determine the policy, and it is always a simple matter to drag the people along, whether it is a democracy, or a fascist dictatorship, or a parliament, or a communist dictatorship. Voice or no voice, the people can always be brought to the bidding of the leaders. That is easy. All you have to do is *tell them they are being attacked*, and denounce the peacemakers for lack of patriotism and exposing the country to danger. *It works the same in any country*" (Goering at the Nuremberg Trials).

The UN's Agenda 21. Just a reminder Agenda 21 calls for a reduction of global population from seven billion to one billion, severe restrictions on resource consumption, an end to national sovereignty, abandonment of the Constitution, presumption of guilt till proven innocent "no inalienable rights," abolition of private property, education focused first and foremost on the environment, restructuring of the family unit, education to create allegiance to the state, limitations on mobility "with upward of 75 percent of the land off limits," Limitations on education and carrier opportunities with "state control of access to higher education and employment opportunities," lack of privacy, "state-owned residential units along rail corridors," or in other words, total slavery.

Knowing this may well save your life! Proof Agenda 21 is being implemented even now. I believe there are numerous examples of this agenda being carried out in our everyday lives. The housing collapse (triggered by the events of 9/11) resulted in the (privately owned) Fed, Fannie and Freddie, acquiring the mortgages of millions of Americans. In Obama's Health Care Bill, he took over control of student loans and levied a 3.8 percent tax on the sale of second homes. Thanks to Bush, Americans can be arrested and indefinitely detained without any legal recourse. Obamacare is nothing short of cloaked genocide as senior citizens will be denied care because the cost benefit analysis says they are too old to warrant the cost of care. Our leaders in Washington hold Mao, who starved sixty million of his own people to death, in reverence; so is it farfetched to think that their takeover of all water rights in the country, coupled with policies that make us dependent on Arab oil and policies that allow genetically engineered non-germinating grains may at some time, in the not too distant future, be used to starve millions of us to death in order to achieve the population reduction called for in Agenda 21! It is all right there for us to see, if we will only open our eyes.

The art of war: The Council On Foreign Relations (CFR) journal says "they will impose a one-world government whether or not we like it. The only question is whether it will be by conquest or consent." That tells us what the elite plan on doing, but not how they plan on doing it. That is where the "art of war" comes in. It tells us how they plan on doing it. Just like the CFR, Sun Tzu says the preferred strategy is to overcome you enemy without bloodshed, but if you must fight, then intellect is the key to winning. It is essential that we understand Sun Tzu's strategy, so we will be exploring it in detail momentarily.

COUNTEROFFENSIVE MEASURES: TAKING BACK THE REPUBLIC

Step two: Know How to Outthink the Enemy

I am absolutely certain the government's strategists are using Sun Tzu's *The Art of War*, so we are going to look at recent political events through that looking glass.

Me: I am sorry, but I just realized that before we get ahead of ourselves, we need to take a brief junket back in time to lay some essential groundwork. I know most people don't like history, but this is essential to our understanding of today's events.

It is as Churchill said, "Study history, study history. In history lies all the secrets of statecraft."

Historical perspective: the origin of the one-world government—the empire of evil!

It was the dawning of the colonial era. The monarchs of Europe were on a mission of conquest. They were establishing colonies around the world in order to enrich their empires by enslaving the indigenous people and stealing the wealth of their nations—their natural resources. They plundered nations for their gold and traded in opium and slaves. The descendents of these Monarchs are in many instances the modern day financial elite. Having for centuries plundered the world's wealth through colonization, today, they do essentially the same thing through free trade and their system of central banks.

What Chinese slave labor has done to destroy America! Why your freedom is disappearing and the dollar is worthless!

"It (the British free trade system) is the most gigantic system of slavery the world has yet seen, and therefore, it is that freedom gradually disappears from every country over which England (the free trade System) is enabled to obtain control" (Henry C. Carey, economics adviser to Abraham Lincoln).

Substitute China for England, and you can see what is happening to drive the US into unmanageable debt.

"Free trade shaves down the workingman's labor first, and then scales down his pay by rewarding him in a worthless and depreciated State currency" (William McKinley, Oct. 4, 1892).

Isn't this exactly what is happening to the dollar? It is being intentionally devalued by the government sworn to protect us!

The True Cause Of WWI!

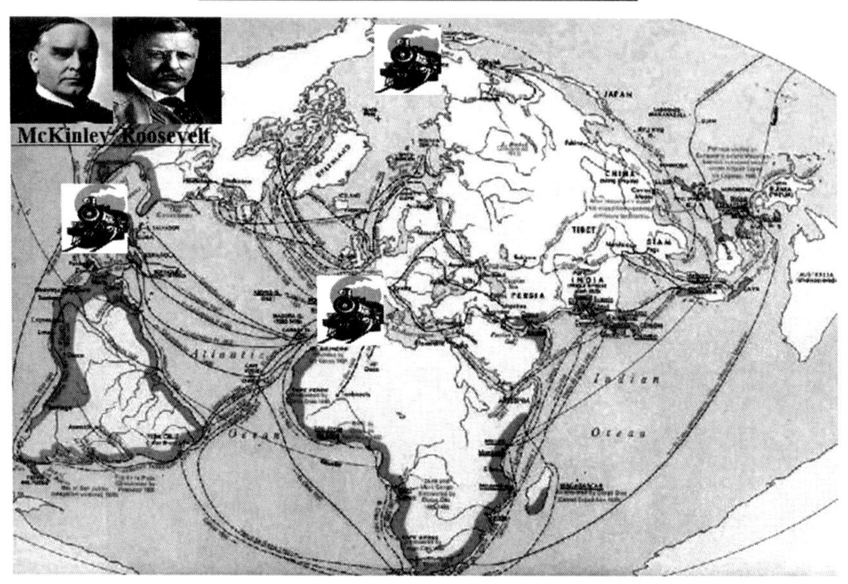

The true cause of WWI: WWI was not about the assignation of Arch Duke Ferdinand as is commonly thought. That was just the pretext. WWI was really about maintaining England's lock on global trade by sea which was being threatened by expansion of America's Transcontinental Railroad System which threatened to spread to, South America, Europe, Asia and Africa effectively making trade by sea outdated and shifting the global power structure. England could not allow that, so they started WWI with the intent of destroying all of Europe and throwing the world into chaos.

Two forms of government lie before us—one, represents freedom; the other, slavery!

The American System of Economics. "Two systems are before the world. One is the English system; the other, we may be proud to call the American System Of Economics, the only one ever devised the tendency of which was that of elevating while equalizing the condition of man throughout the world" (Henry C. Carey, economics adviser to Abraham Lincoln).

What is this quote referring to? Lincoln and McKinley were champions of what they called the American System of Economics. As Lincoln took office, America was entering the greatest period of economic growth and expansion ever experienced by any nation in the history of the world. We were leading the world into the industrial revolution, and we would soon be the first nation in the world to complete a transcontinental railroad in order to quickly and economically transport goods cross-country. This threatened England's virtual monopoly on global trade because the railroad had the ability to make their sea dominance obsolete. This figured in as a contributing factor to the civil war, a war in which England aided the South. Long story short, the South was still dependent on slavery and England's free trade system, while the North with its factories and emerging railroad system wanted to free itself from England's grip.

Me: Please bear with me. I know most people don't like history, but I assure you this is crucial to understanding our current political situation and our struggle with the financial elite.

Fast forward to WWI and thanks to America, England's control of global trade was in jeopardy. America had completed its transcontinental railroad and was sharing both that technology as well as our manufacturing technology with Europe. Japan, Russia, and Germany were embracing the American Economic System and all were modernizing, and most importantly, they were cooperating in building a network of connecting rail systems, which would—when completed—reach across the Bearing Straight, connecting Europe with the North America down through Central America, connecting North and South America across the Mediterranean, connecting Europe and Africa, leaving only Australia still dependent on shipping goods by sea. The English Empire faced the biggest threat in its history. The empire on which the sun never sets had to do something or it was going to lose its lock on global trade and with it its wealth.

Even though the US was the source of the threat, Germany was the key to solving the problem. Why, you ask? Because Germany had been far and away the most successful nation in the world in implementing the American system, and they had become a serious threat to England's power. A plan was devised to start WWI. There were to be no winners, only losers. All of Europe must be devastated, especially Germany. This would drastically slow down the industrialization, but most importantly, it would put an end to efforts to build the railroad system connecting most of the world's continents.

So here is the reason this piece of history is so important. It shows just how ruthless the financial elite are. Sixteen million people were killed, and twenty million were wounded and all of Europe was in ruins, but in the process, Germany was crushed and dreams of connecting the world by rail were crushed. Make no mistake; these men will not hesitate to purge the world of six billion people in order to establish their one-world government and gain control of the world's natural resources. It is crucial that you understand just how truly ruthless our enemy is.

(L-R) Abraham Lincoln, William McKinley, Louis McFadden, Larry McDonald, John Kennedy

All these men opposed the financial elite and were assassinated: Had it not been for the intervention of the Financial Elite into the history of the U.S. and the world, the world would be a much more peaceful and prosperous place. These men must be stopped.

By the way, a quick review. Lincoln was killed because he opposed the central bank of England and issued the Greenback. McKinley was killed to stop the expansion of the railroads through Central America into South America. McFadden was killed because he brought impeachment charges against the Fed for intentionally bringing about the 1929 Great Depression. McDonald was killed because he exposed the Rockefeller's plan to collapse the US in order to birth the one-world government, and Kennedy was killed because he signed Executive Order 11110 to disband the Fed. He issued US Silver Certificates to replace the Fed Notes, and he refused to expand the war in Vietnam. By the way, all three of Kennedy's initiatives were immediately reversed upon Johnson, taking office. Go Figure!

We are on death ground. This is a true account of American history, and it is essential that you know it so you understand that as Sun Tzu would say we are on death ground. This means either we win this battle with the financial elite or most of us will die. It is that simple and that urgent. It is essential that we put aside our differences and unite against our true enemy—our government! I know that seems impossible now, but when the entire truth has been revealed, it will be a possibility.

Oh, one more thing. As soon as McKinley was assassinated, Teddy Roosevelt, who was closely connected to England, stopped plans for the expansion of the railroads into South America. He immediately sent a battle ship into Columbia, seized the Panama Canal, and annexed part of Columbia and renamed it *Panama*. Go figure. As long as these men are allowed to rule over us we will never know peace, nor will we ever be free.

Back to Sun Tzu and the art of war. The intent here is to take Sun Tzu's military strategies and show you how the financial elite has adapted them in order to collapse the US and other sovereign nations around the world from within. If we can understand what they have done to us, it will allow us to resist their tactics in the future, and additionally, we can use this knowledge to discover their weaknesses and use them against them.

The primary tenants of victory in war and in life:

- *Know what is at stake/we are on death ground*. Put your forces in the face of death and they will fight with superhuman resolve because there is no other choice. On death ground, you must fight with *unity and resolve and with moral purpose*! War is a matter of life and death, survival or ruin, not only for the soldier on the field but as much so for the nation and its leaders. Victory comes to the resolute who understand what is at stake. Believe me, the financial elite and their shadow government know what is at stake, and they are committed to victory at any cost!

- ✓ Comments: So based on everything I have presented thus far in this book, what is at stake is our way of life, the future of our children, and indeed our freedom and our very lives, so we can scarcely afford to be *passive. We are indeed on death ground.* We can scarcely allow a government intent on destroying us to divide us and pit us against one another. Most of what we see as our differences are created by the inequalities created by our leaders. If we can see through the lies and deceptions inflicted on us, we can put aside our differences and unite against the real enemy—our government. In our hearts, the American people are kind and generous, and we want to, and we can find the common ground that unites us.
- ✓ A warning: either we stand together or we will surely loose our freedom, our security, and all that we hold dear.

- *Know your enemy as well as you know yourself. The* way a wise leader can distinguish himself is through foreknowledge.
  - ✓ Comments: What this means is you have to know enough about your advisory in order to be able to place yourself in his situation and be able to anticipate what his next move is likely to be. To do that you have to understand his endgame, his political objectives, who and what his assets are etc.—all of which we are going to explore in the next few pages.

- *Know the endgame:* You must know both your endgame and that of your enemy before engaging him. The loser enters the battle without understanding the conditions necessary for victory. In other words, you cannot hope to win a war, if you do not have a fully executed strategy with contingency plans laid out in advance. Believe me, the financial elite are if nothing else strategic, and we must learn to meet them on their terms, and we can.

- ✓ Comments: At this point, we know that our enemy is a group of financial elite who has infiltrated sovereign nations around the world and control banking institutions, key corporations, and key leaders in government, the media and academia, etc. They believe that the global population growth rate is unsustainable, and it is their responsibility to reduce it to sustainable levels (i.e., one billion people), and in the process, they intend to get control of the world's resources and to achieve their objective they must establish a one-world government with the military power to force compliance to their policies, which is why they must gain control of the US or in other words, the US must fall in order for the one-world government to rise.

- *Whenever possible, achieve victory without bloodshed.* The height of skill is to defeat your enemy without bloodshed or at least without direct confrontation. This is best achieved from within and through covert actions and misdirection rather than direct confrontation.
  - ✓ Comments: The CFR has stated that "the New World Order will be built…an end run on national sovereignty, eroding it piece by piece." That is important to know, but in and of itself, it is a relatively useless piece of information. We need to know specifically how they plan on doing it and the human and material assets, which they intend to use to accomplish their objectives. Here I am referring to the shadow government, which we discussed earlier. So as a quick review, they further their plans through the CFR and TC as well as the media, academia, key corporations, unions (e.g., SEIU), and community organizing groups, (e.g., ACORN, etc.).

- *Make your enemy passive.* The goal is to keep the enemy passive, because passivity is a fatal wound. This is what the shadow government has done to the US. They have done it by placating us with creature comforts and entitlements and the illusion that we have a free press, a democratic government, and freedom of choice, when in fact, we suffer the worst kind of slavery, a slavery where the slave is bound by imaginary chains.

"Our great industrial nation is now controlled by its system of credit. We are no longer a government by free opinion, no longer a government by conviction and the vote of the majority, but a government by the opinion and duress of a small group of dominant men. Our great industrial nation is controlled by its system of credit. Our system of credit is privately centered. The growth of the nation, therefore, and all our activities are in the hands of a few men, who necessarily by very reason of their own limitations chill, check, and destroy genuine economic freedom. We have become one of the worst ruled, one of the most completely controlled and dominated governments in the civilized world" (President Woodrow Wilson).

✓ Comments: In America today, we have only the illusion of democracy, only the illusion of freedom, only the illusion that we are in control of our own destiny. In reality a small group of self-serving men control us from cradle to grave and their control has to be brought to an end. As the financial elite put it: "Slavery is but the owning of labor and carries with it the care of labors, while the European plan…is that capital shall control labor by controlling wages" (*Hazard Circular*, July 1862). Isn't that exactly what is happening in America today?

If you knew your government had been taken over by a shadow government intent on destroying our democracy and establishing in its place a communist order dedicated to enslaving you, would you remain *passive* or would you stand up and fight? Congressman Larry McFadden told us exactly that in the following quote. So once you know the truth, will you fight back or *passively do nothing*? That is the question that will determine the future of our children.

"The Rockefeller File is not fiction. It is a compact, powerful, and frightening presentation of what may be the most important story of our lifetime—the drive of the Rockefellers and their allies to create a one-world government combining super capitalism and communism under the same tent, all under their control, not one has dared reveal the most vital part of the Rockefeller story that the Rockefellers and their allies have, for at least fifty years, been carefully following a plan to use their economic power to gain political control of first America, and then the rest of the world. Do I mean conspiracy? Yes, I do. I am convinced there is such a plot, international in scope, generations old in planning, and incredibly evil in intent" (Congressman Larry P. McDonald).

On August 31, 1983, Congressman Larry McDonald was killed aboard Korean Airline flight 007, which "accidentally my a—s" strayed over Soviet airspace and was "accidentally" shot down with no real protest by the US government. The media reporting was scant and short-lived and not a single mention was publicly made about the fact that McDonald had been heading a congressional effort to expose what he called a dangerous international conspiracy. No, my friends, the Russians would not have shot down a commercial airliner without the approval of the US. They would have either forced it to land or forced it to leave Russian air space. They would not have shot it down.

"If we don't fight back, we will just slip into communism like someone in a deep slumber. We can't let that happen. America is a nation of destiny and the fate of the world is in our hands" (Larry Ballard).

- *Use diversion and redirection to gain a strategic advantage.*
  - ✓ Comments: Al-Qaeda did it. No, Al-Qaeda is a scapegoat. Yes, the Muslims hate America, who they call the great, Satan but that doesn't change the facts that they are pawns in a bigger struggle. If our policies toward them were different, perhaps the hatred could be moderated. Yes, we have differences, but our government intentionally exacerbates them in order to use the conflict to their advantage. There

is a saying "My enemy's enemy is my friend." Our leaders use the Muslims to take our attention off of what they are systematically doing to take away our freedom.

- ✓ The problem with the economy is that the rich refuse to pay their fair share. No. The problem with the economy is the government's reckless out-of-control spending that is intended to drive us into bankruptcy. The problem is intentionally losing trade policies and government regulations intended to make US products noncompetitive in the global marketplace.
- ✓ The Whites hate the blacks and hold them down. No. The truth is that the government controlled educational system intentionally creates inequalities. The truth is that the Government Welfare System is not intended to help people get ahead. It is designed to make them dependent, so they can be controlled. The truth is that more white people lost their lives in the struggle to free the slaves than in all other American wars combined. The people are not the problem the government is the problem. They intentionally create divisiveness and hatred. When will we wake up?
- ✓ The problem is the Mexicans. No, the problem is not the Mexicans. America is a nation founded on immigration. It has opened its shores to people of every nationality and ethnicity. The problem is that the government is intentionally flooding America with more Mexican people than it can assimilate without radically altering our culture. All other immigrants have entered the country legally, have learned the language and assimilated into the culture. As with all the other problems, we have discussed the problem rest in government policies designed to create conflict and pit us against each others. This problem as with all the others can be solved, if the government can be gotten out of the way.
- ✓ *A warning: either we stand together or we will surely loose our freedom, our security, and all that we hold dear!*

- *Psychological warfare is as or more important than actual confrontation.* The goal is to make your adversary passive and to break his will through propaganda and brainwashing.
  - ✓ Comments: We are spoon-fed an endless barrage of out and out lies and half truths. The media is little more than a massive propaganda machine, feeding us sound bites designed to draw conclusions, for we, the sheep, who are bread to serve our masters, the financial elite. Education is intended to create loyalty to the state. Crisis after crisis is perpetrated on us to keep us in a constant state of fear and therefore willing to give away our freedom. We are made to be dependent on the state for the very necessities of life in the belief that our dependency will keep us from fighting back. It is urgent, it is vital, it is critically important that we wake up from our stupor and open our eyes as to who the real enemy is and fight back because if we don't, all will soon be lost and everything that our government gave us will be taken away and more much more! They will leave us with nothing. It is as Senator Barry Goldwater said, "Remember that a government big enough to give you everything you want is also big enough to take away everything you have."

- *Use of diversionary tactics.* To move your enemy, entice him with something he is sure to want (e.g., material possessions, security, and comfort. Force him to commit his assets in the wrong place (e.g., in fighting amongst ourselves and with phantom enemies).
  - ✓ Comments: So what does the government have that we are sure to want? They control a large segment of society with entitlements. They control our access to jobs, to energy, to food, to water, to virtually all the necessities of life. They make us as dependent as they possibly can in an effort to control us.
  - ✓ A warning: Again we have to remember that a government big enough to give us everything we want is big enough to take it all away and more!

- *The political context of war: Is always more important than the military context.* It allows you to see the enemy's real objective in the war. Also, you need a political solution to secure peace.
  - ✓ Comments: So what is the government's political context? As we have said repeatedly, it is to establish a one-world communist dictatorship intent on mass genocide and control of the world's resources. Our politicians are not inept. We are not the victim of failed economic policies. We are the victim of a deliberate political strategy to gain political control of first America and then the rest of the world.
  - ✓ As to their political solution: The financial elite don't need one because they intend to use the US Military, NATO forces and a domestic army, such as Hitler's Brownshirts and SS in order to utterly control us. They intend to impose a dictatorship, so they don't need a political solution.
  - ✓ Their endgame is to put (RFID) chips in all of us, so they can know where we are at all times and so we can't buy, sell, get medical treatment, or anything else without government approval. It is the ultimate control mechanism. Add the use of sophisticated surveillance equipment (e.g., cameras on street corners, airports, train stations, etc.) in addition to satellites and miniature drones with surveillance equipment and facial recognition software and our freedom of movement will be almost nonexistent. It will indeed be a "brave new world," and it is coming to America. We are on death ground. We must fight back while we can, but we must do it without bloodshed. Otherwise, they will simply impose martial law and lock us down. Wake up, wake up; the enemy is at the gate, and our lives are at stake.

- *Numerical superiority is not the key to winning a war.* The key is to outthink your opponent and to use his weaknesses against him.
  - ✓ Comments: We have more control than we think. For example, don't underestimate the power of social media as a weapon. Not too long ago, Citibank was going to

charge a monthly fee on debit cards. One woman went on Facebook and told five hundred friends what Citi intended to do and suggested they all move their accounts to nonprofit credit unions. The word spread, and before it was over, 500,000 people were on board, and Citi decided not to implement the fee for fear of further escalation of the protest.

- ✓ Our enemy is the financial elite, so the way to defeat them is to end their control of money. In the next chapter, we will discuss a number of ways to do exactly that.
- ✓ The government intends to take away everything we have. Once we realize that, their strangle hold will be loosened and we will be empowered to fight back. Look at Greece: The handouts have come to an end and what the government gave it is now taking away. It is time to choose slavery or freedom, but freedom will require a fight. It will not be given to us by choice.

- *Attack your enemy from within.* Infiltrate your enemy and attack him from within in the soft underbelly, without him even knowing he is being attacked.
  - ✓ Comments: In the instance of the US, the shadow government is systematically dismantling the Constitution, our civil liberties, and our financial system, and for good measure, they pit us against each other, so even if we see the problem, we will still be unable to put forth a united front of resistance.

  Our enemy exploits our weaknesses, but by exposing his tactics we can neutralize them.

- *How the financial elite and their puppet government and corporate leaders exploit the weaknesses of the masses.* Avoid your enemy's strengths, and attack his weaknesses.
  - ✓ Our weaknesses: They take advantage of our greed. Trappers catch monkeys by putting food in a gourd tethered to a

steak. The monkey reaches into a small hole to get the food. The trap is his greed. You see the hole is not large enough for him to get his clenched fist out, but all he has to do to get free is to let go of the food. In like fashion, the government traps us with their entitlements and by making us dependent on them. Like the monkey, all we have to do to get free is let go. We were once a nation of self-reliant people, and we must be again.

✓ We allow the government to pit us against each other. All we have to do to get free is to recognize that the real enemy is our government and our supposed differences are fueled by the government's intentionally divisive tactics. We have to learn to work together or all is lost.

How we, the people, can exploit the government's vulnerabilities and weaknesses.

- *Moral influence:* The people must be behind their leader or otherwise the war will ultimately be lost. In order to maintain loyalty and discipline, a leader must have the best interest of the collective as the highest principle and not the vested interest of a few. A leader must keep his followers united against a recognized enemy and the dangers he represents. The enemy is our government, not terrorists! Obama's true colors are beginning to show.
  - ✓ Comments: Hopefully, by exposing the government's strategy, we will render them impotent. Our government has shown time and time again that they represent special interest groups lead by the financial elite. Not only do they not have our interest at heart, they see us as a virus to be exterminated.

    "In the event that I am reincarnated, I would like to return as a deadly virus in order to contribute something to solve overpopulation" Prince Philip, reported by Deutsche Presse-Agentur (DPA), August 1988).

- ✓ Our leaders don't serve the American people. They serve the United Nations and other global governance bodies dedicated to destroying America and forcing it into the one-world government.

  "It is the sacred principles enshrined in the United Nations Charter to which the American people will henceforth pledge their allegiance" (President George Bush, addressing the UN).

  "Isn't the only hope for the planet that the industrialized civilization collapse? Isn't it our responsibility to bring that about?" (Maurice Strong, founder of the UN Environmental Program, opening speech, Rio Earth Summit 1992).
- ✓ We must recognize that our greatest enemy is our government, and it is they we must rally against and not some phantom enemies.

- *Expose their lies, and the truth will set us free.* Once we realize that our government is the cause of our problems and not the solution, they will lose much of their power over us. When their lies are exposed, they lose their greatest weapon, which is deception and brainwashing and many of those loyal to them will defect and become assets in the battle against them. We have to remember that as much as we need them, they need us more. The government makes nothing. Its strength is derived from the people, so if we refuse to support them, their power is gone, and they can be defeated. There are only a few of them, but there are billions of us.
- *Arrogance and overconfidence.* They think they are in fact a ruling class. They think we are too stupid, too dependent, and too afraid to fight back. They think their money will be the decisive factor in their victory. It will not. The deciding factor in any war is resolve. We are fighting for our lives and all they are fighting for is power. Their control over us will be ended, if we will only wake up and realize that they need us more than we need them.

- *Our Military vs. NATO.* They expect to deploy NATO troops on US soil. We can't allow that! The American people must wake up to the danger NATO represents. US military forces will not come against our mothers, fathers, brothers, and sisters but NATO forces loyal to the UN certainly will. In order to stand up to NATO we will need some key military leaders, and the soldiers will follow. Also we need to keep our guns as a last resort.
- "Firearms are second only to the Constitution in importance; they are the peoples' liberty teeth" (George Washington). Stock up on ammunition while you still can.
- *End the divisiveness, stand united, and we will be victorious.* Once we realize how they have intentionally pitted us against one another and what they intend to do to us once they take us over, we will be on death ground, and we will become a formidable adversary. We will have the moral high ground, and we will fight as no mercenary or conscripted force ever could.

If we stand united we can be victorious, but as Christ said, "A house divided cannot stand."

One last thing. We must surrender to God and seek righteousness, so that we will have his protection against our enemy. He that has the protection of the Lord will be victorious!

POLITICAL COUNTEROFFENSIVE

Thomas Jefferson knew the real truth. "When the people fear their government, there is tyranny; when the government fears the people, there is liberty." "The spirit of resistance to government is so valuable that I wish it to be always kept alive. Whenever any form of government becomes destructive of these ends—life, liberty, and the pursuit of happiness—it is the right of the people to alter or abolish it and to institute new government."

As Jefferson said, "We cannot long sustain a free civilized society, if we don't have an educated public capable of making informed, moral decisions which reflect the inalienable rights of all members of society!"

"If a nation values anything more than freedom, then it will lose its freedom, and the irony of it is that if it is comfort and security that it values, it will lose that too" (Charley Reese, *Orlando Sentinel*).

"I believe that if the people of this nation fully understood what Congress has done to them over the last forty-nine years, they would move on Washington; they would not wait for an election. It adds up to a preconceived plan to destroy the economic and social independence of the United States!" (Senator George W. Malone [Nevada], speaking before Congress in 1957).

Time to Choose:
Stand and Fight or Lay Down and Surrender?

There once was a nation of destiny
A nation founded on godly dignity
A nation that embraced the world's refugees
A nation most glorious to see

People from around the world flocked to its shores
All were welcome and none were forlorn
Their hopes and dreams they brought with them
The promise of a better land

A land where men could raise their families
A land where they could worship as they pleased
A land of freedom and liberty
A land most glorious to see

Then came men from foreign shores
The old oppressions to restore
Money lenders to enslave
And bind the people with invisible chains

A decision had to be made
The fate of the world was at hand.
Submit and lose their liberty
Or fight to restore godly dignity

Excerpt from the Declaration of Independence:

> "We hold these truths to be self-evident, that all men are created equal, that they are endowed by their Creator with certain unalienable rights that among these are life, liberty and the pursuit of happiness. That to secure these rights, governments are instituted among men, deriving their just powers from the consent of the governed. That whenever any form of government becomes destructive to these ends, it is the right of the people to alter or to abolish it, and to institute a new government, laying its foundation on such principles and organizing its powers in such form, as to them shall seem most likely to effect their safety and happiness."

COUNTEROFFENSIVE MEASURES: TAKING BACK THE REPUBLIC

Step Three: Have a Plan to Fix What Is Broken

Most revolutions, even if they succeed, erode into some form of dictatorship, because when those in power are removed a vacuum is created, because there is no plan in place to run the government, and fix what was wrong with the old system. So our third step will be a "comprehensive political platform designed to restore the republic." It is not rocket science. It's mostly a simple process of replacing those things, which have been stripped away in order to enslave us. Additionally, it takes into considerations that in a highly technological society some provisions are required which were not required in a more agrarian society, like that which existed when the US was founded.

Me: As the title of this chapter infers, we are going to be developing a plan to "return the government to the people." The specific plan is called the **"American Reformation Platform."**

It is not your typical political platform because it is not constrained by what would be allowable under our current political system, which is controlled by "the Financial Elite" and their pawns in government, our corporations, and special interest groups, etc. Under our current corrupt and highly controlled political system, virtually none of what is outlined would be possible. The platform intentionally ignores those artificial constraints to freedom and economic development and outlines instead a plan designed to restore the republic of our Forefathers "one nation under God, indivisible with liberty and justice for all."

You probably won't be surprised when I say that before we can look ahead to the future, we must once again look to the past and discover our roots. In order to restore America to greatness, it is crucial that we understand what made it great in the first place.

The year is 1776 and as Ben Franklin is leaving the Continental Congress he was approached by a woman who said, "Sir, what form of government have you given us?" He replied, "Madam, a republic, if you can keep it." "

Me: What do you suppose Franklin meant by his response? The answer lies in the distinction between a republic and a democracy.

The roots of America's demise: Our Founding Fathers referred to democracy as ***"mobocracy"*** because it is based on majority rule and not the "rule of law, the Constitution." Invariably, the voters discover that they can vote themselves entitlements from the public treasury, at the expense or Peter (the most productive segment of society) to pay Paul (the least productive segment of society). From that point on, elections are decided based on which party and which candidate promises the most handouts from the public treasury. It is what Rush Limbaugh called the Santa Claus Syndrome. Inevitably, the government collapses from failed fiscal policy (debt) and degrades into socialism ending up in some form of dictatorship. Isn't that what is happening to America today?

If only those demanding the handouts could see, that if America continues down this path we will end up like Greece, with 25 percent unemployment, drastic cuts in pensions and other entitlement and violence in the streets.

That is why Jefferson said, "The democracy will cease to exist when you take away from those who are willing to work and give to those who would not." That is why decades later, Karl Marx said, "Democracy is the road to socialism." And I would add that socialism is the road to communism and slavery!

The last statistic I read said that 46 percent of the US population receives some form of government entitlement. To make matters even worse, we have a government committed to driving the US into economic ruin so it can force it into the one-world Government.

While democracy is based on majority rule, a republic relies on a moral, self-reliant, well-informed citizenry willing to be ruled by a set of guiding principles (i.e., the Bible and the Constitution).

That is why James Madison, the framer of the Constitution said, "Religion is the basis and foundation of government" (June 20, 1785). "We've staked the future of all our political institutions upon our capacity to sustain ourselves according to the Ten Commandments of God" (James Madison, 1778, to the general assembly of the state of Virginia).

It is also why Jefferson said, "If a nation expects to be ignorant and free, in a state of civilization, it expects what never was and never will be" (Thomas Jefferson, 1816). And why he also said, "The republican is the only form of government, which is not eternally at open or secret war with the rights of mankind" (Thomas Jefferson, 1790).

So what Ben Franklin meant when he said, "A republic, if you can keep it," is that to exist, a republic depends on—a moral, godly people who are informed and who are willing to abide by the rule of law and enact legislation in the best interest of society at large rather than based on self serving vested interests.

The hijacking of the US political system: "Today in America, our media, entertainment industry, educational system, and government are controlled by the financial elite who us every conceivable form of divisiveness, propaganda, brainwashing, and moral degeneration to make certain that the public is not capable of keeping the republic" (Larry Ballard).

We are their slaves and most of us don't even realize it! As Jefferson said, "We cannot long sustain a free civilized society, if we don't have an educated public capable of making informed, moral decisions, which reflect the inalienable rights of all members of society!"

In America today, that is impossible. Just look at what our government is doing to us. Obama says America is not a Christian nation. He is systematically taking God out of our cultural syntax while at the same time supporting same sex marriage and teaching homosexuality in elementary schools. The rhetoric coming out of Washington is intentionally divisive pitting people of every race, religion, and socioeconomic group against one another because they know it is as Christ said, "A house divided cannot stand."

It is as James Madison said, "Democracies have ever been spectacles of turbulence and contention, have ever been found incompatible with personal security or the rights of property; and have, in general, been as short in their lives as they have been violent in their deaths."

With regard to the ownership of private property, we have discussed how then Senator Obama, President Bill Clinton, and President Bush Junior conspired to allow the banks to intentionally cause the 2008 collapse of the housing market and ensuing depression. We also discussed the fact that privately owned Fannie, Freddie and the Fed are buying up foreclosed properties by the millions for pennies on the dollar.

It is as Jefferson said, "Banking institutions are more dangerous than standing armies. I believe that if the American people ever allow private banks (the Fed) to control issuance of currency. The banks and corporations that will grow up around them will deprive the people of their property until their children wake up homeless on the continent their fathers conquered" (Thomas Jefferson, third US president).

Isn't this exactly what is happening in America today? Please open your eyes and make the decision to join the fight to save this great nation!

Reader's perspective: What is all this talk about America being a democracy? America is a republic, always has been. Just look at our Pledge of Allegiance. "I pledge allegiance to the Flag of the United States of America *and to the Republic for which it stands*, one nation under God, indivisible, with liberty and justice for all."

Me: Do you realize that not a single word in the Pledge of Allegiance applies to America any more. We are no longer a republic. You may recall we covered the fact that in 1933 the US declared bankruptcy and the receivers of the bankruptcy declared that the US had a new form of government a (democracy a communist order). We are no longer united, but are instead, a nation divided, a nation teetering on the brink of a race war. We are no longer a godly, moral nation. Even many of our pastors stand idly by while God is replaced with materialism and vested self-interest, otherwise known as prosperity ministries. Obama is even making the mention of God taboo. And our liberty has never been in more danger. The legal means are in place for the government to enslave us, incarcerate us without due process and at the sole discretion of the president declare martial law and impose a dictatorship. The government controls all the necessities of life and has the means to literally starve us to death. It is time we restored the republic, which our Founding Fathers so wisely gave us. I fear the time is short.

At their admission, what is planned for us is anything but a free society. "The Techtronic era involves the gradual appearance of a more controlled society that would be dominated by an elite unrestricted by traditional values" (*Between Two Ages: America's Role in the Technetronic Age* by Zbigniew Brzezinski).

Isn't this the literal definition of a dictatorship? Stand up before it is too late. If we hope to regain control of our government, we have to come to grips with the reality that:

- we cannot blindly follow our governmental leaders. Both political parties have proven themselves to be complicit in attempting to hijack the US Constitution and the freedoms, which it guarantees.

- the intent of our Founding Fathers was a small decentralized government, not a large centralized federal government that controls virtually everything.
- America was established as a republic not a democracy. All democracies have been short-lived and inherently unstable because rather than being based on law, the Constitution they are based on majority rule, which invariable leads to mob rule.

As Thomas Jefferson said, "The spirit of resistance to government is so valuable that I wish it to be always kept alive. It will often be exercised when wrong but better so than not to be exercised at all. I like a little rebellion now and then. It is like a storm in the atmosphere."

Before I get into the planks of the American Reformation Platform I need to establish that the only hope we have is to clean house in Washington and start over. Washington has sold out to the elite. Bear with me, and we will get to the actual political platform soon enough, but as usual, I first need to lay the groundwork for the case for why we have to abandon the current system.

I invite you to the second American Revolution: May God save America! Our two-party political system is an illusion inflicted on us by the financial elite who select our presidents in exchange for their complicity in their plans to collapse the US to make way for the one-world government.

J D Rockefeller, Carnegie, J. P. Morgan, McKinley, Bryan

The Buying of the First President

The strategy of buying political power by buying the president began with the 1896 election when William Jennings Bryan was campaigning on a strong antitrust platform. The three wealthiest and most powerful men in the US—John D. Rockefeller of Standard Oil, Andrew Carnegie of Carnegie Steel, and Banking Tycoon J.P. Morgan—saw their empire's being threatened and decided to put aside their rivalries in order to protect their interest by buying the office of the president of the United States of America. They put their money and enormous power behind industrialist sympathizer William McKinley and got him elected over Bryan. That was what I call patient zero in the scheme to control the US government by controlling those elected to the highest offices in the land. I am referring to the inception of the shadow government, which today pulls the strings of our elected officials and is the real power on Capitol Hill. Source: Documentary–The Men Who Built America.

This election provided the blueprint for the takeover of the office of the President. The elite determined that if they could control the office of the President and key members of Congress along with the media and the monetary system through the Fed – they could effectively rule America from the shadows! Can you see how our government has been compromised?

Our Presidents are selected not elected: Our Two Party Political System is an illusion inflicted on us by the Elite, who select our Presidents in exchange for their complicity in their plans to collapse the US to make way for The One-World Government. Presidents are groomed, mentored & surrounded with advisors all dedicated to The CFR & TC's goal of collapsing the US and establishing a One-World Government!

Joseph Stalin

Jeb Bush

Our Votes Don't Count

"It doesn't matter who votes, it matters who counts the votes" Joseph Stalin Russian Dictator

Remember those Chad's in Florida! What a coincidence that Jeb Bush was governor of Florida and it was Florida that determined the Presidential election for Brother George!!! Go Figure! *Another*

Coincidence: It just so happens that Brother Marvin had the security contracts at both the Twin Towers & Dulles Airport on 9/11. Those Bush Brothers sure get around.

J. P. Morgan Woodrow Wilson

Wilson broke his promise to the American People when under pressure from banker J.P. Morgan & other banking interest, which put him into office; he signed The Federal Reserve Act giving the printing of US currency over to the Federal Reserve. He later regretted his betrayal of The American People and said:

"I am a most unhappy man. I have unwittingly ruined my country. A great industrial nation is controlled by its system of credit. Our system of credit is concentrated. The growth of the nation, therefore, and all our activities are in the hands of a few men. We have come to be one of the worst ruled, one of the most completely controlled and dominated Governments in the civilized world no longer a Government by free opinion, no longer a Government by conviction and the vote of the majority, but a Government by the opinion and duress of a small group of dominant men.: (Woodrow Wilson) Can you see how the White House has been compromised?

Franklin D. Roosevelt Jimmy Carter

How the CFR and TC became imbedded in Washington politics: The CFR was imbedded into the government during the Presidency of FDR and its control was greatly expanded at the outbreak of WWII when the government assimilated the CFS's international intelligence network into the government, and the TC infiltrated the government when President Jimmy Carter made 26 Trilateral Commission [TC] appointments.

Why you should care: "The New World Order will be built… an end run on national sovereignty, eroding it piece by piece will accomplish much more than the old fashioned frontal assault" [CFR (Council on Foreign Relations Journal 1974, P558)

In other words the collapse of the US will be accomplished from within by infiltrating the government with CFR & TC members dedicated to ending US Sovereignty. Can you see how the White House has been compromised?

Zbigniew Brzezinski Jimmy Carter

President Carter was groomed by Trilateralist Zbigniew Brzezinski and he appointed twenty six Trilateralist to his administration: As the following quote demonstrates Brzezinski was an elitist dedicated to ending US Sovereignty! "The Techtronic era involves the gradual appearance of a more controlled society that would be ***dominated by an elite unrestricted by traditional values***" "*Between Two Ages: America's Role in The Techtronic Age*" (By: Zbigniew Brzezinski [CFR Member, Founding Member Trilateral Commission, Secretary Of State Carter Administration and Security Advisor to five Presidents including Obama.) By appointing TC member Leonard Woodcock Chief Envoy to China carter opened the flood gates to US trade deficits. Can you see how the White House has been compromised?

Bill Clinton

If you want to know what a leader believes find out what his mentors & advisors believe. (Carroll Quigley: Mentor to President Bill Clinton, CFR Member & CFR Historian) Says; "He finds nothing wrong with the CRF's plan of world domination."

"The powers of financial capitalism had [a] far-reaching aim, nothing less than to create a world system of financial control in private hands able to dominate the political system of each country and the economy of the world as a whole. This system was to be controlled in ***a feudalist fashion*** by the central banks of the world acting in concert by secret agreements arrived at in frequent private meetings and conferences." (Quote from Caroll Quigley's Tragedy and Hope.) Can you see how the White house has been compromised?

George W. H. Bush George W. Bush

Why the Bushes are political royalty and traitors to the nation: With friends, family and business partners like these it is no wonder George W Bush Said: "The Constitution is just a God Dam piece of paper!" (George W Bush The White House Blues)

Grandfather–Senator Prescott Bush: Was linked to accusations of *"Trading With The Enemy"* in WWII, and he and George W and George H W were all members of the secret society *'Skull & Bones"* Alleged to groom the elite for key positions in the government & elsewhere.

CFR Member–President George H W Bush addressing The UN pledges allegiance to the very organization dedicated to ending

US sovereignty. "It is the sacred principles enshrined in the United Nations Charter to which the American people will henceforth pledge their Allegiance." Remember The UN is the organization committed to killing 6 billion of us.

George W Bush–Business partner & family friend of the bin Laden family took the FBI off of Osama's trail and refused his surrender. Go Figure! Can you see how the White house has been compromised?

Barack Obama

With mentors like Bill Ayres, Reverend Jeremia Wright, Frank Marshall Davis, and Zbigniew Brzezinski with his background: having attended Muslim school and having recited *"The Muslim Call To Prayer"*, how could Obama be dedicated to anything but collapsing the US?

- Obama Taught *"Rules For Radicals"* A philosophy dedicated to collapsing the US under a mountain of debt! "Lest we forget an over the shoulder acknowledgement of the very first radical… The first radical known to man who rebelled against the establishment and did it so effectively that he at least won his own kingdom "LUCIFER" (From the Forward of Rules for Radicals by Saul Alinsky.) How could a man who endorses Lucifer call himself a Christian?

- Zbigniew Brzezinski: (CFR) member, founding member Trilateral Commission, Secretary Of State Carter Administration, and Security Advisor to five Presidents is now Obama's Security Advisor. With his background how can you call Brzezinski anything but a subversive?
- Frank Marshall Davis: Communist Organizer, mentor to Obama and probably his real father
- Bill Ayres: Obama's mentor & "Founder Of TheWeather Underground" who bombed the Pentagon
- Reverend Wright: Obama's Spiritual leader and the man who said: *"God Dam America."*

Can You See How The White House Has Been Compromised?

Our Presidents are selected not elected: They are groomed, mentored & surrounded with advisors all dedicated to The CFR & TC's goal of collapsing the US and establishing a One-World Government!

Our Two Party Political System is an illusion inflicted on us by the Elite, who select our Presidents in exchange for their complicity in their plans to collapse the US to make way for The One-World Government. Can you see how the White House and Congress have been compromised?

One last thing before we get to the details of American Reformation Platform. We saw a minute ago that all three Bushes were members of the secret society "Skull and Bones" alleged to groom the elite for key positions in the government and elsewhere. Below is a partial list of influential Skull and Bones members form the 1940s–1990s. I bolded the more important men and their positions.

Note: year in parenthesis i.e. (1944) is the year they graduated.

- James L. Buckley (1944), US senator (R-New York 1971–1977); William Singer Moorhead (1944), US representative from Pennsylvania

- John Chafee (1947), US Senator, secretary of the Navy and governor of Rhode Island,
- Thomas William Ludlow Ashley (1948), US representative from Ohio
- **George H.W. Bush** (1948), forty-first president of the United States, eleventh director of Central Intelligence, son of Prescott Bush, father of George W. Bush.
- **Evan G. Galbraith** (1950), US ambassador to France, managing *director of Morgan Stanley*
- Raymond Price (1951), speechwriter for Presidents Nixon, Ford, and Bush.
- **William H. Donaldson** (1953), *appointed chairman of the US Securities and Exchange Commission by George W. Bush*, founding dean of Yale School of Management, cofounder of DLJ investment firm
- Jack Edwin McGregor (1956), Pennsylvania state senator; founder, Pittsburgh Penguins
- **Winston Lord** (1959), chairman of Council on Foreign Relations, Ambassador to China, assistant US secretary of state
- David George Ball (1960), assistant US secretary of labor
- David L. Boren (1963), governor of Oklahoma, US senator, president of the University of Oklahoma
- John Forbes Kerry (1966), US senator (D-Massachusetts 1985–2013), lieutenant governor of Massachusetts, 1983–1985; 2004 Democratic Presidential Nominee; 68th United States secretary of state 2013–present
- Victor Ashe (1967), Tennessee state senator and representative, Mayor of Knoxville, Tennessee, US ambassador to Poland
- **George W. Bush** (1968), grandson of Prescott Bush, son of George H.W. Bush, 46th governor of Texas, 43rd president of the United States.
- **Robert William Kagan** (1980), *cofounder of the Project for the New American Century* (The plan calling for US primacy, the plan written a year prior to 9/11 that was implemented immedi-

ately after 9/11, the plan that was not expected to pass short of a second Pearl Harbor. (Will coincidences never cease?)

- James Emanuel Boasberg (1985), judge, United States District Court for the District of Columbia
- Dana Milbank (1990), political reporter for the *Washington Post*
- **Jon Boulton/Austan Goolsbee** (1991), staff director to and chief economist of President Barack Obama's Economic Recovery Advisory Board

If we continue to labor under the illusion that the US is anything other than a two-party dictatorship, it is just a matter of time before we have a total dictatorship and all our rights are gone. If we hope to save America, we have to stop playing by the financial elite's playbooks and come up with our own. It is called the *American Reformation Platform.*

Overview of political platform.
Rules for patriots.

Phase I: Leadership Issues

- Election Reform

Phase II: Monetary Issues

- Financial Reform
- Trade Reform
- Natural Resource Reform
- Healthcare Reform

Phase III: Social Issues

- Immigration Reform
- Welfare Reform

Introduction to the American Reformation Platform. The American Reformation Platform is comprised of three phases.

- Phase I: *Leadership issues*. Our first step is to take control back from our elected officials, put an end to big government centered in Washington, and put control back at the state level where it was intended to be. To accomplish this, we have to clean house in Washington and start over from scratch or else nothing else we need to do will be possible.
- Phase II: *Monetary issues*. It is crucial that we stop the reckless spending and create a level playing field for America to compete in the global marketplace.
- Phase III: *Social issues*, which the government is using to create division and social strife. We have to find a way to find common ground, and once again become "one nation under God." It is as Christ said, "A house divided cannot stand."

THE AMERICAN REFORMATION PLATFORM

Phase I: Leadership Issues

Election Reform: Overview

If you look at the Bible, which is supposed to be the foundation of our political system, we see over and over that in order for the Israelites to inherit the Promised Land, they had to first rid it of anyone or anything, which would contaminate it and cause the Israelites to backslide. So they were told to kill all the men, women, children, and animals and take no plunder. Please, I am not advocating violence. But what I am saying is that the apple barrel is rotten, and we have to throw out all the apples, which **means everyone in Washington—both Republicans and Democrats**—must go, and we have to start over. So what I am saying is that by election, or what other peaceful means necessary, we have to get rid of all our leaders in Washington and do a reboot of the entire political system, or in other words, it is too late to work within the current political system. A little rebellion cleanses the atmosphere. "The spirit of resistance to government is so valuable that I wish it to be always kept alive. I like a little rebellion now and then. It is like a storm in the atmosphere" (Thomas Jefferson).

America has become a two-party dictatorship. Like I said, the platform I am about to layout is impossible, within the confines of our current corrupt political system, but it is essential if we hope to restore the republic and save America for our children!

It is time for a second American Revolution!

Election Reform: Individual Planks

- Remove all incumbent politicians in Washington, because with very few exceptions, our elected officials in Washington have demonstrated that they place their vested interest and those of special interest groups ahead of those of the public. Simply speaking, we don't know who to trust, so they all have to go.

- Set term limits (two terms) in order to prevent the accumulation of excessive power. Our forefathers never intended us to have carrier politicians.
- Outlaw gerrymandering (restructuring congressional districts for political purposes) because it nullifies the original intent of congressional districts, which was to provide representation to individuals residing in proximity to one another, who were therefore expected to share similar issues.
- Outlaw lobbyist (special interest advocates) because they virtually assure that the interest of the general public will not be represented. *Note*: When our government was founded, we didn't have lobbyist, so I am only advocating a return to our founding principles.
- Set limits on campaign contributions: so super packs (just recently implemented), and other special interest groups can't buy elections.
- Set limits on personal spending on campaigns, so the ultra rich cannot buy campaigns.
- Get rid of electronic voting, because it makes it too easy to fix elections.
- Abolish signing statements and executive orders: so presidents cannot circumvent Congress the way they do.
- Prohibit presidents from having their records sealed in order to hide what they have done (like Bush Junior did).
- Prohibit Congress from approving their own salaries. Again, an unwarranted special privilege.
- Congress must be subject to all laws they pass (e.g., Social Security, Obamacare, and insider trading laws, etc.). Otherwise, they vote in favor of special interest groups and not the general public. *Note*: For example, in terms of insider trading, legislators can pass a bill that they know will make particular stocks go through the roof and yet they can invest in those stocks and make millions, and it is perfectly legal. But if we did it, we would go to jail like Martha Steward did. If Congress is not made

subject to the laws they pass they are by default an elected ruling class.

- Remove all government appointees who belong to the Council Foreign Relations, Trilateral Commission, and Bilderberg Group. Otherwise, they would quickly contaminate the political system and take it over again.
- Require candidates to sign a pledge, supporting an election plank designed to take power from the special interest groups and return it to the public.
- Return to smaller government with more control in the States and less in Washington, which is again the way it was intended to be.

Reader's perspectives: We can never accomplish the things you have outlined. It is just impossible.

Me: You are absolutely right. They cannot be accomplished short of a political rebellion, but that is exactly what I am proposing. I know that the changes just proposed seem radical and impractical, but in truth, they are simply an effort to restore the republic to the way our forefathers intended it to be. Without these changes, it is impossible to have a republic because our current political system is little more than an undeclared dictatorship. It is time to restore the government to "we, the people."

They plan on causing chaos of such magnitude that we will welcome their protection at any cost, even our freedom. We must not let that happen. Consider the following two quotes:

> "We are on the verge of a global transformation. All we need is the right major crisis and the nations will accept the New World Order" (David Rockefeller, Sept. 23, 1994).
>
> Henry Kissinger in an address to the super secret Bilderberg Organization meeting at Evian, France, May 21, 1992 said the following as transcribed from a tape recording made by one of the Swiss delegates:

> "Today, Americans would be outraged, if UN troops entered Los Angeles to restore order; tomorrow they will be grateful. This is especially true, if they were told there was an outside threat from beyond, whether real or promulgated, that threatened our very existence. It is then that all peoples of the world will plead with world leaders to deliver them from this evil. The one thing every man fears is the unknown. When presented with this scenario, individual rights will be willingly relinquished for the guarantee of their well being granted to them by their world government."

> "When governments fear the people, there is liberty. When the people fear the government, there is tyranny" (Thomas Jefferson).

Crisis, crisis, and more crisis. It is no accident. It is part of the plan to make us surrender our freedom. Please stand up, and fight this tyranny before it is too late.

Phase II: Monetary Issues

Economic Reform: Overview

So how do we reform the economic system? As always, the first step in solving any problem is to understand its root cause so you can fix it at its source. Obama wants us to believe that redistribution of wealth is the answer. For once, I agree with him, but we do have a difference of opinion as to how we accomplish that. He wants to place higher taxes on what he calls the rich. The question then becomes who exactly are the rich? By definition, it would be those who control the majority of the money in the country. Surprise, Mr. Obama, that is not the upper, middle, or lower socioeconomic classes. The truth is that the financial elite comprise only 1 percent of the population but they control 95 percent of the world's wealth. And guess what, Mr. Obama, most of them pay little to no taxes. The Rockefeller foundation for example is tax exempt. Go figure. So, if we want to take America and the world back from the financial elite, we have to end their control of the world's monetary system and that is exactly what the American Reformation Platform is designed to do. If you have any doubts that the Financial Elite control the world's money supply, consider the following.

A leaked City Bank Memo dated Oct. 16th, 2005, described the Financial Elite as a ***"Plutonomy"*** which is defined as an economy controlled by the wealthy for their benefit. They disclosed that the top 1% of the population (The Financial Elite) controlled more wealth than the bottom 95% of society and they did not expect that to change unless the masses wake up and demanded a more equitable distribution of wealth.

Obama is right: We do need to redistribute the wealth but not as he exposes from the middle and upper classes. The only group with enough money to make any difference is The Financial Elite the 1%ers who control the monetary system of the world and use their money and power to enslave all of humanity. Their money and power must be stripped away from them, because only then will mankind be free to live in peace and harmony!

Yes, we do need to redistribute the wealth. We need to take it back from the financial elite and share it with the seven billion inhabitants of the world. One family, the Rothschilds are reportedly worth $500 trillion, which is half of the world's wealth. This kind of wealth and power in the hands of a few men guarantees that there will never be a free society. So the intent of this political platform is to do exactly as the Citi memo fears:

Comments: All of these initiatives are *vital*. That is because when you come at an adversary as powerful as the financial elite, you cannot nibble away at them. You have to take clear decisive action and maintain momentum. That is one of Sun Tzu's key military strategies and it is crucial to us taking back the republic.

Thomas Jefferson said, "I place economy among the first and most important virtues, and public debt as the greatest of dangers. To preserve our independence, we must not let our rulers load us with perpetual debt."

Financial Reform: Individual Planks

- Balanced budget amendment to force fiscal responsibility.
- Boycott the nation's largest banks. Most of them are affiliated with the Fed and besides, any bank too large to fail is a monopoly and needs to be broken up in the best interest of the public.
- Pass national usury law to protect consumers from predatory credit card practices. *Note*: At one time, we had usury laws in all but six states, and then a court case allowed financial institutions to incorporate in the six states with no usury laws, and then they could charge any rate they wanted. This birthed our predatory credit card industry with 20–30 and 40 percent usury interest rates.
- Mortgage tied to ***borrower not property*** to end predatory mortgage practice, which requires a new mortgage when refinancing or buying a new home. This practice enriches the banks, and given the fact that the average American moves every five to seven years, it assures that a large segment of home owners will never pay off their mortgages. Here is how it would work. Say you purchased a new home that cost $10,000 more than your previous home. The old mortgage would remain in force at the same interest rate and at the same place on the amortization table. You would take out a new mortgage for $10,000 at current interest rates and at day one on the amortization table.
- Repeal real estate property tax and replace it with a usage tax that does not impart take rights to the government or any other entity. Currently, real estate ownership (title) in the US is based on fee simple ownership, which allows the government to take private property, if real estate taxes are not paid. Historically, real estate ownership in the US was based on "allodial title," which is defined as "an estate held by absolute ownership, without recognizing any superior to whom any duty is due on account thereof." In other words, if a property was paid for, the government had no take rights. The property ownership was irrevocable. Neither the government nor anyone else could take the property. This form of ownership stood in the way of the government's goal of

eventually owning all private property. As it stands now, ***know American citizen owns his home***, ***because ultimately the government can take it, making us all renters not owners***. We need to restore allodial ownership of real estate, if we hope to make "the American dream of home ownership" a reality. As it stands now, in the final analysis, the government owns all real estate in America, and we are all just renters. This must change!

- Close the Federal Reserve, and establish a national bank with currency issued by the US Treasury and backed by gold, silver, oil, or whatever is required in order to prevent the printing of worthless fiat currency. *Note*: This is exactly what JFK did when he passed Executive Order 11110 to disband the Fed, and he printed Silver Certificates backed by precious metals. Also remember, the US used to print its own currency, and it was backed by gold, so all we are doing is going back to the monetary system our Founding Fathers established. By getting rid of the Fed, we will stop private bankers from manipulating the economy through control of the money supply and interest rates, causing boom bust cycles at their discretion. We will also be able to reduce the national debt because we will no longer be paying interest to have our currency printed by the privately owned FED.
- Repeal the illegal income tax because ***100 percent of the tax goes to the private Fed*** as debt service for printing our currency. So if we get rid of the Fed, there is no need for Federal Income Tax, and we can revamp the tax system completely at that time. Remember we established earlier that the 16th Amendment did not give the government the right to impose an income tax and six Supreme Court decisions upheld that opinion.
- Reinstate financial safeguards, such as the Glass-Steagall Act, etc., which when repealed, facilitated the 2008 housing collapse. *Note*: This would break the banking monopolies up, which were formed when banks, security companies, and insurance companies were allowed to merge.

This is the redistribution of wealth the world needs!

Comment: If implemented, these initiatives would virtually end predatory lending in the credit card and mortgage industry and would end control of the monetary system by the financial elite. It would cause massive amounts of money to flow from the pockets of the financial elite into the pockets of "we, the people," where it belongs. It would give us the money to rebuild America and the world. It would also make world peace a possibility Obama's brand of redistribution of wealth is designed to divide the American people, So we become a house divided, that is incapable of uniting against our real enemy—our own government!

Trade Reform: Overview

A quick review: America once the world's leading industrial power has been stripped of its industrial might, and it did not happen by accident. It was done intentionally through intentionally losing trade policies and Fast track free trade agreements specifically designed to disadvantage the US, so we could be driven into economic collapse and forced into the one-world government. As previously quoted: "We've practiced what I call 'losing trade'—deliberately losing trade—over the last 50 years" (Congressman Duncan Hunter, "Exclusive Interview: Hunter Eyes Presidential Campaign," *Human Events*, Dec.4, 2006).

What free trade with China has done to the US economy! Our financial problems began with Carter and the opening of trade with China. As Carter entered office in 1977, we only had a $600 billion national debt. Then came our intentionally loosing trade policies and the planned collapse of the US economy.

Just look at what our government has done to us! National debt by presidents: Carter, $600 b; Reagan, $2.684 t; W. H. Bush, $4.11t; Clinton, $5.662 t, G. W. Bush, $10.7 t; Obama, $17.00 t and climbing exponentially! Most of this debt can be attributed to gutting of the US manufacturing, brought about by the US's intentionally losing free trade policies. America is the only major industrialized nation in the world, not to have a tariff or value-added tax to protect our economy from the ravages of free trade with China!

The financial collapse of America is no accident!

Trade Reform: Individual Planks

- Withdraw from WTO and renegotiate all free trade agreements to make them fair trade agreements.
- Impose tariffs and value-added tax to limit imports and encourage exports so the US can get back on the road to ending the trade deficits, which have so impoverished our nation.
- Eliminate fast track treaty process because it allows Congress to be too easily circumvented.
- Make it illegal to incorporate outside the US to reap trade or tax benefits. This will eliminate much of the incentive for US corporations to take their manufacturing abroad.
- Support US sovereignty. No participation in initiatives imposing global governance (i.e., cap and trade, codex, Agenda 21, Amero union, etc). More on this later.
- Repeal EPA regulations designed to make the US noncompetitive in the global marketplace. They are also used as an end run around failed cap and trade legislation and are intended to tax us for a carbon footprint, which is based on entirely bogus data. As previously discussed global warming is not primarily due to man-made causes. What we are currently experiencing is primarily caused by a cyclical event associated with the sun, and we know this because every planet in the solar system is experiencing the same phenomena. The phenomenon is caused by a period of maximum sun spot activity.
- Capital investment fund with low interest rates to encourage capital investment projects, such as badly needed infrastructure projects.
- Oppose the Security and Prosperity Partnership (SSP) and North American Union because they threaten US sovereignty.

Comments: If measures are not taken to stem the tide of US trade deficits, our standard of living will continue to decline, our salaries will continue to fall, the national debt will continue to rise, and inevitably, the dollar will become worthless, and the US will collapse. Guaranteed! In addition to legislative measures, we should all try to buy US made goods whenever possible.

Natural Resource Reform: Overview

Control of energy and other natural resources is the ultimate form of control. And for that reason, the financial elite and their puppets in government and the energy companies have no intention of giving us cheap clean renewable energy.

From the prospective of the US government, if they lose control of the oil, their geopolitical strangle hold on the rest of the world will be lost forever. The financial elite would cease being our all powerful overlords. Wouldn't that be great? All the sudden, the World Bank and IMF would be much less able to stifle the development of other countries of the world. Ultimately, all wealth comes from nature, so if we let their greed destroy the ecological balance of the planet, there won't be any wealth for any of us.

From the perspective of the oil companies, there is of course the $4–5 trillion per year in lost oil revenue. Equally important is the fact that the financial elite control us by metering out natural resources as a control mechanism. That is why we cannot, from their perspective, ever be allowed to have cheap clean energy. It would free us from dependency on the government, which is something they never want to see happen!

If we want control of energy and the world's natural resources, we will have to literally force the financial elite to relinquish control. I know that sounds impossible, but like I have said several times before, we have more power than we think. The government makes nothing and they depend on us to give them their power.

Natural Resource Reform: Individual Planks

- Oppose cap and trade and participation in the UN's framework convention on climate change because they are nothing more than a means to impose global governance, the largest tax increase in US history, population control, and forced limitations on resource consumption.

- Patent reform to put shelved patents back into the public domain. This would give the public access to energy and medical patents, which corporations have shelved with no intention of ever bringing to market. *Note*: The government has used the "right of eminent domain" (which is supposed to mean for the good of the general public) to, for example, force home owners to relinquish their homes to benefit private domestic and foreign corporations and to allow the sale of US infrastructure to foreign investors. It is time we turned the tables on them and demanded access to energy and medical patents, which have been shelved and which unquestionably benefit the general public.
- No czars: Because they are used to write regulations to circumvent congress and to create regulations, which make the US unable to compete in the global market place.
- Create an international investment fund to develop clean energy solutions to be shared with the world rather than horded as the energy companies have done since the beginning of the industrial revolution and to end scams, such as the one perpetrated on us by Enron.
- Make it illegal to have a revolving door between the White House and corporations, such as Monsanto, with their genetic engineering of food; GE, with their mercury-filled biohazard light bulbs; and Halliburton, which has been complicit in building infrastructure projects which end up driving third world countries into default and confiscating their natural resources; and others which use their positions to get legislation passed, which clearly puts special interest ahead of the interest of the public. These kinds of relationships are examples of lobbyist on steroids, and it has to be stopped. *Note*: This kind of thing is prevented in corporate America with the use of a "noncompete clauses" and a similar strategy could work to end the revolving

door between Washington and their favored corporations. Note: At one time lobbyist were illegal and they should be again.

- The planet is in midst of the sixth mass extinction, "and the time has come when cheap, clean, renewable energy solutions must be taken out of the hands of the financial elite and made available to all of mankind" (Larry Ballard). **The fate of the planet is at stake!**
- God gave us dominion over all the creatures on the planet, and we have a stewardship responsibility, which we have virtually ignored in the pursuit of material possessions.

Note: The following quote accurately describes the government's stance on cheap clean renewable energy. As we have seen, it isn't that there aren't solutions available; it is that the government and the oil companies are not about to give us access to the technology unless we force them to.

The government believes that giving society cheap, abundant energy would be the equivalent of giving an idiot child a machine gun" (Paul Ehrlich, Stanford University). Bunk!

Like I have said before, the only way we will ever get access to cheap clean renewable energy and control of our own destiny is if we wrench that control from the hands of those who would enslave us. By controlling energy and the planet's natural resources, these power crazy madmen are controlling our access to the very necessities of life and that right is reserved for God. They consider us to be expendable, but my Bible tells me differently. This is the time of the harvest, and God has no intention of letting the wicked inherit the earth. He will be with the righteous, if we will repent and surrender to him, and then if we stand against evil, he will be our deliverer, but first, we must be right before the LORD.

Health-Care Reform: Overview

I consider health care to be a financial issue because it represents one-sixth of the US GDP, and if we can reduce health-care cost, that is a huge economic issue. As you will shortly see, our health-care system and our food supply have been hijacked by those who are more interested in profits than our well being. The health-care industry is not interested in wellness because it is not profitable. It is designed to instead wait till we become sick from preventable disease, such as diabetes, cancer, or heart disease, which are related to diets laden with sugar and fat and exposure to foreign substances, such as hormones, genetically modified foods, antibiotics that lower our resistance to infectious diseases and poisons, such as pesticides and artificial sweeteners, such as aspartame. Our health and our very lives are at risk, and we have to get control of our health-care system and food supply. Most of the political instability around the globe is a result of high food prices and food shortages. They tell us that in order to keep food prices down, they have to do the things they do. *Bunk!* If you factor in the cost of medical care and lost productivity directly attributable to their policies, US food costs are arguably the highest in the world. It simply has to be stopped!

Health -Care Reform: Individual Planks

- Repeal Obamacare because it is a Trojan horse for population control and mass genocide. Remember, Agenda 21 calls for reducing global population to one billion, and control of access to health care is one way to get rid of those the government feels are not carrying their weight.
- Prohibit fast-food companies and companies that make sugar laden cereals and poisonous artificial sweeteners, such as aspartame, etc. from advertising to our children. They say they are not responsible for the epidemic of obesity and related diseases, such as diabetes, high blood pressure, and heart disease, but I say different. They brainwash our children and turn them into junk food addicts. ***McDonald's for example calls its customers users***, and they do everything humanly possible to addict our children to their life-threatening products. They are no different from the tobacco industry that, for years, told us their products were not harmful. We got their advertising squashed, and we can do the same thing with these addictive poisonous foods.

- Resend right of corporations to patent life (i.e., food) because it places society at the mercy of corporations for our very existence. Monsanto and three other companies have a monopoly on food production, controlling approximately 80 percent of the world's food supply. Oh by the way, their seeds do not germinate, so the only source for the world's food supply is through these corporations. Additionally, with germinating (legacy seeds) becoming less and less available, if these genetically altered seeds should become susceptible to a disease or become otherwise unavailable, the resulting famine would be biblical in proportion. Maybe even large enough to kill say six billion people. Bingo, population control objective accomplished.
- End the monopoly of health care by AMA, FDA, and Rx Cos. These corporate entities are not interested in curing illness because there is no money in that. No, they are interested in treating illness, illnesses that in many instances are preventable given proper nutrition. For example, through the World Health Organization (WHO) and the Codex treaty, they are endeavoring to deny us access to therapeutic doses of vitamin supplements and nutrients (God's natural healing agents). **Yet, the government has passed a law making it "illegal to treat any disease with anything but a drug" (a poison).**

  According to WTO's and AFO's own projections, the implementation of 2009 vitamin and mineral guidelines will result in a minimum of one billion deaths by starvation and two billion deaths from preventable diseases associated with malnutrition!
- Withdraw from the World Health Organization (WHO) and the Codex treaty because they obligate the US to global governance regulations intended to:
  - ✓ Criminalize the sale of therapeutic dosages of supplements and nutrients. For example, the Codex stipulates, changing the law to make substances illegal unless specified legal. Because of the cost involved in testing this will virtually drive the supplement and nutrient industry out of business.

- ✓ Mandate that every animal on the planet must be treated with Monsanto's growth hormones and with antibiotics!
- ✓ Mandate all or most food must be genetically modified yet. Labeling is not required to disclose genetically modified foods or is testing required to determine if they are safe. If this doesn't put the interest of special interest ahead of those of the public, I don't know what does.
- ✓ Mandate that all food must be irritated unless consumed locally and raw! *Note*: This kills the natural enzymes in the food and destroys much of its nutrient value.
- ✓ Sets limit for dangerous chemicals in food. (But in order to serve the chemical, companies the limits are dangerously high.) In 2001, 176 nations banned 120 dangerous organic chemicals; nine of which were pesticides, and Codex has reintroduced seven of the nine banned pesticides.

Are we going to stand by and do nothing while the government commits mass genocide?

Comments: Implementation of these initiatives will put control of our health-care system and our food supply under our control where it belongs. It is simply too dangerous to have a shadow government and their corporate partners in crime to be able to control the necessities of life, especially when that government is on record as wanting to reduce global population to one billion. Access to food and health care is the perfect weapon for mass genocide, and it must be taken out of the hands of those who would use it to destroy us.

Phase III: Social Issues

Immigration Reform: General Recommendations

It is crucial that we find an acceptable solution to the immigration issue because if we don't, it will tear this nation apart. But at the same time, it is vitally important that any solution we put forth recognizes the government's agenda to use the immigration issue to divide us and to contribute to the collapse of the US so they can force us into the one-world government, because as they say the US is the most significant component.

"The New World Order can't happen without US participation, as we are the most significant single component. Yes, there will be a New World Order, and it will force the United States to change its perceptions" (Henry Kissinger, [CFR] World Affairs Council Press Conference, Regent Beverly Wilshire, April 19 1994).

The solutions that I am recommending here are unlike any others in the American Reformation Platform, because they do not center on reinstating things, which our Founding Fathers put in place to protect the republic.

In order to resolve this issue we will have to do something unheard of in the current governmental lexicon. All parties concerned will have to set down and try to reach a mutually agreeable solution. In this instance, because this is more correctly a social issue than a political issue, I am only going to make general recommendations.

It is my opinion that we must grant all those currently in the country amnesty. But from that point forward, measures need to be put in place to close our borders once and for all and to deny access to social services to anyone who enters the country illegally. If people cannot get jobs, schooling, health care, etc., they simply will not come. In other words, we simply withdraw the invitation.

It is imperative that we deny the government the opportunity to buy the votes of any segment of society, so in this instance, though, I recommend amnesty. I also recommend that voting privileges, not automatically be granted to those who had entered the country illegally. I propose that after five years and conditioned upon passing an English and citizenship test and upon being economically self-sufficient (which means they are not on any government subsidies), they be granted voting privileges. Upon reaching legal voting age, their children would, however, be allowed full citizenship, including voting rights conditioned only on English proficiency.

The reason I recommend English proficiency is that history shows us that bilingual nations do not prosper nearly as well as those with a single common language. The strength of America has been in its ability to assimilate immigrants into the American culture. Therefore, the best solution solves the immigration issue while simultaneously protecting national sovereignty and economic vitality. We need, as they say, "a win-win."

We need to remember that the Mexican people are not our enemies, our government is. A few pages back, we discussed the Security and Prosperity Partnership. We need to remember that its intent is to integrate the US into a North American trading bloc, like the European Common Market, and in the process, end US Sovereignty. When the mask is removed and the truth is exposed, this is what the government's immigration policy is really about. It is the road to socialism and the end of US sovereignty.

Welfare Reform: Overview

As a child, I lived in Welston, the second poorest burrow in all of St. Louis Mo. The neighborhood was primarily black. Matter of fact, there were only two white families on my street—us and one other. Many of the people were on welfare, and I saw firsthand what it does. It is a prison sentence. It takes your dignity, your hopes, your dreams, and your aspirations, but it does something else that is very dangerous. It makes people bitter and angry. It binds you with invisible chains. If you go to work, making a subsistence living, they cut your benefits. You learn to hate the system that keeps you down, but at the same time, you don't dare bite the hand that feeds you. It is the perfect political control mechanism. That is why so many young black men turn to crime. In a land of plenty, they see a system that enslaves them and many lash out and decide that if they are denied the right to earn a living, they will get the things they want any way they can.

Welfare does something even more evil. It destroys the family, the very basis of any civilized society. It creates a system where it is more lucrative to have children out of wedlock than in wedlock, and therefore, children are reared without a male figure in the house, a condition to which psychologist attribute any number of antisocial behavior patterns. Is it any wonder the US has the highest incarceration rates in the world? The system is broken, and it must be fixed, if we are ever to have peace on American streets.

"To put the world in order, we must first put the nation in order; to put the nation in order, we must put the family in order; to put the family in order, we must cultivate our personal life; and to cultivate our personal life, we must first set our hearts right" (Confucius).

Make no mistake. None of this is by accident. It is by design. I remember overhearing two of my black neighbors talking one day. The conversation went something like this:

> Britney, I've got to find me a man. I just have to find me a man. I have to get pregnant. My oldest is turning eighteen soon, and I am about to lose my child support. I just have to get pregnant. I need that money to get by.

This is right out of *Rules for Radicals*. You collapse the system by overwhelming it with entitlements (in this case, aid to dependent children). At the same time, you destroy the family and you create a voting bloc that votes for the party or politician who promises to give the most handouts. Bet you didn't know that prior to FDR's Presidency it was illegal to take tax money from one person and give it to another. In other words Entitlements were illegal.

"There are two ways to conquer and enslave a nation. One is by the sword. The other is by debt" (John Adams, second US president).

"A government, which robs Peter to pay Paul, can always count on the support of Paul" (George Bernard Shaw).

Welfare Reform: Individual Planks

- Incentive to work. Benefits not cut till (reasonable) earning thresholds is reached.
- Able-bodied persons required to work in order to receive benefits but eligible for educational programs.
- Education Programs with tax incentives for employers who hire graduates.

- Aid to dependent children. Yes, in the event that one or more parents die but no aid given to unwed mothers. We have to stop encouraging out-of-wedlock births, and we have to defend the family, which is the core of any moral society. Additionally, as unpopular as it may be, we are going to have to get a handle on the overpopulation crisis, so it will likely be necessary to limit family size to one child by charging extremely high taxes on any family who has a second child. I know this sounds horrible, and it is, but we have to face the fact that we are killing the planet, that there are not enough resources to keep squandering them. In one hundred years of the industrial revolution, we have used over one half the world's oil, which took millions of years to produce, and silver is about to run out, and then there is the clean water issue, which is the largest crisis we face. The aquifers are going dry from overuse. We are in trouble, and we better face the situation while we still have the chance.
- Day care benefits for single moms, so they can work and attend school.

It is as Jefferson said, "The democracy will collapse when we take away from those who are willing to work and give to those who will not."

The invisible chains of modern slavery!

"Entitlements are used to buy votes while keeping those who receive benefits in a perpetual state of poverty and dependence. It doesn't have to be that way!" (Larry Ballard).

Comments: President Clinton passed a welfare reform bill, which set limits on how long a person could receive benefits and put in place provisions to get people to work and end the cycle of generational welfare. Fearing that efforts might be made to resend the legislation, the framers of the legislation even put in wording prohibiting changing the legislation, but President Obama has chosen to ignore those provisions and make changes anyway. Obama promised to cut the budget deficit in half, but instead, he has doubled it, and interventions like this one are responsible. I tell you the intent is to collapse the US under a mountain of debt.

Reader's perspective: I can see where your American Reformation Platform could go a long way toward reinstating America's founding principles, that is if they could be implemented, which would take a miracle. What I don't see is a plan to get America back to work. Political solutions are one thing, but what people want are jobs. Any solution that doesn't put people to work is no solution at all.

Me: If America can reset its moral compass, God can and will step in and help us, and he is in the miracle business. With him, nothing is impossible. There is no reason we should accept our broken, corrupt political system just because a bunch of fat cats tell us what we can and can't do. Like I have said repeatedly, we have more power than we think. Gondi freed the entire nation of India from tyrannical rule by fasting and prayer and with the peaceful support of the masses. Nothing is impossible if we just stand united, so one of the things we will have to discuss later is how do we end the governmental imposed divisiveness and once again stand as one nation under God? We will address that in a little later. On the jobs issue you are absolutely right. Putting America back to work must be part of any political solution. So let's take a look at exactly how we can do just that.

PUTTING AMERICA BACK TO WORK

What America has to realize is that "the cheese has moved." If we hope to reinvigorate our economy, we have to first understand what has changed, and then determine what we need to do to adapt to those chances. Going forward, it cannot be business as usual and neither can we any longer allow our government to intentionally neuter our industrial might. As we have already discussed, any recovery is conditioned on first, ending our intentionally losing trade policies; second, getting rid of the EPA and other governmental regulations, which make it virtually impossible for America to compete in the global marketplace; third, creation of a tax environment friendly to capital investment and job growth.

Our first task is to recognize where our jobs are going and then figure out how we can reverse the trend. Our jobs are going to:

- cheap overseas labor
- automation
- skilled labor forces in other countries
- outsourcing
- foreign nationals working in the US

According to consultants at Mackenzie, the net outcome of this shift in job creation is that since 1990, the recovery rate for recessions has been on the rise. Through the 1980s, it took on average six months to rebound from a recession. Then all the sudden, the 1990 recession took fifteen months to recover, and the 2001 recession took thirty-nine months, and the 2008 recession is estimated to take sixty months—five full years. The question is why?

By the way, if we don't get our out of control spending under control, the 2008 recession will spiral into a full blown depression The worst in US history. The 1929 Great Depression took twelve years to rebound from, and it would have gone on even longer had it not been for WWII. If we don't wake up and get our fiscal house in order, the US could see a total economic collapse with hyperinflation and an economic collapse that would end US sovereignty and force us into the one-world government. We can no longer afford to continue our failed policies. Our problems are real, and they must be addressed with real solutions not the government's typical rhetoric.

Why is it taking longer to recover from our recessions? There are two reasons. The first is increased competition from other countries. As we will see momentarily, we can address this problem by applying some old fashioned American ingenuity. And the second reason is that our economy is becoming less and less resilient. The recessions are getting longer and deeper because they reflect a fundamental weakening of the US economy as we slide deeper and deeper into debt (debt that is intentionally caused by our government's socialist policies which are intended to collapse the US economy).

The eminent collapse of the US economy!

"First comes out of control spending and unfunded entitlements (free handouts and pensions that pay workers as much or more in retirement as when they were working). Then comes higher taxes to pay the interest on the debt caused by the irresponsible spending, which incidentally stifles job growth. Then finally comes massive devaluation of the currency culminating in the government taking away the unfunded entitlements and cutting pensions resulting in social unrest and chaos" (Larry Ballard).

To those Americans who voted for Obama for a second term, I would encourage you to look to Greece to see your future!

Obama says we have to increase taxes on the rich and get them to pay their fair share. The problem with that approach is that it is the rich that create the jobs. If we burden them with tax increases, the response will be not to invest in an economy that does not allow them to get a reasonable return on their investment. Additionally, they don't have nearly enough money to solve our financial crisis. Eventually, we will run out of other people's money and end up like Greece. As discussed earlier, the answer is not to tax the so-called rich. The answer is to redistribute the wealth from the financial elite who controls 95 percent of the world's wealth! The so-called rich don't have nearly enough money to solve America's debt problems. The proposed tax on what the government calls the rich will only generate enough revenue to run the country for approximately one week. It is a ploy and nothing more. It is intended to take our attention off of the government's real plan, which is to tax the middle class into oblivion. On the other hand, the financial elite have enough money to literally transform the world, so that is where we should be focusing our redistribution efforts. And that is exactly where the American Reformation Platform puts its focus.

Additionally, Obama's policies will not help the middle class as he advertises. Obamacare is estimated to cost the average American family $2,500 per year. And according to *Fox News* analysts, Obama's economic solution to the so-called economic cliff will cost the average American $8,000 per year. Americans already have their economic backs up against the wall. They are stretched as thin as possible. According to the same source, one-third of every dollar the government spends is borrowed. Drastic cuts in handouts will occur in the US just like they are occurring in Greece. That is a certainty. Then, all those who voted for "Obama Money" will realize that they were pawns in the government's plan to collapse the US. We have to wake up and start acting responsibly. The answer is creating high-paying jobs, not in free handouts.

So, how can we create jobs and in the process curb our debt crisis?

- *Failed education system.* The "government-controlled" US education system has failed to turn out qualified workers. In 1970, the US lead the world in the number of college graduates. As of 2009, we are fourteenth among wealthy countries. Based on research from Northeastern University, Drexel University, and the Economic Policy Institute, based on data from the Census Bureau's Current Population Survey and the US Department of Labor, about 1.5 million or 53.6 percent, of bachelors degree holders under the age of twenty-five last year were jobless or underemployed. Why?

  The answer is very simple. There is little to no connection to the education US college students get and the demands, which corporations have. We are turning out generalist at a time when automation and technological advancements require very specific skill sets. That is why US corporations say we have jobs, but there are no qualified US citizens to fill them, so they are forced to bring in workers from countries, such as India, China, and Germany. Let's look specifically at Germany to see how they have addressed this problem. *Note*: The jobs programs to follow are taken from CNN 9/23/12 Putting America to Work.

- *Germany's apprenticeship program*. Youth unemployment for those under age twenty-five in Germany is 8 percent. Why? Two-thirds of youth in Germany participate in an apprentice program, which guarantees them that upon completion they will have a job. Not only will they have a job; they are high-paying jobs. Isn't that better than a handout? A job gives you dignity and makes you self-reliant, while a handout lowers your esteem and makes you dependent on your government slave masters. The German apprenticeship program is a cooperative effort between corporations, vocational schools, the government, and trade unions to train a skilled labor force, which meets the needs of employers. Participants get:
  - ✓ three and a half years paid training
  - ✓ guaranteed job offer
  - ✓ free vocational school (paid for by government). Pay attention! This means they graduate debt-free.
  - ✓ a certificate good throughout the industry and may work for any company they please. Eighty-five percent usually choose to stay with the company that trained them.

Note: Germany's success as an exporting company is attributed to its apprenticeship program and the skilled labor force it provides. Automation and technology is how you compete with the cheap slave labor from China, and Germany has shown it works!

Ben Franklin said, "By failing to prepare, you are preparing to fail." That is exactly what America is doing—preparing to fail.

Given that the German apprenticeship program is proven to work, why doesn't the US emulate it? As I have said repeatedly, the US government is intent on collapsing the US economy, so they can drive us into the one-world government because we are crucial to its birth. Beyond that, there are other reasons you don't see the German model emulated here in the US One reason is that it is not cool to be a blue-collar worker. Americans have forgotten that America was founded on apprenticeship programs like those in Germany, and we need to go back to our roots. The day of the unskilled laborer is gone forever. Vocational job training is essential to individual employment opportunities and to the economic health of any technological society. An even more important reason you don't see this model in the US is that it requires cooperation between corporations, vocational schools, the government and trade unions. In today's intentionally divided America that cooperation is not possible, but if we hope to put America back to work and solve our debt crisis, it had better be a concept we adopt. We simply have to stop fighting and start cooperating, or we are finished as an economic force in the world and are destined to become a third world country. Our cooperation is that important.

- *Government subsidies to develop technology.* They can be hit or miss as in the case of the failed Solyndra solar panel company that was given half a billion by the federal government and went bankrupt. Another problem with subsidies is that since the investment is in a specific company as opposed to a technology to be shared with many companies, when successful, it tends to create a monopoly, which is often not in the best interest of the public because it imbues too much power in a single entity. I believe a better model is Research Hubs.
- *Research Hubs are the wave of future.* The cost of research is shared between participants allowing development of technologies, which in many instances would be too expensive for a single company to afford. Also, the technology is then able to be applied in a variety of ways benefiting the economy and society in ways that simply would not happen, if the research was horded. Lastly, it tends to reduce the dangers associated with creation of monopolies.

We have one notable success story here in the US, and we need to encourage more state governments, corporations, and universities to embrace this model. In 1990, the State of New York, NY State University, Albany, and over three hundred "nanotechnology companies" joined forces to develop a research center at University of Albany with spectacular results. To date, the state has invested $4 billion, but participating companies have invested over $13 billion.

The project has created 15,000 jobs in NY State with $1.4 billion in annual wages going into the state economy. The average nanotechnology job pays $92,000 per year.

Note: America has always been known as an innovator but our current competitive cutthroat R&D approach is outdated. Research Hubs are the model we should be using to develop the technological breakthroughs that will take the world into the twenty-first century. There is an unforeseen benefit from the Research Hub model, especially if it is adopted on an international scale to tackle issues of global concern, like developing cheap clean energy solutions and addressing the worlds looming water crisis. If society continues its current course of hoarding technology, the disparity between the haves and have-nots will continue to cause social strife and ever escalating wars. The pathway to peace on planet earth is to take control of technology out of the hands of the few and share it with the many. Coincidentally, in the wisdom of our Founding Fathers that is exactly what the American Economic System was intended to do.

"Two systems are before the world—one is the English system (free trade) and the other we may be proud to call the American System Of Economics, the only one ever devised the tendency of which was that of elevating while equalizing the condition of man throughout the world" (Henry C. Carey, economics adviser to Abraham Lincoln).

Either we elevate and equalize the condition of man throughout the world or the wars, which our greed, will cause will eventually destroy us all.

"Is there any man, is there any woman, let me say any child here that does not know that the seed of war in the modern world is industrial and commercial rivalry? (President Woodrow Wilson).

- *The Netherlands' flexicurity system* is a work transition and training program intended to retrain or find jobs for employees who are laid off due to economic downturn or technological obsolescence. It is considered to be a major reason unemployment in the Netherlands is so low. Unemployment in the Netherlands is only 5.3 percent compared to 10.4 in the European Union and 8.1 in the US. Both employees and employers benefit.

- Employer Benefits:
  - ✓ Employees can be hired and fired relatively easily.
  - ✓ It is generally cheaper to retrain an employee or help him get another job than it is to pay unemployment benefits.
  - ✓ The national labor pool is maintained so when there is an upturn in the economy there are trained employees available so jobs can be kept in the Netherlands.
- Employee Benefits:
  - ✓ Security net for employee. Rather than simply being laid off or fired like here in the US, they are sent to what they call the "mobility center," which is a cooperative service offered by multiple employers where they attempt to place them in another partner company.
  - ✓ If the employee has to take a lower paying job, they sometimes even pay the difference in salary for a period of time.

Unemployment in the Netherlands has dropped 60 percent since the 1980s.

Note: Another benefit of the Netherlands work model is that they offer flexible work schedules with 77 percent of women and 25 percent of men working part-time. This means there are more jobs available, and it also means people are able to use technology advancements to afford themselves both an income and leisure time. In my opinion as technology advances and fewer people are able to do more, working part-time will become the norm.

- *Lost opportunity in the tourism industry*. Following 9/11, the US tightened its visa requirements supposedly to improve security, yet it left the border with Mexico wide open. The two actions are simply inconsistent, and I believe it is just one more example of the intentional destruction of the US economy. As a direct result of the government's actions, the US lost one-third of our share of the global tourism business. The tourism business is booming. China, India, and Brazil have rapidly growing middle classes that want to travel outside their countries. According to the Chinese government, eighty million Chinese are expected to travel outside China in 2013.

If the US were to recapture its lost share of the tourism industry since 9/11, it is estimated to generate 1.3 million jobs, which is 20 percent of all jobs lost since the 2008 recession.

- The Solution:
  - ✓ Easier access to visas
  - ✓ Massive advertising campaign marketing US as tourism destination
  - ✓ More destination locations, such as Orlando and Vegas

- *US falling behind on growth indicators.* According to the 2002 World Economic Forum:
  - *Infrastructure.* Five years ago, the US infrastructure was ranked fifth in the world. Now, we are twenty-fifth, and most of America's infrastructure is for sale to the highest bidder. For example, China spends 9 percent of GDP on infrastructure, while the US spends only 2.4 percent. America is crumbling. Our bridges are falling down, our water mains are bursting and our levies are breaking. *Note*: Historically growth in GDP pretty much tracks on a one-to-one ratio with investment in infrastructure, so it is a near certainty that the country that does not invest in infrastructure will not grow.
  - *Burden of government regulations.* The US ranks seventy-six with a score of 3.3 on a scale of 7. Clearly, the US is burdened with job killing regulations many of which have been passed by bureaucratic czars who are used to circumvent Congress and implement regulations through the EPA, which are nothing short of an end-run on the failed cap and trade legislation.

- *Tax burden.* The US ranks 69 out of 144 countries. And our tax burden is increasing at an alarming rate.
- *Research and development.* Federal funding for research and development is half of what it was in 1960

CONCLUSIONS: HOW TO PUT AMERICA BACK TO WORK

- Revamp our educational system, so we are turning out graduates with the skills companies want and need.
- Develop apprenticeship programs modeled after Germany, which will mean the government, companies, schools and unions will have to learn to cooperate with one another.
- Embrace the Research Hub approach on a national and international level and share technology with the world, so the disparity in the standard of living of individuals and nations can be reduced and along with it the ever present threat of war.
- Embrace the Netherlands' flexicurity system as a way to lower unemployment and retain a skilled labor force during upturns and downturns in the economy.
- Lower taxes so individuals will have more money to spend to stimulate the economy and companies will be incented to invest in new technologies. Seventy percent of GDP is based on consumer spending, so it is only common sense to put disposable income in the hands of consumers in order to vitalize the economy.
- Eliminate unnecessary job killing regulations designed to make the US noncompetitive in the global marketplace.
- Withdraw from Free Trade Agreements and negotiate Fair Trade Agreements with tariffs to protect domestic manufacturing.
- Smaller government with more control at state level.
- Streamline process for getting visas so the US can regain its lost share of the global travel industry.

- Invest in America's infrastructure, which will put people to work in the construction industry and provide the foundation for future growth.

I am sure there are additional things we could do to stimulate the US economy, but this is a good start. All of these things are doable, if we will have the courage to stand up to our government and tell them to get out of the way and allow prosperity to blossom.

Reader's perspective: I have to say I never could quite understand how America could have gotten in the mess it is in. At least now I know.

Me: Yes, thank God that at least the American people finally know what has been done to drive then into slavery. But now we know something else as well. We know how to put Humpty Dumpty back together again which is certainly something all the governments men have no intention of doing. So know that we have the knowledge the question becomes will we accept the responsibility. The walls of the temple of finance have been knocked down will you help rebuild them so Humpty can be hole again, so America can once again be the land where dreams come true the land where people can live in peace and raise their families and worship God?

SURVIVING THE FUNDAMENTAL TRANSFORMATION OF AMERICA

Your personal preparedness and survival strategy!

America is about to find out to, their dismay, what Obama meant when he said, "We are five days away from the fundamental transformation of America."

The question I am most frequently asked is, "What can I do to protect my financial assets?" But the question we really need to be asking is, "How can I survive a global economic meltdown leading to a totalitarian global government?"

If you don't look at your preparedness plan from that perspective you will be ill-prepared to face what lies ahead. Having said that, I ask your indulgence because the next several pages are somewhat of a review, but I want the horror of what is coming to premeditate your spirit so you will be prepared to make a "total change of mind-set!" No half measures will save you or your loved ones!

Obama's globalist handlers envision a fundamental transformation not just of America but of the entire planet. The entire global economic system will be morphed into a new system, which will be unlike anything we, Americans, have ever experienced. When it actually occurs, that change will be swift and dramatic. It will affect the entire planet. There will be no safe havens, none! The only hope lies in having prepared in advance for what is coming. We will discuss "exactly what you need to do" as soon as we lay some additional groundwork. Get ready!

Chaos will be fostered in order to force us to accept a totalitarian government in exchange for restoration of civil order!

If you and your loved ones are going to survive what is coming, you first have to understand exactly what Obama means by fundamental transformation. Then you have to prepare a comprehensive survival strategy, which includes financial strategies, mental and emotional preparedness (a complete change of mindset) and contingency plans for how to survive in a society where all the rules of society have broken down and chaos reigns. This is indeed a "brave new world," and it requires rugged individualism (self-sufficiency from the government) coupled with a return to the type of support system our pioneering forefathers embraced (a combination of self-sufficiency and interdependence of family and neighbors). When the monetary system is brought down, our material society will crumble, and we will have to adapt or perish. It is that simple. When paper money becomes worthless, and it will, we will need alternative forms of exchange.

In order to understand exactly what we will need to do to survive, we first have to understand what is coming, so let's get to it, and we will get back to preparedness in a while.

Obama's Agenda: America is being systematically destroyed from the inside, by the very people sworn to protect and serve, "by our own government, by our own president!" You are about to get a glimpse into the true meaning of Obama's "Fundamental Transformation of America," a transformation, which will make the economic misery and hardship of the Great Depression and the oppression and tyranny of the Mao's Cultural Revolution look like child's play. This book will provide you with a survival plan, which could well save your life and that of your loved ones.

The plan of the globalists is to:

- intentionally collapse the worldwide monetary system in order to create global chaos,
- force us to accept a global government and global credit system controlled by implanted (RFID) chips.
- make us willingly "give up the constitution and our liberty" in exchange for the promise of peace, security, and order,

"For when they shall say peace and safety: then sudden destruction cometh upon them, as travail upon a woman with child: and they shall not escape" (1 Thessalonians 5:3 KJV).

- impose a capitalist/communist totalitarian dictatorship,

  "And he causeth all both small and great, rich and poor, free and bond, to receive the mark in their right hand, or in their foreheads. And that no man might buy or sell, save he that had the mark, or the name of the beast or the number of his name" (Revelation 13:16, 17 KJV).
- RFID technology will give the government the means to fulfill Revelation 13:16, 17 thus fulfilling the government's evil plan as outlined in the Bible over 2,000 years ago. Once we all have (RFID) chips the government will be in a position to:
- implement the UN's Agenda 21, which calls for:
  - elimination of personal property. (The state intends to own first all mortgaged property and eventually all property.)
  - limitations on mobility (restricted travel and restricted areas)
  - control of all natural resources (as an ultimate control mechanism)
  - the "culling of the population" from its current level of seven billion to one billion. (Mass genocide on a level never before imagined.)
  - All those the state deems "dangerous or of no value" will be either imprisoned or killed; the primary targets will be the elderly, those deemed to be nonproductive, the uneducated, intellectuals, Christians, veterans, and dissidents.

The remaining sheep will be driven into submission!

The president can, at his discretion, declare martial law and the Congress cannot challenge his authority for six months which is plenty of time to do as Hitler did and impose a dictatorship!

The National Defense Authorization Act (NDAA) opens the door for the arrest, interrogation, and indeterminate detention of US citizens arrested on US soil without any legal representation. It completely flies in the face of the American judicial system's framework of "*the presumption of innocence till proven guilty.*" This presumably gives the government the authority to call a dissident a terrorist, and he can then be locked up forever just like in Communist China. We are treading on very dangerous ground.

The new terrorists are *you and me*. A Department Of Homeland Security memo has been sent out to law enforcement officials all over the country. It describes the future threat to America as Right Wing Christian groups (reminiscent of the demonization of the Jews in WWII Germany), prolife groups, Second Amendment Groups, and returning veterans. In other words, anyone likely to stand up against the government is being targeted, but conspicuously absent from this list is any mention of Islamic extremist. Go figure. But remember, we have a Muslim president. After all, Obama bowed to the King of Saudi Arabia, signifying Islam is superior and Christian America is subordinate. By the way, the new head of Homeland Security is a Muslim! What does that tell you?

In China, the organs of political prisoners are auctioned off to the highest bidder. With legislation, such as NDAA, this could happen in America in the not too distant future.

Welcome to Obama's fundamental transformation of America. The only way to survive what is coming is to *adopt a complete change in mindset.*

You will have to open your eyes and see the truth of what is planned for America. There will be limitations on income, energy consumption, mobility, freedom of speech, freedom to congregate, and there will be no inalienable rights. Freedom, as we know it, will become extinct. What few rights we will have, will be granted by the government and subject to revocation at any time. Those deemed to be a threat to the state will be subject to indefinite detention, torture, and execution without any legal representation whatsoever.

You will have to come to grips with the fact that "the material prosperity" which America has enjoyed, will be abruptly and permanently ended. That "the freedom we have enjoyed," will be taken away. That America will "no longer be the land of opportunity," but instead, "America will be a land of limitation, hardship, and oppression!"

The good news: the collapse will come in phases and each phase will require a specific strategy, so you have time to plan and prepare!

Before I get into your personal preparedness plan, I want to digress, yet again, and go back in history to the "Great Depression and Mao's Cultural Revelation" in order to give you a perspective of what to expect. If you know what is coming, you can plan for it. Otherwise, you will be a victim.

History demonstrates that when the great depression befell America there were three outcomes for people.

1. Those that knew in advance that the crash was coming, and prepared accordingly were able to bridge the collapse (protect their wealth) and actually build wealth by buying assets in the aftermath of the collapse for pennies on the dollar. (That is possible today with the right plan.)
2. Those who were debt-free or had jobs that were essential were able to get by but just barely. (You will learn where the job opportunities will be.)
3. The unfortunate majority suffered for twelve long years in abject poverty and endured very real hardships. (This is the fate of all those who do not heed God's final warning and prepare for what is coming).

I want to give you a glimpse of what it was like during the Great Depression, but keep in mind what is coming will be much, much worse because on top of the poverty we are talking about implementation of a totalitarian dictatorship!

> *The Great Depression brought unimaginable suffering to millions and the financial elite are doing it again. But this time, it will be much worse!*

Roosevelt's *New Deal* relied on borrowing from the very Fed, which caused the depression. Borrowing money from the Fed at interest didn't work then, and for the same reasons, neither has Obama's Stimulus worked. WWII ended the depression, not FDR's New Deal spending. You simply cannot borrow your way out of debt. Given our enormous debt, all the Fed has to do is raise interest rates, and they can trigger a crash at will so you need to be prepared now because when the end comes, you won't have time to react!

The plight of the American people during the Depression. The Great Depression created an America hitherto unimagined. This great nation had represented the hopes and dreams of millions of immigrants who had left their homes to come to this country to forge new lives. This was a nation built on the hopes and dreams of people who believed in rugged individualism.

Now we are a nation who has become dependent on the government from cradle to grave, and the government fosters that dependency as a means of control.

America was the land of opportunity and eternal optimism, but in the throes of the Great Depression, it had become a nation of people numbed by the reality of unbelievable financial hardship. It was a nation of people in disbelief, a nation of people who were almost too dazed to know what to do. In order to gain even a small measure of the severity of the Great Depression, we need to take a look at how it impacted the lives of a generation of Americans who would forever have their lives defined by the bleak reality that they had lived through the Great Depression.

By 1932, the Depression was in its fourth year, and no matter what the government did, it didn't seem to work. Over ten million people, or approximately 20 percent of the population, were unemployed and were locked in the grips of depression, despair, gloom, and the inevitable loss of self-esteem that besets a person when he has no hope or when his nightly companion is fear of starvation. It wasn't just the uneducated or unskilled laborers who were affected. The depression had no respect for age, race, gender, or education; some people were just luckier than others. In aggregate, the unemployment rate in the heartland cities neared 50 percent.

Economic chaos is coming to America!

You can expect 50 percent unemployment in the near future! One of the precipitating causes of the Great Depression was that the money was concentrated in the hands of a few mega rich robber barons who kept wages down and prices up resulting in under consumption, leading to unemployment and the Great Depression. Today, 70 percent of GDP is based on consumer spending, so if people don't have money to buy consumer items, the economy collapses, pure and simple. Add in higher taxes, depreciation of the dollar and inflation and you have the perfect financial storm. As if that wasn't bad enough. The US owes more money than all the nations of the world combined. That makes the US a financial pariah and the nations of the world are determined to combine forces and bring America to her knees. And all of this is being orchestrated by the financial elite in order to bring about enough chaos to birth the New World Order.

Social workers consistently reported that, despite the fact that people had lost jobs through no fault of their own, unemployed men experienced not only depression, but also feelings of guilt and self-recrimination. They felt that in some indeterminable way, they had let their families down, they had failed their children, and they were somehow "less of a man," because they didn't have a job. If their wives worked and they didn't, the situation was even worse as a role reversal occurred, and the husbands became subservient and submissive to their wives, the breadwinners. The entire family structure was turned upside down, and it often resulted in separation or divorce, with the husband eventually leaving. Tens of thousands of unemployed men, labeled "hobos," hit the highways and railways, looking for work. With heads bowed in shame, they stood in soup lines; they huddled in box cars and around camp fires, their clothes tattered, their shoes lined with newspaper to plug the holes. They anguished and lamented and prayed for relief from their torment, but their prayers went unanswered. Those who stayed scrimped and scraped. Often, families would move in together to share expenses. Every penny was precious. Food was basic—no frills, socks were darned, clothes were patched—nothing went to waste. People went about the business of survival, and it was a harsh business, which nightly visited them with feelings of despair and hopelessness.

I found this quote by Frank Walker, president of the National Emergency Council (1934) to be especially heart-wrenching. "I saw old friends of mine, men I had gone to school with digging ditches and laying sewer pipe. They were wearing their regular business suits as they worked, because they couldn't afford overalls and rubber boots. If I ever thought 'there but for the grace of God go I,' it was right then."

There was a tragic irony to the depression. In Oregon, apples fell to the ground and rotted for want of buyers. In the breadbasket, wheat also went unsold. Striking farmers overturned milk trucks and blocked deliveries of cattle and hogs to the stockyards in Omaha. In the cities, this was contrasted by visions of tens of thousands of men standing in soup lines. In the cities, people scrounged in trash cans for scraps of food. The pity of it, such want in a sea of plenty. Across the country, family farms encumbered by debt went on auction blocks by the thousands, as banks first foreclosed and then tried to recoup some of their losses by turning around and auctioning them to the highest bidders.

Mass starvation is on the horizon! Expect food shortages in the near future, not because there is no food, but because when the dollar collapses, there will be no money to buy it with! Get prepared!

A second housing collapse is on the horizon! As hard as it may be to imagine, what is coming will be even worse than the 2008 collapse or the Great Depression. The financial elite, and their cronies at the Fed and in Washington, intend to own every mortgage in America! The privately owned Fed is buying $40 billion in mortgages every month and privately owned Fannie and Freddie (who were bailed out with tax payer money effectively nationalizing them) are the "investors" behind virtually every short sale and foreclosure in America. Another aspect of this property grab will be to consolidate the banks down to just a few banks that are "too big to fail," the banks owned by the financial elite through the Federal Reserve, the World Bank, and IMF. This is the biggest property grab in the history of the world.

If at all possible, pay off you mortgage and put aside money to pay your taxes! (Precious metals not cash as it will be worthless.)

Much of the tragedy of the American people was reported by Loretta Hickock, on assignment for the White House, to travel across America and record the plight of Americans in the Depression.

In a summary report written on New Year's Day 1935, Hickock recounted her worries about a "stranded generation," men over forty with half-grown families who might never get their jobs back. Through loss of skill and through mental and physical deterioration, owing to long periods of enforced idleness, the relief clients—the people who had been longest without work—were gradually forced into "the class of unemployables," like rusty tools, abandoned, not worth using any more. "And, so they go on – the gaunt, ragged legion of the industrially damned, bewildered and apathetic, many of them terrifyingly patient" (Lowitt and Beaslen, *One Third of a Nation*. 361–63).

Hopkins concluded "the elderly through hardship, discouragement and sickness as well as advanced years, have gone into an occupational oblivion from which they will never be rescued by private industry" (Hopkins, *Spending to Save*, 161).

Misery of unparallel proportion is headed to America! As bad as the Great Depression was, this time around it will be much, much worse, because this time, there is an agenda to cull the population of six billion people, and those in power will have dictatorial power. This is the reality of life under communism! By any measure of human suffering, the Great Depression was an event never experienced by any generation of Americans before or since. The real tragedy is that it was intentionally brought about by a group of greedy bankers and they are doing it again and we are standing by and doing nothing.

Time to choose: fight back or be exterminated!

In Oct. 1933, Hickok wrote to Eleanor Roosevelt from North Dakota, "These plains are beautiful, but oh the terrible, crushing dumbness of life here. And the suffering, for both people and animals… Most of the farm buildings haven't been painted in God knows how long! If I had to live here I'd just quietly call it a day and commit suicide… The people up here… are in a daze. A sort of nameless dread hangs over the people" (Richard Lovett and Maurine, eds. *One Third of a Nation*).

A warning from the past: Believing that the Federal Reserve had brought the Great Depression on the American people on purpose, Congressman Louis McFadden began bringing impeachment proceedings against the Federal Reserve Board, saying of the crash and depression, "It was a carefully contrived occurrence. International bankers sought to bring about a condition of despair, so that they might emerge the rulers of us all."

Not surprisingly, Congressman McFadden was assassinated (poisoned at a state function) for standing up against the financial elite.

This brings us to Mao's Cultural Revolution and its promise of "power to the people." Imagine their surprise when the very people who helped bring Mao to power were starved to death. They were as Lenin called then "useful idiots." This is communism, and the Obama administration holds it in adulation and the free market system in contempt. "The free market is nonsense. We kind of agree with Mao that political power comes largely from the barrel of a gun" (Manufacturing czar, Ron Bloom).

A Confluence Of Events Is Forming Which Will Result In: The Economic Collapse Of The US And The Rest Of The World!

Our Materialism Is A Poison That Is Destroying Society & Threatens Our Very Souls!

Collapse Of The Dollar Is Inevitable!

- The International Monetary Fund [IMF] announced Plans to replace dollar as world's reserve currency! Feb. 10 2011
- PIMCO [largest private buyer of US Treasuries]: divested their position in treasuries!
- FED monetizing debt: buying 90% of treasury notes!
- 41 cents of every tax dollar goes to pay interest on national debt!
- FED has increased the money supply 300%
- Washington has raised the debt ceiling 11 times in 11 years.
- Standard & Poor's has lowered our credit rating.
- Obamacare contains 20 new or increased taxes target at the middle class.

Hyper Inflation Is Inevitable Along With Food Shortages!

The Perfect Storm. Words of Encouragement.

What is coming is necessary in order to separate God's righteous from Satan's evildoers. Though these things must come to pass, God is giving you a survival plan. If you read this book and heed God's warning, he will use what is coming to strengthen your faith and save your soul.

"All things work for good for those who love him" (Romans 8:28 KJV).

Finally, your personal preparedness plan!

I am sorry it has taken me so long to get to your preparedness plan, but I wanted to make sure that when we did get to this point, you would understand the gravity of what lies ahead. It is nothing short of the fundamental transformation of the world. We are faced with devising a survival strategy, which will see us survive global chaos and the formation of a government intent on severely limiting resource consumption and culling the population by six billion people. The future will be a hostile environment, and though we will be looking at how to protect our assets, there is much more than finances that we have to consider. For those of you who are Christians, you will ultimately have to decide if you will take the mark. If not, you will have to be capable of living completely off the grid, independent of the government. What we are about to explore will require a *change in mindset*. We will have to be prepared financially, mentally, emotionally, and spiritually!

The planned collapse of the US and global economy.
Phase I: The Downward Spiral
Phase II: The Crash
Phase III: The Transition Period
Phase IV: The Totalitarian Dictatorship

HOW TO SURVIVE COLLAPSE OF THE US AND GLOBAL ECONOMIES

Phase I: The Downward Spiral

What to expect: Over the next two to three years, the economy will be systematically collapsed. Much talk is made about taxing the rich, but make no mistake; the intention is to bleed the middle class dry and back them into a corner where they are so desperate that they will have to choose between buying food or paying their mortgage. This will cause a second real estate crash and millions more hardworking Americans will lose their homes as real estate prices plummet yet again. When the government is ready to collapse the US economy, the Fed will raise interest rates which will hyperinflate the dollar, and over night, the economy will go into a tail spin, and a default on the national debt will be threatened, just like with the Stimulus.

In order to bring about these desperate circumstances, you can expect the government to dramatically increase taxes. Food prices will soar as a result of devaluation and inflation. Gas prices will go up for the same reasons, except you can also expect some sort of manufactured crisis, which will drive gas prices through the roof. (Say Saudi Arabia, America's largest oil supplier, topples, and Middle East Oil supplies are cut off, and Obama has not allowed development of the Keystone Pipeline, oil exploration in the Gulf, or the opening of federal lands in the Western US, resulting in a devastating oil shortage.) In addition, millions of Americans will be forced into part-time employment, as employers cut hours in order to avoid paying for health insurance under Obamacare. The outcome will be less discretionary money to fuel the economy, which will result in higher unemployment and more borrowing to pay unemployment benefits and other entitlements. Currently, approximately 46 percent of the population receives some sort of payment from the government. You can expect that number to be upwards of 70 percent as the government's entitlements makes us dependent on them. Entitlements will be paid, up to the point that the economy actually collapses, because the government knows that if they cut entitlements, there will be riots in the streets, and they don't want that till the very end.

Eventually, the government will remove the debt ceiling, resulting in the unbridled printing of money, which will cause massive inflation and the collapse of the US economy. This is what always happens in the final death throes of an economic collapse.

In this phase, the number one objective is to protect/preserve your assets. The strategy is to be debt-free and to get your assets out of potentially worthless paper assets and put them into tangible assets, which will retain their value and bridge the economic crisis.

The sixty-four-thousand-dollar question is how do you achieve that sleight of hand? For those that have faced the reality of what is coming and have protected their assets, this will be an opportunity for the riches of the wicked to be transferred to the righteous as God allows those with cash to buy bad debts.

"And the wealth of the sinner is laid up for the just" (Proverbs13:22 KJV).

For God giveth to a man that is good in his sight wisdom, and knowledge, and joy: but to the sinner he giveth travail, to gather and to heap up that he may give to him that is good before God" (Ecclesiastes 2: 26 KJV).

This is exactly what God intends in these turbulent times, and this book will give you the necessary wisdom. But God will only give the opportunity to those that he judges as "good before him." So search your heart and get it right; then, God will help you protect your finances. Otherwise, no matter what you do it will be for naught!

Questions and Answers

- *What exactly do you mean when you recommend getting out of paper assets and going into tangible assets?* For purposes of our discussion, a tangible asset is anything that has intrinsic value in and of itself by virtue of its desirability or its usefulness. In this instance, a tangible asset might be food or a commodity, such as oil, grain, or precious metals. It does not include paper assets because they only represent something of value or as in the instance of currency, a promise to pay, which is worthless unless backed by a tangible asset, such as gold or silver. Otherwise, the promise is only as good as the holder's faith in the promise. If that faith is lost, then paper assets are only worth the paper they are written on and nothing more.

  The US dollar will soon be worth only the paper it is written on, so in order to protect your wealth, you must store your wealth in tangible assets till such time that the economy stabilizes.
- *Do you recommend investing in gold and silver?* The short answer is yes, but some explanation is required. Gold and silver have

historically been a store of value. Our currency was originally backed by gold till President Nixon took us off the gold standard, so the dollar could be systematically devalued, in order to drive the nation and its citizens into unmanageable debt.

As we have discussed, the financial elite intentionally caused the Great Depression and the 2008 housing crash, and they now intend to bring about a second housing crash followed by a stock market crash and a global currency collapse! Then, they will issue a new currency, but in order for a world in chaos to accept the new currency, it will have to be backed by something of value, such as gold, silver, and possibly, even oil.

This could save your life. Put your money where the financial elite put their money! So with this in mind, where do you suppose the financial elite and the various governments of the world have their money? Not in worthless paper but in gold and silver and other stores of value!

In short, the financial elite and the super power countries of the world are getting out of worthless paper, particularly the dollar and into tangibles (gold, silver, and natural resources). The Rothschilds have so much gold that they literally control the market. The Fed (owned by the financial elite owns the money in Fort Knox. We cannot audit the Fed or tell them what to do. They are above the government; supposedly established to represent "we, the people." Over the last few years, the Chinese have increased their gold reserves to thirty times what it previously was. There is speculation that at some point they may issue a gold backed currency. India and China are now buying oil from Iran in gold, not US dollars. We recently gave China an oil well off the coast of Brazil, and we gave Russia a large portion of Alaska's Purgo Bay Oil Fields.

Our creditors are demanding payment in something other than worthless dollars! The crash will happen with no warning, so be prepared!

One day, you will wake up and find out that the Fed has raised interest rates, and it will be over. "The death of the dollar will be at hand!" In 1929, they called in the margin loans and during Carter's term they raised interest rates, with devastating consequences.

History will repeat itself! If we want to preserve our assets, we need to do what the movers and shakers of the world are doing. They will be the ones to trigger the global economic collapse, and you can bet your last dollar they intend to profit from it!

History will repeat itself. The financial elite will do exactly what they did in 1929. They pulled their money from the stock market, put it in gold and set back, and waited for everything to collapse. Then they converted their gold back into currency and bought entire companies and vast holding of real estate for pennies on the dollar. Do what they do, and you will come out on the other side of this man-made crash with a good portion of your assets intact. You may even come out wealthier than before the crash, especially if you are a person that is "good before God!"

- *Which is the better investment, gold or silver?* Again, that depends on you individual situation. If you are super wealthy, gold is a better storehouse of wealth because of its higher price. On the other hand, if you need a loaf of bread, silver is a lot more practical medium of exchange. If you think you may use either gold or silver as an interim currency, then I recommend you get US-minted coins. They are recognized as legal tender and will be far more acceptable as a medium of exchange than bars or rounds, which would have to be assayed to determine their value.

  To answer your question in a more direct fashion, I believe silver is a much better investment for the average person for the following reasons:

  - Gold is subject to fractional reserve banking practices but silver is not. Remember, precious metals—gold and silver—are the only real money. Paper money is fiat currency, so in order to get the public to support their fiat currency, the government has to artificially suppress the price of gold and silver. A few super wealthy investors can suppress silver prices like the Hunt Brothers did years ago, but gold suppression is more complicated. Here is how it works. If for example a person deposited $10 into a bank, according to Fractional Reserve Lending Practices that bank could then loan out $90s, money they created out of thin air. The banker gangsters do the same thing with gold, but because they don't hold physical silver in central banks, it is not subject to the same manipulation. Central banks lease their gold to bullion banks, and then they use double accounting loopholes to count the gold twice. Then, the bullion bank can in turn lease the gold to another bullion bank so that the same gold can be fictitiously owned by any number of people. So if you do not hold physical gold in all probability, you hold a worthless piece of paper. This allows the government and the banker gangsters to sell large quantities of nonexistent gold over and over in order to artificially suppress gold prices. *Can you say crooks?* This scam is about to get exposed. Suspecting that their gold may not actually be in the Fed in New York, Venezuela recently asked to take possession of their ninety-nine tons of gold, and Germany asked to take possession of their three hundred tons. They were told it would take seven years for them to get their gold. I don't know how trusting you are, but to me that translates into "we sold your gold."

- Silver reserves are dangerously low. The US geologic survey estimates that unless silver prices are allowed to go up that the world will exhaust its mining supply by 2020.
- Above ground, silver reserves are exhausted. At one point, there was a ten-year supply of above ground silver and now there is less than a year.
- Silver is a critical industrial commodity. For example, because of its attributes as a electrical conductor it is critical to the manufacture of electronics. Can you imagine our modern world without electronics? Silver is vital; gold is not.
- US silver mining production is likely to be reduced for several years due to a huge landslide at the Kennecott Mine, which accounts for 16 percent of US production.

- With both silver and gold prices suppressed and hyper-inflation looming. All precious metals can be expected to increase dramatically in value when the dollar dies as it will shortly do. This is the end of the road for the fiat currency, and when people realize that fact, gold and silver will go through the roof, but I expect that for the reasons discussed above that silver will significantly outperform gold.
- We may see the day silver is as valuable as gold. Gold is currently trading at $1,400 per ounce and silver at $24 per ounce, so just imagine how happy you would be if silver sold at the same price as gold, which it might over the next few years, because the best way to conserve silver use and boost production is to increase the price. If we woke up one day and there were no more gold, life would go on relatively unchanged, but if silver supplies were exhausted, it would dramatically change our lives.

• *What if the government confiscates the gold or silver?* (They likely will!) In 1933, in the depths of the Great Depression, the US declared bankruptcy, declared a bank holiday, and made it illegal to own gold. US citizens had to turn their gold in or face up to ten years in prison and/or a $10,000 fine. (Silver was not called in.) Even so, those with gold were far better off than those with their wealth in paper assets, because in most instances, the paper assets were worthless, whereas the gold was turned in at an exchange rate favorable to the government crooks, but nonetheless, their gold was a store of value for those who had it. After the government got their hands on the people's gold, they raised the price of gold 65 percent, which meant those that had gold got 45 cents on the dollar but that is far better than getting stuck holding worthless paper. Don't forget that when the economy collapses, values may well plummet to as little as 10 percent of where they were pre-crash. This said, even with 45 cents on the dollar, you may well be able to turn around and buy assets for 10 cents on the dollar and have a net increase in your wealth. I should note that eventually, once the government has put in place their global dictatorship, they will once again take us off gold going instead to credits issued by the government and monitored by your RFID chip (the mark).

Jews in Germany were able to use gold to buy their way to freedom. In these turbulent times, everyone who can should have some gold or silver as a hedge against the collapse of the dollar. As to how much, that depends on your financial situation. You can't eat gold. You can't drink gold, and gold won't cure your medical problems, so take care of the basics first, and then look to investing in gold or silver. You do need some gold or silver to pay your taxes or else even if your home is debt-free, the government will still take it!

- *Gold and silver can be extremely volatile, so what if I get caught holding a large quantity and prices fall?* I can guarantee you that when things stabilize, gold and silver will go down appreciably in value, but it is much more likely that before that, the government will seize it to back a new currency, in which case you will likely be given an exchange rate (just like what happened in 1933). History repeats itself with great regularity when circumstances repeat themselves. No matter what happens to gold and silver prices, they are a safer place to put your money than in paper, which will become worthless. Silver is the better long-term investment because of its short supply and industrial uses.

You may be surprised to know your assets are not diversified because at the end of the day, they are all in worthless paper!

I am sure you have heard the saying "Never put all your eggs in one basket." That said, diversify your assets! Diversification is the basis of asset management and a good strategy in any market. A word of warning to those of you who think you are diversified because you have your money in stocks, bonds, real estate, a whole life insurance policy, a pension fund or 401k. All of these assets have one thing in common. They are at their core paper assets. If you want to be truly diversified, you need to put a portion of your assets in tangibles. More on this later.

Another lesson from the Great Depression! When the stock market crashed, it took forty-five years for the market to return to its pre-crash value. The lesson is this. Many stocks went off the board and the companies went out of business. However, some companies, though they lost value, remained solvent and rebounded. If you are going to leave a portion of your wealth in the stock market, then you need to learn from the Great Depression. People suffered severe emotional trauma, and they leaned on alcohol and tobacco as a solace so those companies tended to do better than most. In periods of severe economic crisis, like the Great Depression—which lasted twelve agonizing years—people simply cannot afford any luxury items. Given this simple fact, companies that made luxury items were the hardest hit. Only items that were absolute necessities were purchased, and so it will be again. Ask yourself what you cannot live without, and if you invest in the stock market, invest in companies that make those items (i.e., food production and manufacture, pharmaceuticals, commodities) as long as their demand will not be impacted by a downturn in manufacturing, utilities, etc. Also, even in these categories, you should investigate which companies have large contracts with the government or are heavily in bed with the government. Most people will work for the government, and the government will be the largest buyer of goods and services, so invest where they do the majority of their business. For example, Monsanto is in control of a large portion of the world's food supply, and they are in bed with the government, so my money is on them as a survivor. Also, GE is developing the smart grid, which the government will eventually use to control our energy consumption. They are also in bed with the government as witnessed by the fact that they paid no corporate income taxes for the last several years, and the government mandated their mercury filled biohazard fluorescent light bulbs. These are just a couple of examples. Do your own research, or get someone to do it for you.

I do not have a securities license so I cannot give you specific recommendations. Talk to a financial advisor, but make sure he does not get paid by the transaction, and (very importantly) make sure whoever you choose understands what is coming and will advise you how to protect your assets based on the assumption that the dollar will collapse.

Note: When the economy collapses the US will be the biggest loser. There will be a huge transfer of wealth away from the US to Asia and other emerging countries. Here is a bit of advice that could not only keep you from losing your wealth, but could see you get rich. "Follow the money"! There is a system called 'Money Mapping" which tracks where all the big investors ***[The Insiders – The Financial Elite, The Politicians, The Corporations, and The Government]*** are putting their money. They know who will benefit from what is coming because they are the ones bringing it about. If you get the right investment company they will know what I am referring to and they will have software to track where the money is going so you can follow it.

- *The Bible tells us that the day will come when we will throw our gold and silver in the streets, so why do you recommend investing in them?* I believe that to be an accurate statement, but I do not believe that will occur till the final phase of the takeover by the one-world government. Eventually, when the government has consolidated their power the government, banks and corporations will make slaves of us all. The mechanism by which they will do that is the RFID chip. Once it is mandated, in order to buy or sell, you will have to have an RFID chip. At that point, there will be no further need for currency. We will be given credits by the government and corporations who will control everything. Get ready!

- *Do you recommend stockpiling survival items, such as food, water, medicine, guns, and ammunition, and the like.?* Yes, but that is a topic for later discussion.

- *What about investing in foreign currency as a hedge against the devaluation of the dollar?* As stated earlier, China has entered into trade agreements with roughly half the world's population to trade international commodities in Chinese currency. Until recently, such trades have been conducted exclusively in US dollars. This coupled with the fact that China has arguably replaced the US as the world's number one economic super power and one could easily conclude that it is an excellent idea to buy Chinese currency. But this is where knowledge of the endgame of the financial elite becomes invaluable. I believe that all indications are that for the indeterminate future buying Chinese currency as a hedge against the dollar could in fact provide protection from a falling dollar. I used to have a client who traded international currencies for a living. It is complicated, and it is definitely not something the average person can do on his own.

This said, I want to caution you that at a time of their choosing, the financial elite intend to collapse the entire global monetary system by intentionally collapsing the quadrillion dollar derivatives market. When they do so, there will be little to no warning, and if you get caught in any paper asset at that time, you will likely lose your shirt. This said, I am not a trader. Most of my real world experience is in the real estate market, where I was both an investor and licensed broker. In this instance, my comments come from research and from a study of history. In this regard, I should note that the reason there is a world reserve currency (i.e., the US dollar); is to prevent currency speculation, so as the world goes off the dollar there is likely to be currency speculation, which could make playing in that market risky. On a slightly different vain, you can expect China and others to artificially manipulate the value of their currency in order to gain trade advantage. This introduces the possibility of trade wars, which could introduce additional risk factors. Lastly, as I stated earlier, at a time of their choosing they will collapse all currencies, and if you are in paper assets at that time, you will lose everything you have.

- *What if I have assets I want to pass on to my children?* You better make provision immediately. Currently, inheritance assets are exempt up to $5.120 million, but it is going to be dropped to $1 million with the rate over a million going as high as 55 percent. This is nothing short of theft of our children's futures. Contact an estate planner and find out about gifting money to your children immediately. Also look into a trust or tenancy in common to pass on real estate.

- *Is my home a tangible asset and how does it fit into my investment/survival strategy?* Most people would say your home is a tangible asset, but unless it generates a positive cash flow (and it does not), then it is actually a liability, not an asset. Think about it. If your home is not paid for, you have a monthly mortgage to pay and even if it is paid for, you still have, maintenance, and utilities, and if you should get behind on your property taxes, you will find out the hard way that the ultimate owner of your home is the government. We are all just renters. That said, it is still preferable to own than to rent, especially with what is coming. Your home is your safe haven. At least, it should be. The key to real estate ownership has always been *location, location, location.* In the past that has been based on such criteria as proximity to jobs, services, and good schools, which generally meant big cities or their surrounding suburbs were the most desirable locations. In the near future, as the economy collapses and the social order breaks down, it will be safer to be in the country with access to food and water and if at all possible, you should be off the utility grid. Some cities will literally become ghost towns. If there are no jobs, people will just walk away from their homes leaving them derelict. Just look at Detroit.

Note: Given what I just said, farmland and small farms (farmetts) have been increasing in value at the very time other real estate has experienced devastating losses. That is because people with money are getting places in the country as a safe haven against riots in the big cities caused by food shortages. I recently bought an eleven-acre farmett. The financial elite live almost exclusively in rural settings. According to Pastor Lindsey Williams, who has connections with the financial elite, many of them live in remote regions of Alaska. As I said before, do what the elites do.

Earlier, I presented a scenario in which a confluence of events would see the government raise taxes and interest rates and buy US mortgages and banks would in turn invest in the highly speculative/leveraged derivates market, and at a time of their choosing, they would collapse the real estate market and currency markets. Now, I want to give you some more basic reasons the real estate market will absolutely collapse, leaving millions more unsuspecting Americans homeless.

Given what I am about to disclose my recommendation is to own a home for safety reasons, but you should not put assets in real estate, thinking that it is a hedge against an economic collapse, because it is not. Put your money in tangible assets in order to bridge the coming economic collapse. Then after the collapse, you will be able to buy real estate for pennies on the dollar, just like was the case in the Great Depression. History is a good indicator of the future.

Why real estate is not the place to hide your money!

1. The real estate market is intrinsically tied to the dollar (a paper asset that is only worth something as long as people have confidence in it). Therefore, if the dollar collapses (as it will), the real estate market will collapse too (guaranteed). Why? Because the credit market will dry up and interest rates will go up, which 100 percent of the time causes the real estate market to crash!
2. As state and local governments are threatened with default (as many are), they will raise real estate taxes (as many have), and it will affect property values (as it has and will continue to do). Also, they will default on the bonds, causing a crash of the bond markets.
3. As taxes go up—which they are (i.e., payroll tax, Obamacare, carbon taxes, and let us not forget the 3.8 percent real estate sales tax on second homes that was imbedded in Obamacare, etc.—and inflation and devaluation continues (as they are), there will be less discretionary money to spend on consumer

items. Since 70 percent of GDP is based on consumer spending, this will create a spiral where inventories will rise, jobs are lost, unemployment benefits go up, deficit spending goes up, and more and more hardworking Americans are forced to choose between paying their mortgage or their taxes, or putting food on the table. You have to eat. You don't have to pay your mortgage, especially not for the approximately 40 percent of US homeowners who are upside down on their mortgages.

4. Expect more defaults as the last of the adjustable rate mortgages reset and mortgage payments go up on homes, whose taxes have increased, and whose value had fallen. The perfect storm.
5. The easy money days are gone. Banks require near perfect credit scores and more money down. As a result, nearly 30 percent of all mortgage applications are rejected. Fewer mortgages means fewer home sales, less demand, longer time on market, and ultimately, lower sales prices Currently, 2/2014 home sales are up because of pent up demand, but even so, prices are still being held down because of the other factors I just indicated. This will be a short-lived resurgence.
6. There are still homes that have been foreclosed on by banks, but they are being kept off the market because if they were dumped on the market, housing prices would tank and the bank's portfolio of performing mortgages would be threatened. The result would be that a substantial number of the mortgages would go upside down, and then the mortgagees would decide to walk away from their mortgage.
7. The baby boomers are downsizing, and there are no buyers for their expensive, large, high maintenance houses, because the upcoming generation is smaller, can expect to make less, pay more in taxes, and incur higher utility bills. These homes are albatrosses.
8. The next generation is graduating with $1 trillion dollars in school loans. Poor job prospects, and thanks to Bush, even if they declare bankruptcy their student loan is not forgiven. They are indentured servants, which is exactly what the government wants.

9. There are more multigenerational households, which mean fewer home buyers. The American dream of home ownership is dead.
10. As the dollar dies, foreign investors are fleeing the US for Asian countries, which means less demand and lower prices.
11. There is an inescapable income to expense ratio. As cost of living goes up (as it is), we will reach a point where housing prices must fall. It is inescapable. Additionally, think about what Obama's 3.8 percent real estate sales tax (on second houses) will do to a housing market that is not appreciating and even worse depreciating. It is a death blow as it was intended to be. Remember that one of the goals of the UN's Agenda 21 is to end private ownership of real estate.
12. I will leave you with this thought: The American manufacturing sector has been gutted and as one time Presidential Candidate Ross Perot said, "Until The price of labor here is on par with the slave labor in other countries, jobs will never come back." (No jobs at least no decent paying jobs mean a dead real estate market. An inescapable reality.)

- *What about rental property, is it an asset?* If it creates a positive cash flow, it is an asset. And with interest rates being so low, it is hard for retires to live off of interest income so rental income can be an attractive alternative. However, things are not what they used to be. A little personal experience. I sold several rental properties in Chicago because even with 50 percent down, I found myself unable to generate a positive cash flow. Here is what happened. This is a scenario that is playing out all over America. Illinois state taxes went up 65 percent as Illinois struggled to avoid default. Meanwhile, property values fell 40–50 percent on my properties while at the same time real estate taxes went up 40 percent and my association fees also went up, as unpaid association fees were passed on to paying property owners. Lastly, rental prices fell. The moral to this story is that with what is coming, there is no guarantee that your rental properties will be able to generate a positive cash flow. Even if it is paid for, there are no guarantees because you can expect to generate less in rents than before the crash and the government may impose rent freezes like it did in the Great Depression. History is a great teacher, if we will only pay attention.

- *What if I can't be debt-free? What do I do?* The answer to this question depends on how much money you have and how much it cost you to meet your basic needs. It is a form of asset management. Ask yourself what you absolutely need in order to stay alive—no luxury items, just survival items—and how much money you need to provide your family with those items (e.g., food, water, clothing, shelter, utilities, gas, medical supplies, etc.). Take care of the survival items first, and then divert what is left to debt reduction. Given what is coming, you are recommended to stockpile survival items because the time will come when they will either be too expensive to afford, or they may not be available at all. For example, when Russia fell, people stood in lines all day to buy a pair of shoes or a loaf of bread. I recommend a minimum of a six-month supply of survival items! Once you have taken care of your stockpile of survival items, you can turn your attention to debt reduction. Some things are more important to pay off than others.

- *So what are the most important items to pay off?*
    - *Should I pay off my house?* The first thing most people think about paying off is usually their house, but given what is coming, that is probably not the best choice. Due to the dramatic fall in housing prices, 40 percent of all mortgages in the US are currently upside down. In the months ahead, many of these people will be forced to consider walking away from their mortgage and renting. This will be especially true if we have a second housing collapse and housing values take another noise

dive (which I am absolutely positive will happen). *Note*: It can take one to three years to foreclose on a house during which time, you typically don't make payments. I am not recommending walking away from your house, but if you have to, then at least be smart enough to save the money you would normally be paying in mortgage payments and put it aside toward future rent payments and survival items.

Generally, if you walk away from your personal residence you do not incur a tax liability. But this may not always be the case, so it is something you definitely want to check on with a lawyer or tax expert. You do, however, generally incur a tax liability on a (non-owner occupied property), but again, this requires expert council.

If you just owe a few thousand on your mortgage, you may be tempted to make extra payments in order to pay off your mortgage. I do not recommend that because your mortgage is a ***closed end loan***, which means that once you pay into it, you can't get your money back out unless you refinance. But in a falling real estate market, there will not be any appreciation and banks will not be doing many refinances. Credit will be extremely tight. The better option is to put the money aside in a tangible asset (say silver), and when you have enough to pay off your house, make a lump-sum payment.

So now, your house is paid off. You own it free and clear. *Wrong*! The American dream of home ownership is a ruse! The government owns your home, and if you don't believe me, fail to pay your property taxes and the government will sell the lien, and if you can't redeem it, you are out in the street faster than you can say, "Presto Change-O." This said, you must put aside enough money in tangible assets (i.e., gold or silver) to allow you to pay your taxes! You should also keep some cash on hand, but not too much.

- *Should I pay off my car?* Again, we are looking at survival strategies. If it is a second car and you don't absolutely need it, then don't pay it off. Sell it and use the money for survival items. If on the other hand it is your only car and you depend on it to get to work; then, you want to pay it off ASAP. ***Unlike your house, your car can be repossessed with no legal rigmarole.*** Fall behind a month or two and Presto Change–O, your car is repossessed, and if you depend on it, you are up the proverbial creek without a paddle.
- *Should I pay off my credit cards?* This is an ***unsecured debt*** so the credit card companies are not going to come and take back your big screen TV, but if you default on your credit card debt, you will screw up your credit (which, depending on your circumstances, may or may not be important to you) and you will incur a tax liability with greedy Uncle Sam. In a survival situation, the first loan you would likely chose not to pay would be an unsecured loan (i.e., your credit cards vs. your house or car, which will be taken away if you don't pay).

Phase II: The Crash

What to expect: When the financial elite believe that the free market system is sufficiently in debt and that there is absolutely no hope of a recovery, they will collapse the global monetary system and literally every currency in the world will be collapsed simultaneously!

At this point, virtually, all paper assets will become worthless! This will include your stocks, bonds, 401ks, IRAs, whole life insurance, mutual funds, pensions, including Social Security, etc.

- *So what do I do if I have my wealth in these assets?* This is going to be a bitter pill to swallow and one that many of you will simply not be able to cope with. The answer is to get out of all paper assets and put your wealth in tangible assets (i.e., cash in your whole life insurance. Use the money to buy tangibles, and if you want life insurance, buy term insurance. If you absolutely insist on keeping some of your wealth in the stock market, then remember what I said a while ago. Invest only in companies that are in cahoots with the government and those that make necessity items. They will likely not go out of business and eventually they will rebound, but even then we have to be concerned with the government nationalizing key industries. Many investment brokers are recommending transferring assets to growth markets, such as China and India, but if I am right and they collapse, the entire global currency market by collapsing the quadrillion dollar derivatives market no paper assets on the planet will survive the collapse. Remember, since the US (the world's reserve currency) was taken off the gold standard by Richard Nixon in 1971, all the world's currencies have been fiat currency backed by nothing but a promise to pay, that they cannot possibly keep, because the entire global economic system is nothing but a Ponzi pyramid scheme destined to collapse under its intentionally created debt burden. Get out of all paper!

Additionally, the financial elite will have opposition to establishing their utopian one-world government. Even as I write this, WWIII looms on the horizon, and if the Bible is right, we will eventually see Russia and a consortium of Muslim countries make a play for oil against the Anglo-Saxon financial elite and their leader, the antichrist. They will be defeated, but then, China with their two-hundred-million-man army will make a move, so, if this scenario plays out, you tell me what currency anywhere in the world will be safe in the face of such instability. I say again, invest in tangibles and get out of paper.

Many people I have spoken with say they are not worried because they are diversified. I say in the final analysis there are only two asset classes—paper and tangibles. You can't eat paper. In the final analysis, all fiat currency will be worth the paper it is written on and nothing more. Gold and silver are the only real money, not worthless paper. Put your money where the financial elite put their money, which is in gold and silver not paper. No matter how things shake out you can be sure of this: the elite are intentionally causing this global collapse, and they don't expect to come out of it poorer for their efforts. So I say again put your money where they put theirs, which is in gold and silver.

The financial elite controls the money supply, the availability of credit, and the interest rate. Through these three mechanisms, they are able to control currency devaluation and inflation and they are able to collapse the real estate market, stock market, and currency markets at will. Do you remember how during Carter's presidency the Fed raised interest rates and over night the economy took a nose dive and the real estate market all but dried up for several years? And the 1929 stock market crash occurred just as quickly when the financial elite dried up the credit market and massive margin calls were triggered, which collapsed the stock market overnight? Once the global debt is sufficiently high (At a time of their choosing), they will raise interest rates (as of Aug. 2013, Bernanke is warning that the Fed intends to do just that), triggering an economic collapse of the US, which will spread around the world because of the amount of US dollars in circulation. Eventually, they will collapse the quadrillion dollar derivatives market, causing the entire global currency market to collapse and literally all paper assets will be obliterated and *chaos* will break out all over the world!

The collapse will happen so fast that if you have not already taken measures to protect your wealth, it will be too late! Commerce will literally come to a halt because without money, nothing will be manufactured or shipped. There will be no food on the shelves, and riots will break out in most major cities. Bands of marauders will roam the streets. Martial law will be declared and UN troops will be brought in to restore order. Obama has ordered 2,700 tanks for urban deployment. Gee, I wonder what they could be for. Our civil liberties will be suspended, and the nations of the world will be under the grips of military occupation. Then, they will step in and offer to restore order by creating a new currency backed by gold, but the price will be the relinquishing of our freedom!

Gee I just remembered that is exactly what Rothschild did in England when the King came to him for a bail out. He said sure King old buddy, old pal, but I want control of the printing of the currency which of course by default meant that from that day forward the King was a figure head and the real power behind the throne of England was the Rothschilds. It will be the same this time around except they won't be the power behind the throne they will be the rulers of the entire freaking world. If that doesn't give you nightmares I don't know what would.

"Today, America would be outraged if UN troops entered Los Angeles to restore order (referring to the 1991 LA Riot). Tomorrow, they will be grateful! This is especially true if they were told that there were an outside threat from beyond, whether real or promulgated, that threatened our very existence. It is then that all peoples of the world will plead to deliver them from this evil. The one thing every man fears is the unknown. When presented with this "scenario," individual rights will be willingly relinquished for the guarantee of their well-being granted to them by the world government" (Henry Kissinger, Bilderberger Conference, Evians, France, 1991).

The number one objective is to have a strategy to cope with the temporary breakdown of essential services and the resulting breakdown of social order! Utter chaos will likely ensue till such time that a new currency is issued and products and services are once again available. This could take a few weeks, or it could also take several months, but what is for certain is that nothing will be as before. The power structure of the world will have shifted. The middle class will be virtually obliterated; all except for those few who saw it coming and took steps to protect their assets. Regardless of whether a person has money or not our freedom will be gone. We will be subject to a dictatorial government, which will take ever increasing measures to take away our freedom and make us submissive!

Questions and Answers

- *What should I do if I live in a mayor city?* There is no one right answer. If you live in the suburb of a large city and you had some place to go, you are advised to get out of Dodge. But say you live in the heart of New York. You might not be able to get out of the city, so you may have to hunker down. But whether you stay put or leave the city for the country, you face the same issues. You need a supply of food, water, medical supplies, warm clothing, and a means of protection from marauders.

  Items to consider:

  - *Boogie bag:* This is a small light weight bag, which you keep packed and ready to grab and go in case of an emergency. They contain all the essentials for short-term survival. You can make one yourself or they can be purchased with the essential items included. Do some research.
  - *Water:* You can't survive without fresh water. Believe it or not, the time is coming when you will go to the faucet and there may be no water, so what do you do? Depending on your situation, you may not have the space to store an adequate supply of fresh water, so you may need water filters. Go online and do some research. There are also chemical water purification kits available, which use iodine, bleach, etc. If you live in a single family home and you plan on staying in it, you may want to consider a rainwater collection system of some type, but whatever you do, water is priority number one!
  - *Food:* I strongly recommend a minimum of six months supply. You should consider nitrogen packed or dehydrated food because it not only has a long shelf life (twenty years or more), but it is compact, lightweight and requires less energy to prepare than raw food. If you have to be on the move, it is the only practical food supply. Again, I urge you to go online and do some research. The military also has

meals ready to eat (MREs). They are expensive, but they have their own heat source, and each meal is approximately two thousand calories.

- *Energy:* Heat, light, and thermal gear. We may have rationing of gasoline, electricity, and natural gas so you need to make provision. If at all possible, you should have more than one heating source (e.g., a wood burning fireplace or cast iron stove is a good start). If you live where you can have a large propane tank, it is a much better intermediate backup fuel supply than gasoline, which is too difficult to store in large quantities. *Note*: A propane generator would supply you with enough electricity to run your essential electrical appliances, such as your refrigerator for several months. If you are currently on natural gas and you want to cook with propane, you need to know that you would have to retrofit your burner jets, which is no big deal.

  Once the smart grid is operational, the government will be able to ration electricity, so you do not want to be exclusively dependent on the electrical company. There are also solar-powered generators that have recently come out. Depending on where you live a solar oven is an inexpensive way to cook your food.

  For light, you may want to look into battery-powered LED lighting. They use less electricity than conventional lighting, and if you have a generator you can recharge batteries to operate the lights. You may also want to get some kerosene lamps, candles, etc.

  You will also need warm clothing and bedding. Go online and investigate outfitters who supply all weather gear. There are some amazing materials, which are lightweight and will keep you warm in extreme temperatures, and even cool you in hot temperatures.

  Without knowing your individual situation, I cannot make specific recommendations, but I urge you to do some research.

    - *Medical needs:* If you are dependent on prescription medicines, it goes without saying that you need to have a back up supply. A few helpful hints: You need a well-supplied first aid kit. It is not only for trauma, but should also be for prevention. You should have antiseptic to prevent cuts from getting infected. You should have antibiotics in case of infection. *Note*: You can buy fish antibiotics that are inexpensive and don't require a prescription. Do some research. You also want vitamins and supplements to boost your immune system because you will be under stress, which weakens your body's natural immunity.
    - *Self defense:* If you cannot defend yourself, you are putting yourself and your loved ones at risk. When there is no food, the law of the jungle quickly kicks in. If you cannot protect what you have, you might as well not have prepared, because it will be taken away from you. The obvious self protection is a gun, but there are nonlethal options as well. Wasp spray will drop an assailant at a distance of up to fifteen feet more effectively than pepper spray and as well as a small caliber gun. For close quarters, a taser or a knife are good options. Again, all I can say is do some research.
- *Do you recommend moving to the country?* No place will be guaranteed to be safe, but the advantages to the country over the city are considerable. You can be close to food, and water and you can have better access to alternate energy sources. We can expect many of the large cities to experience riots and bands of roaming marauders. The further away from civilization, you are the safer you will be, but in any event, you need to be prepared to protect yourself from those who are desperate because they have not prepared for the chaos, which will reign.

Phase III: The Transition Period

What to expect: It will take several months for the government to restore order and to consolidate their power. It will be like when Hitler came to power. Once martial law is declared, the Constitution will be abolished and the president will assume dictatorial powers. All the necessary laws to allow this are in place, including allowing UN troops on US soil. They will use Hitler's playbook. You can expect an occupation force, like Hitler's Brownshirts (Homeland Security and the UN). And again, just like in Nazi Germany, you can expect youth camps to be established in order to brainwash the youth.

The number one objective is long-term self-sufficiency, depending on the government very little or not at all! In the aftermath of an economic collapse, things will not just go back to normal. With few exceptions, there will no longer be a middle class. There will only be the poor and an autocratic ruling class, so the question is how do we live in such a situation?

Questions and Answers

- *If I have to work what will be the best jobs?* We can expect a replay of the Great Depression which saw nearly 50 percent unemployment as demand for luxury items, cars, houses, and manufactured goods of all kinds plummeted. As a result unemployment, in these customary high-paying job sectors was very high.

  The government will be the largest single employer. The other job sector most resistant to the collapse will be in the area of essential goods and services (i.e., utility companies, teachers, first responders, medical personnel, food production, basic clothing production etc., but there will even be cuts in those areas).

- *What skills will I need for long term self-sufficiency?* You will need the skills, which our pioneering forefathers had. You will need to be self-sufficient (i.e., you will need to know how to grow a garden, can and preserve your own food, and a myriad of other survival skills). I recommend you buy a book that teaches basic survival skills. It is highly unlikely any one person will be able to acquire all the necessary skills, so in addition to a library of how-to books, you need to develop a network of people with survival skills. There are a lot more of those kinds of people in the country than in the big cities, so yet another reason to get a place in the country. You will also need the necessary tools and raw materials appropriate to the tasks at hand. For example, you will need non-genetically altered seeds (legacy seeds) along with gardening tools. Whatever the task, you will need supplies and tools.

- *What survival items will be most essential?* In a nutshell, you must address your basic needs for food, clothing, shelter, and energy. In phase two, we were looking at stockpiling these items, but now we have to look at long tern sustainability, which means we must grow our own food, make and or mind our own cloths, repair our own house, and machinery (or trade with others who have the requisite skills).

  It will be very important that you be off the grid if at all possible. Let me use myself as an example of what you need to do for long-term survival. I moved from the city to an eleven-acre farmett with a large garden and a commercial orchard. I learned to can my own food. I have my own well and septic system. I burn my trash. I have a wood burning fireplace. I am putting in a wind mill. I have two large propane tanks piggybacked together with enough propane to last me approximately a year. I have a propane generator as an alternate electrical source. Water is essential to life. Without electricity, I cannot get my water from the well because it is too deep to use a hand pump. This is the case with many wells so that is why you absolutely need a means of electricity. I am also putting in a rain water collection system. About the only thing I don't have are solar panels. I may put them in later, but with technology where it is now, the payback is quite long, so I went with other energy solutions for right now. If you want to be 100 percent energy self-sufficient you probably need both wind and solar, and you definitely need batteries to store your electricity.

- *What about barter items as an alternate currency?* Over the course of history, everything from seashells to tobacco has been used as currency. Following the crash, you can expect a brisk black market. I highly recommend you invest in a stockpile of barter items (i.e., alcohol, cigarettes, seeds, food, ammunition, medical supplies, anything that people will need to get by). Other than gold and silver, these are the ultimate tangible investments. As peak oil and the government's forced reduction of resource consumption collide, our current oil driven agricultural system will become impractical. It will no longer be possible to ship food around the world. Food will be locally grown and consumed using a lot less pesticides and fertilizers, so organic gardening and hydroponics will become the key to locally grown food supplies. I strongly recommend you stockpile non-genetically altered seeds for not only your own food needs, but also for barter. Food and water are the ultimate necessity items.

- *What about security issues?* We have already talked about self protection (i.e., guns, pepper spray, wasp spray, tazers, and knives. You may also want to get a large dog, put in surveillance cameras, get a security system installed, and forming a community watch. Security is essential. In a slightly different vane; do not put any valuables in a safety deposit box in a bank. It is just a matter of time before the government declares a bank holiday, and just like in 1933, they will open our safety deposit boxes and confiscate our valuables.

Phase IV: The Totalitarian Dictatorship

What to expect: I believe that the establishment of the New World Order marks the beginning of the tribulation, and I believe it will occur prior to 2017 (more on this later). Many Christians believe they will be ruptured away and not have to suffer through the tribulation, but I believe scripture supports the possibility that we will be tested and only those that endure to the end and are proven righteous will inherit the kingdom. In other words their might not be a Pretribulation Rapture. It is better to prepare for the worst and pray for the best. The enemy wants the Christians to enter the tribulation unprepared, so he will be able to force all but the most devout to accept the mark rather than starving to death. Once their power is fully consolidated, you can expect RFID chips to be implemented along with deployment of "drones" (the size of a bee with facial recognition software), and then just like the Jews in Nazi Germany were rounded up and sent to death camps, all those on the governments hit lists will be rounded up. Many people will have to go underground—another reason to be prepared. This will be a time when every person will have to ask the following question: "For what shall it profit a man, if he shall gain the whole world and lose his soul?" (Mark 8:36 KJV).

The number one objective will be how to survive off the grid (underground if necessary).

That is if you intend to refuse to take the mark and become part of the New World Order. Otherwise, if you take the mark and if you are among those that the government has a use for, you can get use to your new life of servitude. If, on the other hand, you are "one of the useful idiots" the government has no use for, you can prepare to go to a work camp or leave this earth.

If by the time phase four (the occupation) begins and you are not prepared, it will be too late. At this point, your only choices will be to submit or live off the grid and trust in God. Phase four is the tribulation and things will be horrifying. The Bible says in Mathew 24:21 NKJV, "For then shall be great tribulation, such as was not since the beginning of the world to this time, no, never shall be."

All I can say is that God called me to warn his people. So let those with eyes to see, see and ears to hear, hear. Remember God cannot lie! Therefore, prepare according to his warning to you! The material world as we know it will fall and there will be great tribulation. That is a warning from God!

PART 5

UNDERSTANDING GOD'S ULTIMATE PLAN

SPIRITUAL COUNTEROFFENSIVE

The Harvest Is At Hand: God's Final Warning!

The time of the harvest is at hand
For there is much sin in the land.
The wheat and tares they grow together,
But the nations and the people stand not together.

Hatred and war threaten to ravish the land,
And hunger and pestilence are at hand.
God calls to his people to submit to him,
But most head not his voice and live in sin.

The time of the harvest is at hand.
The sickle is ready to be thrust in
Who shall be counted among the righteous?
And who among the wicked?

Who shall be among the first fruit?
And inherit the Promised Land.
And live with the spotless Lamb.

Who shall know the second death?
And be judged by the Lamb
For he was called and did not head
Choosing instead the wages of sin.

COUNTEROFFENSIVE MEASURES: TAKING BACK THE REPUBLIC

This brings us to the fourth and final strategy for taking back the republic.

Step four. The American people must come together with one accord

Lastly, in order to keep America from being intentionally collapsed and driven into the one-world government, we must put into place measures to "restore unity, equality, peace and liberty." Only then can we hope to maintain national sovereignty and take the United States of America into the twenty-first century. Otherwise, we will surely be absorbed into the tyrannical one-world government, and our freedom and quite possibly our lives will be forfeited.

What your government has planned for you isn't pretty. We are all on death ground and either we fight back or die!

The differences that we think separate us are all artificially inflicted on us by our government in order to divide us, because they know that a house divided cannot stand. If they can divide us, they can neutralize us, and if they can neutralize us, they have already defeated us, or I should say we have defeated ourselves. So I say again, are we smarter than a monkey? We must face the reality that to our government, we are all as Mao said, "Useful idiots." Our government considers us nothing more than chattel (personal property), slaves with no rights. We are as Kissinger said, "Pawns," in a chess game of global dominance. There are simply too many of us, consuming too many of the elites' natural resources, so most of us must die, and the survivors must live in poverty as indentured servants/slaves so that the elite can live in luxury. And just to make absolutely certain we are clear, those who voted for Obama because you wanted entitlements/handouts, the government considers you dead weight, and you will either be killed or sent to labor camps. You are the useful idiots Mao spoke of—too bad—but that is the truth of the matter. So in light of the truth, we had better all of us—black, white, Mexican, rich, and poor, young and old. "We, the people," had better come together in one voice with absolute resolve and take a stand or we will all suffer and die together. Like it or not that is the truth of the matter. We are all one in the eyes of God, and we better start acting like it or perish. It is that simple. Cooperate or become slaves. Cooperate or die. There is no other outcome. That is the mindset we must all come to grips with, if we want to live. We are all on "death ground," and we had better fight like we are fighting for our lives because we are. In this book, God has given you the information you need in order to fight the good fight, now it is up to you—fight or die; that is our only choice. But remember, if we turn to God, he will help us, and no enemy will stand before us. Remember, the elite need us as much or more than we need them. We don't need them. We can stand on our own two feet, and we will be better off for it. We need to return to the founding principles of self-sufficiency and neighborly cooperation of our founding fathers because that is where our strength and happiness reside. May God bless you all!

Our government has done everything they could to create every possible form of division. If our nation is to survive, we must create an environment of cooperation and equal opportunities, which can be done once we understand that it is our government who is the enemy of the American people, and not each other. We are all in this together, and if we hope to survive the onslaught planned by our government, we had better learn how to put aside our differences and stand as "one nation under God indivisible with liberty and justice for all."

The balance of this book is about salvation, because God tells us not to fear him that can destroy your body (our government), but fear he that can destroy both body and soul (God, the Creator). This book would not be complete if I did not look to that most important of all human aspects our immortal souls.

GOD'S SECRET BIBLE CODE REVEALED

Before I jump into what God's secret Bible code is, some explanation is in order. The story starts about a year ago. God instructed me to move from Chicago, Illinois to Branson, Missouri where he said he would position me for the release of this book. I don't usually question God, but I had written two earlier books, and I had been unable to get them published, so I self-published them, which meant they went exactly nowhere. I had also done several PowerPoint presentations because years before, God had promised to establish me with a speaking platform to deliver the message that he had given me in my twenties when I had the near-death experience I mentioned earlier, during which he told me, "When you have salt and pepper hair, the US will be on the verge of collapse, and I shall call you to deliver a message of salvation to my people."

I honestly thought I had somehow missed God's timing, and he wasn't going to use me. I said, "God, the 2012 election is nearly here, and nothing I can do now will, in any way, impact the election, so isn't it too late?" The next morning, about five, I got my response. Thus said the Lord, "Do as I say. Have I not called you and prepared you for low these many years? All things are according to my time not mans. Am I not your God and does not my words accomplish that which I intend? Despair not, nothing you have done is in vain. Soon will come the time to release the message I shall give you. 1st the nation must come to a point of despair and then the word will be released."

So I did as God said and moved to Branson, Missouri, and waited. I camped out in a condo for nearly six months, looking for a place to live to no avail. Then, one morning at five, God woke me and said, "Get thee up and go to your computer. Today, I have fulfilled your prayers. The house you have asked me for is waiting for you, but you must act quickly."

I can just imagine that some of you might be asking what does any of this have to do with a Bible code. In absolute terms, nothing, except that God wants you to see that he is faithful and he never lies, so that when we do get to the Bible code, your faith will be bolstered. God had told me that when I got to Branson, I was to prepare an ark as a safe haven for what was to come. I had very little money to work with given that I had lost most of my wealth in the real estate collapse. Given that I was to prepare an ark, I had a very specific idea of what I wanted in a house. I wanted five- to ten- acre with a house with an in-law situation and a garden plot. And I wanted to be in the country, yet close to town. In six months of looking, not a single home had even come close to what I wanted, and most of them were in horrible condition, and even so, they were out of my price range.

God is amazing. Just listen to what he did for me. The house he had for me was a foreclosure, and it was priced way, way below market value. I need to interject something here so you understand what a miracle this was. I was a real estate broker for twelve years, so I know a few things about real estate. Foreclosures are not always the great deals people think. Here is how it works. When a bank forecloses on a home, they are allowed to get the mortgage amount and the cost incurred in the foreclosure process and sales expenses and nothing more. The vast majority of the foreclosures on the market in recent years have been because the homes were purchased around the time of the housing bubble, often with little down so the owners were upside down. What this can result in is that many foreclosures actually come on the market above the fair market value. You have to have a very unusual situation for a house with a low mortgage to be foreclosed on. So with that in mind, here is what happened. The property God promised me came on the market on a Friday. Over the weekend, it had twenty-four showing with people coming from as far away as St. Louis and Kansas City. By Monday, when the bank opened, there were multiple offers, but God had promised the property would be mine. Long story short, I was the only cash offer, so I got the house. Based on fair market value, I picked up the house for about forty cents on the dollar.

Oh, one more thing. There was an adjacent parcel of land that ran right up against the side of the house creating a potential encroachment issue, which could have significantly impacted the value of the property. God promised me he would allow me to get that property and solve the problem. I trusted God and bought the house, believing that the problem would be solved. Later, after I moved in, I found out that my next door neighbor had unsuccessfully attempted to buy the parcel. God promised me the land, so I approached the owner any way, and long story short, I got the land and was able to protect my property value. Oh, I also got a bonus from God! In the process of buying the land, I learned how to buy leans for pennies on the dollar. Little did I know, that that skill would allow me to rebuild my real estate holdings by picking up properties for pennies on the dollar! God is good!

Not only did I get a great price, but I got even more than I asked for. Isn't God great? I wanted a newer home. But all the ones I looked at were out of my price range. Well this home was actually built in 1980 as an earth home, but a few years ago, the son of the original owner tore off the roof and expanded the foundation and built a new home on top of the old one, so in reality, I have two homes. Upstairs, I have three bedrooms and two baths, plus of course a living room, kitchen, and dining room. Then downstairs, I have another kitchen, living room, dining room, two bedrooms, and two additional baths. I can sleep fourteen people. Oh, God also threw in a commercial orchard and a two-thousand-square-foot garden plot. I live on a mountain top in the Ozarks, which means that I essentially live on top of a big rock so to get a two-thousand-square-foot garden is unheard of. The previous owners had brought in a bull dozer and created a flat area and hauled in top soil. Remember God said, "Build an ark," so with that in mind, all I need is a wind generator, and I will be completely off the grid. So a guy who lost almost everything in the real estate collapse got his dream home and is debt-free, living in the Bible belt and to top it all, I have a million dollar view. If we are faithful, God will answer our prayers.

Then, in September 2012, a prophet friend of mine called and gave me a word. He said, "Thus saith the Lord, 'The time is at hand. For all of next month I shall visit you with revelations and instructions for the book I have given unto you to write.'" Sure enough, the revelations and dreams started flooding in. I took copious notes and followed my instructions to the letter. The most important instruction was to take one month and read all the prophets and compile a selection of verses by category. God said, "When you do this, I will give you a deeper understanding of the Bible, which I want you to share." As I said earlier, he also instructed me to tell the truth exactly as he showed me regardless of who it offended, so if I have offended anyone, I apologize, but God said, "The truth will set you free," so my instructions were to tell the truth no matter what.

God always confirms what he tells me, so about a month after, I had started writing the book, and I went to church and the pastor gave me a prophecy. Remember, I had just moved so I was checking out a lot of churches to see where I would decide to go. The pastor didn't know me or anything about me. He said, :This saith the Lord, 'I shall use you to deliver a message to my people with power and clarity.'" I hope that is what I have done.

God's Secret Bible Code Revealed

As in the beginning so at the ending
Life's answers are woven in the fabric of time
The knowledge you seek, your ancestors do keep
Their victories and losses reveal the divine
To those who are obedient the path shall be known

One came before you to show you the way
His virtue is the key to unlocking the divine
Walk in his footsteps, and your way you will find
His angels will protect you; no enemy will stand before you

But before he intervenes, your faith and
courage he must test
Your purity and devotion must be shown
Then when you step out in courage and purity
Divine intervention and miracles will you be shown
No weapon forged against you shall prosper

The victory shall be yours
The Promised Land you shall inhabit
The promise of the righteous shall be at hand
Peace and prosperity shall prevail in the land

Finally let's get to the Bible code. Sorry for the diversion, but I wanted you to see how faithful and amazing God is. Anyway, here is what God showed me. A lot of people say they can't understand the Bible, so this makes it very simple to understand. If you look at the Old Testament, it repeats the same two messages over and over. The more frequently God repeats a thing the more important it is.

First lesson: God prepared the Promised Land for the Israelites, but only the righteous were to be allowed to inhabit it. The righteous being those that are virtuous and keep God's covenants. For example, that is why when Joshua entered the Promised Land, he was instructed to kill all the men, women, children and animals, and take no plunder. The first fruit was to go to the LORD, and if the people were obedient then he would reward them.

"Now go and smite Amalek, and utterly destroy all they have, and spare them not: but slay both men and women, infants and suckling, ox and sheep and ass" (1 Samuel 15:3 KJV).

That was because God did not want the Promised Land contaminated. Only the righteous could inhabit it. Even before they got to the Promised Land, God purged the Israelites of the disobedient for the same reason. Only the righteous and obedient could be allowed to enter the Promised Land. For example, in Numbers, we see that Korah rose up against Moses, and the Lord opened the earth and swallowed him and his entire household.

"And they gathered themselves together against Moses, and against Aaron. And said unto them, ye take too much upon you, seeing all the congregation are holy, every one of them, and the Lord is among them; wherefore then lift ye up above the congregation of the Lord" (Numbers 16:3 KJV).

Then, a few verses later, we see God's reaction to the disobedience. He determines that he will decide who is holy (righteous) and who is not, and those that are not shall be swallowed up by the earth for only the righteous shall be allowed to enter the Promised Land.

"And it came to pass as he [Moses] made an end of speaking all these words, that the ground clave asunder that was under them. And the earth opened her mouth, and swallowed them up, and their houses, and all the men that appertained unto Korah, and all their goods" ((Numbers 16:31 KJV)).

The lesson for us today is that there are many, if not most, who attend church regularly and profess to love the LORD and to be righteous and holy who are not, and they shall not be allowed to enter the Promised Land when Christ comes the second time to establish his kingdom on earth. God grants us mercy and forgives us our former sin, but thereafter, he expects us to walk in righteousness. If we don't, we will not be allowed to enter the Promised Land—guaranteed.

"And they came unto thee as thee people cometh and they stand before thee as my people and hear my words, but they will not do them; for with their mouth they show much love, but their heart goes after their covetousness" (Ezekiel 33:31 KJV). Greed, lust, and materialism.

Second lesson: From the Old Testament is that God will come to the rescue of the righteous and fight our battles, but first we have to step out in faith, and God must be given the glory for the victory so that man does not become prideful.

"And the lord said unto Gideon, The people that are with thee are too many for me to give the Midianites into their hands, least Israel vaunt themselves against me, saying, Mine own hand hath saved me. Now therefore go to, proclaim in the ears of the people, saying, Whosoever is fearful and afraid, let him return and depart early from mount Gilead. And their returned of the people twenty and two thousand; and their remained 10,000" ((Judges 7:2 KJV).).

And God continued to cull the numbers till he got to three hundred men.

"And the Lord said unto Gideon, By the 300 that lapped will I save you, and deliver the Midianites into thine hand: and let the other people go every man unto his place" (Judges 7: 7 KJV).

The lesson for us today is that many, if not most of the inhabitants of America, are not only, not righteous but they also lack faith. We cow down to our government in fear instead of trusting in God and standing against the evil. Therefore shall we remain blind to the truth and therefore shall God not intervene to save us. God is calling us to revival, and he is calling us to stand in the gap and proclaim Jesus Christ, and if we will do these things, he will utterly destroy our enemies (the financial elite and their pawns in our government) before our eyes. It will be as with David and Goliath.

So in summary, the lesson from the Old Testament is that only the righteous may enter the Promised Land, and that applies to the second coming when the saints will reign with Christ for one thousand years. And if we will step out in faith against the unrighteous, the Lord our God will defeat our enemy no matter how strong he may appear. The victory is ours. We have God's word, and he is incapable of lying. If we read the Old Testament, looking for these themes to be repeated over and over, as they are, then we will truly understand God's message to our generation. Have faith and stand up and be counted. The time is short, and the time is coming when the door will be closed, and even if we repent and surrender to God, he will reject us because we did not answer when he called.

God's final warning!

> "Strive to enter in at the straight gate: for many I say unto you, will seek to enter in, and shall not be able.
>
> 25 When once the master of the house is risen up, and hath shut to the door, and ye begin to stand without, and to knock at the door, saying, Lord, Lord open unto us; and he shall answer and say unto you. I know you not whence you are.
>
> 26 Then shall ye begin to say, We have eaten and drunk in thy presence, and thou hast taught in our streets.
>
> 27 But he shall say I tell you, I know you not whence ye are; depart from me all you workers of iniquity.
>
> 30 And, behold, there are last which shall be first, and there are first which shall be last.
>
> Luke 13:24 KJV

That takes us to the New Testament and the lessons God has given us to go along with those from the Old Testament. But like before, I need to give you some background before we get started, so you see just how marvelous God is. In the introduction, I told you that where necessary, I would share my life story, if it would give glory to God. I was born to a father who was an alcoholic and a very abusive person. No details are necessary except to say that I slept with a baseball bat under my bed, and I never ever went to sleep before my father came home, and I found out if he was drunk or sober, melancholic or angry. My mother was a beautiful woman. For you old timers, she was the spitting image of Loretta Young. The problem was that she was arguably the most negative and helpless person I have ever known. She loved me in her own way, but she saw me as her care giver rather than as a son who himself need love and care.

The physical abuse in my family was bad, but the mental abuse was much worse. My father had an IQ of 185, which put him in the genius category, but he never went to college and was trapped in a mindless job as a construction worker. This, I believe, was in large part the cause of his dysfunctional and self-destructive personality. His IQ was a real problem for me because when I was born, my head was caught on my mother's pelvis and my skull was split open, and I also had oxygen deficiency. The result was that a part of my brain was damaged, and I had a learning disability. In some areas, I was as smart as my father, but I couldn't learn anything that required rote memorization. Where this came out most obviously was that I couldn't spell worth a hoot, still can't. When he was drunk, he would follow me around the house for hours, calling me a dumb punk and asking me if I could spell shit. I can tell you from firsthand experience that the old saying, "Sticks and stones can break my bones but words can never hurt me," is absolutely untrue. It hurts a lot. As to my mother's contribution to my mental health, her dream was to go to New York and be a fashion model. How that relates to me is that I was unplanned, so she blamed me for costing her, her dream, so her refrain to me was, "If I hadn't gotten pregnant with you, I would be a famous model." Gee, thanks, Mom.

So once again, I can imagine that you are saying, "What does any of this have to do with the lessons from the New Testament?"

Actually, it has a lot to do with it. You have no doubt heard of "self-made men" in the context of a man who rose from poverty to become wealthy.

Well, I am a self-made man, but in a completely different context. I found myself in my early twenties with no direction, no sense of identity, and no idea what I was going to do with my life. The only role models I had were those of completely dysfunctional parents who only had negative lessons to teach me, certainly none of which would ever lead to happiness or success. What I didn't realize at the time, being unsaved was that in God's universe there are no mistakes. His ways are not ours. That which does not kill us makes us stronger.

Remember when in the beginning of the book I told you I had a near-death experience in which God gave me the assignment of calling those with ears to hear to salvation. Well, there was another outcome from that experience. Over the next three years, I read the Bible, Talmud, and Koran and went on to read many autobiographies of men I admired, as well as history, science, and philosophy books. A whole new universe opened to me. I found I could have as many mentors as I wanted. I could emulate highly moral and successful people and literally rebuild my persona from the inside out. But the truly miraculous thing was that one day I was praying to God for guidance, and he said to me, "My son, read my holy word and look to find what made my son sinless and try to emulate him in all that you do." Obviously, no man can emulate God or Christ, but a lost confused, young man found that he could develop character traits that he never even knew existed, much less displayed in his life. As with the Old Testament, God instructed me to read the New Testament from beginning to end in a month, and this time, I was to write down and categorize all the virtues from the New Testament. I came up with a list of approximately fifty virtues, which I culled down to what I call the twelve great virtues. Once I had my list, I determined to do my best to integrate them into my personality and see if I couldn't literally remake myself from the inside out. I took each virtue and focused on it for a month, trying to exhibit it in my everyday life, hoping that I could develop new habit patterns that would overwrite the negative ones I had learned as a child. I did this for a year till I had completed all twelve virtues. I won't lie and tell you that at the end of the year that I was some sort of goody-two-shoes, but I will tell you that over the course of my life, I have continued to endeavor to learn to apply the twelve great virtues in my life, and I honestly believe it has served as my moral compos and has made me a better more caring human being. I also believe that it was God's will that I had this experience, so I could share it with a world that has lost its moral compos and is spinning out of control. The twelve great virtues are as follows:

The Twelve Great Virtues

- Humility
- Discrimination
- Devotion
- Precision
- Forgiveness
- Courage
- Sincerity
- Kindliness
- Charity
- Tolerance
- Persistence
- Efficiency

The twelve great virtues are the most powerful set of values or habits in the world. If you apply them in your life until they are habitual and instinctual, there will be no limit to what you will be able to achieve. One day, you will look down from the clouds and realize that somehow mysteriously, while you weren't watching, you were transformed from a scared field mouse into an eagle soaring high above, surveying his domain and knowing that there is no limit to what you can achieve.

"Life evolves or life dies for there is no standing still.

If we don't grow, we wither away and die
a slow death of despair.
So to live is to grow and to grow is to change.
This is the key to finding happiness."

—Larry Ballard

Definition of the "Twelve Great Virtues" Necessary for Spiritual Growth.

- **Humility** is the ability to look beyond ourselves. When we attain humility, we come to understand our role in the grand scheme of things. We become naturally unpretentious, grateful, and finally capable of true love. It grows out of adversity coupled with surrender to a higher power.
- **Devotion** is a spiritual commitment of faithfulness to an object of devotion that we hold above ourselves. Devotion represents our first step in truly giving ourselves to someone or something that we hold higher than ourselves. It is God consciousness. It is the fountain deep inside where God gives us an understanding of our true purpose in life.
- **Forgiveness** is application of God's grace where the wrongs of another are put out of remembrance and the other person is given a clean slate. Once a person learns that un- forgiveness is a chain of bondage that robs us of happiness it is easy to take the next step which is to understand that hurt people hurt people not because they are bad, but because they are in pain. Once we understand this forgiveness is easy.
- **Sincerity** is at the core of our self-worth. It is the faculty to be open, honest, genuine and free of hypocrisy or vested self interest. It is essential to any healthy relationship. It is an extension of Christ admonition to treat others as you would be treated.
- **Charity** is the process by which we become more benevolent. Charity denotes a genuine concern for others and the desire to help those less fortunate than us. It's an expression of care

and giving that moves us further from an "I" orientation to the "other" orientation of Christ. All I can say is that you can never out give God so to give is to receive and to receive is to understand that God is watching over us all.

- **Persistence** is the ability to stay the course despite delays, obstacles, and adversity, for only through continued effort can we succeed. It is essential to developing faith. It is ultimately what separates success from failure. It also builds faith.
- **Discrimination** is the process by which we learn to discern and distinguish how things in our environment interact, their similarities and differences, and how they affect each other, and then to apply that knowledge in a humanitarian fashion. It is what I would refer to as the art of intuitive analysis. I ask God to show me the heart of a matter and he usually does if I will wait on him.
- **Precision** teaches us to learn to optimize our time and to distinguish differences and to discern the relevance of those differences. This is the basis of informed decision making.
- **Courage** is the ability to move beyond our fears. Without courage, we would reach a point where obstacles, difficulties, and opposition would eventually cause us to give up and simply quit. But with courage, we persist. With resolute determination, tenacity, and stubborn persistence, we continue unwilling to acknowledge defeat. For me courage is inseparably linked to faith and a belief in the fact that there are forces above our understanding which keep the cosmos in balance.
- **Kindliness** requires that we consider the emotional needs of others. That we learn to be supportive, sympathetic, nurturing, and caring, and that we extend ourselves to others. For me kindliness emanates from learning to see life through the eyes of others and having empathy for their situation by virtue of the hardships you yourself have overcome.
- **Tolerance** is the process by which we learn to consider opposing points of view, then to begrudgingly tolerate them and eventually to be open to the possibility of changing our own point of

view. It is fundamental to growth. To me it as simple as asking myself what Christ would do in a given situation,

- **Efficiency** is the process whereby a person achieves a desired outcome with the minimum expenditure of effort. Efficiency is not possible without the application of persistence, precision, and discrimination, which together with mans natural inquisitiveness is responsible for most of mankind's advancements.

The twelve great virtues provide us the necessary skills for success in the material world and help us to develop our characters so that we are able to continuously grow and evolve. In addition, they provide us with a framework that we can use to re-script our brains so that, regardless of our early programming, we can realize our potential. If you look at truly successful people, you have known or that society has revered; I believe you will find that they exhibited most if not all of these traits. They are the basis of spirituality and righteousness.

I urge you to take these virtues or character traits and develop them into habits. Once they have become habitual, they will be your expression of reality, a reality that attracts positive events and people to you, a reality that ensures your success. If you learn to express these traits in your dealings with others, you will be a supercharged magnet that will attract positive people and outcomes into your life. You will be capable of achieving greatness. In so doing, you will cease to be part of the problem. You will instead have become part of the solution, a solution that enriches your life and all those you come in contact with. Your brain can accept only one reality at a time. If you focus on the virtues, which are by nature positive, the negatives will be washed away into the shadow of oblivion. These traits are in fact predominant habits of most truly successful and happy people. And are the key to your entrance into the Promised Land.

"We are what we think, and what we think
controls the emotions we feel.
Therefore, the quality of our consistent
beliefs defines the quality of our life!"

—Larry Ballard

By living life and making my fair share of mistakes, I find myself in the autumn of my life a lot wiser than I was in the spring of my life, so I want to share this with you as well. They are my rules for finding happiness, and after all, if we don't have happiness, what is life but a hollow experience? It is as George Carlin said, "Life isn't about the number of breaths we take, but the moments that take our breath."

Key Enabling Emotions

"If you learn to routinely express these emotions in your communications with others, you will substantially improve the quality of your interpersonal relationships and the quality of your life!"

- Open-mindedness
- Acceptance
- Flexibility
- Cheerfulness
- Passion
- Understanding
- Caring
- Giving
- Forgiving
- Sincerity
- Confidence
- Love

Key Enabling Rules. To be happy and win the game of life, learn to incorporate these rules of conduct into your daily lives.

- Design your life vs. reacting to circumstances
- Accept responsibility for your actions
- Get motivated (cost of not achieving your goal)
- Spend your *time* on what makes you happy
- Focus on balance and happiness first and money second
- Make sure your goals aren't in conflict
- Be flexible and willing to change

- Become that which you pursue
- Focus on your strengths vs. your weaknesses
- Focus on the pleasure you want to feel
- Live in the present
- Take action (Have a written life plan)
- Strive to control events vs. responding to them
- See end result and set priorities accordingly
- Reward yourself every step of the way (keeps you motivated)
- Be grateful vs. fearful (key to abundance)
- Live within your means (save first and be debt-free)
- Spend less than you make and invest the difference
- Use your emotions to facilitate growth
- Control what things mean to you (your rules)
- Choose your words carefully (be nonthreatening)
- Learn from your mistakes (constant growth)
- Surround yourself with supportive people (mentors)
- Find your higher purpose your (kingdom assignment)

If you add the "to-be attitudes" to what I just outlined, I believe you have the essence of the New Testament and what Christ came to teach the world.

> And seeing the multitudes, he went up into a mountain, and when he was set, his disciples came unto him:
>
> 2 And he opened his mouth and taught them saying
> 3 Blessed are the poor in spirit: for theirs is the kingdom of heaven.
> 4 Blessed are they that mourn: for they shall be comforted.
> 5 Blessed are the meek: for they shall inherit the earth.
> 6 Blessed are they that do hunger and thirst after righteousness: for they shall be filled.
> 7 Blessed are the merciful: for they shall obtain mercy.
> 8 Blessed are the pure in heart: for they shall see God.
> 9 Blessed are the peace makers: for they shall be called the children of God.

10 Blessed are they that are persecuted for righteousness sake: for theirs is the kingdom of heaven.
11 Blessed are ye when men shall revile you, and persecute you: and say all manner of evil against you for my sake.
12 Rejoice, and be exceeding glad: for great is your reward in heaven: for so persecuted they the prophets that came before you

Mathew 5:1–12

Bible Cliff Notes

The key to inheriting the Promised Land.

Below is the compilation of Bible verses, which God had me compile when I read the prophets. But first, the Cliff Notes Version. Think of this as your instruction booklet for preparing for what is to come. God is calling his people. Let those with ears hear and those with eyes see.

Thus said the Lord:

- The wages of sin are death.
- Repent and receive salvation, for the time is fast approaching when it will be too late to repent.
- To those that have made materialism you're God: I shall reject you.
- You shall be judged by your fruit, and not the words which proceed from your mouth.
- Repent and obey my commandments, and I shall show you the truth and the truth shall set you free.
- Only my sheep shall hear my voice.
- Only the righteous shall inhabit the Promised Land and receive life eternal
- Him that believe in me and abide my word, him shall I provide for.
- If you will step out in faith, and stand against the evil that pervades the land, I the Lord God will heal the land and restore that which has been destroyed.

- In the Promised Land, peace shall prevail and there shall be no sin, no pain and no sorrow for those things will have passed.
- I do not lie, and my word does not return void.

Actual scriptures from the Bible Cliff Notes about the wisdom of the Old Testament Prophets as given to me in revelation by God!

God's word never returns void. Thus said the Lord, I am the beginner and the finisher. Evil shall not prevail.

"So shall my word be that goeth out of my mouth; it shall not return unto me void, but it shall accomplish that which I please, and shall prosper the thing where I send it" (Isaiah 55:11 KJV).

God's final warning! Thus said the Lord, Repent and obey my commandments and I will show ye the truth and it shall set ye free.

"Surely the LORD God will do nothing, but he revealeth his secret unto his servants the prophets" (Amos 3:7 KJV).
Sin separates man from God! Thus said the Lord, Only my sheep shall hear my voice.

"O Lord, to us belongeth confusion of face, to our kings, to our princes (government) and to our fathers, because we have sinned" (Daniel 9:8 KJV).

"Yea, thou hearest not, yea, thou knowest not, yea from the time that thine ear was not opened; for I know that thou wouldest deal very treacherously and was called to transgress from the womb" (Isaiah 48:8 KJV). (Rotten Apples must be thrown out.)

"None calleth for justice nor any pleadeth for truth; they trust in vanities (riches and power) and speaketh lies; they conceive mischief and bring forth iniquities. (Bad fruit.) Their feet run to evil, and they make haste to shed innocent blood; their thoughts are thoughts of iniquity; wasting and destruction are in their path" (Isaiah 59:4, 7 KJV).

Warning to the lukewarm church and those who trust in their riches! Thus said the Lord: Ye shall be judged by your fruit, be it good or bad Thus said the Lord, To those of this generation who have made materialism your God, I shall reject thee!

> And unto the angel of the church of the Laodicean write: These things saith thee amen.
>
> 16 So then because thou art lukewarm, and neither cold nor hot, I will spew thee out of my mouth
> 17 Because thou sayest, I am rich, and increase with goods (materialism). And have need of nothing: and knowest not that thou art wicked, and miserable, and poor, and blind and naked! (The prosperity churches and name it and claim it churches are leading their flocks astray).
>
> Revelation 3:14, 16–17 KJV

> "And they came unto thee as thee people cometh and they stand before thee as my people and hear my words, but they will not do them; for with their mouth they show much love, but their heart goes after their covetousness"
>
> (Ezekiel 33:31 KJV).

Thus saith the Lord: Ye will be judged by your fruit, not your hollow praises.

"I the Lord search the heart, I try the rains, even to give man according to his ways, and according to fruit of his doings As the partridge sitteth on eggs, and hatchet them not: so he that getteth riches, and not by right, shall leave them in the midst of his days, and at his end shall be a fool" (Jeremiah 17:10 KJV).

Thus said the Lord, Many who call themselves saved will not enter the Promised Land because they worship not me, but the things of this world.

The grapes of wrath shall be poured out upon the nations! Thus said the Lord: I will pour out Tribulation upon the land that my people may repent and turn to me.

"I spoke to thee in thy prosperity: but thou sadist, I will not hear" (Jeremiah 22:21 KJV). (The US)

"As it is written in the law of Moses, all this evil is come upon us; yet made we not our prayers before the Lord our God, that we might turn from our iniquities, and understand the truth" (Daniel 9:13 KJV).

God is calling for revival in America and around the world. This saith the Lord: I will judge you by your actions not the words of your mouth.

"Therefore hath the Lord watched upon the evil, and brought it upon us: for the Lord our God is righteous in all his works which he doeth; for we obeyed not his voice" (Daniel 9:13 KJV)

Thus saith the Lord: Your rulers shall lead you into captivity. America has the president they wanted and deserve, and it is about to reap the whirlwind.

"Therefore shall I number you to the sword, and ye shall all bow down to the slaughter; because when I called, you did not answer; when I spoke, ye did not hear; but did evil before mine eyes, and did choose that wherein I delight not" (Isaiah 65:12 KJV).

The wages of sin are death: Thus saith the Lord:Your end shall be as that of Sodom and Gamorrah.

"Let her therefore put away her whoredoms out of her sight and her adulteries from between her breast. [Same sex marriage, pornography, and breakdown of the family unit" (Hosea 2:2 KJV).

"Lest I strip her naked, and set her as in the day that she was born, and make her as a wildness, and set her like a dry land, slay her with thirst" (Hosea 2:3 KJV).

God's judgment on the nations can be stayed if we repent! Thus said The Lord, Salvation comes only after repentance.

"If that nation against whom I have pronounced, turn from their evil, I will repent of the evil I thought to do unto them" (Jeremiah 18:8 KJV).

"But if the wicked will turn from all his sins that he hath committed, and keep all my statutes, and do that which is lawful and right, he shall surely live, he shall not die" (Ezekiel 18:21 KJV).

"All his transgressions that he hath committed, they shall not be mentioned unto him: in his righteous that he hath done he shall live" (Ezekiel 18:22 KJV).

Only the righteous shall inherit the Promised Land: Thus said the Lord, From the time whence the harvest begins, no longer will the sinner and righteous be together for sin must be obliterated that righteous may prevail. From thence forward shall I shut the door and my mercy will be withdrawn.

Repent and receive God's mercy! Thus said the Lord, Only my sheep hear my voice.

"Behold, I stand at the door and knock; if any man hear my voice and open the door, I will come in to him and will sup with him, and with me" (Revelations 3:20 KJV). *Last call.*

"Let the wicked forsake his way and the unrighteous man his thoughts and let him return unto the LORD, and he will have mercy upon him; and to God, for he will abundantly pardon" (Isaiah 55:7 KJV).

God is our deliver and our protector! Thus said the Lord, He who believeth in me and abide my word, him shall I protect and for him shall I provide.

"Hearken unto me, ye that know righteousness, the people in who's heart is my law; fear not the reproach of men, neither be afraid of their reviling." (Isaiah 51:7 KJV).

"For the moth shall eat them up like a garment, and the worm shall eat them like wool; but my righteousness shall be forever; and my salvation from generation to generation" (Isaiah 51:8 KJV)

"He delivered me from my strong enemy, and them that hated me: for they were too strong for me" (2 Samuel 22:18 KJV).

> "21 The Lord rewarded me according to my righteousness: according to the cleanness of my hands hath he recompensed me.
> 31 As for God, his way is perfect; he is a buckler to all them that trust in him.
> 32 For who is God, save the LORD? And who is a rock, save our God?
> 33 God is my strength and power and he maketh my way perfect."
>
> 2 Samuel 22:21, 31–33 KJV

The victory is mine: Thus said the Lord, I will bring down the corrupt governments of the world, but my people must first stand against them in faith and then I God will intervene as with Jericho and they will fall.

"Not by might, nor by power, but by my spirit, saith the lord of host" (Zechariah 4:6 KJV).

Only the righteous shall take part in the first resurrection. Thus said the Lord, In order to enter the Promised Land I instructed the Israelites to kill all the inhabitants, all the men, women, children and animals and take no unclean thing [bounty]. So shall it be with the second coming. No unclean thing, no unrighteous shall be allowed to contaminate the Promised Land.

"And their shall in no wise enter into it anything that defileth, neither whatsoever worketh abomination, nor maketh a lie: but they which are written in the lamb's book of life" (Revelation 21:27 KJV).

> "And I saw thrones, and they sat upon them; and I saw the souls of them that were beheaded for the witness of Jesus and for the word of God, and had not worshiped the beast, that neither his image, neither had received his mark upon their foreheads, or in their hands: and they lived and reigned with Christ a thousand years. 5 But the rest of the dead lived not

> again until the thousand years were finished. This is the first resurrection. 6 Blessed and holy is he that hath part in the first resurrection; on such the second death hath no power. But they shall be priest of God and of Christ, and shall reign with him a thousand years"
>
> (Revelation 20:4–6 KJV).

Thus said the Lord, Know ye that those who come before the throne for the second resurrection I the Lord know all that ye have done and will judge ye according to your sins.

What the righteous must do! Thus said the Lord, Live peaceably with your neighbor and have mercy, love and forgiveness in your heart. These things do I demand of the righteous.

> "These are the things ye shall do; Speak ye every man the truth to his neighbor: execute the judgment of truth and peace in your gates 17 And none of you imagine evil in your hearts against his neighbor; and love no false oath: for all these are things that I hate, saith the LORD"
>
> (Zechariah 8:16–17 KJV).

> "He hath shown thee O man, what is good; and what doth the Lord require of thee, but to do justly, and to love mercy, and to work humbly with God"
>
> (Micah 6:8 KJV).

Why bad things happen to good people. Thus said the Lord, I place thee in the refiners fire that I may purify thee and make thee holy and righteous.

> "Behold I have refined thee, but not with silver; I have chasten thee in the furnace of affliction"
>
> (Isaiah 48:10 KJV).

"I form the light and create darkness: I make peace and create evil: I the Lord do all these things"

(Isaiah 45:7 KJV).

"Not only so, but we also rejoice in our sufferings, because we know that suffering produces perseverance; perseverance, character; and character, hope"

(Romans 5:3 KJV).

"Our fathers disciplined us for a little while as they thought best; but God disciplines us for our good, that we may share in his holiness"

(Hebrews 12:10 KJV).

"No discipline seems pleasant at the time, but painful. Later on, however, it produces a harvest of righteousness and peace for those who have been trained by it"

(Hebrews 12:11 KJV).

There Can Be No Good Without Evil

Ask ye why doeth evil prevail in the land?
Why fore is evil rewarded with power and riches?
While the righteous struggle and suffer.
Battling ever battling to no avail
Is there no justice. Is God a liar?

The evil are tempted and their greed doth prevail
A bargain is struck and payment is given
Their riches abound and power as well
But the devil is a liar and a deceiver
And what he giveth he shall surely taketh away
And in its place agony and pain
A lesson hard sought and soon not forgotten

> But to the righteous, long suffering and testing
> Shall give away and God's promises shall be kept
> No longer will your pain and tears be remembered
> With him shall you walk in bliss and harmony
> Angelic music shall you hear to sooth your spirit
> A love beyond imaging shall you be given
> And then you shall know what the blood did purchase!

The antichrist shall reign but a short while. Thus said the Lord, Know that he that prevails to the end shall be judged righteous and shall inherit the kingdom.

"And there was given unto him a mouth speaking great things and blasphemies and power was given unto him to continue forty and two months" (Revelation 13:5 KJV). *The purification of the earth.*

"And it was given unto him to make war with the saints and to overcome them: and power was given him over all kindred's, and tongues, and nations. And all that dwell upon the earth shall worship him, whose names are not written in the book of life of the Lamb slain from the foundation of the world" (Revelation 13:7–8 KJV)

Thus said the Lord, The sinner shall be blinded and follow after the evil one, but my righteous shall prevail.

How The Bible Says We Will Know The Antichrist?

- He shall come at the time when knowledge shall be increased. [now]
- He shall come in peace [be elected receive Nobel Peace Prize]
- He will think to change the times and laws [fundamental transformation]
- He shall magnify himself above all [the anointed one]
- He shall exalt himself and do as he pleases [anointed one - rule by executive order]
- He shall obtain the kingdom by flatteries [movie star status]
- He shall speak blasphemy against God. [mocked Christianity & Sermon On The Mount]

- He shall make war with the saints [Muslim pretending to be a Christian]
- He shall do according to his will [executive orders, circumvent Congress]
- He shall cause all to take his mark [healthcare is a Trojan Horse for RFID chip]
- He shall not regard the desires of women [he will support Sharia Law]
- Trouble from East & North [laying groundwork for WWIII]
- He shall break his promise & become strong with a small nation [Israel]
- He shall put his palace on the holy mountain [To Be Seen]
- We shall cry out because of the King we chose [our President]

Who Other Than Obama Fits Even ½ oF These Descriptions?

Supporting Scriptures: For how we will reorganize the Antichrist.

"And he shall *speak great words against the most high* and shall wear out the saints of the most high, *and think to change times and laws*; and they shall be given unto his hand until a time and times and the dividing of time" (Daniel 7:25 KJV).

> "And the king shall do according to his will; and *he shall exalt himself, and magnify himself above every God* and shall speak marvelous things against the God of gods, and shall prosper till the indignations be accomplished; for that that is determined shall be done
>
> 37 Neither shall he regard the God of his fathers, *nor the desires of women*, nor regard any god: for *he shall magnify himself above all.*
>
> 44 But *tidings out of the east and out of the north shall trouble him*: therefore he shall go forth with great furry to destroy and to utterly make away many.

> 45 And he *shall plant the tabernacle of his palace between the seas in the glorious holy mountain;* yet he shall come to his end and none shall help him.
>
> Daniel 11:36–37, 44–45 KJV

> And in his estate shall stand upon a vile person, to whom they shall not give the honor of the kingdom, but he shall *come in peaceably* and *obtain the Kingdom by flatteries.*
>
> 22 And with the arms of a flood before him shall they be *overflown from before him*, and shall be broken; yea also the prince of the covenant.
>
> 23 And after the league made with him, he *shall work deceitfully*: for he shall come up, and *become strong with a small people.*
>
> Daniel 11:21–23 KJV

"But thou, O Daniel, shut up the words, and seal the book, even to the time of the end: many shall run to and fro, and *knowledge shall be increased*" (Daniel 12:4 KJV).

"And he causeth all both small and great, rich and poor, free and bond, to *receive the mark* in their right hand, or in their foreheads. And that no man might buy or sell, save he that had the mark, or the name of the beast or the number of his name" (Revelation 13:16–17 KJV).

And ye shall *cry out in that day because of your king [Presiden*t] which ye shall have chosen you; and the LORD will not hear you in that day" (1 Samuel 8:18 KJV). *The US will suffer under the hand of our president.*

The time of the harvest is at hand.

"Put ye in the sickle, for the harvest is ripe: come get you down for the press is full, the vats overflow; for their wickedness is great" (Joel 3:13 KJV).*Only the righteous shall inherit the Promised Land*

"If any man worship the beast and his image, and receive his mark in his forehead or in his hand. The same shall drink of the wine of the wrath of God which is poured out without mixture into the cup of his indignation; and he shall be tormented with fire and brims, one in the presence of the holy angles, and in the presence of the Lamb" (Revelation 14:9–10 KJV). *Any who take the mark are dammed.*

"And the Lord my God shall come and the Saints with him. And the Lord shall be king over all the earth; in that day shall there be one LORD and his name One" (Zechariah 14:5, 9 KJV).

Thus said the Lord, In the day of the harvest, there shall be *no more need for evil for my righteous shall be separated* and peace shall reign upon the earth and the evil shall be cast out.

In the end, God shall bring peace upon the earth!

"And he shall judge among many people, and rebuke strong nations afar off; and they shall beat their swords into plowshares, and their spears into pruning hook; nation shall not lift up a sword against nation, neither shall they war anymore" (Micah 4:3 KJV).

Our wars are brought upon us by our leaders for their greed, and God shall put an end to it.

"And God shall wipe away all tears from their eyes: and their shall be no more death, neither sorrow, nor any more pain: for the former things are passed away. He that overcometh shall inherit all things: and I will be his God, and he shall be my son" (Revelation 21:4 KJV).

"For as the earth bringeth forth her bud, and as the garden causeth the things that are sown in it to spring forth so the LORD will cause righteousness and praise to spring forth from all nations" (Isaiah 61:11 KJV).

"And the LORD shall be king over all the earth: in that day shall there be one LORD, and his name one" (Zechariah 14:9 KJV).

Thus said the Lord, In the day of my coming, there shall be no more sin and therefore no death, no pain and no sorrow.

The time is coming when God's grace will no longer be granted, and it will be too late to receive salvation.

24 Strive to enter in at the straight gate: for many I say unto you, will seek to enter in, and shall not be able
25 When once the master of the house is risen up [Christ Has Come], and hath shut to the door, and ye begin to stand without, and to knock at the door, saying, Lord, Lord open unto us; and he shall answer and say unto you. I know you not whence you are.
26 Then shall ye begin to say, We have eaten and drunk in thy presence, and thou hast taught in our streets.
27 But he shall say I tell you, I know you not whence ye are; depart from me all you workers of iniquity.
30 And, behold, there are last which shall be first, and there are first which shall be last.

Luke 13:24 KJV

Thus Saith The Lord: I shall trouble the land to bring forth repentance and revival and those that heed not my word shall not enter the kingdom thereafter.

The Harvest Is At Hand!

The crops have been planted and water given
Good seed has been chosen and planted with care
Under the sun's warm rays, the seeds do sprout
The promises of harvest can be seen upon the land

Then look thee closely and a surprise you will see
Seeds never planted have mingled with thine
Bad plants they yield, poisonous to man
Though they grow together, at harvest they must be untwined
One to the fire and one to the feast

But the truth be known these are not plants
These are the wicked and the righteous entwined
Raised together so the truth may be known
Man cannot know good less he also know evil
He cannot be found righteous, less he overcome evil

From the foundation of time, God has purposed the harvest to determine his chosen that they may sup with him.

THE TRIBULATION

Will there be a Pretribulation Rapture? We all want to believe there is. But what if there isn't? Are you prepared for that possibility?

This is probably one of the most controversial questions in the Christian religion, so I am not going to claim to have the answer, because the scriptures can be used to build a case for either side of this the greatest of all Christian debates. However, in what follows, I am going to take the position that there is not going to be a Pretribulation Rapture. I am going to take this position because I would rather see God's people "pray for the best and prepare for the worst." That way, my message can do no harm to the body of Christ.

The devil is a liar, and it would be just like him to deceive us into believing there will be a Pretribulation Rapture so we will not be prepared mentally, emotionally, spiritually, or materially, and when the rapture didn't come, have our faith fail us, and we fall into the devil's snare. In order to build the strongest case possible, I will speak as though there is no question that there will be no Pretribulation Rapture. I apologize in advance, if I offend anyone, but when God called me for this work, he explicitly told me not to be concerned for what any man thought of me. I was told to deliver the message he gave me with power and clarity and let those with eyes to see, see and those with ears to hear, hear and as to the rest, they could not say they were not warned, so his judgment would fall on them. The one thing I can say is that God will rapture no man lest he first accept Christ. Repent and then pick up the cross, and do his absolute best to live a righteous life. Just because a person calls himself a Christian does not mean he is saved. God only wants the righteous because otherwise the tares will be mingled with the wheat and the whole point of the tribulation, and the harvest is to separate them so God's kingdom on earth can be established, and a millennium of peace and harmony can rain upon the earth.

Overview: Here we go. The case for why there will be no Pretribulation Rapture. The truth is that nowhere in the Bible did God bless any people unless he first tested them to prove them righteous. Jesus, the disciples, and the prophets were all tested, so it is pure foolishness to think that we will not likewise be tested. Though evil and righteousness exist together, they are always separated in the end with evil receiving its just rewards and righteousness its just rewards. Only the righteous shall inherit God's promise, and the only way God can prove us is by testing us in the furnace of affliction. That means there is no easy way out through the rapture. It is a lie from the pit of hell. God always rewards us fairly according to our fruits. The devil on the other hand is a liar and a deceiver. There will be no Pretribulation Rapture. Only those that endure to the end shall inherit the Promised Land. The scriptures below are very clear in supporting this position. Anything else is a deception!

As long as we continue to be rebellious, the Lord will keep the truth hidden from us. We choose to believe in the rapture because it is easier than facing the truth! (It is prophecy deceit).

8 Now go, write it before them in a table, and note it in a book that it may be for the time to come forever and ever.
9 That this is a rebellious people, lying children, children that will not hear the law of the Lord.
10 Which say to the seers see not; and to the prophets Prophesy not unto us right things. Speak unto us smooth things prophecy deceits.

Isaiah 30: 8–10

No man knows when the Lord is coming, and they shall not escape the travail! (No easy way out/no rapture).

1 But of the times and seasons, brethren, ye have no need that I write unto you.
2 For yourselves know perfectly that the day of the Lord so cometh as a thief in the night.

3 For when they shall say peace and safety: then sudden destruction cometh upon them, as travail upon a woman with child: and they shall not escape.

1 Thessalonians 5:1–3 KJV

36 But as the days of Noah were, so shall also the coming of the son of man be.
37 For as in the days that were before the flood they were eating and drinking, marrying and giving in marriage, until the day that Noah entered into the ark. (Those who were not right with God were destroyed in the flood. Why should this generation be spared?) (No rapture.)

Mathew 24: 36–37 KJV

The evil one, "the great deceiver" will make war with the saints. But those that endure to the end shall inherit life eternal. How can Satan war with the saints, if they have been ruptured? The promise of the rapture is an easy way out, which promises that unlike all others in the Bible, we alone won't have to pass through the refiners fire. (No easy way out/no rapture.)

11 And many false prophets shall rise, and shall deceive many.
12 And because iniquity shall abound, the love of many shall wax cold.
13 But he that shall endure unto the end, the same shall be saved.

Mathew 24:11–13 KJV

7 And it was given unto him to make war with the saints, and to overcome them: and power was given him over all kindreds, and tongues, and nations.
8 And all that dwell upon the earth shall worship him, whose names are not written in the book of life of the lamb slain from the foundation of the world.

Revelation 13:7–8 KJV

He that overcometh shall inherit all things: and I will be his God, and he shall be my son.

Revelation 21:7 KJV

Affliction is necessary because it refines us and produces a harvest of righteousness and peace. (Only the righteous who have been tested shall inherit the Promised Land and life eternal. It was the same with the exodus. Only the righteous were allowed to enter the Promised Land.)

> Behold I have refined thee, but not with silver; I have chasten thee in the furnace of affliction.
>
> Isaiah 48:10 KJV

> 10 Our fathers disciplined us for a little while as they thought best; but God disciplines us for our good, that we may share in his holiness
>
> 11 No discipline seems pleasant at the time, but painful. Later on, however, it produces a harvest of righteousness and peace for those who have been trained by it.
>
> Hebrews 12:10 KJV

We will have to prove our righteousness by suffering and persecution, just as Jesus, the prophets, and the apostles did. Then we shall be rewarded according to our fruits. We must be tested to determine who the wheat is and who the tares are, who will burn in the fiery pit and who will receive life eternal. (No get out of jail free card/no rapture.)

> 9 For when thy judgments are in the earth, the inhabitants of the world will learn righteousness.
>
> 21 For, behold the Lord cometh out of his place to punish the inhabitants of the earth for their iniquity: the earth also shall disclose her blood, and shall no more cover her slain.
>
> Isaiah 26:9, 21 KJV

> 24 Then said Jesus unto his disciples. If any man will come after me, let him deny himself, and take up his cross, and follow me.
>
> 25 For whosoever will save his life shall loose it: and whosoever will lose his life for my sake shall find it.

> 26 For what is a man profited if he shall gain the whole world, and lose his own soul?
>
> 27 For the Son of man shall come in the glory of his father with his angles; and then he shall reward every man according to his works. (*We are rewarded when Christ comes, not before.)*
>
> Matthew 16:24–27 KJV

God caused Elijah to kill the false prophets of Baal. "The false God of materialism is about to fall and poverty and hardship shall be upon the land." Those Who worship materialism will suffer the same fate as the false prophets of Baal. They are blind and wicked and shall not inherit the kingdom. Many in the US will suffer this fate, if we do not repent and submit to God.

"It is *our* heart and soul, our human compassion, our personal connections that makes a man rich? When will we ever learn that a man is rich according to who he is and what he believes, and not according to what he has?" (Larry Ballard).

> And Elijah said unto them, Take the prophets of Baal; let not one of them escape. And they took them down to the brook Kishon, and slew them there (1 Kings 18:40 KJV).
>
> Because thou sayest, I am rich, and increase with goods. And have need of nothing: and knowest not that thou art wicked, and miserable, and poor, and blind and naked! (Revelation 3:17 KJV).
>
> And they came unto thee as thee people cometh and they stand before thee as my people and hear my words, but they will not do them; for with their mouth they show much love, but their heart goes after their covetousness (Ezekiel 33:31 KJV).
>
> *(America has been seduced by greed and materialism, and we must repent or be brought utterly to our knees. America is the lukewarm church that God said he would spew out. We were used to evangelize to the world, but now, we have turned away from*

> *God just as the Israelites did so many times and suffered the consequences of their wrongdoing. Why should America be any different? We elected what may well prove to be the antichrist, and now, we have to reap the fruit of the deception that has befallen us.)*

> 23 Then said Jesus unto his disciples, verily I say unto you, That a rich man shall hardly enter into the kingdom of heaven.
>
> 24 And again I say unto you, It is easier for a camel to go through the eye of a needle than for a rich man to enter into the kingdom of God.
>
> Mathew 19:23–24 KJV

Heed the warning of God and get prepared! The evil one will use materialism to control us. Those who refuse the mark of the beast shall not be allowed to buy or sell. When the rapture turns out to be "a lie and a deception," those who have believed in it will be at the mercy of the deceiver, which is exactly where he wants them. Did not Joseph put grain away in preparation for the famine? Why should it be any different now? Head the warning of God.

> 9 If any man worship the beast and his image, and receive his mark in his forehead or in his hand.
>
> 10 The same shall drink of the wine of the wrath of God which is poured out without mixture into the cup of his indignation; and he shall be tormented with fire and brims one in the presence of the holy angels, and in the presence of the LAMB.
>
> Revelation 14:9–10 KJV

Once, God warns us "we are held accountable for our actions." The question is will you choose "the false god of materialism" and the false promise of the rapture, or will you choose to endure to the end, prove your righteousness and receive gods protection? There is nowhere in the Bible where God rewarded a people without first testing them and refining them, so they were worthy! Why should it be any different now?

"Surely the Lord will do nothing, but he revealeth his secrets unto his servants the prophets" (Amos 3:7 KJV).

Choose salvation and nothing else matters. God wins, and if your name is in the Book of Life, you win too; otherwise, you lose along with Satan. I leave you with this verse to ponder:

> And fear not them which kill the body, but are not able to kill the soul: but rather fear him which is able to destroy both soul and body in hell (Mathew 10:28 KJV).

GOD'S FINAL WARNING

The Government's Endgame Is to
Cull the Population and Enslave the Survivors!

When knowledge abounds and
chaos is upon the land, the time is at hand!
He shall come in peace, a charismatic man,
full of promises and flatteries
His promises shall be like the dew that
evaporates with the coming of the sun
In a time of trouble, he will come,
promising hope and change
He will think to change the times and the laws of the land
In truth, he comes not to save but to destroy and enslave

Once his power is enshrined, his true nature will you see!
He shall come from a great nation and come
against a small nation
He shall speak blasphemy against God
and seek to war against the saints
Neither shall he regard God, nor the desires of women

From the East he will come to rule from the West
He shall make both high and low to bow down before him
He shall bring war, pestilence, and starvation in his path
Untold numbers shall fall before his sword
as he purges the land
A river of blood shall be seen across the land, and men shall
no longer be free!
He walks among us and the time of woe is at hand
Who shall submit and take his mark, and who shall perse-
vere till the end?

Come together every nation and creed, and solve these problems or perish!

Political and economic issues. We must face the fact that:

- *We must get rid of our corrupt leaders and never again allow career politicians, who serve themselves, not we, the people.* God let us have the president we wanted. And now, he is going to use him to bring us to our knees and to repentance! However, the time is short for repentance, for soon will come the time when God will say, "Depart you evil doers for I know you not." God's final warning is at hand, and that is why he called me to write this book now, and why he gave it the title *Eyes Wide Open: God's Final Warning.*
- *We must address overpopulation. It threatens all life on the planet.* It took ten thousand generations for the population to reach two billion, and now, in the span of one generation, global population is seven billion, and in another generation, it is estimated to be approximately twenty-five to thirty billion, which is an extinction level event. There simply are not enough natural resources (especially fresh water) to support that level of population. Either we voluntarily solve the population problem or the one-world government will solve it for us, by systematically exterminating six billion of us. The time for action is now.
- *We must not let our government sell us the hoax of man-made global warming.* Our government wants to use the ruse of global warming to impose tax burdens, which will be so onerous as to result in utter servitude. Global warming is a cyclical event related to the sun. Many of the natural disasters attributed to climate change, may actually be caused by our own government, as a means of creating sufficient chaos to get us to accept their "one-world government." *Note*: Technologies such as HAARP can cause earthquakes, tornados, hurricanes, droughts and floods, etc. Such technology cannot be allowed to remain in the hands of a government committed to causing chaos in order to drive us into a one-world government dictatorship.
- *Per capita resource utilization must be reduced.* We must learn to live in harmony with the environment and that will mean significant changes in lifestyle. It does not mean accepting cap

and trade because global warming is not man-made. Resource consumption and overpopulation, not a bogus carbon footprint are the core issues. Either we bring resource utilization in line with the planet's ecological system or we will experience a total ecological disaster of unparalleled proportion. No more disposable society. Products must be made to last, and when they break, they must be repaired not disposed of. This will dramatically change the basis of our economic system, but that is okay because it needs to be overhauled anyway.

- *We must take control of cheap clean renewable energy technology or forever be slaves.* And the technology must be shared with all mankind. Otherwise, we will remain the slaves of the financial elite, and the social and economic disparity they cause will keep the world in a state of constant war till eventually, we destroy ourselves.
- *We must get control of the necessities of life from the government and corporations.* Because they will use them to cause starvation and mass genocide as a means of population control. They control access to "food" through genetic engineering and through the legal means to seize farm land. They have taken control of "all water rights" through executive order. Also, technology exist, which could allow cheap clean desalination of sea water, which is the key to global water shortages, which is the most serious problem facing the planet, but they deny us access to the technology. They control access to "health care" through, implementation of Obamacare, which will be used to deny access to healthcare to the elderly as a means of mass genocide. They control access to "energy" by denying us access to cheap clean renewable energy solutions and making us dependent on an energy grid, which they will soon be able to be control remotely (the smart grid). There are energy solutions, which would allow us access to energy on demand without need of an energy grid. Either we take control of the necessities of life or we remain at the mercy of a tyrannical government intent on forcibly reducing global population to one billion. Can you say mass genocide?

- *We must elevate and equalize the worldwide standard of living or continual war and oppression will prevail.* As long as there is a major disparity in the standard of living around the world, there will be escalating conflict. We have the technological means to do as the American Economic System did over one hundred years ago, and that is "equalize while elevating the standard of living for all mankind."
- *We must redistribute the wealth of the world from the financial elite to the masses or forever be oppressed.* As long as the financial elite control more wealth than the world's poorest 95 percent, there can never be peace or freedom in the world. There can only be slavery and oppression. We have to stand up and demand a more equitable distribution of the world's wealth. When we do, the world will experience a renaissance. This vision of redistribution of wealth, not Obama's is the key to prosperity and a better life for all. Obama's policies lead to division, oppression, and ultimately, slavery. The "American Reformation Platform" explains exactly how we can take back control of our currency and put a stop to control of the world's wealth by a few evil Robber Barons and their minions.
- *We must get rid of the shadow government that utterly controls and enslaves us.* This means we must get rid of all our carrier politicians, especially the president and most of our congressmen and senators and start over after we have passed sweeping election reform. The shadow government must be completely eradicated, which means the Fed must go, and there can be no more banks, which are too big to fail. No corporations can be allowed to utterly control us by controlling access to food, medical, energy, and other necessities of life. We must get out of all global governance organizations (i.e., the UN, NATO, World Bank, World Trade Organization, World Health Organization). Lobbyist and special interest groups must be done away with. Anyone remotely connected to the Council Foreign Relations, Trilateral Commission, or Builderberg Group must be banned from politics. The American Reformation Platform outlines

exactly how all of these initiatives can be achieved, and America can be restored to its founding principles.

Wake up, wake up before it is too late!

Social and spiritual issues:

- *We must reestablish the republic by once again becoming one nation under God, indivisible with liberty and justice for all.* We have allowed the government to take control of the media and the educational system (effectively brainwashing us). Likewise, in the name of *"Fairness"* we have allowed them to undermine our Christian and family values, which are the core of our moral foundation, and represent the fundamental principles upon which this nation was founded, and which made it the greatest nation in the world. America has become a modern day Sodom and Gomorra, and unless we wake up and repent and turn to God, we are in for some extremely rough times.
- *We must take back control of the educational system and the media.* We are the victims of the worst kind of propaganda and brainwashing, because we labor under the illusion that we are being told the truth, when in truth, we are being fed a constant barrage of lies and half truths, by those who would rule us. The key to creating a docile, complacent, society is to brainwash the people and our children are the principal target. The public school system is designed to dumb down our children, to eradicate individuality and creativity, and create a generation of complacent drones who mistakenly give their allegiance to a government intent on making them harmless docile sheep, who will do what they are told, without questioning it or challenging it. The government is grooming a slave generation and we have to put a stop to it.
- *We must end entitlements of every sort. They are a poison ointment used by the government to control and enslave us!* We must once again become a nation of self-reliant people, who cleave to the nucleus family, and our Christian faith, not a corrupt govern-

ment intent on our destruction! If our economic system wasn't utterly controlled by the financial elite, we would have no need for entitlements, because we would all enjoy a better standard of living, because the wealth of the world would be more fairly distributed, and liberating technology would be available. Our educational system could be focused on turning out students with skills, which would guarantee them employment. We could end or at least substantially reduce wars, and the economic drain, which they impose, because wars are invariably about taking something from someone else. In a society where technology and resources were more equitably shared, there would be less provocation for war, because there would be less to gain. Most importantly, the government would no longer be able to pit us against one another, and society could truly become civilized. And the list of benefits goes on.

- *We must impose the brand of separation of church and state, which our Founding Fathers intended.* Currently, the government uses the ploy of separation of church and state as a weapon to destroy our Christian values and to undermine our freedom of speech (i.e., churches, veteran's organizations, and schools all receive government funding with the provision that they will refrain from engaging in political affairs). This is nothing short of gagging those most likely to oppose the government.

    Our Founding Fathers intended exactly the opposite. They intended that the state would not be able to encroach on peoples religious values because they understood that "America was established as a republic not a democracy."

    A republic versus a democracy! A republic is a nation governed by the "rule of law, the constitution," not majority rule, which is democracy or as our Founding Fathers referred to it mobocracy. They understood that invariably all democracies, in the history of mankind, had ended in violence culminating into a dictatorship. The reason for this is that eventually, the least productive members of society figure out that they can use their vote to put into office those who will irresponsibly give them handouts (entitlements) in exchange for power, even if it destroys the nation. Sadly, this is where America is today, and why entitlements must be ended! A republic is only possible when you have a moral population willing to abide by the rule of the law, "the constitution" and who cast their vote based on what is in the best interest of society at large and not some "self-serving special interest group." This is why Obama and our rulers in Washington are doing everything they can to destroy Christianity and family values, the core of our moral fiber.

- *We must stand united, or fall pray to the oppression of those who would rule over us with tyranny and death.* And we must wake up and realize that the government is intentionally causing racial, religious, and economic dissention in order to keep us at each other's throats rather than uniting against our real enemy our government.

America, which will you choose, freedom or slavery? If you want freedom you will have to fight for it, and you will have to unite as one people under God!

> "If a nation values anything more than freedom, then it will lose its freedom; and the irony of it is that if it is comfort and security that it values, it will lose that too" (Charley Reese, *Orlando Sentinel*).

> "I believe that if the people of this nation fully understood what Congress has done to them over the last forty-nine years, they would move on Washington; they would not wait for an election...It adds up to a preconceived plan to destroy the economic and social independence of the United States!" (Senator George W. Malone [Nevada], speaking before Congress in 1957).

These words of warning are truer than ever, and the situation couldn't be more urgent!

Also, you now have the knowledge you need to fight back against our corrupt government. You have the truth and a complete political action plan. If we are going to win this battle, we need God's help, and in every instance in the Bible, in order for God to intervene, the following was necessary.

- *The people had to repent and cry out to God*, which means we have to "reject materialism" and instead put our faith in God Almighty!
- *We have to obey God's laws*, which means we must return to the "Christian values," which made America the greatest nation the world has ever known.
- *We must have the courage to stand up and fight the good fight*, "with faith" that the armor of God will assure our victory. Remember, all adversity is simply a test to prove our righteous. If we prove our righteousness, God will fight our battle, and the battle will be supernaturally won, no matter what the odds!

Now all has been heard, here is the conclusion of the matter: Fear God and keep his commandment, for this is the whole duty of man (Ecclesiastes 12:13).

When the Second Great Depression comes and, heaven help us, when the end-of-time tribulations come on us, we will be rewarded "according to what our deeds deserve" (Jeremiah 17:10 KJV). I don't know about you, but I want to be rewarded, not punished. I want God's blessings on me and mine, and I am writing this book because I believe God called me to gather the lost sheep, like myself, so that we may receive his blessings and his protection. Please for your sake, take this message from God seriously!

America, the truth has been revealed to you, and you have been warned! Will you choose Satan and the "false god of materialism" or will you choose "Jehovah, the living God"? Time to choose! Open your eyes and ears and know the truth and repent unto God and receive salvation or choose to remain blind and non-repentant and suffer the consequences. It is up to you.

I appeal to all nations of the world. Much of this book has been written from my vantage point as an American, but I want to reiterate something I have said several times in this book. The Shadow Government of which I have been speaking is global in scope.

They control the US, Europe, China and Russia and in one way or another all of the sovereign nations in the world. They have suppressed technological development in Africa and target its population for genocide. Today they are jockeying for control of the oil rich Middle East. They pit nation against nation and cause most of the chaos we see in the world. To them we are just pawns on a global chess board. Currently they have the world in check and are moving with fervor to establish the one-world government which signals check mate, game over, slavery imposed on the entire world. We are all in this together. Not only do the people of America need to come together as one people, but all the people of all the nations of the world need to come together against the forces of evil which would enslave us. Then the peoples of all nations need to join hands and usher in a new era of cooperation where we share technology and tackle the problems facing the world from a single united point of view, and if we will open our eye as to who our real enemy is we can do that without bring enslaved. I know that sounds a bit utopian, but not so much so if we can come to the realization that we are on ***"Death Ground"*** and if we don't unite we will be either killed or enslaved. So the choice is stand by and do nothing and be killed and enslaved, or stand up and fight and have a chance of gaining our freedom. I am with Patrick Henry, "Give me freedom or give me death." Where do you stand?

Thus said the Lord, Ignore this warning at peril of your sole!

> The harvest is at hand. God is about to open the eyes and ears of the righteous so they be not deceived. Then, the remnant will be tested and proven by their fruit. Most will be found wanting. Will your name be one of those in the Book of Life?
>
> —Larry Ballard

SUMMATION TO A JURY OF MY PEERS

I want to thank the members of the jury (the American public) for your participation in what is arguably the most important trial ever to come before the people of a nation or the world!

The prosecution has laid out its case and now all that remains is to summarize the facts as established so that you the jury can render your verdict.

THE CHARGES: HIGH TREASON AND MASS MURDER

Charges as presented: That the "Washington political establishment" has forsaken its solemn oath to "protect and serve the people of these United States of America" and have conspired with private banking interest, their corporate affiliates, and the UN to establish a shadow government, which by secret agreements and covenants conspires to collapse the government of first, the United States of America and then the rest of the sovereign nations of the world and drive them into a highbred super capitalist/communist one-world dictatorship.

The prosecution has established: Based on submission into evidence of the UN document entitled "Agenda 21" that their goals are to end national sovereignty (treason), abandon the Constitution (treason), reduce the global population to what they consider to be sustainable levels, which is one billion or less (mass murder/genocide), reduce resource consumption to what they consider sustainable levels (confiscation of national resources, which by right of eminent domain are the rightful property of the general population).

As to their motive: They represent that the planet is facing a mass extinction event on par with that of the extinction of the dinosaurs, so they contend it is their responsibility to purge the world of some six billion souls. In real terms, they have decided that in order that they, "the self-appointed elite," may not only live but live in luxury that it is their intent to murder some six billion people and hold the remainder in poverty as their slaves. Even if the contention of a mass extinction event were true (which it is) they have no right to assume the role of judge, jury, and executioner. This is a problem, which faces all humanity and should be redressed by all of humanity working in one accord to solve the problem for the betterment of all, not an elect few. No matter what their justification, their actions constitute *treason and mass murder*. They made no effort to inform the public of the problem of which they have been aware of since the 1970s, but have instead acted in secret toward a solution beneficial to them and in exclusion of the rest of humanity. How can this be considered anything less than crimes against humanity?

Their agenda: Having established their motive; it remains to establish that they had means and opportunity and in fact carried out their plans. We have heard testimony from those in positions to know [quotes from honest government officials, corporate leaders, and others as to exactly what their agenda is. In summary, their agenda is to:

1. *Seize control of the Global Monetary System* through establishment of a network of Central banks, the World Bank, International Monetary Fund, and United States Agency For International Aid which has systematically taken over the issuance of currency from the sovereign nations of the world and thereby secretly ceased control of their various governments. In specific regard to the US they ceased control of the US Monetary System when their pawn President Woodrow Wilson, having been elected based on his pledge not to inflict the people with a Central Bank, betrayed the American people and instead kept his secret promise to banking interest, which financed his campaign. He inflicted the people with the "Federal Reserve Act,"

which took issuance of currency away from the US treasury and put it in the hands of private bankers who henceforth not only issued our currency, but charged us interest for doing so. They have, since that day, controlled the money supply and interest rates, and by these means, have regularly caused boom bust cycles in the economy resulting in the fleecing of the general population to benefit special interest groups and line the pockets of the elite, including our elected officials in Washington who can legally become wealthy by participating in insider trading.

One notable example of the intentional creation of an economic collapse was the Great Depression of 1929, which was blamed on the Fed. Realizing what the Fed had done, in 1933, Congressman Louis McFadden, the chairman of the United States House Committee on Banking and Currency, made a twenty-five-minute speech before the House of Representatives in which he introduced "House Resolution No. 158, Articles of Impeachment" for the secretary of treasury, two assistant secretaries of the treasury, the board of governors of the Federal Reserve, and the officers and directors of the twelve regional banks. McFadden said of the crash and depression, "It was a carefully contrived occurrence. International bankers sought to bring about a condition of despair, so that they might emerge the rulers of us all." Shortly after making that speech, he was poisoned and the charges were not perused further.

As to Mc Fadden's charges that "they wanted to emerge the rulers of us all," the prosecution has established that in 1933—in the depths of the depression—the US declared bankruptcy, and pursuant to "The Emergency Banking Act," the US Republican form of government was dissolved, and the receivers of the bankruptcy (the international bankers) instituted a new form of government known as a democracy, a socialist's communist order. That is why ever since then, US leaders in Washington have done everything in their power to collapse the US from within through creation of unmanageable debt, destruction of the nucleus family, and Christian values—the pillars upon which America was founded.

A more recent example of an intentionally created financial collapse can be seen in the events surrounding the 2008 economic meltdown. The prosecution has established that the actions of then Senator Obama, and Presidents Clinton and Bush conspired to force banks to loan money to high-risk borrowers, repealed landmark legislation, which allowed the mergers of banks, security, and insurance companies to create what has been referred to as financial institutions, which "are too big to be allowed to fail," therefore obligating the American public to bail out these corrupt institutions. And in advance of the collapse, President Bush blocked efforts of all fifty governors and state attorneys to pass anti-predatory lending legislation, which would have obverted the financial collapse of 2008.

2. *Debase the currency.* In 1971, President Richard Nixon announced that he was temporarily taking the US off the gold standard. Nearly fifty years have passed and the gold standard has never been reinstated. So since 1971, the world has had a "fiat currency" backed by nothing but hot air. The result has been a criminal expansion of the money supply to such an extent that today the dollar has been devalued to where it is worth an estimated two cents compared to its value prior to implementation of the Federal Reserve and their issuance of our currency. This is nothing less than the criminal fleecing of the entire world because as the world's reserve currency, what happens to the dollar affects the monetary system of the entire world.
3. *Create unmanageable debt* as a means of driving the US and other sovereign nations of the world into their one-world government.
    - *Intentionally losing trade policies:* The prosecution has established that a cast of players including Henry Kissinger, Richard Nixon, Gerald Ford, Nelson Rockefeller, Jimmy Carter, and others played a hand in taking the US from being the world's wealthiest nation to being the world's largest debtor nation with a debt larger than all the other nations of the world combined. These men all played a role in seeing to it that the US practiced "intentionally losing

trade policies" intended to gut US manufacturing and create trade deficits in order to crush US economic supremacy and drive it into unmanageable debt.

- *The imposition of fiat currency:* Likewise, the prosecution has established that every year, since Nixon took the US off the gold standard, the US has run a budget deficit. This deficit is in large part due to unfunded entitlement programs. But the real story is how the elite hijacked the entire monetary system.

John F. Kennedy, realizing that the US monetary system and government had been hijacked by private banking interest, notably the Federal Reserve referred to them as "this establishment that virtually controls the monetary system, that is subject to no one, that no Congressional Committee can oversee, and that not only issues the currency, but loans it to the government at interest." He went on to issue Executive Order #11110, disbanding the Federal Reserve and issued "Silver Certificates" to back a new currency. He further said in a speech to the American people seven days before his assassination, "There is a plot in this country to enslave every man, woman, and child. Before I leave this high and nubile office, I intend to expose this plot." I should also note that he was in the process of reducing the power of the CIA, and he made it clear he had no intentions of committing additional troops to the Vietnam conflict.

Following Kennedy's assassination, the traitor Lyndon B Johnson rescinded Executive order #11110 and had the Silver Certificates pulled. This criminal, treasonous act once again put the money supply under control of the shadow government who are on record as holding the belief that "if they can control the issuance of money, it doesn't make any difference who writes the laws." Or in other words, by controlling the money supply, by default, they controlled the government. Which is exactly what Alan Greenspan, Fed chairman, admitted to when he was asked about the proper relationship between the chairman of the Federal Reserve and the president of the United States, and he responded, "Well, first of all, the Federal

Reserve is an independent agency and that means basically that, uh, there is no other agency of government, which can overrule actions that we take, in so long as that is in place…what that relationship is frankly doesn't matter."

So ladies and gentlemen, you have a clear admission by the chairman of the Fed that our presidents are simply figureheads and the government is in fact run by the private bankers here in referred to as the shadow government. The government of the United States has been hijacked by a group of men who are on record calling for the dissolution of all sovereign nations of the world and establishment of a one-world government run in feudalist fashion (a two-tier economic system with no middle class, only the rulers and the ruled—their slaves).

4. *Lay the groundwork for imposition of martial law and open dictatorship:* The single most blatant example of this resides with George W. Bush. The prosecution has established beyond a reasonable doubt that 9/11 was a false flag event perpetrated by President George W. Bush, Vice President Cheney, elements of the US military, CIA, FBI, and CIA operative Osama bin Laden, personal friend and business associate of the Bush family. The motive for the attack was to further a military agenda laid out in a document entitled "Project for the New American Century" (PMAC) written a year prior to 9/11 and thought not to be approved short of "a Second Pearl Harbor." PMAC details the government's plans to:
   - increase military spending (following 9/11, the Pentagon got a $48 billion dollar budget increase—mission accomplished)
   - bring about regime change in countries unfriendly to US policy. (Iraqi dictator Saddam Hussein was offered an oil deal similar to what the US has with the house of Saudi but turned it down and went so far as to threaten to sell oil denominated in other than US dollars, then along comes 9/11 and problem solved. The US is in control of Iraq's oil supply just like it wanted—mission accomplished.) That

could just be a coincidence except for the fact that it was disclosed that plans were put in place to attack Iraq prior to 9/11, which was just the justification for the invasion.
- outline the need for strategically positioned military bases. Bingo. Iraq is strategically positioned between the Tigris and Euphrates Rivers, has access to the Persian Gulf, and is in missile range of Israel and Russia.

How this relates to imposition of martial law resides in the fact that Bush pulled the congressional version of the Patriot Act and replaced it with one written by the White House, one which was modeled after Hitler's "Enabling Act," which he used to usurp the German Constitution and eventually declare himself dictator. You will remember that Bush is on record as saying that the Constitution is just a goddamn piece of paper, so he obviously does not hold its principles in high regard.

So subsequent to 9/11, the US is faced with a government who, in the name of "Homeland Security," (the same phrase used by Hitler) can arrest US citizens without charges and imprison and even torture them with no legal recourse. The president can declare martial law and neither the legislative or judicial branches of government have any say in the matter for six months. The government can take control of all water rights and even enter your home and confiscate your food. What do these things have to do with making America a safer place? Nothing, but it has everything to do with making the population completely dependent on the federal government for the necessities of life as the ultimate means of control. We now have foreign troops practicing urban crowd control exercises on US soil and UN military gear is being stockpiled in the US like the military does before a deployment. What do they know that we don't?

Lastly, thanks the recent Snowden scandal, we found out that the US is gathering information on US citizens, and it is believed to have used that information to compile a list of people it considers dissidents. Again, a tactic used by Hitler who had such a list, and if you were on it, you could expect a visit by the Gestapo or SS during the night, never to be herd of again. This scandal goes way beyond illegal wiretapping and speaks to testimony given by Aaron Russo, political activist and personal friend of Nick Rockefeller. He testified that according to Rockefeller, the elite intend to establish a communist one-world government and utterly control the population by requiring implantation of a radio frequency chip in order to buy, sell, travel, or do just about anything.

5. *As to the charges of mass murder and intent to commit genocide:* Some three thousand plus souls were lost in the tragedy of 9/11. The prosecution has proven beyond a reasonable doubt that the government covered up their involvement in 9/11. That their explanation that the Twin Towers and building 7 collapsed due to the heat of the fire is scientifically impossible.

Demolition experts testified that the only thing capable of bringing down a steel building in free fall fashion, the way the towers and building 7 came down, is by controlled demolition. They testified that never in history has a steel framed building collapsed from a carbon based fire, which would include a fire fueled by jet fuel, because the temperatures are not nearly high enough to cause that to happen.

As proof of controlled demolition, they presented photographic evidence that the columns in the basement of the towers and building 7 were cut at forty-five-degree angles, there were explosions on an upper floor moments before the collapse, and that tons of molten metal were found in the towers and building 7, all of which is consistent with controlled demolition. They further testified as to the absence of these events as related to buildings 4, 5, and 6 which did not collapse despite cataclysmic damage far in excess of the towers or building 7. We established motive for the collapse of building 7, which had only minor damage, as being the destruction of criminal case files of Enron and other white color crimes connected to the banking industry. We provided expert testimony that a 757 could not possibly have hit the Pentagon because the hole in the facade was simply too small. Air traffic controllers testified that based on the maneuverability of the plane, they all thought it was a military plane, most likely a drone. We heard testimony from the coroner on the site of the crash of flight 93 that there were no bodies and no wreckage, and it appeared to be staged crash site. We heard charges from the families of the victims that the government obstructed the investigation in order to hide their involvement. I could go on but time does not allow.

Regarding the invasion of Iraq and Afghanistan, we have testimony that invasion plans were made in advance of 9/11, and 9/11 was only the excuse for the invasion, which was to further the objectives of PMAC. We have heard from Henry Kissinger that the government considers military men to be dumb animals to be used as pawns. We have established that more than anything else, what the US Government considers to represent as its essential interest is oil and that it now has control of Iraq's oil fields and a pipeline deal has been struck with US oil concerns to build a pipeline across Afghanistan to the Caspian Sea.

Why these facts are important to the case against the government is that as we have established the reason for invasion of Iraq and Afghanistan was not as represented, to protect the US homeland. Instead, it was to gain control of oil reserves to enrich the elite. Given these facts, the wars in Iraq and Afghanistan were wars of opportunity perpetrated for financial and political gain, and therefore, they constitute a grievous injustice to our military personnel who were used as pawns. Therefore, the blood of every single person killed in the conflicts is on the hands of the US government, and they are guilty of war crimes.

Additionally, we have heard testimony that it is the responsibility of certain designated entities controlled by the US to exterminate populations, especially in third world countries as part of their agenda to address what they consider to be the overpopulation problem. And lastly, based on the UN's Agenda 21, we know explicitly that once they impose their one-world government, they plan on embarking on their extermination of some six billion souls. This constitutes a mass genocide event of unparallel degree.

In Summation: Based on the evidence presented, it is your responsibility to return a guilty verdict, convicting all those concerned of crimes against humanity most importantly of which is their intention to commit mass genocide of most of the human race. This does not constitute all the evidence in this case but it summarizes the most salient events so that it may be made abundantly clear that we are not dealing with any form of incompetence. We are dealing with a specific agenda carried out by a self-elected elite who are on record as saying that:

"The technetronic era involves the gradual appearance of a more controlled society. Such a society would be dominated by an elite, unrestrained by traditional values". Soon it will be possible to assert almost continuous surveillance over every citizen and maintain up-to-date complete files containing even the most personal information about the citizen. These files will be subject to instantaneous retrieval by the authorities" (Zbigniew Brzezinski). Translation: we will be their slaves. Now, how do you feel about the government collecting data on US citizens?

Carol Quigley, Georgetown professor, member Trilateral Commission and mentor to Bill Clinton, wrote that the goals of the Financial Elite who control central banks around the world are "nothing less than to create a world system of financial control in private hands able to dominate the political system of each country and economy of the world as a whole…controlled in a feudalist fashion by central banks of the world acting in concert by secret agreements arrived at in private meetings and conferences." Translation: the shadow government runs the world and our presidents and Congress are irrelevant.

And lastly, we have a warning from the past that went unheeded. It is my hope that as the prosecutor in this case, I have presented sufficient evidence that you will at last heed this warning from an American patriot who gave his life to issue it. "The Rockefeller file is not fiction. It is a compact, powerful and frightening presentation of what may be the most important story of our lifetime—the drive of the Rockefellers and their allies to create a one-world government, combining super capitalism and communism under the same tent, all under their control...not one has dared reveal the most vital part of the Rockefeller story that the Rockefellers and their allies have, for at least fifty years, been carefully following a plan to use their economic power to gain political control of first, America and then the rest of the world.. Do I mean conspiracy? Yes, I do. I am convinced there is such a plot, international in scope, generations old in planning, and incredibly evil in intent" (Congressman Larry P. McDonald). You will remember that shortly after making his speech the commercial airliner McDonald was on was shot down when it supposedly strayed into Russian air space. I would note that Russian Dictator Mikhal Gorbachev is on record as being in favor of formation of the one-world government. The Russians would not have risk shooting down a commercial airliner when they could have just as easily forced it to leave Russian air space or forced it to land, that is, not unless they had the green light from American officials. Though it cannot be proven, this was likely a political assignation to keep him from doing what Kennedy had threatened, which was exposing the shadow government.

I leave you to contemplate your verdict.

AFTERWORD

I feel led to give you one last warning. I believe that God has shown me that soon, very soon, probably in 2014 (around the midterm elections and certainly before the end of Obama's second term in 2016, the financial elite will make their move to establish their one-world government. I am not saying this is the inspired word of God, but I feel strongly that this timeframe is accurate. All Obama is waiting for is to trigger the right crisis, and he will deploy UN troops and impose martial law. Remember, *The Art of War* says, "It is always preferable to win without bloodshed or at least minimal bloodshed. Why NATO troops? Because US troops are not going to stand against their mothers, fathers, sisters, brothers, and neighbors, but NATO forces will not hesitate to do whatever is necessary to take control of America."

For the last two summers, NATO troops have been conducting urban crowed control training exercises, and Obama recently ordered 2,700 urban assault vehicles and asked for 15,000 Russian troops. Additionally, tens of thousands of UN assault vehicles have been shipped to the US and are awaiting deployment and Homeland Security has ordered a billion rounds of ammunition. Couple this with the Halliburton contract to build detention camps and storage sites for millions of coffins, and it sure looks like plans for a US invasion and occupation are under way. I tell you martial law can't be far away. Draw your own conclusions, but I honestly believe we will see NATO troops on US soil, and it will be soon. They will come in peace, but in reality, they will be an army of occupation. First America then the rest of the world.

One last thing. The one-world government considers the American people and our military to be their enemy. Kissinger said the US was crucial to establishing the one-world government. Here is what I think he meant. They want our military industrial complex, our global bases and our weapons, but our soldiers are expendable because they will not do their bidding. Additionally, they want the US agricultural complex. Our largest export is food, and China is not currently capable of feeding all their people, so they need our farmland either as leverage against China or as payment for the outstanding debt we have amassed with them.

* * *

We must put aside our differences and come together as one people, or we will surely die or be enslaved!

Please, if you believe what I have laid out in this book, tell everyone you know. Go on Facebook and tell all your friends, go on the internet, go on YouTube. We have to wake up the people of the world to the fact that their governments have been taken over by a shadow government that represents the greatest threat we have ever had or ever will have. We also have to recognize that we all have a common enemy, the shadow government. We have to put aside the divisions which have been intentionally created by our governments and recognize as Sun Tzu said in *The Art of War*. *We are on death ground*, and if we don't come together as one people and fight for our lives, we will surely die and or be taken into slavery.

A final thought. The problems I have laid out in this book are real, and America and the world had better wake up and face them or we will most certainly suffer the consequences. The Cinderella story is over. The material frenzy is coming to an end. We truly are facing an extinction event. Any time a species has no natural predator it proliferates out of control and that is exactly what has happened to us humans. We can no longer look a blind eye to the problems we have created, and we can no longer allow our corrupt governments to lay their plans to enslave us. We can no longer hide our heads in the sand. I am reminded of the book by Kubler Ross where she outlines the five stages of grief—denial, anger, bargaining, depression, and acceptance. Most of America and the world is in denial, but that is about to give way to anger as the global economy collapses, and there are food shortages, leading to riots.

That will be followed by bargaining when troops are sent in to quell the riots, and when we realize the troops are actually an army of occupation, that will result in overwhelming depression. Only those who are at the fifth stage, acceptance, will be mentally, emotionally, and materially prepared to face what is coming. I hope you will not just put this book down and go about your life as usual. It is my ardent prayer that you will take heed of God's warning and get your house in order by preparing for what is coming, by standing up against the evil that is the shadow government and the UN, and most importantly repent to God and get down on your knees and pray that he intercedes on our behalf. I don't know any of you, but nonetheless this book is written out of love and concern for all of humanity individually and collectively.

Fight For Freedom Or Surrender & Be Enslaved

Will you stand up and be counted? Will you fight for freedom, or will you willing submit to the forces of evil? Will you take the mark of the beast and surrender your sole, or will you "***Persevere To The End***" and inherit the promised land? Will you let your children be sold into slavery?

May God protect his people, and may you be one of those who heeds the warnings, which have been reveled by the inspired word of God!

May God bless you.

PS

LATE BREAKING NEWS: According to Pastor Lindsey Williams (and others) who have connections inside the Financial Elite, 204 countries have agreed to implement a reset of the global currency system (expected to occur summer/fall of 2014). This will result in the US ceasing to be the world's reserve currency. Williams says this will in turn result in an immediate devaluation of the dollar by 30% and end the ability of the US to print counter-fit currency to fuel it's reckless spending and entitlement programs.

The result will be a massive currency shortfall, which like in Europe will result in the government confiscating all pension funds, IRA's and 401k's. The expectation is that in order to avoid riots they will tell us we will continue to receive our monthly pension checks, but since the government will control the pensions that can change at any time. With a 30% devaluation of the dollar the middle class will have to decide to either pay taxes and their mortgage or buy food. This will lead to a massive housing bubble as millions of people loose their homes over the next year or two. Before it is over all mortgages will be owned by the government so unless your home is paid for you will eventually loose it. This goes for you car as well and anything that is financed.

The currency devaluation will not immediately result in bank closures. That will not occur till at a time of their choosing (probably 2015 or later after Obama Care is fully implemented) when they raise interest rates and implode the global derivative market which will collapse the global monetary system and usher in the New World Order. If you are not out of paper you are going to loose virtually everything and as Jefferson said "be homeless in the nation our fathers conquered". Our government poses the greatest threat this nation has faced.